FAMILY FICTION

Mark Rasdall

Published by Burwell Web Communications Ltd

CONTENTS

"...One child grows up to be
Somebody that just loves to learn
And another child grows up to be
Somebody you'd just love to burn..."

From *Family Affair*, Sly & the Family Stone

CHAPTER ONE

'I had only visited a hospital ward once before. That was when Dad accidentally put a metal fork through his right foot. I didn't see all the blood – it had all gone by the time I got there – so why tell me all about it?

Miss Hall, the goth physics teacher, had come into her classroom and beckoned me with her finger. The whole class had immediately fallen silent, so she could have just asked out loud, like a normal person. Maybe that's why I've never understood physics: the people who do clearly operate in a different dimension.

Mr Smith, the Head Teacher, had tried to make a name for himself (well you would do with a surname like that wouldn't you?) by offering to rush me straight to the hospital in his car; only the blue lights and siren would have been missing. Thankfully Miss Hall had already asked Reception to call a taxi. People said that Mr Smith wasn't as ordinary as you might think.

Dad had been able to talk of course; much more so than Nan can now. They'd given him a sedative so he couldn't speak that clearly, and much more slowly than usual. I'd understood him well enough though. His damaged foot was hidden below a mass of white bandages, shaped like an oversized boot. No blood was showing through, so I assumed everything was under control.

I had hoped that Mum would come and join us,

although Dad didn't ask me to phone her. Presumably, he knew. Mum didn't.

They'd discharged Dad a day later. These days he'd have been lucky to have even got taken off a hospital trolley by then if you believe everything you hear on the News. I helped with the dressing as best I could. Thankfully it healed quite quickly and Dad's doctor said he could go back to work. It would probably have been a week or two earlier, but you know how difficult it is to get an appointment with a GP?

They are obviously very worried about Nan. She'd been found outside – in the garden of course – by the Postman. He'd brought her a magazine (almost certainly the Radio Times) which wouldn't fit through the letterbox. He'd knocked, but when nobody came to the door, he'd assumed she'd be outside so he went through the side gate, calling her name. She didn't answer. Of course, she didn't: she was lying in a patch of pink and white azaleas, unable to move or speak.

Miss Hodges wasn't at home for some reason, so nobody really knows how long she'd been lying there. It was the Postman who phoned for an ambulance which then rushed her into Worcester – almost certainly on blue lights!

Nan would have loved that – she never missed the various hospital documentaries on television that followed a small sample of patients and their out-of-body experiences while specialists dealt with the damaged human flesh on the beds in front of them.

Now it's Nan herself who is lying here. Her face looks much the same, even though her lips have gone a bit blue. She hasn't said very much to me since I've been here. The various machines keep beeping at her – trying to communicate in their special language, no doubt – and graphs keep getting drawn on a monitor to which they and she are connected. The shapes of the flashing images seem to be much the same each time, and an exhausted-looking young black nurse in a crumpled blue dress has just been in and confirmed that there has been 'no change.'

Everything smells a bit. A metallic smell. I did think about opening a window, but I'd probably get told off for bringing fresh air in. I can't smell Nan at all, not like old people often do, especially if they're poorly. Nan often used to make me promise that I'd tell her if she or her house smelled of anything it shouldn't. How could that possibly happen? I buy Nan little packs of soap every Christmas, and the house always smells of flowers.

Because I am now 18 and listed as 'next of kin', they have told me what they do know, although I don't think they wanted to. At the same time, I don't understand why Mum or my uncles haven't been given that responsibility. It doesn't bother me at all. Nan has always called me her 'special one.' Now it's just the two of us. Nan must have been right unless she'd confused 'special' with 'only.'

Apparently, Nan had suffered from low blood pressure for years and had been taking medication for it. I have occasionally seen Miss Hodges giving her pills in the kitchen, to be honest. Sometimes, despite the pills, it can make you dizzy, and they thought initially that Nan had had a fall and hit her head.

They've changed their minds about that now and decided that Nan is suffering from some kind of internal bleeding which has affected her intestines. They haven't said much more than that; neither have the machines.

As I was looking around the small room – clean but a bit tatty, with faded green paint peeling in the corners – I became aware of a slight movement on the pillow beside me. Nan has turned to face me, struggling to remove the transparent mask from her mouth.

"Hello, Nan! How are you feeling?" My heart is racing faster than the graphs and in a straight line to that of the old lady. "I'm not sure you should be doing that."

She is staring at me intently; not blinking. Determination seems to be making its final stand in holding her eyelids open. She is beckoning me to come closer to her until she is just a couple of inches from my mouth. She is trying to speak but I can't hear what she is saying. Gently lifting the mask upwards, though not removing it entirely, I can see Nan trying again and eventually – mercifully - the words do come this time. The sentence is exhaled in a whisper.

"Everything is yours. Just look in the little house... promise me!"

I nod vigorously, waiting for further instructions. None arrive.'

***

Normal people wouldn't immediately associate this outwardly peaceful spot in the western reaches of Worcestershire with screams of fear, bleeding, butchery and death. But not all people are 'normal' whatever their society or culture deems that to mean. The wooded hills of the Malverns loom over them to the south, casting their shadows over everything, even on a day like this.

Daniel Reed hasn't visited Bishop's Lacy since he left the area to head west to university. Although the pretty hamlet consisting of mainly grey, stone cottages around a single shop is only a mile or so from his former home in the village of Marcombe, like the cars and lorries occasionally running along the valley road below, it has largely passed him by.

The countryside is as green and lush as ever; the clouds have performed their duty on leaving the Welsh hills way below them, replaced now by a clear blue sky and an early summer sun. It warms their backs and the backs of their legs. The only black marks on the horizon are his suit and her dress.

He and Charlotte are standing in front of the Wilkins shop. The whitewashed building with pink and white awning and large sheets of frameless glass is exactly as he remembered it. The only other shop here had been, bizarrely, a pet shop. He hadn't been allowed a pet as a child. Unlike the butcher, his father hadn't liked animals. That shop has gone now, converted back into the other half of a semi-detached house, though the new brickwork belies the arch over an opening that once existed there.

The remaining shop is empty today, of course. Spotless silver trays gleam in the morning sunshine, but he can see that the paint is peeling in places and the wooden facia board – also white - has not weathered well; flecks of the oriPetral brown paint showing through it. The family name is still spelled out in large black, block capitals.

Peering through the slightly blurred glass Daniel can

see Harry - a great bull of a man. As children they'd compared him to the real animals in the fields beyond, daring each other to consider out loud – and almost within earshot - where his horns had disappeared to. He hadn't been unfriendly to them or anyone else, but nobody in their right mind would have crossed him.

Even now he appears to be arguing with Joe, the eldest of his two sons. His finger is wagging as he rages at him, just inches from the younger man's face. Daniel remembers Joe as a shy, overweight child and a magnet for bullies. His playground safety was only guaranteed by him being the son of Harry. All the same, he could stand up for himself well enough if push came to shove.

"You have to stop her from doing this!" Harry is imploring, no, demanding of his son.

Pale next to his father, who is as red in the face as he always was, Joe is silent and, though Daniel doesn't hear anything else, he sees not only anger in the older man's face but disappointment.

Charlotte doesn't recognise either of their faces of course.

***

A few minutes later they are sitting at the end of one of St David's pews.

"I'm not sure I've ever been in here before." Charlotte gazes up at the wooden rafters above her head in an exaggerated fashion, her grey hair forming its own small curtain behind her. She then turns to see the plain walls closing in around her before facing the stained-glass window behind the altar at the front of the church. Both – through the miracles depicted before that simple cross dominated everything that came afterwards - are supposed to offer the promise of a better future.

Daniel isn't at all sure whether this is the case, though he is perfectly certain that it brings no comfort to his wife; not that it ever did.

"We have been in here before, darling." Although this place is managed by her brother, they haven't often been inside it, but he knows that it's important to keep telling his wife the truth, even if she cannot recognise it as such. Just allowing her to drift is the worst thing they can do. Equally, overly correcting can very easily stress her. It's a tight balancing act for all of them and the rope is being pulled tighter.

His wife is in what the doctors have described might be the final stages of Pick's Disease – a form of dementia – though they don't know this 'for certain.' They never do, even though so many futures come and go. Whatever people in buildings like these might believe, science does tell them that it's terminal.

He grasps her hand, still warm from their walk down the hill, and is rewarded by a smile: unadulterated and unrehearsed.

"Do you remember when we went to the carol service in Worcester Cathedral last Christmas?"

She smiles benignly. No words accompany it.

"You were just like a little girl again; all excited!" He tries to fill the void that life has been seemingly so determined to place between them.

"You were so angry!"

"Not with you," he is encouraged that she can

remember anything about it, "With the people who put themselves in charge of such events. All they did was tell us at every opportunity how much it costs to maintain the building and how we could become supporters and set up Direct Debits. The leaflets were placed right next to the crib just in case we'd missed the leaflets on the tables next to every exit or a different set of 'festive' leaflets neatly folded up inside the carol sheets."

"The message got through though."

Now he is uncertain whether she is mocking him or not. Gloriously, deliciously uncertain.

"And not a shepherd in sight..."

She doesn't respond; shows not a flicker of recognition. She stares ahead now, quietly, reminding him only of where he is and why he is here. He doesn't pray anymore but can't help wishing that it will be a long, long time before even the briefest flickers of either happiness or sadness are extinguished forever.

The organ is playing discreetly in the background as other mourners file in. Fred Wilkins – the younger of the butcher's sons – makes eye contact with him and nods. They haven't seen each other for years but childhood associations outrun time like no other "Thanks for coming," he mouths, "I'll catch you after."

Fred's wife or partner, who Daniel has never met, is taller than him, dressed in a sober, black trouser suit and looking suitably anxious. Despite the judicious use of makeup, he can see redness around her eyes.

Joe is already seated alone at the front of the church, big and solid in the face of ephemeral notions. 'He mustn't have married.' Daniel muses as a middle-aged woman pats him on the shoulder.

He turns towards the aisle, not recognising the woman at first, and yet there is something in her eyes that he knows he has seen before. She is dressed in a dark blouse and jacket over what might be black jeans. Her once naturally dark hair is now unnaturally black.

"Long time, no see!"

That phrase alone unlocks the mystery of the mysterious stranger. With a creeping horror that he tries very hard to keep away from his face, he realises that he is looking at their sister, Pat ('never Patricia'). He hasn't seen her since leaving Aberystwyth and this isn't the look he remembers. Not at all.

She cuts a skeletal figure, slightly bent over. Her falsely orange skin looks leathery, and her cheeks seem to have been sucked by an invisible force within.

"Absolutely! So sorry that we must meet again in these sad circumstances." He is trying to be politely formal and referring to the imminent burial of her mother but catches the waver in his voice, still recoiling from the ravages that have turned such a pretty young girl into an almost unrecognisable crone from a much darker place than this.

"This must be your wife?"

He is relieved to turn away from the yellowing teeth, and all-seeing gaze. "Yes. Yes, this is Charlotte." He realises he is half-standing: half-polite, half-kneejerk reaction to flee rather than fight.

Charlotte smiles benignly.

"Well, better get settled!" The sentiment is expressed as

a snarl, seemingly aimed at Charlotte, who is mercifully oblivious to such nuances.

Pat is followed by a tall, lean man, dressed in a crumpled dark suit that might once have fitted him, and a younger girl – about Claire's age – in a neat navy-blue jacket, darker blouse and grey pencil skirt. She smiles briefly at Daniel and Charlotte, but the man very studiously avoids all eye contact.

Funerals can do that though, he considers. Everyone reacts differently to everyone.

Another couple of people slink into the pew in front of them. She is tall and angular, dabbing her nose with a tissue, while he is smaller, grey-haired, and focused.

The organ music has stopped suddenly, its analogue efforts replaced by a digital track: production perfection not witnessed since that long-ago day in the font.

Charlotte's brother Fergus looks older than the last time they saw him. This is indisputably bound to be the case, although the speed of his physical decline appears to be matching hers from within.

"I would like to welcome you all here today as we celebrate the life of Brenda Wilkins, devoted wife of Harry and beloved mother of Joe, Pat and Fred."

Fergus had once told Daniel how the theatrical nature of services such as these had initially appealed to him, not having the brain of a barrister nor the flair of a stage actor himself. It had also gone some way to making up for the crushing, isolating bureaucracy imposed by the man-made business requirements of the Church of England organisation. However, this was no passion play. Suitably sombre, everything today appeared to be black and white, but mainly black.

"... and although we lost Harry just over four years ago, Brenda was stoical in her attitude to life, and I think we can all learn from that," Fergus is getting into some sort of stride now (or endless loop), "If Harry had been the pillar of the community in which they made their home, then Brenda sought out the pillars of faith to sustain her through her final years on earth..."

The woman in front of them is slowly shaking her head. Daniel isn't sure if this is out of grief and that final realisation that Brenda isn't coming back which events such as these are so expert at providing, or whether faith itself had been an issue for Brenda. The older man beside her remains perfectly still; dressed like a small pigeon and stuffed like one.

After each of those present individually confirms that 'I will ever give to thee' from the collective rendition of 'Guide me, o thou great redeemer' which has crept over the Welsh border for the occasion, they file out behind Brenda's coffin which, with family members close behind, is ferried away by sleek black limousines. It could have been a scene out of The Godfather, Daniel muses irreverently (without the assassins, obviously).

As they walk slowly back to the car, Charlotte holding on to him tightly as she has increasingly started to do now, eschewing any pretence of self-sufficiency let alone independence, he spots the couple who had been sitting just in front of them.

The woman is towering over the man who has taken his jacket off now that the formal part of the day has ended; now that the midday sun is wondering whether he is a mad dog or an Englishman.

His black tie is still knotted tightly over a damp white shirt: he is English then. Daniel can hear the woman's voice - thin and nasal. She appears to be gesticulating wildly, her long, bony fingers pointing in all directions on a kind of random circuit.

The man remains quiet. Perhaps he is listening to her, or perhaps he is just reflective.

"I did manage to get a word with Hazel, but she cut me off as usual."

"Except this isn't usual, is it?" The man looks up at her. "I mean this is the occasion of her grandmother's funeral. She's hardly likely to want to converse with you today or most probably anybody else."

Daniel notes the man's use of language. It doesn't sound natural in 2019. He's just been proofing a story where one of the characters was seemingly locked in a world of Pickwicks or Pumblechooks, and yet he and the plot took place in California in the 1950s. In trying to highlight that the character was English rather than American, the writer had lazily fallen into a stereotype without updating the page.

"I didn't go into detail – not with all of them hovering around." She snaps back at him. "The point is that we both know there was another will and it's up to her to find it."

"More pertinently it's her decision whether or not to search for it."

There is no light or shade in his voice. Perhaps there has been little to compare or contrast it with in his life.

"She might have been more interested if she'd known what was in it."

"Indeed, but she didn't; doesn't. And I'm afraid you are not at liberty to tell her."

"Brenda will be turning in her grave already; I know she will."

The man fails to respond this time; presumably, this eventuality is beyond his level of expertise.

The two of them climb into a red Ford Focus – her folding her head in elaborately as she's had her hair done for the occasion – him slipping neatly into the passenger side. Daniel can tell by her head action, even from glancing through the rear window, that she is continuing to prosecute her case even as she engages gear, reverses out of the parking space much more quickly than necessary, and accelerates away from them down the hill and out of sight.

"So much for respect for the dead!" He exclaims.

"When people are convinced that an injustice has been done to themselves or someone they love or care for, they exhibit even less respect for the living."

Daniel stares at his wife, open-mouthed, his eyes smiling.

***

"I still don't understand why we need a Cold Case Unit here." DS Flowers is sitting at his desk on the second floor of the main West Mercia Police building on Castle Street in Worcester. Unsurprisingly it's fraying a bit around the edges, having been the Constabulary's Divisional Headquarters for more than eighteen years now. Still, their space is far nicer than the much more cramped (and very sweaty) spaces of many of the other stations he's visited, and unimaginably more so than those depicted in the numerous 'crime dramas' on TV.

He is bent over his computer, but he hasn't been reading anything on the screen for at least half an hour.

"Why not here? West Mercia covers such a broad area?" DS Taylor places a mug of steaming liquid on the corner of his desk and carries hers to the one adjacent to his.

"I suppose so much of it is rural as well, isn't it?"

"More out-of-the-way places to hide the bodies you mean?" She takes a sip and makes the usual grimace.

"Sorry. I suppose that is what I meant! When we were aligned with Warwickshire Police it seemed like we were called in to investigate many more urban crimes – if only to support them."

"Seems more than a year ago that we went our own way again."

"And much of Shropshire and Herefordshire is out of the way of prying eyes isn't it – hillbilly country!"

"You'll be sent for PC training if you keep going on like that, Sergeant! Taylor is enjoying the banter with her colleague once more. Life has been even more lonely without him. It's taken him nearly eighteen months to properly get over the death of his brother, Rob, who had been afflicted by Spina Bifida since birth and died relatively suddenly from acute renal failure amid other complications. "Besides, don't forget Telford & Wrekin!"

"How could I? Linda never stops reminding me that our patch does butt up against some pretty busy parts of Birmingham too."

"I wonder if she'll ever go back. I know I wouldn't."

"Handsworth?"

"Closer to Smethwick. My parents still live there, yeah. A bit too lively for them these days, especially as they've slowed down so much. Can't see them moving now though. At the same time, I'm not sure that people ever go back to Birmingham. I've always had the sense, not that Linda was running away when she came down here, but that something bad happened up there."

"Me too. There's a very private part of her life that's not for sharing. The Super came from there too, didn't he?"

Taylor nods. "I'm not sure which part he's from. He never talks about it, and I've never been in a position to ask. I don't know anyone who's ever met him socially either when his guard might have been down.

I do know the powers that be felt that a shared facility along the lines of the West Midlands Regional Organised Crime Unit wasn't the right model for cold cases. Presumably local knowledge – and I do mean local knowledge – is what's needed most?"

"Do you think our work on the Julie Beech case will have been a factor?"

Taylor is instantly transported back to the case of the missing girl who had finally been discovered after more than forty years buried under the ground. She shudders at the recollection, especially of Julie's sister, Grace, who had kept the secret rather than simply the memory alive.

"It may have done. There have been other successes too, though I'm not sure that's the right word for them. Certainly, it brings some kind of closure for those still living, but I think they'd prefer it if those particular doors had never been opened in the first place. Having said that, I read that someone is reported missing in

Britain every 90 seconds with the majority being found safe and well, yet 1% of missing person cases are still unsolved 12 months later."

"And Mr Reed? Do you think he'll be involved?"

"Only on a case-by-case basis, I imagine, cold or otherwise."

***

There is a discernible pause at the other end, and he thinks the line has gone dead or, worse, that it is a cold caller. Then a familiar male voice fills his ear:

"You're not going to let her get away with this are you?"

He is gripping the receiver now, pleased it is the landline. Had it been his mobile phone, he'd likely have accidentally turned it off by now, pressing hard against the side buttons simultaneously; subjectively. He doesn't need to reply yet. The caller won't expect him to.

"She deserves nothing – less than nothing if you ask me!"

He hasn't. Not only because of the mathematical certainty that his logic is flawed – and thus not open to question - but because there is only ever the same series of set answers for every eventuality the caller can imagine; and imagination was a problem, not a solution. Still, he remains quiet.

"What I mean is this: if you don't put a stop to this straight away, she'll worm her way in – they both will. You know that don't you?"

The caller volume is rising, as it usually does at times like this. At times when the script no longer offers the safety of lines of words, but rather the unmistakable requirement to read between them.

He says nothing. He rarely does, even when he knows that the caller is probably right in what he says, as opposed to what he might even now be planning to do.

***

Daniel is relieved that 'Lucy' (Lucille to her friends and those few members of her family she still bothers to stay in touch with) is not there. He feels just a touch of guilt that it is because of Charlotte that Fergus's wife has made herself absent, but, given the relief that there will be no 'scene' because of her, is easily able to assuage it.

"Monthly meeting of the Flower Arranging Committee I'm afraid. Very little is allowed to get in the way of that. Drought possibly..."

Charlotte has never really got on that well with her brother, but there was always a certain degree of sibling care for him. As a young man, he had been quite lost. Now, as an older woman, she would never again be able to find him.

Daniel recalls the many times when they had made extensive journeys so as to be 'just passing' his house. Satisfying herself that he was present mentally as well as physically they had returned home, saying little, but at peace – at least in the short term.

Fergus is even now searching her face, finding less perhaps than the last time he saw her.

"How have things been?" He throws this out as a general question to both of them; playing safe.

"Fine, thanks." Daniel can do bland, especially as Charlotte has failed to register the question, let alone respond.

“Tea?” Even safer. He watches as a portlier version of the man he first knew shortly after he met Charlotte ambles back into the kitchen, leaving them sitting on the metal patio chairs outside. Mercifully it is mid-afternoon and the sun is more focused on evening warmth than afternoon heat.

Moments later he is presented with an old white mug, not chipped, but with a once bright red slogan that is still more likely to have said ‘Joy Fades’ rather than ‘Jesus Saves.’ If Lucy had been present, they’d have been presented with twee little china cups with impossibly small handles. She did it to both test the dexterity of her guests and to save on tea. Few asked for second cups.

Fearing another quiet impasse, Daniel picks up the reins. “I haven’t seen the Wilkins boys for years. Joe doesn’t change, does he?”

“He still manages the shop with Big Steve. We call in there now and again.

“Pastorally?”

“Pork sausages – still the best in the area.”

“And Fred?”

“Still messing with peoples’ lives I’m afraid.”

“I’m sorry?”

“He’s an estate agent. Plays with their dreams far more than I ever could.”

“Is he doing well? With the real estate I mean, not the make-believe.”

“He must be. He often works in Hereford now.”

Any other vicar that Daniel has ever known would

have physically bristled at such flat rejection of their profession, or let it be known by what they said next - or the way they said it. Not Fergus. There is no hint of irony, no local nudge nudging. Daniel knows that his being family has nothing to do with it. A flat bat is what you always get. Maybe that's why Fergus has never 'progressed?' Much to the dismay of Lucy no doubt and the social mapping she had planned for herself (if not necessarily the two of them).

"I didn't recognise Pat at first."

"Nor me. I must admit that none of them attend church and although I might run into Hazel now and again, I haven't seen Pat for what, probably years? If we were in that branch of the church that likes to confess to so much, I'd have to say that I do feel slightly guilty about not visiting her more often."

"I'm sure you have plenty of other people to minister to."

Without missing a beat, the sudden cloud that has come over him appears to lift. "Especially those who are less... problematic."

"Hazel's the same age as Claire, isn't she?"

"I think so. Yes. She told me back in the wintertime that she was having to make university choices. Not sure where she decided to go. I do know that she was worried about leaving Brenda, for some reason. She was certainly very close to her grandmother. Claire must be getting ready to flee the nest too?"

"York if her grades work out. Not long for her to have to wait now."

"I imagine the waiting is the worst part. I've never

been very good with patience; can talk about it until the proverbial Herefordshire cattle come home, but the unknown…"

"I'd have thought, you know, that believing must help?"

"I'm not sure it is a gift in the way yours is a gift."

"That can go either way too. I may sometimes be able to see things that most people can't, usually by detecting energy in objects and mostly in response to a request or on a need-to-know basis. Again, the endings aren't always happy ones."

Fergus stints back in his chair, glancing over at his sister again. Charlotte simply remains staring straight ahead. She's been sipping her tea quietly and neither man is anxious to disturb whatever peace she may have found in doing so.

"A woman was sitting in front of me at the service – very tall – and a much smaller man with her?" Daniel knows that he is avoiding the main issue at play here which is trying to work out how well or not Charlotte really is. He takes some comfort from knowing that this is not at all the same as avoiding her.

"Oh, I imagine that would be Kathleen Hodges: she was Brenda's carer for several years. Again, I didn't know her very well I'm afraid, but I saw them together in the village a few times, and in Brenda's garden of course. She loved that place like no other, I think. No idea who the man would be. I'm fairly certain that Kathleen never married; actually, I don't think I ever saw her with anyone other than poor Brenda."

"The two of them seemed to be having quite a tete-a-tete outside the church."

"Marginally better than French kissing in the vestry I suppose!"

Daniel smiles his approval. Fergus has always displayed a certain degree of cynicism – from the pulpit as much as in private. Charlotte had worried that it might destroy him; Daniel sees it as a natural counterweight to the fairy tales he is force-fed: not by those in the congregation who necessarily want to believe them, but by his various managers and supervisors who most certainly need them to.

"We seem to have entered a new – quieter – phase?" Fergus half-whispers the question, presumably out of respect for his sister. Not that she would have argued the case. Not now. Not anymore.

"Possibly. The disease is so unpredictable though. They told me (us) that when they first diagnosed it. Behaviour patterns, timeline: there just haven't been enough cases to predict either with any real degree of accuracy. The anger has largely gone now. Difficult to tell how confused she often seems to be. She still has her moments but might just be resigned to the inevitable defeat."

"Or inner peace?"

"I wish I could believe that; I honestly do. Sometimes I even wish we could have some of the feistiness back. It's so quiet now for the rest of us."

"I guess Claire is feeling much the same?"

"She's not coping well with her mum being so quiet. She's never known her to be like this – neither of us has. Years ago, I'd have sometimes craved a quieter life, you know, without the discussions which usually became arguments over cases she was handling at work. I'd come home in the early hours after the paper started rolling and there she'd be, typing away, as though the keys were her real enemies, not the people she was in dispute with."

"It must all seem a long while ago."

"The paper? Yes, but I've got used to that now. I keep myself busy enough with the proofreading of course. It's not for everyone; sometimes your mind works too quickly and fills in blanks, without realising there actually are blanks that need filling, but I enjoy it. I just never really appreciated how much I liked Charlotte interrupting me, though it used to drive me mad at the time (most of the time)."

"You mentioned the writing to me once before…"

"Creative writing, you mean? That's still on hold – part of the same block, probably. If I couldn't see what was happening to Charlotte who was there right in front of me every single day, I don't imagine I'd have fared much better with make-believe."

"It might come back. You never know."

"I know. Although I've managed to carve a career out of words, I never planned to become a creative writer. It's in there, for sure, but never what you might call a 'lifelong ambition.'

"Perhaps you were afraid of it – needed more structure, especially given the gift you were blessed with. Something like that takes you to places most of us will never be able to go and, God knows, I try each time I conjure with the supernatural. At the same time, I could understand why you would seek out an anchor back here on earth."

"You don't do so badly when it comes to reading minds!" He laughs and is pleased to see Fergus blush slightly. "I think there's a lot of truth in what you say. I've always felt that it was a gift to be treated with care, rather than trying to push it too much. There are all kinds of explanations for why things get blocked: stress is the usual culprit, isn't it? In my case, it was probably down to the business with the newspaper – being relegated to the snippets and then snipped altogether. I may never have had a life plan, as such, but I've also never known the disappointment that could last a lifetime if it hadn't been achieved."

"Are you still working with the police?"

"Occasionally. If they need me, they know where I am."

"The senior chap you mentioned after the Weston-super-Mare incident a couple of years ago? You were helping him to find his son?"

"Hunter-Wright? Well, I was, am, but we haven't got very far I'm afraid."

"You've not been able to make any kind of a breakthrough?"

"Yes and no. He presented me with a record early on – an LP if you please."

"Nothing wrong with a bit of vinyl."

"Nothing at all, and we're not talking a little here. Hunter-Wright's front room was effectively a music room. One of the walls had racks of albums, literally from floor to ceiling. There must have been over two thousand titles."

"And I bet he plays a lot of them still. You know, many people show off their shelves of records – like a kind of rite of passage – but play their CD equivalents when their guests have gone. Too much hassle to get the thing out of its sleeve, wipe the dust and static off with a cloth then lower the needle onto the turntable at the right speed, only to discover the last disc you played was a 45 and the speed's all wrong." Fergus seems to be talking from experience – recent or otherwise.

"I'm not sure he'd ever make that mistake, and not just because he's a policeman. There wasn't a speck of dust on the deck's perplex lid, so I think you're right about the first bit at least."

"No chance of fingerprints then?"

"Time to move on, I think! When I was over there one evening, he suddenly pulled a sleeve out of one of the rows. I think he wanted it to appear to be at random but you remember whenever you wanted to pull out an album from a shelf or rack, it would usually pull out the record on either side slightly, and then you'd over-compensate when you put it back in its place by pushing it in but reaching behind and pulling those same records forward slightly so that you wouldn't see which record you'd played last?"

"I do, yes!" Fergus's eyes are shining. "I only really have CDs now and usually look for music to stream for services but, yes, I can visualise exactly what you mean."

"Well, the records on either side were already protruding slightly. I reckon it was a record he turns to often or wants to be able to find quickly when the mood takes him."

"Who was it by? Sorry: who was the singer?"

"It was a Motown compilation. It seems that they were amongst Michael's favourite songs when he was a boy."

"And you heard something different?"

"No. I heard one of the same songs – 'I'll be there' – by the Jackson Five."

"And?" Fergus is leaning forward now, genuinely interested in what he has to say. It hasn't always been this way; years ago they had merely tolerated each other for Charlotte's sake.

"It was playing somewhere else, quite a long way from here, but I know Michael was listening to it."

"You've no idea where?"

"I do actually – have some idea. The place name Waterloo kept coming into my mind, but I couldn't see the station or any other familiar London landmarks along the river."

"Could it have been Flanders?"

"Or South Brussels if you believe Ryan Air!" Daniel allows himself a brief smile before continuing. He is pleased to see the smile reciprocated, despite the seriousness of the subject matter. Perhaps that's how priests cope with so much pain. "It wasn't there. There are buildings all around – some modern, some much older – and a green hill."

"Ah, well there you are!" Fergus claps his hands and leans back again, as though one of the great mysteries of life has just been solved.

"I did see a man in a dark uniform, though. It seemed like he was watching over someone. I'm not sure if this was Michael or he was the one being looked after."

"For his benefit or that of others?"

"Indeed. I haven't told the Detective Superintendent any of this in case he's being held captive."

"Surely he'd at least like to know that his son is safe?"

"True, but I don't want to set him off accessing prison records and so forth if I'm wrong. I'm not sure about it and this isn't an exact science. I've often got it wrong, unfortunately. Even when I first mentioned London he was on the 'phone straight away with some old 'colleagues' from the Met. I'm pleased that he has such faith in me, but it's the hope that kills you in the end, isn't it?"

Fergus is quiet for a while before answering this hypothetical question (or is it?). "But you do believe the boy is alive?"

"I do. Yes. We may never find him though. Equally, he may never want to be found. I've no idea of the circumstances which led to his leaving in the first place. I'll have to ask Hunter-Wright at some point given that the boy's mother has since died.

Another surreptitious glance towards Charlotte before Fergus continues. "Maybe he wants to come home – has done for some time – but doesn't know how to do it. Time can heal (how many times do I hear myself saying that to my parishioners) but it can also become the biggest obstacle of all if you let it."

"Especially given that he was so young at the time."

"How old was he when he went missing; remind me."

"He was just twelve years old. He'd be in his early

thirties now."

"So many years of suffering." He turns to look at Charlotte again. She is still staring benignly towards the Welsh hills. "And yet I do wonder if this is what peace looks like."

***

"So, when are you going to tell the others?" Debbie Harcourt holds her husband's hand tightly as they stroll through the park, each enjoying the last of the evening sunshine. Enjoying the warmth that comes from being in each other's company. It hasn't always been like this, but the dark clouds appear to have moved away for now.

"It's up to Rupert. To be fair to him he's become as frustrated as I have at working the role without the rank."

"Too few foot soldiers?"

"Something like that! We make a good team though."

"Will they bring in a new DI?"

"I've already insisted on it. I also told him that I wanted at least two of them to join me in the new unit, as well as a DC (a Detective, not a Disappearing Constable). Serious Crimes will need at least a Detective Inspector in place; should technically be a DCI of course."

'It's your time now. You always told me that promotion in the police force was down to lucky breaks."

"I'm not sure the victims or their families would see them as lucky."

"Maybe not, but not knowing the truth – never knowing what happened to their loved ones would surely be far worse?"

"What if I can't keep it up?"

She gives her husband what can best be described as an old-fashioned look.

"No! I mean what if promotion blunts my thought processes, and takes me too far away from what I'm good at? I have seen a fair few detectives – good detectives – who've become conflicted somehow."

"I don't think you'll ever be able to prioritise a spreadsheet over any case; cold or otherwise. Rows and columns are all very well, but they need you to fill in the cells and re-calculate what you're looking at, especially when others can't see what's right in front of them."

"I thought you were taking evening classes in bread making, not great literature!"

"I haven't noticed you complaining about the bread rolls..."

"Thank you for still believing in me." He turns to face her, enjoying her returning smile, her face raised slightly in readiness for the kiss she instinctively knows is coming her way. It isn't that Debbie hasn't always had faith in him, she just hasn't always been able to show it. He's put her through a lot and sometimes it has seemed that indifference has been the defence mechanism she's needed to cope with the pain: his pain mostly.

"All I'm saying is that you've nothing to prove to them now, Martin. Any of them. Now's the time to stake your claim – especially while Rupert's still around. He must be coming up to retiring soon?"

"In just under a couple of years, I think. He told me when I first joined that he intended to retire at sixty; I don't imagine much has changed. Well, lots has changed of course! Only reinforces his intentions I expect, though what he'll do without the job I don't know."

"You might be saying the same in a few years!"

"I've got you. It's completely different. Thank goodness."

She squeezes his hand even more tightly. The setting sun has coloured the Malvern Hills pink in the near distance; the flimsy clouds above them still bearing more of an orange tinge.

"Could one of your team go for DI?"

"I hope they might go for it, yes. West Mercia is all about promoting from within..."

"Eventually!"

"Well, that too, yes." He laughs out loud. "I think Linda would probably be the favourite but each of them is capable of making the step up."

"How is Ian now?"

"I think he's OK most of the time. I do catch him gazing out of the window sometimes, but he probably always did. When someone becomes so seriously ill - and especially if they die - you associate pretty much all their behaviour with that grief, don't you? I mean it's hard to go back to what they were like – really like – before it all happened."

"It would certainly take over your life. I imagine people like Ian wish they could turn the hands of the same clock backwards too. Things are never going to be quite the same though, are they?"

"Very deep! You'll be writing poetry next."

"Does Ian still find comfort in poetry? You mentioned it often when his brother first became poorly."

"I haven't asked him since Rob died."

"Some Detective Chief Inspector you're going to make!"

CHAPTER TWO

Claire Reed walks down the stairs quietly, not wanting to wake her mother. It's been a relatively busy day for her – she doesn't go on many visits or, in turn, enjoy many visitors here at home now – but it has still taken her a fair while to fall asleep.

Her father has drawn the curtains and the small lamps on either side of the sofa have been switched on: golden orbs in the growing darkness outside.

"You don't have to sit with her until she physically goes to sleep you know." Her father smiles gratefully as he hands her a blue mug of hot chocolate. The mug bears the legend 'Hope' in pink lettering on one side; the side that is turned away from her.

He tells her this most evenings but they both understand that this is their little ritual. She, in turn, makes his coffee if he has been on the 'mum run.'

"I love it that we still have hot drinks at night, even after such hot days."

"It was a scorcher today, wasn't it? Even Uncle Fergus allowed us to sit in the shade. Not like him at all."

"I'm sure he's an undercover druid."

"We'll try and get hold of him at the summer solstice next year – see if he's at home."

Claire smiles at the familiar banter. They are both fond

of Fergus, especially if they can manage to get him on his own. “How was she?”

“Fine. I’m not sure how much of it she took in, but she did say she’d seen someone she recognised today. She couldn’t tell me who it was. Not sure if that necessarily means she didn’t know, or just couldn’t find the words to articulate it.”

“Could have been one of many!”

“People or words?”

Claire laughs but the humour doesn’t reach her eyes. Daniel had noticed the huge bags under her eyes before they’d left for the service that morning. “Hope you get a better sleep tonight.”

“I’ll certainly try. I’ve stopped reading the Kindle at bedtime now. I thought the ‘phone might have been the problem but seemingly not.”

“You can never have too many screens!”

“You’ll be proud of me…”

“I am proud of you. We both are.” He comes to sit on the sofa beside her and she leans into him, resting her head on his shoulder as she has done for so many years now. Reassurance and reassuring in equal measure.

“I took a book from one of the shelves in your room.”

“A book. An actual book! Great. Which one?”

“Death is all in the mind.”

“Can’t imagine why I might have bought that one… should help you sleep though.”

They laugh, carelessly and carefree, though that clearly isn’t the case at all.

Daniel notes that the last of the birdsong outside has finally subsided. The days are getting shorter now, but nobody seems to have told them yet.

Claire moves quickly to sip her drink.

"She wouldn't mind, you know."

"Mum?"

"Daniel nods, leaning back and closing his eyes momentarily. "She'd want you to be happy. Does want you to be happy. If she can hear us upstairs, she'll be smiling too."

"I know. It's just..."

"It doesn't feel right?"

"Yes, that, but also, I suppose I keep wishing it was the three of us, you know, sitting down here like we always used to, late into the evening. Making sense of the world."

"You mean Mum pontificating and driving us both senseless!"

"Maybe I've got memory issues too!"

Daniel puts his head to one side and looks at her quizzically, saying nothing.

"I'm sorry Dad; I didn't mean..."

"I know you didn't." He gives her a warm hug and can feel droplets of moisture on his cheeks which his own eyes have not expelled. He tries to lighten the mood – for both of them.

"At least we seem to have got through the pieces of paper phase!"

"Oh, I know. I still don't understand what that was all

about."

"The lines?" He remembers clearly how he'd come downstairs one afternoon, just before Claire had arrived home from school (something to do with an internal clock?). Charlotte was sitting in the middle of the floor, surrounded by at least 70 sheets of paper, torn from an A4 writing pad (80 lined pages with feint margin). Many remained blank, looking up at him forlornly as he entered the room as if asking him to try to work out precisely what was going on there. Some had squiggles towards the top-left of the page, the lines on others roughly traced over with a blue pen.

Claire had duly arrived home, observed the chaotic scene, and gently asked her mother very tenderly if everything was alright. Charlotte had shaken her head quietly but offered up no other explanation. It hadn't happened again.

"Quite a lot of the paper was crumpled up into balls as well, wasn't it?"

"I think some of the anger was still inside her. It possibly still is. I certainly wouldn't have wanted to be on the receiving end!"

He's rewarded by his daughter's smile; has been for more than 18 years now.

"You're doing just fine. We're doing fine, or at least we're doing the best we can. Carry on making the most of Mum. One day it will be quiet up there and she won't be."

"I think that's it. I've been worrying about how you're going to cope when I go to Uni. If I go."

"Me too – how you're going to deal with it all - but you

will, and of course, you're going. You'll be installed in York before you know it."

"I could stay here. Worcester has a perfectly good course."

"Not where your heart is though is it?"

"No, you're wrong. It's exactly where my heart is, even though my head knows the course in York would be a better one for me, especially if I do want to go into counselling one day."

"We should still look for accommodation in both places though, given they're the only two you'd want to go to. You know, have a backup plan."

"I might be going through clearing yet; then it's just a case of what's left. Much easier in some ways."

"I'm sure it won't come to that."

"And that's what's making me feel so bad. I've been worrying about the results for months now. It still wakes me up at night and then I just can't get back to sleep. I do try the breathing exercises the specialist showed Mum, but they don't work. Then my mind gets to thinking: how selfish am I wanting to move away when you'll still be here and Mum couldn't go anywhere now, even if she wanted to."

He lets her cry, even handing her his handkerchief which, based on previous experience, she rightly rejects in favour of a pack of tissues.

"The angst over A-level results and even anxiety over moving is perfectly normal. What's going on with Mum – and the timing of it – isn't your fault or yours alone to worry about. None of us, including Mum, can do anything about it happening or when it's going to happen; just that it will."

"I hope it's still a long time yet."

"So do I, darling."

"I don't even know if she can understand me when I pour it all out to her – all the college stuff. I hope she can but, then again, what if it's making her sad too?" She continues to sob: a pitiful sound in the warmth and comfort of their cosy sitting room.

"I find that it's best to assume she can hear and understand everything; also, that she'll immediately forget everything she has been able to process. Sometimes she'll surprise us and sometimes not."

"How do you cope with the silence Dad?"

"By continuing to talk to her; hanging the words in the air for her to reach up and grasp if she still wants to. And, if she doesn't, well, it breaks the silence, doesn't it?"

"You're wasted as a proofreader."

"Better than being a proofreader who used to get wasted quite regularly. I can never make that time up to Mum – or you."

"I don't remember any of that and I'm sure it wasn't nearly as often as you're making out."

"The sooner you begin your psychology course and get some insights into the way we store memories the better!"

***

Having signed the Crime Scene log, Harcourt watches PCs Millie Rome and Jennifer Kent extending the blue and white ticker tape from the front of the garden to the rear. The word 'Police' is printed on it at regular intervals, but it's largely superfluous. Everyone knows what the colours mean.

Brenda Wilkins' garden next door is in full bloom just as she was taken from it. The purples of the foxgloves sway gently in the early morning breeze, faded now but still providing relief from the old stone wall that separates the gardens here. So innocent they seem, yet each flower contains its own particular form of poison.

The lawn could probably do with a cut, though it isn't anywhere near as desperate as some of the houses he's visited in Worcester. The residents of such places have no doubt seen 'going green' as an opportunity for weeds to cover the rusting metal skeletons of once-useful devices or fragments of concrete and rubble that were never really going to serve any use.

A small wooden cabin sits at the far end of the garden. He can see piles of orange flowerpots piled up behind the small window, ascending in size. In due course, an estate agent would probably market it as a 'home office.' Balls of green garden twine and black plastic seed trays are neatly stored against the back wall. Their work in the spring has been completed until next year's seedlings require a home; before they too would be planted in the various pots and other planters dotted around the garden. Except that this isn't going to happen now, or at least not on Brenda's watch.

A few weeds are showing in the borders but, again, far from a rampage. The rain showers over the previous two nights have kept everything looking fresh. Thunder has been predicted but it hasn't materialised yet (if a weather phenomenon can take on a material form?). It's going to be another humid day and Harcourt can already feel sweat on his lower back, pinning his light blue shirt to his skin, which unfortunately means he'll need to keep his jacket on for now.

"No sign of a break-in, sir," Linda Farren has joined him in the adjacent garden, projecting her usual appearance of being cool and calm. Harcourt could act calm – do calm – but staying cool was much more of a challenge.

"What about neighbours on the other side?" He points towards the chalet bungalow to his left. Of yellow brick and white wood panels adorning the dormer windows, it is almost certainly an in-fill build from the late sixties or early seventies.

"An elderly couple: Mr and Mrs Portugil. They didn't see or hear anything untoward but, sadly, she's quite deaf anyway. I got the impression they were still stressed over Brenda Wilkins' death, even though it was through natural causes."

"Nothing remotely suspicious about that one?"

"Not according to the medics. She could have fallen over at any time, apparently. Given she spent so much time out here and looking at the uneven paths over there, I'd say it was the proverbial accident waiting to happen."

"Family?"

"Two sons and a daughter. Her husband died a few years ago. One of the sons is local. The daughter and another son both live on the other side of Worcester now; out towards Stratford."

"And Kathleen Hodges was Brenda's carer, right?"

"It appears so, yes. House-to-house is only just starting

to get going, but it's a small village and those we have been able to contact say that Miss Hodges spent much of her time in Brenda's house or, more likely, her garden."

"So, she could just have been a friend or a good neighbour, for example?"

"Or a nosy neighbour?"

"Who called it in?"

"A gentleman who didn't want to be named. Had a strong Northern Irish accent though, so shouldn't be too hard to locate if he's local."

"And what exactly did he say?" Harcourt doesn't like witnesses who don't wish to be named.

"Just that Kathleen was unexpectedly missing and would we come round to the house as quickly as possible."

"Two key parts there then. The first is the use of the word 'unexpectedly.' Either Kathleen never really went out – apart from across to Brenda next door – or this person was expecting to see her, only to discover that she wasn't here."

"The front door is locked, and all the windows shut so calling out to her from the front wouldn't have worked; he goes around the house and tries to look over that wall to see into the back garden. He'd have had to have been quite tall, sir. That's a pretty high wall."

"To keep nosy villagers from looking in!"

"Unless he stood on something."

"Which, handily, he brought with him, expecting to have to use it instead of entering by the front door?"

"Or he wasn't alone? Maybe someone helped to lift him

up?"

"Which wouldn't have looked at all suspicious at that time of night? What time did the call come through."

"10.14, sir. You said there were two key parts to what the witness told us?"

"Ah, yes. Why would he ask us to come round to the house 'as quickly as possible?'"

"Perhaps he thought that Kathleen was still in the house – maybe he thought she'd fallen like Brenda Wilkins did and was unable to come to the door."

"We'll have to check her medical records – I'll get Taylor on to that too. Maybe this is a low-pressure area?" He looks at his colleague expectantly, but her face is blank. "Low blood pressure, Sergeant.

"Sorry, sir."

"No need." He smiles his encouragement before his face turns into the scowl that Farren is, to be honest, much more comfortable with. "It's just that if you think someone has gone missing, your first thought would be to get uniformed officers all over the local area (at least at first) looking for her, wouldn't it?"

"Unless, as you say, he had good reason to believe she was actually inside the house."

"In which case, why say she was 'missing?' Wouldn't you say something along the lines of you were 'worried for her safety?'" Again, no hidden thought processes manifest themselves on her smooth cheeks. "If it was a missing person, we got here quickly, didn't we? We still advise people to wait 24 hours don't we (at least unofficially) unless a child is involved?"

"We do, sir, and this was the suggestion our call handler made to the gentleman. She reported that he rang off straightaway."

Harcourt is liking the 'witness' less and less.

Farren fills the void for them both. "One of our patrol cars was on its way back from Hereford where they'd been called out earlier that morning to the 'Mad as the Marches' festival. 'Clash of the Texans' had decided to turn up unannounced to play a free gig, but someone put it out on Facebook, and they were quickly inundated."

'Clash of the Texans' in the border country! Give me strength, thinks Harcourt. There'll be a Mexican uprising next.

Farren is continuing. "The officers took a detour here on the way back to Worcester and saw the body over the wall."

"They were tall then, I'm guessing."

"Not particularly sir, they parked up alongside the wall and one of them stood on the roof."

'Who would insure a police car' he considers. He looks around him once more. Certainly, this garden pales in comparison with the cacophony of colours and scents next door; most would. However, it is neat and the borders are well-kept. Flagstones are largely covered in small pots of assorted bedding plants. The cheerful faces of marigolds and pansies are clearly enjoying the sunshine much more than he is. What took place here? What did they see?

They are enclosed in a rough square of the ticker tape including a small white tent erected close to the house.

He heads over there, purposefully.

"Sir, before you go in there..." Farren has headed him off from the side of the garden closest to the other boundary wall, beyond which runs the main High Street through the village. Quiet now. Probably always quiet.

"What is it?" He turns to face her.

"Over here. Something you should see."

He follows her past a series of small green 'ornamental' shrubs and finds himself looking at a collection of brightly coloured garden gnomes, fishing lines cast out in front of them.

"I've never understood why people have these in their gardens."

"Nor me, sir. Mind you, where I was brought up, they'd probably have been stolen and had packets of drugs thrust up their backsides. Nobody suspects gnomes of trafficking. Not usually anyway."

"Perhaps that's why they always look so happy?"

His sardonic comment elicits only a cursory shake of his DS's head. "Not all, sir." She points to a blue-jacketed member which (who?) appears to have lost their fishing rod. In its place, it appears to be holding something far more deadly: a steel knife with an ugly serrated edge, perhaps twelve inches in length.

"Get it bagged up, will you."

"Sir. And sir." Farren touches his arm gently. "It's nasty in there; just so you're aware."

He nods and heads back towards the tent, removing his shoes and adding the dreaded blue plastic overshoes, along with matching gloves.

As he lifts the flap, one of the SOCO officers exits the tent with a cursory acknowledgement. Unfortunately, she is unable to take the terrible stench with her. Harcourt has seen many dead bodies, most in real life but several in his dreams. The long, broken body of Kathleen Hodges is lying in an arc shape on a deep crimson patch of stone, which didn't start this life that colour. The holes from which the blood has escaped appear to be gaping open in the stomach area. To the naked eye, he can see at least three wounds, made by a knife or other sharp implement.

Other liquids have discoloured her white summer dress, and small amounts of matter sit in irregular piles at the top of her right leg and on the ground beside it. Thanks to the morning heat it seems that the rigor mortis stage has come and gone, the skin area over the abdomen – exposed by that side of her dress having ridden up – is already slightly discoloured.

He notes the excited, uncoordinated movements of flies and other insects gathering on the outside of the tent's thin fabric, the shadowing effect ghostly on the victim's face (or what he can see of it).

The slabs of the victim's hands have been severed and placed over each eye; single fingers protrude from both ears and, if he is not very much mistaken, it seems that her mouth has been stitched up. He can just make out the brutal, haphazard stitching of what looks like fishing line through each lip.

Nothing else is haphazard about it. In direct contrast with Kathleen's erstwhile neighbour, nature has not taken her life, seemingly at random or at least according to some other timetable hidden from them. Another person or persons has deliberately sent a message here: see nothing, hear nothing, say nothing.

***

"Have you heard the news, Joe?" Old Mrs Sanders is eyeing up the meat.

"What news would that be?" He knows that she will tell him everything in due course - is dying to tell him about the body – while pretending to be a genuine customer. She isn't the only one.

Jackie Megson, not having had anything else to do for years now, had set himself up as the unofficial reporter at the scene. He has reported that at least three police cars and an ambulance arrived earlier that morning. He'd just been able to make them out from his bedroom window, three doors down and two across. He'd quickly got dressed and brushed his teeth (Ma and Pa would never have forgiven him if he'd failed to do so, even though they were long in the ground) but did skip breakfast for now.

All of this background information has been delivered breathlessly in order to lead Joe and Steve up the garden path and into Kathleen Hodges' garden itself. From there, approximately twenty-three minutes later, a stretcher had been carried out by paramedics – a chunky man and a much slighter woman (marvellous what they do these days isn't it?) and loaded into the ambulance. Jackie was fairly sure that the colour of the long, zipped-up bag on top of the stretcher was dark blue. What he was much more certain about was that it wasn't moving.

Now Elsie Sanders is keen on a piece of the action.

Joe would like to have been able to say how great it was that footfall had increased that morning, but apart from Jenny Meadows unexpectedly buying a chicken, sales have not kept up with the pace. Besides, it seems wrong to associate commercial gain with someone else's misfortune. He isn't an undertaker.

"Kathleen Hodges?"

"What about her?" He catches sight of Steve, head-to-toe in as yet clean white overalls, looming in the doorway leading to the freezers in the back room.

"She's dead!"

"Who told you that?"

"It's all over the village; I'm surprised you haven't heard anything about it!" She breaks off to cough noisily into the sleeve of her faded pink cardigan. Her ample bust, housed in a flowery 'summer' dress, is resting on the top of the counter. She isn't the only one to do this. Joe used to find it vaguely disgusting. Very occasionally he would lose his temper and then they'd know about it alright. These days he feels nothing at all, just relieved when she and her like finally decide to leave them in peace.

"Have the police confirmed that it's her?"

"I don't know for certain, but it's obvious, isn't it? Apart from that solicitor chap she barely ever had any visitors. Besides, she's hardly likely to have killed one of them and laid them out in the garden before scarpering, is she?"

"Could have been a family member?"

"Would have been a distant relative then; like I say, nobody saw many comings or goings, apart from your poor mother of course." She gives him a coy look, either trying to be sensitive or provoking him into a deeper conversation than the one they've had so far: one that could provide her with much more information for the gossip round that will inevitably follow.

Steve suddenly moves forward, his huge bulk akin to a silent polar bear as he deposits the rack of pork chops into their allotted space in the display unit, gently moving three sprigs of artificial green herbs to make way for them.

"You won't be selling many of them today?" Spittle accompanies this confident assertion, coming to rest on the surface of the glass counter in small globules of sticky liquid which sit there defiantly, daring either of the two men to wipe them off while she – the valued customer - continues to stand there.

Neither of them responds, knowing from experience that she will become increasingly desperate to solve her own little riddle. Not for the first time, Joe wonders if old wives must undergo specialist training in myths and legends, or whether they just grow old and bored with little else to fill their days other than make-believe.

He stares back at her, noting the stepping stones of black fillings in her straw-coloured, misshapen teeth.

"No 'r' in the month!" She cackles before mercifully turning her back on them, their blank faces and, naturally, the pork chops.

***

Harcourt swings the car into the parking space that has finally become available after at least twenty minutes of slowly – painfully - driving around in circles. A shiny, dark Range Rover toots him loudly as it passes behind. Alright, so he's never quite managed the signage. Thankfully, not everything at the hospital revolves around a one-way system.

Shortly afterwards he is considering again how much Dr Jenny Graham resembles a Scandinavian goddess, or maybe even a member of ABBA. Her naturally blonde hair sits above an elfin-like face made up of seemingly flawless skin with absolutely no makeup ever required. As in Sweden, the air around them in her 'office' is cold, and so is she.

"I hope you're not going to make a habit of this?" Her crystal blue eyes are hard and go perfectly with the accusatory words that have left her lovely mouth.

"What? Phoning you at work?"

"You know exactly what I mean!" She doesn't sit nor does she invite him to do so, but the muscles have softened slightly. "You and your colleagues might think it's funny to label every case you send to me a priority, or 'rush job' to give it the vernacular I think you'd be more familiar with."

This is what he came here for. He catches himself; no, of course, it isn't. The banter is always entertaining though. "How are your parents? Still out in Stratford."

"My parents are both fine, thank you. Just old. In answer to part two of your inane question, yes, they still live in Arrow which, the last time I looked, was a small village at least ten miles from Stratford-on-Avon."

"Arrow! That's right. Debbie and I went to an evening concert in the grounds of Ragley Hall, just down the road from there. It was good. Bach, I think, or maybe

Beethoven? Must be at least three years ago now."

"How time flies." She is even less impressed with his classical music knowledge than his clumsy attempt at unwanted conversation. "Shall we get back to the matter in hand?"

"Of course. Where were we? Ah, yes. The circumstances surrounding Miss Hodges's death did give us just cause for wanting your pathology report back as soon as possible."

She is noticeably much more at home with his detective-speak, although it hasn't appeased her. "I'm afraid you've had another wasted journey then, Inspector. No lab on this earth would be able to turn something like this around in, what, less than six hours?"

"But you mentioned on the phone that you had been able to take a quick look at the knife?"

Finally, she sits back down on her ash-grey swivel chair. He'd like a similar one to replace his own at work. Debbie had seen one at IKEA but, this being the NHS, it had as little chance of being purchased from there as his would by those who held tight to the purse strings of the police service.

"I had a cursory look." She spits the word out as though it were a cherry stone. "The knife found at the scene could certainly have been used to make the four stab wounds to the body. I'll have to check further before I confirm that."

"You said four stab wounds!"

"Four does usually come after three – in my limited experience anyway."

Harcourt ignores the sarcasm – he's endured it for years now. He did tend to rise to it at first but keeps his feet firmly on the ground these days. "I only saw three stab wounds, all of which were in the stomach area."

"And lower abdomen if we're being strictly accurate, yes. However, there was a further wound to her left thigh, severing the femoral artery on that side just below the groin. You wouldn't have seen it when the dead body was in situ as it was covered by her dress, although the amount of blood might have been a clue."

"I assumed that was from the other wounds."

"Which is why some professionals assume nothing. One of the upper wounds passed the left side of the sternum and penetrated the left ventricle of the heart. It would have stopped beating pretty much immediately. There would have been much less blood at the scene had this been one of the first wounds. The bleed out came from the thigh initially."

"Would Kathleen still have been conscious at that stage?"

"I have every reason to believe so. There is a small abrasion at the back of her skull consistent with her hitting her head on the concrete patio when she fell or was pulled over. There is also severe bruising around the neck area to the front and some kind of green fibres. As I have said, these wounds need much closer examination, and we'll swab of course."

"But very likely that the killer was right-handed?"

"Given the location of the wounds, yes. They were made from the bottom up i.e. the perpetrator was not standing over her face when the wounds were made.

I'd suggest that Kathleen was pulled over from behind, possibly with a rope or scarf – fibres will help us with that – and then the killer came around the side of her body when she was on the ground and stabbed her."

"If he had come up on her from behind, no doubt surprising her, why not just carry on with the ligature he was using and strangle her? It would have been a lot less noisy for one thing."

"Perhaps that would have been too quick. The way the scene was staged does suggest an element of theatricality does it not? Given the risks involved I'd say this was personal, that those messages were meant for an audience to see, don't you? Strangulation would almost have been too easy."

"Kathleen was six feet two inches tall, so that does imply we're looking for someone tall."

"If she was standing up at the time, yes. Do think again about the need for things to be acted out – to be on a stage. If he did stab her in the thigh initially, he could have been talking with Kathleen as the blood began to flow out of her body, telling her what was happening and why."

"Sounds like the work of a sociopath. Fits with the subsequent amputations too."

"Certainly, some kind of antisocial personality disorder, although the attack and the subsequent performance suggest to me that you are more likely looking at psychopathic behaviour, given the planning or at least premeditated nature of this event. I certainly don't believe you are looking at a sudden call to random violence. It wasn't a frantic attack. There is a message here that needed to be delivered and it was."

"So, you think he may have stabbed her that first time before getting impatient that the bleeding out was taking so long so finished the job by stabbing her through the heart? Wanted to be out of there?"

"Or perhaps, once he'd read his lines to her and assured himself that she understood his reasoning – warped though it might well have been - and saw that she was losing consciousness, he saw no point in waiting any further time. The second set of stab wounds was intended to form the end of the Act. The dramatic finale if you like.

He made more than one incision as couldn't be sure he'd hit the heart itself. Three chances to do so rather than one. He would have found it easier to go on stabbing once he'd started; not that I think he was lacking any self-confidence or experienced any shame in what he was doing whatsoever."

"This is truly cold-blooded."

"Planned according to some narrative that told the killer it had to be done. That he – or she – really had no choice. You just have to work out the narrative."

"Could a woman have done it?"

The short pause before the pathologist replies describes the affront to her sex more than any subsequent words could. Eventually, she responds, simply: "If she were big enough and strong enough, why not?"

"And the knife itself?"

"Looks to have been wiped completely clean. Again, the lab might find something. We'll need to be patient."

"Anything else?"

"Regarding this unfortunate woman's body?"

She always manages to make him feel thoroughly chastised by the end. "Yes. Please."

"You were right in your guestimate. She will have been killed the previous evening, probably between about 10 and midnight. Again though..."

"You'll need to check."

"Precisely."

***

'Beat on the brat with a baseball bat, oh yeah...' How many times – especially in the last few years – would Hunter-Wright cheerfully have done that? All of them are dead now of course. Long live The Ramones and good to see them still getting airplay.

He switches off the radio and gets out of the car, hearing the familiar high-pitched poop poop noise as he locks it with his remote key. Oh, to be back in 1976!

DI Hunter is waiting for him in his office. He stands as his superior enters, Hunter-Wright filling the space with his early morning presence, both physical and psychological.

"You said it was important." He doesn't do pleasantries, never has.

"Yes, sir. I'm sorry if I interrupted anything serious?"

Hunter-Wright ignores the apology and the apologetic way in which it was delivered. It's no secret in the station that he plans to be there less, what with his retirement to plan for and the garden to tend to. Why Miriam has neglected it so, he cannot fathom.

As for 'retirement,' he already works from home two

days per week, mainly on budgets and strategic plans to finance and execute the Force's development going forward over the next five years. It had been his brainchild that they should set up the new Cold Case Unit here in Worcester. It had also been his idea that Harcourt should run it, not only because he needed a reason to finally promote the man, but because, at the same time, he had always found him far too quiet and recessive for mainstream policing.

"So, what do we have?"

Harcourt describes the crime scene in far too much detail for a driver personality like Hunter-Wright; then again this is what they are both paid to do: to inform and, sometimes much more importantly, to listen.

"Not the kind of crime scene you would expect on a sunny morning in a sleepy village like Bishop's Lacy!"

"No, sir."

"Even though we're trained to attend every scene with an open mind."

"Yes, sir."

"And the knife? What did the pathologist say about it?"

"Jenny Graham confirmed that it could have been used as a weapon, yes."

"Could have? Was it *the* weapon, or wasn't it? In my experience, all knives are potential weapons."

"It's too early to be sure, sir."

"Did you not have the whole thing accelerated?" How he's going to miss this! In reality, he's missed it since suspects sat on the other side of the table, watching every muscle twitch, and eye movement, picking them up on every grammatical inconsistency. Perhaps he should go into proofreading like Daniel Reed?

“I did, sir, of course. However, even Jenny can only do so much in the time she’s given. She’s promised to get the post-mortem done as quickly as possible.”

“Good old Jenny eh!”

Harcourt feels the detestable flush on his face, caused by this detestable man. Whatever he does or doesn’t do in the years he has left, he vows again never to forget who his colleagues are. Who their real enemies might be.

“Indeed, sir. She was able to say that the knife had been wiped clean but that obviously, the lab would conduct further forensic analysis.”

‘Conduct.’ He briefly visualises Harcourt as the conductor of an orchestra. Silence abounds.

“You said that you were especially concerned about the amputations? Did the pathologist share any thoughts on them?”

“Again, it’s too early, sir. However, rather worryingly, I did feel they bore all the hallmarks of some kind of gangland killing – or at least that’s what the killer or killers wanted us to believe.”

’Rather worryingly!’ Pass me that baseball bat right now and I’ll show everybody how it should be used.

“In Worcestershire?”

“We do know that Organised Crime has its fingers in many pies here, sir.”

“And ears!”

“Yes, sir.”

"You hadn't considered I suppose that this could be the work of some mad person who has read too many books and/or seen too many crime dramas on the television?"

"Of course, sir."

"What's your theory then, Inspector?"

He knows the employment label will needle his colleague, even though it's about to change.

"None as yet, sir. DS Taylor is gathering background information on Kathleen Hodges."

"Nothing on social media I assume. Unlikely that she'd be posting pictures of food or fashion items on Instagram."

"A lot of older people do have Facebook accounts, sir." He can see his superior bristle at the thought but ploughs on. "It helps to keep them in touch with friends and family." Harcourt realises his mistake immediately and frantically tries to tack back to safer, shallower waters."

Hunter-Wright is thinking of a fly caught up in a spider's web. Isn't there an Alice Cooper track about that?

Harcourt swallows. "Nothing has come up initially, but clearly, we need to go much deeper."

"Like Jenny Graham?"

Why can't he just let this drop? It just isn't funny anymore; in fact, it never was.

"We're also going to ask Joe Wilkins if he can throw any further light on Kathleen, given she was his mother's carer and spent so much of her time with her. Farren and Flowers are heading out there this morning."

"He has the butcher's shop in the same village as our

unfortunates?"

"Yes, sir. He worked with his father – Harry Wilkins – pretty much since his school days. He took ownership of it when Harry died just over four years ago."

"Do we think they're connected – the deaths of Kathleen Hodges and Brenda Wilkins?"

"We can't rule that out, sir, but there is absolutely nothing at this stage to suggest that to be the case. The doctors in the hospital signed off on the cause of Brenda Wilkins's death as sepsis, brought about initially by a fall. This caused internal bleeding which was undetected at first. By the time it was the immune system had overreacted and started to attack her intestines. It seems that it became out of control very quickly."

"So, we had no reason at that stage to suspect Kathleen Hodges of pushing her over?"

"Brenda's GP confirmed that she'd been suffering from low blood pressure for years. We'll check this out with Joe, sir – see if there had been any other unreported instances."

"Was the knife they found at the scene a butcher's knife?"

"It is the kind of knife that butchers are known to use, sir."

"Right. Shall we make the announcement?"

"Announcement, sir?"

"About our new venture, assuming you hadn't forgotten?"

"I hadn't, sir. Thank you, sir."

***

Ten minutes later, the four of them are sitting facing Hunter-Wright who has just formally announced that the new Cold Case Unit would come into operation at the end of the summer.

"I don't need to tell you how hard DI Harcourt has worked on cases such as these in recent times and so it was an absolute no-brainer that he should head it up as Detective Chief Inspector."

The spontaneous round of applause which follows is for Harcourt, though it is Hunter-Wright who waves it away as though all the credit for the promotion and new position is down to him.

"Thank you. Finally, because of this development, we shall need to make some further changes."

Now he has their attention; he watches their concentration levels rise through Flowers sitting up in his seat, Taylor scribbling something in her notepad other than the shopping she might need on her way home, and Farren's quick hand through her dark, wavy hair before wiping away otherwise invisible dust mites from the front of her navy-blue skirt.

"Unfortunately DC Hanrahan has gone off sick again: stress! It seems like just a few weeks since he came back from that stress fracture of the leg, although Records inform me it is just over seven months. This is naturally very disappointing and I will do my best to get a new DC seconded to this department as soon as possible but these things take time.

Nor do we yet have the go-ahead to bring in a new DCI. As you know, DCI Harcourt had been acting-up for some time now, but we're going to have to continue much as we did before for the time being. So, we'll need a new DI as soon as possible. This will have to be advertised across the force internally. I hope I can rely on some internal applications much closer to home."

***

"I wasn't expecting that." DS Flowers has turned on to the A44 heading towards Leominster, glad that the sun which had been blinding him all the way down to the river bridge is now to his left and slightly behind him. He had been expecting a traffic build-up at the lights in St John's and hadn't been disappointed.

"Why not? We need someone to lead our unit too – I can't imagine Hunter-Wright wanting to get fully operational again any time soon. He turns 60 at the end of the year, doesn't he? I think the DI – sorry, DCI – said he'll have completed 42 years of service?"

"Must be something like that. He's been in Worcester for nearly 20 years. Crazy when you think about it!" Flowers suddenly feels as flustered as he had when Farren first joined them. His hormones have been causing mayhem recently, though he's been blaming it on the sap rising since early spring. "I assumed they'd already have someone lined up as DI. You know, from outside."

"I suppose Hunter-Wright would prefer continuity and it would cost him less. He should know, he's in charge of the budgets, isn't he?"

"Pay scales are pay scales though."

"They are, but if one of us got the job, he'd have one less DS to pay. He didn't mention that, did he? Keeping the same number of people as before."

"We also need a permanent Detective Constable – or at least one with a bit more staying power than Marvyn Hanrahan! Still not a full enough complement to do the job efficiently though, is it? DCI Harcourt spent a lot of time convincing them of that. That's how we managed to get you."

"And worth every penny, I'm sure."

They both laugh as the last of the endless city sprawl reluctantly lets them out of its grasp as they head out into the countryside, bathed in morning sunshine below blue skies that might never have seen clouds. Brown signs soon remind them of Elgar's birth over a hundred and fifty years ago in the village of Lower Broadheath to their right. He'd felt like an outsider throughout his life. Flowers does too, though how or why he has become such an enigma to those few people who are normally around him remains a case that possibly only he can solve.

"It wouldn't be for me though?"

"Cold cases or promotion, or both?"

Flowers brakes suddenly as a stoat decides to hedge its bets and make a run between oncoming traffic on both sides to reach the far hedge.

"Was that a stoat or a weasel?" Farren rearranges herself on the passenger seat, pulling her seatbelt over her blouse.

Flowers tries not to look but does take a furtive glance across at her before replying. "A stoat. Weasels are usually smaller and have black tips on their tails."

"Quite the naturalist!"

"Just familiar with my habitat! You were saying…"

"Oh, yes. I wouldn't want to be working full-time on cold cases. I mean it's the slow lane, isn't it? You must come to dead ends – if you'll pardon the pun – all the time, with nobody still alive to interview. I think I'd find that frustrating."

"It has its rewards though, doesn't it? Solving cases that were seemingly going nowhere, filed away in some cabinet locked in a storeroom that people rarely enter. At least having a dedicated team that comes along and re-examines them gives those that are still around closure that they probably never expected to get."

"And justice."

"Absolutely."

"I know. I'd just rather be dealing with things that are happening now or things that I can help to prevent from happening again. That's the buzz of it for me."

"' A Bee from her hive one morning flew,

A tune to the day-light humming;

And away she went, o'er the clear, bright dew,

Where the grass was green, the violet blue,

And the gold of the sun was coming.'"

"That's beautiful. Was it one of Rob's favourites?"

"It was. It's from 'The Bee, Clover, and Thistle' by a lady called Hannah Flagg Gould."

"Do you still…"

"Read poetry? Of course. I don't think my brother would ever forgive me if I didn't. Besides, it allows me to remember him in a nice way: uplifting not sad. I often imagine he's still sitting there beside me, in some meadow, sunshine on our faces."

"With bees humming all around."

"Bees are very hard workers, you know. We can take a lot away from them."

"Can that include honey?"

They laugh again as the Black Mountains of Wales loom up in the distance, and human settlements become sparse.

CHAPTER THREE

She sits up in her bed, pulling the pillows up behind her so that she can lean back again and gaze out of the window. The morning mist has cleared to leave a bright, clear morning. She could be looking at a countryside painting with the distant Cotswold Hills framing the scene far better than the window itself does.

The white, wooden shutters are wide open. He must have opened them for her. She remembers when they were first installed. His idea, not hers. Gave them more privacy he had said and kept the bright sunshine at bay. Gave the house a 'New England' kind of look. She hadn't been convinced. She quite liked the old England.

The cornfields seem to her to be like seas of gold. Farmers will be counting their chickens despite the proverbial warnings and weather forecasts that usually get doom exactly right and fine days wanting.

She's walked through those fields so many times, book in hand, seeking out a sheltered corner where she could read the afternoon away, alone. Always alone. Like now.

The pile of books on the bedside table beside her is growing. Multi-coloured spines for everyone: the fat and the thin, the special and the spineless. She smiles inwardly, and outwardly though there is nobody there to share it. So many words and yet so little time left.

***

Joe Wilkins lives in a small, detached cottage of grey Welsh stone at the top of Rectory Lane

Neither detective can see a rectory, nor a larger-than-average-sized house that has since been converted for ordinary people to inhabit. No doubt the DI would have done his historical research before heading out, or walked back down the lane, his endearing interest in most things historical suitably piqued.

Old wooden barrels sit on either side of the front door, deep red geraniums in each welcoming them with their beautiful colours contrasting with the stone, and that kind of summer morning fragrance that no branded, artificial household or personal spray has ever been quite able to adequately trap.

Although tall and solidly square, Farren notes that Joe's voice is higher than she would have expected as he somewhat reluctantly invites them inside. She is also surprised at how light and airy it feels. She had expected it to be a bit cramped and gloomy like so many similar cottages she has now visited in the area. The clue is usually in the size of the windows: authentically quaint to look at from the outside, and practically useless to see through from the inside. Maybe it's because she's still not used to the country lifestyle? Perhaps she won't allow herself enough time here to become accustomed to it? The jury is still very much out on that one.

Joe leads them into an expansive, modern kitchen which is bathed in sunlight. Looking up, she notices two large skylights and quickly realises that this is a modern extension at the back of the cottage. There is also a glass conservatory beyond it which enhances the feeling of space and an 'outside-in' perception the architect had supposedly been aiming at.

A middle-aged woman in white jogging pants and a tight white top is sitting out there on one of the two wicker chairs. She is flicking through a glossy magazine, a large mug on the glass table beside her. She barely acknowledges their presence and makes no move to join them.

Without being invited they each take a chrome stool by the sleek breakfast bar, all in smooth granite. Not a stain in sight and everything is in its meticulous place. Fresh flowers are arranged in a vase at the far end and trailing green spider plants sit along the conservatory's glass wall, giving the impression of separation.

"This is a lovely space!" Flowers leans forward onto the bar, as though about to order a drink.

"Thank you."

"Your wife's doing?" Farren nods towards the woman.

"Camilla!" He seems amused but the smile is just as quickly put away again. "Hardly."

He isn't going to elaborate or offer them refreshments. Standing somewhat menacingly in front of the expensive-looking cooker, his broad arms folded across his chest, he isn't expecting them to stay either.

"We won't take too much of your time."

They will both confirm later that this had met with no obvious body language response whatsoever.

Farren continues, calmly, almost more slowly than she might otherwise have spoken. She has never been one to be intimidated; many of her erstwhile colleagues soon discovered that. A woman has been killed and left outside in her pretty, private garden, open to the elements, in what had looked like a horrible death resulting in a carcass pecked over by crows and possibly worse.

"We're investigating the murder of Kathleen Hodges."

"Murder?" He seems to have been knocked out of his stride for the first time – not that he has moved.

"Given that she was your mother's carer we were hoping that you might be able to help us with some background information."

"Why me? I do have a brother and sister, as I'm sure you know."

Flowers makes a note of this before serving the next ball towards the receiver. "We do, sir. We may talk to them in due course. It made sense to us to begin here as you live in the village and were, therefore, closest to your late mother, as well as Miss Hodges."

"I wouldn't say we were closest."

Farren has already had enough. Patience isn't her strong suit. She would never have made a good poker player. "But you know what we mean! We believe that your brother – Frank – lives in Upper Handley and your sister in Pershore, each on the other side of Worcester, whereas you stayed local."

"What are you implying by that?" His rising hostility is shown by his rocking from one leg to the other.

"We're not implying anything, sir." Flowers enjoys playing the role of the 'good cop' peacemaker, especially alongside Farren who doesn't. "It just seemed that given the proximity of their houses relative to both yours and your shop, yours was as good a place as any to start."

"At least we're good enough for something out here." Again, the words are fired back over the net without emotion but are not lost on their targets.

"You're not at the shop today, sir?" Flowers again.

"I can see why you became a policeman."

"Is it closed?"

"We only close on Sundays; was the same when my father ran it. I saw no reason to alter it. People get used to things. They don't generally like change. My colleague and I share shifts apart from Fridays and Saturdays when it's generally busier. I'm down there this afternoon."

"Sounds like a very flexible solution." Farren watches Mrs Wilkins lift the mug to her lips. She could kill for a coffee. Perhaps better not to interrupt the flow of this conversation though.

"Was Miss Hodges a regular customer?"

"Fridays. Regular as clockwork."

"Presumably she shopped for your mother too."

"Sometimes she did. I used to see to it if not. Anyway, if Mum had needed anything she could have come by herself. She wasn't an invalid. Just needed a bit of help in the house, that's all."

"And Kathleen provided that help?" Flowers again.

"That's generally what carers do isn't it?" The response is withering.

"Not necessarily." Flowers is also feeling thirsty now. "A home help wouldn't see themselves as a carer, for example."

"Kathleen used to pop in when Dad was alive; make

sure he was OK while Mum was out for the day – bus to Bromyard or maybe even Hereford. She started doing bits of dusting, washing up. That's how it started. As Mum became a bit more frail, she used to help her wash and so on. Mum never had any problems with her that I know of. Neither did Dad. Satisfied?"

"I'm sorry if this is still quite raw for you, Mr Wilkins. It's only been three weeks or so."

"18 days."

"You miss her."

"We all miss her."

"Including Kathleen. I imagine her days seemed very empty after your mother died. It can't have made it any easier living next door, looking across at an empty house and so on."

"If she found it difficult, she didn't say."

'And you were never going to ask' thinks Farren.

"Can you tell us what Miss Hodges was like, sir? You probably knew her as well as anyone."

"I didn't know her well at all. She seemed friendly enough whenever I went around to see Mum. She didn't have a lot to say and neither did I."

"Bishop's Lacy is quite a small village though," Flowers persists, "Not too many secrets!"

"Don't believe all that crap about 'community spirit' you might have read about in the papers. In my experience people prefer to try to keep themselves to themselves; the gossipmongers see to that. They say that one swallow doesn't make a summer. Well, around here one step out of the ordinary – one step out of line – and they're on it, banging on all the jungle drums they can find. Sorry, I probably shouldn't say things like that these days, should I? That's just how I feel."

"Alright. Well, many thanks for your time, Mr Wilkins." Farren finds his outburst curious and not necessarily in keeping with someone grieving for their mother. Maybe Brenda did have something to hide – some secret she jealously guarded perhaps. What if Kathleen had found out about it? The neurons in her brain are fizzing which is exactly why she joined the police.

She had hoped that Camilla might have come in to join them by this point, if only for curiosity's sake. "Would your wife be able to add anything do you think?"

"I think not."

***

They walk back down the narrow lane, dusty again after the recent rain. Farren is studiously looking directly ahead while Flowers half turns to see Joe Wilkins standing outside his house, watching them (to make sure that they keep on walking?). He bends to pluck a wilted leaf from one of the plants, rolling it round and around in his fingers, not once letting them out of his sight.

The lane is still cobbled in places and the heel of Farren's left-hand shoe catches between two of the ancient stones. She loses her balance momentarily and leans backwards to compensate for the unexpected forward movement. Flowers darts forward to take her arm, steadying her if unsteadying him.

"Thanks." Her response is appreciative, nothing more.

Flowers quickly removes his hand and just as speedily

begins to talk in a low voice. "He's gone back inside – finally."

"What did you make of him?"

"Same as you did, probably. Defensive. Like getting blood from a stone."

"There's plenty of that around here."

"Blood or stone?"

Farren laughs. "Both. He was very singular though, wasn't he? I can't believe that woman didn't even come in to say 'hello' to us."

"Perhaps she didn't want to intrude?"

"In her own home? You'd think curiosity would have got the better of her if nothing else."

"Maybe they'd argued before we arrived, and she stayed out there on purpose?"

"Or maybe she wasn't his wife?"

Flowers hadn't considered this possibility, just made an assumption about their relationship. DI Harcourt was always encouraging him to 'throw all of the jigsaw pieces that you can see up into the air and see if they make the same pattern when they land. If you're still puzzled, something is missing.'

He still has a long way to go and hopes that Harcourt won't be too far away from them in his new role. As mentors go there was only really his mum before the DCI. He carries her words of worldly wisdom with him every day, but she prefers romance fiction to crime novels.

"I'll show you the crime scene." Farren is striding ahead, purposefully, and free of cobbled stones now.

A few minutes later they are standing on tiptoes, just enough to see over the wall and into Kathleen's back garden, Brenda Wilkins's lies beyond it. The gently fluttering ticker tape remains as a reminder to admiring passers-by that bad things have happened in this village.

"Brenda Wilkins was the gardener of the two then?"

"Or maybe she had more time on her hands to get out there? You know what it's like with gardens: before you know it, they've surrounded you." Farren has never had a garden but has heard plenty of her colleagues moaning about the need to weed and mow when all they've wanted to do is sit and watch the football.

"I guess Kathleen would use the little gate up there to cross from one garden to the other?"

When she'd been here before with Harcourt Farren had noted the small, black metal gate that appeared to have made a relatively recent entry. The cement lines on each side of it held it in place in the old wall and it showed as yet few signs of wear either from sun or rain – or both.

"And easy enough for someone to pass from Brenda's garden the other way too." Farren nods, thoughtfully. "Quite sheltered from these bushes on Brenda's side. I mean, it's not completely covered, but you don't have a direct view of her back door from here or that part of the garden. If someone wanted to avoid being seen from the road here, they could do so relatively easily when passing from Brenda's house to Kathleen's." She steps down and rubs the backs of her legs, aware that Flowers is watching her.

"Much more so than from Kathleen's side," he agrees, also stepping backwards so that his feet are flat to the ground again, his hamstrings continuing to burn. “Maybe the perpetrator wanted to catch Kathleen by surprise and cut down the risk of being seen. What’s beyond this wall to our left?”

“An old garage. That dilapidated white building you can see next to it also belongs to the garage. We haven’t interviewed the owner yet, although it looks as though it would be quite difficult to climb up on that side and drop down into either garden. You certainly couldn’t do it without being seen from here, because of the height. The bushes aren’t that tall.”

“Give them time, though!”

Farren doesn’t respond. She has spotted a small, grey-haired man bounding along the pavement towards them.

“Can I help you?” She turns to face him before he’s quite reached them; being seen to be ready and prepared for action is a proactive move she has found to be quite useful in the past.

“I do hope it might be the other way round.” Dressed in a grey shirt and thin pink tie over immaculately pressed khaki chinos, the man holds out his hand. “Simon Short.”

Flowers smiles inwardly at the appropriateness of the man’s name and fights hard not to show it. He does notice that there are no patches of sweat on the man’s shirt. He is either pretty fit for his age or has parked his car just around the corner, out of sight.

Farren shakes his hand. She is pleased that it is not as damp and limp as she had anticipated, rather it is pleasingly dry – and very firm. “DS Farren, and this is DS

Flowers."

"Ah. I thought you must be connected to the unfortunate events that have taken place here. I wasn't sure whether you were from the insurance company or not."

"Why. Has somebody put a claim in already?" Farren is intrigued. It is certainly a possibility, but a bit of a leap, nevertheless.

"I have absolutely no idea."

They wait silently for him to elaborate, just as he appears to be waiting for them to ask him questions.

Flowers needs to move this – and possibly the man – on. The sun is blazing down on his exposed neck, and he needs to get away from this spot; into the shade at least. Covering his eyes so that he can see Mr Short more clearly, he asks, perhaps a little more abruptly than might usually have been the case: "Who would stand to benefit from the death? Do you know?"

"Kathleen's death, do you mean?"

"Either would be handy." Farren joins in. "We're at an early stage of our enquiries." She's less interested in the answer because they'll soon find all the information they need (Taylor might already have done so), more to see how much this man knows.

"Kathleen had no family that I am aware of. Certainly, she entertained no relatives that she told me about."

"What about friends, excluding yourself of course? Were you aware of any recent visitors or even people from her past who might have wanted to cause her any trouble?"

"I wasn't her keeper you understand. My principal involvement in Kathleen's life was to feed the cat when she went on holiday, which wasn't all that often, it has to be said (her taking holidays not me feeding the cat). Brenda saw to that. She knew what she was doing when she turned on the taps. Kathleen used to say that she'd have been so racked with guilt there'd have been little enjoyment in taking a vacation. As to her distant past, I really couldn't say as I wasn't part of her life back then."

"Sorry, can I just ask how it is that you did get to know Kathleen?" Farren is also feeling the heat now.

"Well, of course, I didn't initially." The silence again, as though he wishes to be seen (heard) as a storyteller wanting to drag out the tension for as long as he possibly can. Neither detective is in the mood to play the game by responding so he continues, a little reluctantly it must be said.

"It was my wife who knew her first. She – my wife, Rosie – was a nurse at the Royal. Kathleen had been admitted for a minor ailment. Women's things..."

He looks up at Flowers but enjoys no typically male reciprocity such as raised eyebrows or awkward shuffling of feet so continues more quickly.

"They got chatting and found they had much in common – tennis and small Japanese fish – and that we lived in the same village. Soon after she was discharged, Rosie took her along to the tennis club in Piston Harbury and the rest, as they say, is history."

"They became good friends." Farren is so bored.

"Right up until my wife's sudden death, yes."

"I'm sorry to hear that – your wife's death I mean."

"Thank you, she had a heart attack. Very sudden it was. Being in the right place at the right shift time was some comfort."

"It must still have been a shock." Farren is wondering where all this is going.

"It was, yes. But I am minded that she didn't suffer too much. Certainly not like poor Kathleen."

There is an almost imperceptible glance between Farren and Flowers. No details have been disclosed. Though the imaginative press rarely worries about such things, she hasn't read anything yet. "What do you know about Kathleen's death Mr Short?"

Her sudden formality appears to alarm him. "Nothing at all, Sergeant. I was curled up in bed with John at the time."

Again, the time of likely death has not been disclosed because the pathologist has not, as far as either of them knows, got back to Harcourt.

"John?"

"Le Carré! Jolly good writer, though I do admit I frequently have to turn back to remind myself of who was whom, or who was pretending to be somebody they weren't. Better that than the film which was laden with flashbacks, however."

"And where was this, sir."

"At home."

Farren is, for sure, almost at the end of this story now, whether Short is ready to conclude it or not. If there is to be no twist in the tale, she is prepared to close the book. She knows who she is and strongly suspects Short to be a time waster consumed by too much of it on his hands.

"Where is 'home', sir." Flowers gallantly takes up the reins.

"Snots Road. Oh, don't worry about the name, Sergeant. It's short for Snorts Road. There used to be stables there in the last century – the nineteenth that is – and the name derived from the sound the horses often made. Of course, young boys quickly developed their own, peculiar version, and that's the one that sticks in your mind, isn't it?"

He beams at their serious, almost disbelieving faces.

"Well, it's been interesting to meet you, sir." Farren is at her wit's end now. "If there was nothing else..."

"Oh, but there is! Indeed, there is." He has their attention but knows it won't be for long. "Kathleen was obsessed by Brenda Wilkins's will."

"How do you mean 'obsessed'?" Farren is doing her duty, dutifully.

"Wouldn't stop going on about it."

"Presumably everything got left to the children, Harry Wilkins having pre-deceased her?"

"That may well be so, or at least what the will that was read to them states."

"So?"

"Kathleen knew that there was another will. A different will. A later will."

"Why would she have changed her will? I assume it would have been a continuation of their joint intentions – hers and her husband's."

"Quite so, but Kathleen was certain of its existence and,

what's more, so am I."

"Why is that, sir?"

"Because I signed and witnessed it."

***

Harcourt listens intently to his colleagues' feedback before swinging into action – metaphorically and also using his office chair. "We'll need to get over to the solicitors handling probate for Brenda Wilkins first. After that, we'll need to contact the other two children – Fred and Pat. Let's also see what comes back on the fingerprints that Forensics managed to lift from Kathleen's property."

"And Joe, sir?"

Farren is there with her notepad balanced on her knee, pen poised to strike as usual. She'd have made a formidable journalist if the Force hadn't made its enquiries about her first and offered her a job. For all her apparent dedication and fastidiousness though, Harcourt has never been entirely convinced that she loves police work. Perhaps none of them do?

"Given what you've reported back, I think we'll let him stew for a little while. You could usefully go and see his butcher chum..."

"Steve Baker, sir."

"The same. We might check that Joe is at home first; if what he said about shifts is true then it might be more informative to get Mr Baker on his own."

"Would you like me to join DS Farren, sir?" Flowers is as eager as ever, and not just over the prospect of making another trip to Bishop's Lacy.

Harcourt watches him blush as usual before replying. "I think we'll keep you in reserve to tackle the mysterious lady in the back garden, Ian. We'll do it in reverse: check that Joe is in the shop first and then you could casually appear at his home. Gabby, what have you found out about Kathleen Hodges – apart from the fact that she appears to have been brutally murdered?"

"Thank you very much, sir." Taylor sits upright, clearly pleased to have been given the opportunity to contribute. "Kathleen Hodges was an only child, born in Bromyard in 1960."

"Only fifteen years younger than Brenda, then?" Farren interrupts.

If Taylor is annoyed at her flow being interrupted, she doesn't show it. Perhaps she is just being professional. "Correct. Kathleen's father – Arthur - worked in the local branch of Barclays. He didn't progress far and neither does he seem to have moved much between branches, apart from a brief stint at Leominster at the start of the Seventies."

"Not ambitious, then?" Harcourt this time.

"Or nobody was ambitious for him?"

"Point taken. Carry on."

"Very little on his wife – Melissa. There are no recent employment records for her, and she had paid no NI at all since the 1950s – even then, barely any to make a significant contribution to her state pension."

"She didn't receive one then, or a hugely reduced one?"

"She didn't because she died when she was 58 (Arthur was 61)."

"Seems a bit young, even by the standards of the time, what, the late 80s?"

"1988, sir. A fatal car crash just this side of Hereford."

"Suspicious?"

"Cut and dried. They were hit by an oncoming lorry after a shopping trip. The radio in the lorry's cab was going full blast and it is thought that he just lost concentration. All three died at the scene. No other explanation was forthcoming. No sign of stroke or heart attack or any undiagnosed medical condition. He just ploughed straight into the Hodges's car. They obviously wouldn't have expected it and had no time to swerve or take any other kind of evasive action. They didn't stand a chance, sir."

Quietly, they each picture the scene of carnage in their own way: the impact, the aftermath with emergency services unable to make any of it better before the wheels of justice that would have come into play shortly afterwards. Harcourt, in particular, seems lost in a re-imagining of such horror.

Taylor presses on. "Apart from those facts, we can't find anything untoward. We can certainly continue to search for any friends or neighbours who might be able to give us something more, but any contemporaries are going to be into their eighties by now, or at least late seventies – even if they still live nearby."

"No. You're right. If we don't have anything clear-cut to go on, it would just be a waste of resources for now, and you know how much Hunter-Wright hates those three words when put together. We can go further back if anything comes our way in the meantime. Did the parents have any siblings on either side?"

"That's just it, sir. Both were only children too. If we had some kind of social media profile, we might have been able to find out more about them and the lives they led."

"Or a memory of a birthday celebration years ago, and reminders of the date years after they'd died!" Harcourt's playfulness has dissipated. The room has become colder, despite the sun creeping around the window to the south of the building. "OK. Kathleen has no other living family to speak of. What about friends, former work colleagues?"

"She seemed to live a very solitary life. She went to school in Bromyard but didn't go on to college. She got a job in a primary school close to Bishop's Lacy in 1979 which is when she moved there. She bought and lived in the same house all her life. We've found bank records going right back that show her father putting down a significant deposit for her."

"I guess you'd want to do whatever you could for your only child." Harcourt remains grave.

"Or he was a bank robber?" Flowers's attempts to lighten things haven't helped any more than the sunshine now pouring through the window.

"She obviously didn't have much more about her than her father did?" Farren remarks, adopting the same serious approach as her superior.

"Or, as the DI – sorry, sir." She looks across at him, clearly embarrassed.

"You're fine, Gabby. Please continue."

Noticeably relieved, Taylor does so. "As the DCI remarked earlier, perhaps neither of them had the chance to make something of themselves. Or maybe security and a peaceful life were all they ever really wanted."

"Did Kathleen train as a teacher then?" Farren is hastily covering her tracks.

"She became what we might now call a 'teacher's assistant' or 'classroom assistant' I think it is. She left the school just under five years ago."

"Presumably to enjoy an early retirement?" Harcourt is leaning on his desk, his hands together as if in prayer, though all of them know that would not be the case.

"That's what I thought, sir, yet almost immediately she is taken on by a recruitment company – Careers, they're called. They put what looks like a hashtag through the second 'e' so that you would most likely see 'Carers.'"

"I wonder how much some London branding agency charged them for that."

"No idea but they're based in Bromyard."

"And we know that she never married."

"We do. We'll continue to ask about close friends. Nothing, how shall I put it, 'sentimental' was found in her house. Some china ornaments of girls and boys, but these look much older - more likely hand-me-downs (or cheap items considered too precious to leave behind) from her mother. No letters of any note on the sideboard and no photos of holidays to go on – not even of her parents. There were a few pictures on the wall which could just as easily have been bought from any junk shop. Again, none of them were valuable."

"Apart from to her?"

"Of course. It just seems very strange that she hadn't

accumulated more 'stuff' in a house she'd lived in for so many years. My house is bursting and I'm not that old - really."

This relaxes all of them, even Harcourt slightly. "And no sign of a break-in?"

"No, sir. All windows had window locks which were in place. The front door was locked with no signs of any attempts at forced entry. The back door was open, as you found it."

"Strange that the windows were locked shut, in this weather?" Harcourt glances the question off each of them.

"Could be the thunderstorm warnings." Flowers offers.

"Possibly, though locking everything up would have made the humidity level in there horrendous, surely?"

"Maybe that's why she went outside, only planning to go back inside when the rain came." Farren tries.

"Which it didn't," Taylor responds, abruptly.

"Or she locked everything up because she was planning to leave the house for some reason?" Flowers doesn't want to be left out of the pitching of possibilities.

"But there's nowhere to go to from the back garden – no escape. It's bordered on all three sides, and there's no back gate." Farren again. "We were only just tall enough to be able to see over the wall."

"Response officers had to use their vehicle," Harcourt confirms, grimly, "When they first got there everything seemed to be locked up, so they drove round to the side and got over the wall that way. That's how they knew the front door was locked from the inside, with the key still in the lock. Maybe Ian has a point, though. Perhaps she did intend to leave and just went outside to check everything was OK before she did so. She'd have locked the back door and then headed out from the front, wouldn't she?"

They each nod. The unanswered question in the air is whether this had been her intention and, if so, where she had planned on going.

"It does seem certain that the murderer came from Brenda's side; that much I think we can assume is true. Forensics have swabbed both back and front doors on both sides, so we'll see what, if anything, they reveal.

Great work Gabby. Let's follow up on the agency and check out the school; see if we can ascertain why Kathleen might have left the school when she did. I don't believe in quiet lives, or at least a family tree with so few lines of enquiry. Somebody, for some reason, chose to kill Kathleen and make it look even more sinister than it actually was. Either that or we're looking at some kind of gangland moll from 'The Long Good Friday.'

None of them respond.

"And going back to Simon Short, sir?" Farren is bending forward, prepared to hang on his every word.

"We do need to look at him. 'Small man syndrome' – by name and by nature?"

"That could certainly have something to do with it." Farren smiles, acknowledging that vertically challenged men often didn't view the world in its correct perspective.

"I don't particularly like the way he suddenly turned

up when you were in Bishop's Lacy. It feels like he might have been stalking you or at least staking out the houses, waiting for an opportunity. Seems off to me."

"I thought he might have been just another nosy villager at first," Farren articulates the DCI's distaste, "You know: aroused when something out of the ordinary has happened for the first time in six decades."

"You're enjoying being out in the country then?" Harcourt's sarcasm is mollified by his smile.

"I am. The Frome Valley is absolutely beautiful, especially at this time of year. I imagine it's a bit bleak in the winter, though."

"You've not been over that way before?"

"No, sir. Further down, yes. My parents used to take us on camping holidays in the Forest of Dean. The trip out to Bishop's Lacy reminded me a bit of the Wye Valley, but that's a long time ago now."

"Too quiet for you, though? I mean that's why you left Selly Oak to come and join us here in Worcester for a bit more action wasn't it?"

"It is, but I knew there would be a lot of rural cases too."

"Or nutcases?"

"I'm sorry, sir. There was just something about Mr Short. He seemed to know much more than we've yet put out in the public domain. I'm not convinced he's told us everything he knows either."

"I agree with Linda, sir." Flowers nods his head. "He spoke peculiarly too."

"Olde English? Touch of Gaelic perhaps?" Again, Harcourt is smiling, but he does want to establish whether the pair of them have got a bit carried away with a potentially important witness they happened not to like.

“Nothing like that, sir.” Now Flowers shakes his head, blushing slightly. “No. He just didn’t seem real somehow – and, no, this is nothing to do with poetry and daydreams. What I mean is, he seemed otherworldly.”

“Maybe he reads too many books? Gives him too many ideas?”

“He did mention John Le Carré.”

“Well, there you are then: none of us is who we seem to be.”

The three of them wait for him to continue, but he too seems to be momentarily detached from the room, from them.

“What do you make of the whole will thing, sir?” Farren takes up the slack.

“We certainly need to follow it up, though with whom I’m not quite sure yet. The children certainly, but let’s see what the solicitor handling the family’s affairs has to say about it first. DS Taylor, would you care to accompany me?”

Taylor jumps up, beaming. “I’d be happy to, sir.”

If he wasn’t very much mistaken, a frown had taken up temporary residence on Farren’s lovely face – fleeting and gone again almost as soon as it arrived – but it was there for all to see. Harcourt saw it, even if the others didn’t. He wasn’t mistaken and, what’s more, he understands exactly where it came from.

***

She tries to clear her mind yet again. There's a small white cloth under the pillow. She wipes it across her damp face, then closes her eyes and tries to focus. Someone once told her to imagine that everything in front of her was a white screen. A blank screen. Anything that tried to creep in from the top or bottom or either side had to be pushed out of sight. Only when that happened, could she begin.

It doesn't take her long. There wasn't very much on the screen to start with. A woman is trying to enter from the left-hand side. An older woman. Somebody she once knew though from where or when she cannot work out. She doesn't like her. She knows that. She mustn't concentrate on this person though as it isn't her. This is what he told her – the man with the dark-rimmed glasses in the big house. The one who used to shut the curtains each time they went into the room. The woman needs to go. Somehow Charlotte pushes her out of her vision again. She mustn't open her eyes in case she's returned without Charlotte realising it.

She knows she must start with something called 'basics.' Well then, people are made up of letters. Each part of them has a trail of letters attached. The labels used to identify them are made up of letters. Letters form words which people use to describe what they've seen, heard, spoken about, written or read. Those letters are rearranged according to where they live – where they've come from – but their function remains the same: to give meaning to the life all around us, for each of us. To add meaning where there is confusion or doubt. She knows this, just can't always make the words work properly and wonders if she ever will again.

Charlotte does remember that her husband is something to do with making sure that the right letters are used, or used in the right way. There's a right way and a wrong way, but she doesn't understand what difference it makes, or why. Daniel and the young girl who is often here in the house don't seem to have to think about it. They just know. So why doesn't she?

A tiny girl is standing on the table at the far end of her bed, next to the thing that makes the room light when all the light has gone from the sky outside. It probably isn't the same girl who often walks into her room. This one doesn't move. Just stands there waiting for her to say something or perhaps she wants Charlotte to leave so that she can have the room to herself.

A soft voice from long ago and far away keeps telling her that letters form secret codes that somehow unlock mysteries. Maybe, if she could just work out the code, everything would be alright again. There are four of them, children - and a dog. One of them is called Julian but she can't remember the names of the others. They live in castles and big houses and tall houses by the sea with lights at the top. Charlotte is there with them somehow, only she isn't. She's all grown-up now and, besides, she's here – in this room. The voice is her own and nobody else seems able to hear what she is saying.

She has tried to use the notepad next to her. Honestly, she has. The long metal thing slips quite naturally between her fingers as if it's been there before. It feels familiar if not comforting. That part of it is fine, but what to do next?

She cannot remember how many letters there are but does recall them having shapes – each of them different unless they sit side by side, or stand. Neither can she remember how to make the shapes work. There was something about a 'p' sitting on a line with its tail below it, and possibly a 'd' reaching up to the line above it. She can see a line through her window, but it isn't the same. Headless, blue, red and white people are swinging on it in the wind. Not the same at all.

There's a computer on the table too – next to the girl. Maybe it belongs to her? It has another name too, but she cannot remember what it is. One evening when she was sure that the girl was looking the other way, she'd crept out of bed and lifted the lid. The letters were all hiding inside, jumbled up but in straight rows. Thrilled with the discovery, she'd used her big finger to hit each of the letters in turn. Excitement had quickly turned to disappointment as nothing happened: she couldn't make them work. Perhaps they were already asleep?

Sometimes she can hear the sounds of words, even though she's pretty sure there's nobody else in the room. She can hear them and sometimes hears herself sending them back without her brain ever really needing to get involved.

It isn't always like this, but it is sometimes. The secret is definitely in the letters. When they choose to hide life is a mystery to her.

***

"Nothing at all?" Harcourt knows that this is a superfluous question.

"You mean 'nothing' on its own is insufficient?"

"Yes, he'd asked for that."

He mouths to Debbie that he'll be back at the dinner table in a minute or two. She in turn mouths 'Don't worry' as she pops his loaded plate into the microwave, ready for the familiar – much later - follow-up phase.

"So, the work of a professional?"

"Or that's what they're trying to make you believe, along with all of the other little touches."

"Somebody who knows how to handle knives then; to thoroughly, almost forensically clean them?

"They always believe that something can be 'forensically cleaned!"

"This could have been the murder weapon though?"

"It could have been, yes. The rips in the outer skin match exactly the teeth pattern of the serrated cutting edge.

She is so cool, enjoying the coolness between them, and yet he cannot help but picture her face rather than the damaged one of Kathleen Hodges. Perhaps it's a natural reaction that his years of experience and training haven't quite managed to stamp out. "Is there anything else from your examination that you can tell me – only if you think it's useful of course?"

"I'd hate to feel useless." She waits for his reaction, as this is how they usually play their little game, but his dinner is going cold, and Debbie is beginning to smoulder. Thankfully she takes the non-verbal hint and continues a little more swiftly than before. "The cause of death was essentially organ failure due to massive blood loss. The trauma to the stomach area resulted in three distinct knife wounds. I would say that the knife was inserted and withdrawn quickly on each of the three occasions. There was surprisingly little external bruising around the wounds."

"Violent or mechanical?"

"Strangely, I've often thought that stabbing a seemingly defenceless woman was an act of violence."

This isn't improving his mood, and Debbie is now glaring at him (in that way she has).

"Not... a frenzied attack; that's what I meant."

"In that case, yes. Deliberate and controlled. Cold-blooded killing as opposed to rage I would say."

"And the limbs?"

"Her hands and fingers were severed post-mortem. She wouldn't have suffered any further."

"Anything from the fishing line or whatever it was the murderer used to stitch her lips together?" He hears a sudden gasp from the table and turns to see that Debbie has dropped her fork into her bowl of pasta and is taking a long gulp of Pinot.

"It certainly looks like part of a fishing line; we'll do some further analysis of it. No other evidence from anything fishing-related has come my way so probably plucked from the grasp of the garden gnome and replaced by the knife. We'll have to get back to you on that. As to DNA, which I expect you are more interested in, nothing for us to sample I'm afraid, on either human or other materials."

"Disappointing."

"Such is life – and death."

CHAPTER FOUR

Taylor heads over the River Teme, which gives its name to the winding picturesque valley she has been told about so often but never explored. There seems so little time in her life to do so, what with the regular trips back to visit her parents in Birmingham and domestic life taking its chances on her time when she isn't on duty.

She's been thinking about her father a lot lately. It isn't just that he's slowed down; her mother thinks he's about to stop. Both women are concerned about it although Dad is as philosophical about it as ever, telling them both to 'stop your worrying.'

She tries to push him (them) out of her mind. Not out, exactly, more to the back of her mind for now. They would never be allowed to leave her completely.

The unfolding landscape suggests a regular supply of rainfall, although Harcourt had once told her that the Malvern Hills acted as some kind of air pressure filter. Forecasts predicting rain from Wales often didn't quite make it to this, one of England's western outposts. Still, the neat green fields seemed to be in pretty good shape to her.

An old sign with rusting edges confirms the Herefordshire border as the bracken on the hilltops gives way to acres and acres of green fields stretching down and away to her right. Wood-framed yellow buildings – wannabe Tudor or otherwise – and the occasional oast house cling to the foothills while, as she approaches Bromyard itself, a similarly faded advertising hoarding on her offside expounds the delights of the 'Bromyard Town Criers Festival.'

Mercifully this has already passed, she muses, as she passes a road sign to Bishops Frome on her left, and a brown sign just below it, encouraging drivers to drink in the delights of the Frome Valley Vineyard. Far more to her taste.

Bromyard is the 'Jewel in the Downs' according to its welcome sign. She heads towards a car park in the Town Centre although the Sat Nav doesn't particularly like her doing so, satisfied as it is that she has already 'reached her destination.'

She parks behind Bromyard Public Hall which also boasts a Heritage Centre. St Peter's Church looks on helplessly as, consulting the notes she had written before leaving the police station, she heads off on foot in the opposite direction, past 'The Old Vicarage.' A blue plaque reliably informs her that it had been converted to offices in 1967, which the local council have occupied for the last fifty years.

The town – or this part of it at least – is made up of a muddle of independent stores, such as may have been found in small towns like this years ago. Peeling paintwork and, on closer examination, rotting wooden windowsills prove the point. To some, this would be described as trendy, but to Taylor, everything is just a bit drab and has that left-behind air about it, which is very different to 'quaint.'

A collection of almshouses erected in the seventeenth

century (help, she's turning into Harcourt) sit at the foot of Cruxwell Street. She obediently turns right and heads up towards the High Street before spotting the Carers offices up ahead. It sits in a cluster of newish brown-brick buildings which also features a shiny therapy clinic. Opposite them, a dreary grey building is given over to insurance offices. 'Ah well, if the therapy doesn't work...' Taylor is in a wicked mood today.

There is only one door into their part of the building, above which a peeling, white sign spells out the word Careers, with the aforesaid hashtag obliterating the second 'e.' Unfortunately, its font size is quite a bit bigger than the other letters and so all eyes are drawn to it, rather than the remaining word and mistakenly assume that #ers is some kind of cryptic Twitter tag.

Just inside there is a small desk with a long grey metal strip on top helpfully confirming in black capital letters: 'Reception.' It is unmanned but a dumpy woman of average height soon arrives. Dressed in a neat, red skirt and white blouse she introduces herself as the Chief Executive and asks, rather officiously, if Taylor has an appointment.

Trying not to stare at the small but obvious gap in the young woman's upper front teeth, Taylor glances briefly at a row of vacant chairs on the right-hand side of the desk, before presenting her warrant card. "I'd like to ask you a few questions about Kathleen Hodges. If you can spare me the time of course."

The woman fixes an icy smile on her face before leading Taylor to the opposite side of the room where two further desks sit at right angles to each other. An older, diminutive woman with dirty blonde hair tied up into a bun sits, furiously hitting the keys of her laptop without looking up at either of them.

The same style of grey metal strip adorns each desk, only these now incorporate names. The blonde woman is 'Glenda Hollybush – Senior Training Manager' and the friendly, outreach person is 'Sybil McCaffrey – Chief Executive Officer.'

A grubby orange anorak hangs, incongruously, on a peg above and behind Sybil's desk. This must be the higher-grade part of the office, then, as no such pegs seem to exist anywhere else in the corporate space.

Taylor is waived towards a high-backed wooden chair which may have come from one of their kitchens at home. She looks through an open door into a small cell-like room to her left. Devoid of windows it has no furniture apart from two further kitchen chairs separated by a miniscule wooden coffee table.

"That's Glenda's domain." Sybil has caught her looking. "It's our purpose-built training suite."

At the mention of her name, Glenda has stopped typing and is looking at Taylor with mild curiosity.

"How many of you work here?" Taylor begins, addressing her question to neither of them in particular.

"It's just the two of us," Sybil answers before Glenda can project the words through her open mouth which quickly reverts to its default thin, ribbony shape.

"Well, then, I'll take as little of your time as I can."

"It's no problem. We haven't anything in our diaries for the rest of the week." Glenda is visibly pleased to have a distraction, yet Sybil is glaring at her colleague in the same way as a football centre half might glare at a goalkeeper who has just allowed the football to pass through their legs. “We’re all about one-to-one training here.”

“That must be time-consuming?”

Glenda continues to beam at her. “Yes, well it is, and it isn’t. Depends on how quickly our candidates pick everything up really.”

“They have to go through a rigorous testing procedure before you’ll take them on?” Taylor is trying to keep a straight face while dreading the earnest response she knows is coming.

“It is, and not everybody is suited to becoming a carer you see. We had one candidate with a broken arm which made lifting difficult; another one who was deaf.”

“We’re well-known in the area for our expertise,” the CEO interjects, strategically, “We’ve won awards for it.”

“Oh!”

“Yes,” Glenda continues the thread, excitedly, “Last year we won the East Herefordshire Healthcare Brochure of the Year competition.” She sits back to bask in the glory of such an accolade, while Sybil’s acknowledging smile is suitably bashful.

“I’m here to talk about Kathleen Hodges.” Taylor is pleased to hear her voice holding up and sounding suitably authoritative. “We believe that she is on your books.”

Glenda glances at the glossy manual in front of her - bearing the legend ‘we care so that you won’t be scared’ - before trying to hide her mistake. “I’d have to check our records.”

"Please do." Taylor smiles nicely.

"What, now?"

"If you don't have anything else on, or at least nothing more urgent."

Sybil clicks her tongue disdainfully. "This is most unusual and I'm not sure if last year's Data Protection Act..."

"It does." Taylor needs to move this on. "It covers your ability to let me know whether an individual is part of your business or service provision as in a specialist recruitment agency such as this. Believe me, I have spent months studying the new regulations."

Whether being recognised as a fellow specialist or not is the catalyst, Sybil cleverly gives her colleague the go-ahead via raised eyebrows. The manual probably refers to this as an example of meaningful dumbness.

"I'll have to open the file," her clearly disgruntled colleague exclaims, "And that means closing the other window."

"When one window closes, another is sure to open." Taylor is startled to hear Harcourt's sarcasm in this riposte.

A few minutes later Glenda manages to multi-process by scrolling down her screen as well as speaking out loud, triumphantly. "Yes. Here it is. April 2014. Hodges, Kathleen. Could that be her?"

"Almost certainly." Taylor nods her encouragement, "Can you tell me anything more about her?"

"Can I? Do you mean, can the computer?"

"No, well, yes, both I suppose."

"I can't, but the computer does say that she lived in Bishop's Lacy if that's any use to you?"

"You don't remember her then; not even after training her?"

"We have so many people who come through our office, Sergeant," Sybil has sat back in her comfy office chair, looking decidedly smug, "It would be difficult to remember all of our candidates."

"Tall, angular, she would have been in her early 'fifties."

"As I said, it's not easy."

Exasperated, Taylor tries a different tack. "Do you know who she first worked for?"

Glenda turns back to her screen, the epitome of concentration confirmed by her gripping her tongue between her teeth. More scrolling ensues before she looks back up at the detective. "No."

"Has the record been deleted or corrupted somehow?"

"Everything is above board here; I can assure you." The CEO has misunderstood the word, the implication, or possibly both.

"No, I meant: has some of your data been lost? You must surely keep records back further than this for compliance purposes?"

The two of them look at each other, caught off guard and confused. No grey metal strips can provide enough cover for this unexpected turn of events. Sybil eventually puts out the fire which, presumably, is why she is the Chief Executive after all.

"All of our back-office files are stored off-site."

Or maybe she just has a good memory for buzzwords.

"For security purposes." Glenda can't afford to be completely left out.

"Have there been any incidents then, thefts in the area?"

"The old man in the cheese shop on the market square did say he thought he was a bit short of Caerphilly," Glenda is on a roll now, "He told Iris in the flower shop. There's also the sheep rustling of course."

Taylor has had enough. "Was... is she still registered with you?"

"Who? Kathleen Hodges?" Glenda has asked the question entirely innocently.

"Yes!"

"No," Sybil answers definitively. "I'd know if that was the case."

"Ok. Thanks. Incidentally, how can you be so certain?"

"Because we currently have thirteen carers out there. Two of them are male and of the other eleven, none goes by the name of Kathleen, though we do have three Shirleys."

***

"All OK with DS Farren?" Harcourt glances across at Flowers. Even with the visor down, the mid-morning sun is nearly blinding him and he's glad for even the slightest respite.

"She's fine, sir. Why do you ask?"

"Just wondering what she thought about the new unit being set up." He is teasing the young man, putting him on the spot.

"She hasn't said much about it, to be honest." He replies dishonestly, hoping the redness on his neck might be mistaken for sunburn. "She's as industrious as ever, though." He adds quickly.

'Industrious?' His DS uses some strange words and has always had this somewhat ethereal quality about him. Harcourt recognises that he also has the uncanny ability to think laterally – perhaps that's all part of it – and has quite often looked at something entirely differently from the rest of them. His paperwork is adequate too. He could certainly go somewhere if he wanted to. Therein lies the problem: does he truly want to and, if so, where?

They pass the rest of the journey in relative silence. The tension seems to have been released from the younger man's body, like air from a balloon, and Harcourt leaves him in peace (if that's what it is). They cross the Avon and take a left at the Fladbury crossroads, mercifully heading north now and away from the sun for a while.

Harcourt hasn't been this way for some time. He does recall an afternoon trip to the picturesque village back in the winter months. Some called it 'Floodbury' for obvious reasons. They'd walked from its eighteenth-century mill across the fields and up into the neighbouring village of Cropthorne where Debbie had insisted on an ice cream despite the cold wind. He always forgets how pretty it is out here.

They head up the hill and take a right onto Hill Furze Road. The tiny hamlet of houses, farm, and glamping site (whatever that is?) is quite bohemian in appearance. An off-the-beaten-track kind of place, despite the road running right through the middle of it. They proceed in an easterly direction until they reach the tiny hamlet of Upper Handley. Some of the houses here are old and some are enormous. It is through the gates of one of the latter that they turn, parking up next to a large, silver Mercedes saloon which gleams in both the reflected sunshine and, no doubt intentionally, all of those who pass the property.

The house itself is lovely to look at and probably no more than five years old. In creamy Cotswold stone, a low, slightly darker wall appears to run around it, with only a single gap for a path leading up to the front door of solid-looking brown oak. Several windows look out on them from each side and their beautiful arched counterparts follow each other along the first floor. Wooden shutters have been added reminding Harcourt of a long-ago trip to Cape Cod when they'd decided to 'splash the cash' before spending much more of it when moving to Worcester. His last holiday had been spent in Dorset.

The house occupies a flat plot of perhaps a couple of acres, mainly laid to lawn. Harcourt notes that the pretty flowers along each border appear to be perfectly spaced, their colours contrasting in a way you might see them displayed on the front of a seed packet. This is a statement garden, almost certainly tended to by a professional gardener rather than a loving owner. Unlike Brenda Wilkins's garden, there is nothing quirky or haphazard here in the way that foliage drapes across walls or fences or buttercups and daisies allowed at least their own reservation in part of the lawn which here is a Photoshopped green and immaculate.

Equally, there are no children's slides or trampolines whose artificial colours might assault the senses in the way that they and their users are designed to do. There are no ponies in the paddock to the left where the grass has been scythed to an acceptable height rather than trodden down by either two or four-legged creatures.

Fred Wilkins is opening the door as they approach it. He is wearing a crisp white shirt over elegant dark trousers, supported by shiny brown brogues. “Good morning, how may I help you?” He has a broad grin on his face, but Harcourt detects an insincerity in it. Maybe he keeps it in one of the drawers of the lovely pine ‘telephone table’ which sits just inside the door. ‘When did people stop having dedicated tables for their phones?’ he wonders, checking that his mobile is sitting comfortably in his inside jacket pocket.

They each show their warrant cards. The smile doesn’t flicker – confirmation that Harcourt is right. Nobody likes being visited by the police, whatever the reason might be.

He leads the two detectives past a large study, flooded with light. Like the garden it is well-organised. No papers or files strewn over the polished walnut desk here. They enter a huge open space with a kitchen at one end, separated by a long wooden table and chairs from a comfortable-looking lounge area of sofas and regulation widescreen TV at the other. No plants or greenery of any kind has been allowed to grow into this space.

“Do sit down,” Fred beckons them to the dining table, either recognising this as a formal meeting in which he’d need to take notes or because the comfortable seating area might have encouraged them to stay longer than strictly necessary. Fred indeed does produce a notebook and flashy gold-coloured pen, as do the detectives (both black Biros, one chewed at the end).

"We won't take too much of your time, sir." Harcourt pulls his chair up deliberately, noting the lack of coasters and therefore the unlikelihood of tea or coffee. "We're investigating the recent deaths in Bishop's Lacy and think you may be able to provide us with some background information."

"That's fine," Fred continues to beam at them, not even flinching over Harcourt's deliberate use of the plural form of death, or the word itself which usually takes the smiles off people's faces. "I've got a viewing at 1.00 so plenty of time."

"A viewing, sir?" Flowers is sitting on the other side of Harcourt with Fred, naturally, at the head of the table. It enables him to look around that part of the room that his boss has his back to. Bi-fold doors lead out to a large wrap-around stone terrace with a lawn beyond. He can see an expensive-looking barbecue and ubiquitous grey wicker seats gathered around it as if expecting to be fed at any moment. He'd noticed several bookcases filled from top to bottom along the hallway – but not in the study – and there are several more between where they are sitting and the first of the cream sofas. Again, the shelves are full.

"Yes. I'm an estate agent." Fred brings them back to this end of the room. "Not far, though, just over in Elmley Castle. About fifteen minutes if I obey the speed limits!" He laughs out loud, but only to himself.

"How long have you been in that line of business, sir?" Harcourt is doing his best to keep his tone as neutral as possible. He still hasn't quite got over how they were messed about when moving to their current home, having to pay more than £10,000 over the asking price after the seller's agent 'with a nose for these things' had encouraged the vendors to raise it just before the contracts were due to be exchanged.

"Most of my life, really, Detective Chief Inspector. I did dabble in hedge funds early on, but it was always property for me."

"Sales or rentals?" Flowers asks the question innocently enough.

Fred scoffs, exchanging what he hopes is a mutually understandable glance with Harcourt before replying. "Sales of course. I manage other people who handle rentals: in Evesham, Pershore and Worcester. I've personally handheld the opening of a new office in Hereford too if that's of any interest? "

It isn't. It isn't really a question either, just an opportunity to elevate himself above those many unfortunate younger people who currently have no chance whatsoever of getting on the 'property ladder.' Harcourt doesn't like posturing. "Your parents must have been proud: being able to afford a place like this?"

For the first time since they've been there, the smile drops, though he continues to talk as though it hasn't. "I hope so. Dad never really said much, and Mum, well..."

"We're very sorry for your loss. It must still feel quite raw." Harcourt has dipped into his dictionary and phrasebook and come up with humility.

"It is and it isn't. Life goes on, doesn't it? Sorry, I didn't mean that to sound so crass."

"We know what you mean."

"It's probably the only way I can cope with it. I mean,

she'd had a few falls, but I suppose I thought she'd go on forever."

"Had you visited her recently, sir?" Flowers is not being insensitive, Harcourt knows that.

Fred, bristling, doesn't. "Not for a while, Sergeant. We saw her at Christmas, obviously, and I must have spoken to her at least once a month on the phone."

"It must have been a comfort knowing that Joe lived just up the road from her." Harcourt is less interested in the obvious fact that all roads on a map can lead quite easily to Bishop's Lacy, and more how he will react to the much closer proximity of his brother.

"I'm not sure that Joe saw much more of her than we did. He's very busy too, what with the shop and everything."

"You moved away but he didn't."

"I wasn't aware that the free movement of people was somehow a crime - unless you believed in all that Brexit nonsense?"

He is getting agitated now, Harcourt perceives. A good sign. "Of course not. I was just wondering why Joe chose to stay, especially as your sister left too - Patricia, I believe."

"There's no pattern there at all. People grow up in a certain place and then choose to leave when they grow up. Sometimes they stay. She and I left the village, but Joe didn't. That's it. Joe was always going to run the shop. Dad made that quite clear to all of us from an early age, even though each of us had to work in there when we were growing up – especially Saturday mornings."

"Did you resent that?" Harcourt perseveres. "Not having

to work in there. I mean, you were being passed over: the family business your father had built up going to your elder brother. He didn't leave it to the two of you?"

"It wouldn't have made any difference. Joe was welcome to it. I was pleased to get out; get away. I had much bigger fish to fry."

Harcourt mischievously wonders if this would still have been the case had Harry been running a fish and chips shop. "And your sister?"

"She went away to college and was never the same after that."

"In what way?"

"You'll have to talk to her."

"And her husband, Charles?"

"Ex-husband I think you'll find." He gives Flowers a malevolent glare, accompanied by what he believes to be a winning smile.

"Is he still on the scene – part of the wider family – or is he considered by the rest of you to be in its past?"

"I don't think any of us 'consider' him at all, Chief Inspector, including my sister. He moved out of the family home and my niece chose to accompany him."

"Except that's not quite right is it, sir?" Flowers is keen to prove that he has done his homework – all of it. "Patricia left first, leaving Charles Band having to sell the family home."

"How painful you make it all sound, as though it's come straight out of one of the mountains of books my wife seems to get through each week. Yes, technically she may have left him, but none of us are angels, are we?"

"Meaning?" Harcourt doesn't like the way the man is addressing his colleague. Time to remind him who is really in charge here.

"Just that there's no smoke without fire is there? It's easy for everyone to assume that my sister, with her multitude of problems, must therefore be the sole cause of their relationship breaking down. He wasn't there for a lot of the time. Perhaps she could have done with a little more help?"

"Where was he?"

"Out working I assume. Gardening. It takes people over and becomes not just the most important thing in their lives but the only thing. My mother got the bug and after that nothing and nobody ever came close, apart from Hazel perhaps. She spent a lot of time out there with her. As for Charles, well, he was a friend of the earth; far too busy to be friends with anybody else."

"And yet Hazel stuck with him. Quite unusual in paternity disputes?"

"There was no dispute, Inspector, Pat (she's always been Pat, I don't think even her Birth Certificate names her Patricia. You'd probably know that better than me by now) was having trouble coping with life in general. It was easier all round if Hazel stayed with Charles."

"Harder for him, though, in cost-of-living terms I mean."

"Charles adores his daughter. I don't think he'd have seen it in that way at all. Sadly, I'll probably never get to experience such joy."

Harcourt can see, hear the conversation being closed down.

"You mentioned 'we' earlier, sir. Is there a Mrs Wilkins?" Flowers is rewarded with startled glances by both Fred and Harcourt.

"I'm sorry." Fred glares at the younger man, opening and closing his fists as he does so: an equally encouraging sign in the context of the interview. The pen remains unused, glinting in the sunshine now though.

Flowers refers to his notepad in which he has been making copious notes. "You said that you weren't sure that your brother saw much more of Brenda than *we* did."

"Oh. Right." A flicker of a smile reappears – more naturally this time. "I did mean 'we' as in my wife Suzanne. She's usually here but popped out just before you came."

Flowers is undeterred by suspicion or intended sleight. "Anywhere in particular?"

"Not sure. It'll be somewhere on her own, though; she doesn't do well with crowds."

"We may need to interview her in due course," Harcourt remarks, kindly, "Whoever it is will come alone."

"Right. Well, if there's nothing else... "

It appears that Fred needs much more time to prepare for the 'viewing' after all. This character reference has not gone particularly well for him. At least Harcourt and Flowers can seek out a coffee at the Craycombe Business Park he saw signs for just before they turned off the main road. "There is sir, actually. One last thing."

"Go on." Fred moves his own, blank, notepad subtly to one side: a distinct clue that this really will be the last thing on the agenda.

"Your mother was cared for in recent years by her neighbour, Kathleen Hodges. Can you tell me anything about her that might be of interest?"

"It depends on what you're interested in I suppose." He places his hands together sighs and takes a deep breath as though he is about to impart some meaningful philosophical observation on life. "I only met the woman a couple of times – very tall."

"Anything else?" Flowers continues to scribble, not wanting his eyes to give anything away.

"She always seemed to be there."

"At least she was on the couple of occasions you visited?" Harcourt's need is less for confirmation than to rile the man into telling them honestly what he thought of Kathleen Hodges

If he recognises this, Fred is not going to give them the benefit of it. "I thought she was a bit of a nosy neighbour, to be honest. Joe probably did too."

"Getting a bit above her station, sir?" Flowers is still scribbling in his notepad.

"Why do you say that?" Fred's hands are wide open now in mock surprise and affront on the dead woman's behalf.

"It was just a turn of phrase, sir." Flowers and Harcourt both know perfectly well that it wasn't.

"Mum must have liked her, and I suppose that's all that matters now."

"Not really, sir," Harcourt again, "Kathleen Hodges is dead and what matters is that we find her killer as soon as possible."

Fred looks at him and then at Flowers, disbelief etched on his face or pencilled in. He is an estate agent after all. Eventually, he concludes the meeting. "All I can tell you is that Mum's garden was her world and the flowers and veggies in it were far more important to her than any person could ever have been."

***

"A bit of a loaded statement, I thought?" Harcourt is slowly buckling his seatbelt while watching Fred disappear behind the front door in his rear mirror.

"*Any* person, you mean, sir?"

"I did." He turns the ignition and they set off, indicating right. "He also clearly knew about Kathleen's death yet showed no curiosity about it whatsoever."

Flowers nods. "He wasn't especially curious about why we were even here today, was he?"

"If he thought we were looking at Brenda's will, he might have been more open with his questions but even more guarded with his answers."

"Are we? Looking at the will I mean?"

"As you know when we're investigating a crime, we must look at absolutely every angle; with murder, it's every angle upside down, clockwise, anti-clockwise and refracted through every piece of scientific and technological equipment we have available to us.

We have a murder crime scene that the pathologist believes to have been staged to send us all a message – or a warning – and nobody acts in that way or communicates it without good reason. We call that good reason 'motive.'

"You think a different will from Brenda Wilkins could have given someone motive to kill Kathleen Hodges?"

"It's one of those angles, certainly. We're off to Brenda's solicitor this afternoon, though that won't be as straightforward as it sounds, given they're such a cagey lot. I didn't want to give Fred any inkling of any of this, though. We're keeping our powder dry on both it and the state of the body we found. As they say in Fred's trade: 'We're very interested in it, and we'll let him know in due course.'"

"Our much less cagey friends in the media don't seem to have any further details – or at least haven't published anything yet; just a statement of fact."

Harcourt smiles inwardly at the younger man's use of 'media' and 'published.' In his day – which it still is, thankfully – it would have been 'press' and 'printed.' Media proliferation does have its advantages, though. With people broadcasting directly, in whatever medium, the press no longer has control over what people see, hear and read. Or at least that's the theory.

He smiles as he replies, not wanting to seem more patronising than he knows he often is. "Just because they haven't put anything out there other than the facts doesn't mean that they're not building up their fictional picture of what did happen in that back garden. You can't do much more with facts, can you? Not enough to captivate your readers – or viewers – anyway. Lack of further juicy details leads quickly to speculation, and they won't be backwards in coming forwards on that."

"He seemed OK about his brother inheriting the butcher's shop, didn't he?"

"He did, although it appears that he and the others expected it – according to Fred at least. How people handle the unexpected is usually more interesting. No wonder the TV series was such a hit."

"Sir?"

"'Tales of the Unexpected.' Roald Dahl!"

"Sorry, sir, I thought he wrote 'James and the Giant Peach.'

For someone professing to enjoy literature, Harcourt is amazed at how limited the reach of his sergeant is; still, they'd all been young once.

Flowers isn't sure what it is that he has or hasn't said, but knows it was somehow the wrong response, so grasps the safety net of the investigation. "Fred Wilkins was still pretty off though, wasn't he, sir? Business-like you might say if you were being kind."

"Unlikely for an estate agent. Maybe he was expecting us; in which case someone had warned him, and we now have another elusive woman on our hands whom we haven't yet been able to talk to directly. Let's see if you can make any progress with Joe's wife..."

"Camilla!!"

"That'll be the one. You and Linda need to get back over there; let's see if she can work her charm on this Steve chap in the butcher's shop. I'll drop you off at the station once we've had an important debrief."

"Debrief, sir?"

"Coffee, Ian. You'll need to be wide awake."

Flowers wonders how his superior could possibly know when he's all there physically but less so mentally.

Perhaps it's this that gives Harcourt his superiority over him?

***

"Dunno." Jamie Bright shrugs his shoulders. In his mid-twenties, possibly, the legend on his off-white t-shirt belies his name: 'I get paid for being laid ... under a truck.'

Taylor re-phrases her question nicely: "The ladies who live on the other side of the wall – do you know either of them?"

"No."

"You've not seen them? They don't come round this side?" She hasn't informed him that both are dead, so as not to lose him in the same rumour mill that he just might have been aware of.

"Why would they come round here? It's not exactly the place you'd go for a walk, is it? Besides, if they didn't have cars..."

Taylor's interest is piqued; the lunchtime growls in her stomach momentarily quietened. She hadn't mentioned any vehicles (isn't entirely sure yet that Kathleen didn't possess one).

"What makes you so sure that they didn't?"

He sneers as he replies. "Because they'd have parked them in the lean-to over there. When people come to visit those houses, that's where they park – overnight I mean. I think it's supposed to be shared between the two houses."

"You've seen cars parked in there?"

"Occasionally."

"What about two nights ago?"

"What about it? Was there an eclipse or something?"

"You didn't see any cars parked there?"

"No."

"You're sure?" CSI officers had photographed the two different sets of tyre tracks she can clearly see now in the dirt and dead leaves that had somehow survived the winter.

"Completely. I was out with my mates in Worcester. 'On the lash' as we youngsters like to call it."

Taylor ignores the ageist inference. She is frustrated that this conversation, such as it is, is going nowhere. She squints at the old garage in front of her. There isn't much there: a hydraulic ramp sits in the centre with ancient oak benches on either side, each laden with tools, oil cartons – some covered in cobwebs – and dusty A4 files.

Metal pipes containing only marginally more metal than holes provide a sad demarcation line between it and the old barn-like structure next to it. This is empty save for an ancient rusty plough which hasn't seen fields for possibly decades.

The high metal roofs almost butt up to each other but the slope of each is severe. More than 60 degrees she'd estimate. It may have been possible to climb up somehow and shin down the wall beyond and into either Kathleen or Brenda's gardens, but neither roof looks strong enough to take the weight of much more than a stray cat, let alone a grown man or woman.

It would also have been unlikely for an assailant to make their descent without hurting their legs or knees, such is the height involved, and certainly not unseen or unheard. They could have used ropes but there is nothing obvious to knot them to on this side of the building or either gable.

She lowers her gaze and Bright assumes she is looking at the files. "All a bit run down, isn't it? I'm only here twice a week for the odd MOT."

"Who owns it?"

"Old Mr Portugil just around the front. He comes round in the mornings that I'm here to let me know what's coming in that day. The place is closed the rest of the time. No point in opening if nobody knows it's here is there? Most use the local Kwik-Fit now anyway."

"Not too busy then?"

"Nah."

"Given so few people use it, you must be able to tell me if any strangers have visited lately, or just people hanging around you haven't seen before?"

"Not that I can recall. Like I say, I'm only in a couple of days a week – sometimes only one. Mr Portugil might know. Anyway, what's all this about? I don't think anything's been nicked."

He stops chattering for a second and Taylor watches the redness take over his vacant face. 'Now he's got it,' she assesses.

"You're not connected to the Department of Transport, are you? Is this something to do with Mr Clarkson's brakes? I did put it down as an advisory."

"No, nothing like that." Taylor has to admit to feeling just a little disappointed, not to mention concern for the unfortunate Mr Clarkson. She'd have to check with Traffic when she got back; to see if there had been any incidents reported.

"What then?" Bright is frowning at her, waiting for an answer.

"'What then?' is right. Many thanks for your time. She walks away, secure in the knowledge that he is not at all thankful, even though he is white, and even though he is male.

***

Daniel is sitting just outside the patio doors, scrolling through his feed of the latest news stories on his iPad. He can hear any movement inside the house from here and, besides, the front door is locked, and the key is hidden in an old biscuit tin which only he and Claire are aware that they still possess. The tin still features a romanticised picture of the Scottish Highlands on its lid with a meandering train consisting of purple LMS carriages snaking across the foothills, below a message in large italics urging biscuit lovers everywhere to 'escape to the hills.'

The sun is making him squint a little, but it's so lovely to feel it on his face after sitting in his north-facing study for the past two hours. He's only going to be out there until the coffee's brewed anyway. It used to be one of their little domestic rituals – making tea and coffee and trying to catch each other out with subtle changes of blends or beans.

He's currently proofreading a novel about a young woman who is trying to bring theatre and dance to a remote rural area in Norfolk. He'd thought initially it was going to concern the reimagining of Billy Elliot as a scarecrow learning to tap dance his way through a potato patch, but it has turned into something much more sinister. The unwelcoming, unfair demands, and generally ungrateful attitude of some of the parents she tries to befriend make it seem unlikely that the school will survive (or at least at this point and he's already two-thirds of the way through the book).

A select few are only interested in their children succeeding to the detriment of others while the majority have failed to achieve anything of any great interest and don't see why their offspring should have opportunities that they did not enjoy. The wider point being made by the author is of closed-off tribes where each family knows everybody else's business and tries to present it as a 'community.' Outsiders simply upset that balance or, worse, might find out the truth.

The book is quite well-written apart from some difficult colloquialisms which he and most purchasing readers would struggle over, and Daniel suspects that the author has experienced a good deal of this first-hand, even though the publisher's blurb tells him she is married with a toucan and lives in Truro.

The first, welcoming whiffs of coffee beans being drowned in scalding water entice him back inside just as he spots an article with the title: 'Neighbours in death' and a short piece detailing the deaths of an elderly woman called Brenda Wilkins and her erstwhile next-door neighbour Kathleen Hodges. The source is simply listed as Newsquest which now owns a range of titles in the area, including his old newspaper. Undeterred he reads on.

It states that Brenda died of 'natural causes' but that the

police have revealed no details about Ms Hodge's death, which the journal finds 'disturbing.' The piece ends with the question on everybody's lips (they hope!) 'Just neighbours, but are the two women's deaths related?'

Daniel doesn't recognise the byline – someone called 'Jo Waffle.' Unfortunate, but maybe not unknown. He sits back, easily recalling and rewinding to the start of the scene outside the church just a few weeks ago and then the one in Fergus's garden. That had been a lovely hot day too. He remembers Fergus telling him that Kathleen had been Brenda's carer and, even more clearly, how upset she'd seemed outside the church – seemingly much less so about the dead than those still living.

He picks up his mobile phone from under the white plastic seat – Charlotte thought (thinks!) that wicker chairs are an extravagance – where he had placed it to keep it out of the direct sunshine. He dials his friend Kate Harcourt, a journalist on the local *Evesham News* whom he has known for years.

"That's Worcester News's story." She'd answered on the second ring as though she's been waiting to hear from somebody else; somebody more important?

"I know, but you're all part of the same newspaper group, aren't you?" There is a short pause during which Daniel hears a door opening and closing again and Kate saying 'thanks.' A slight pang of jealousy grips him somewhere inside, its unwelcome fingers only prised off by the overwhelming guilt that always follows such events.

"Sorry!" She is back on the line (airwave?), but it is only Charlotte's face that Daniel now sees. A sad, uncomprehending face.

"I hope I wasn't disturbing anything?" They both hear the timid acceptance of rejection honed during their wretched teenage years.

If Kate recognises this, she doesn't admit it to him (or to herself). "Not at all. I'd been waiting for an Amazon delivery. The tracking message online said it would be here before 10.00 and it's, what, after 11.00?"

"11.07" he replies, happily. "You might have to give them feedback. They're always asking for it."

"They certainly are. Now, the deaths in Bishop's Lacy. What is your interest?"

Typical Kate. Nice and friendly to talk to but always to the point, whatever the weather. "It's just that Charlotte and I went to Brenda's funeral and I'm pretty sure I saw Kathleen Hodges there."

"Not surprising if they were neighbours?"

"And again, outside. She was arguing with someone about a will."

Now Kate is actively listening. "A will? Who's. Brenda's?"

"I assume so. I don't – didn't - know her at all, but I've known Brenda all my life. Her husband ran the local butcher's shop. We lived just across the fields when I was growing up."

"Ah, yes, of course. I remember now. Charlotte's brother still lives over there, doesn't he? The vicar?"

"That's him. God bless him."

"So how did the argument end?" Kate too is a woman of her words, not promises.

"I'm not sure if it really did – not then, anyway. They just got into a car and drove off."

"And now she's dead. Interesting."

"It might be something and nothing. I just wondered if you knew anything more about it?"

"I don't but I can ask Joseph."

"Joseph? Sorry, I thought the journalist was a woman: Jo."

"He sometimes uses the 'e' sometimes he drops it. Depends."

"On what?"

"You haven't come across many non-binary people, have you?"

"I have to admit I haven't." He is sweating a little now, even though the huge, black sunshade towering above and to the side of him, shielding the patio table, is beginning to get down to work.

"You will. In time."

"OK. Let me know if you turn anything up?"

"Have you contacted the police by the way? Sounds like it could be very useful information if there's anything suspicious about Kathleen Hodges's death."

"I haven't yet. I thought I'd phone you first."

"Always a good plan!" He can hear her smiling (if that was possible). "Let's keep it between us for now then. I'll phone you."

"Thanks." He hits the red button, wishing it was green all over again, and secretly hoping that Kate will continue to identify as a woman.

A voice is calling him from upstairs.

***

"Joe always dealt with her, not me." The voice is softer than Farren had imagined for such a big man – easily around six feet five.

"But she was a regular customer?"

"Every Friday morning."

She is leaning over the counter now, straining to hear the words he prefers to whisper. Maybe he is frightened of being overheard; if so, which words and by whom? She throws out a question which isn't as pointless as it may sound. Unchallenging as it is, it might put him a little more at ease.

"Did she order the same kind of thing each Friday?"

"Yes."

"Such as?"

"Meat."

She watches him running his thick fingers through the beef mince, as a fisherman might squish maggots in excited anticipation of a big catch. The wonders of the food chain! She needs to change tack. "Did she buy for Brenda Wilkins as well?"

"You'd have to check with Joe."

"But Brenda had to pay for her meat; Joe didn't make up a weekly order for free."

"Joe has a business to run. Brenda understood that. It's not easy with Aldi Price Match here, and veganism there."

He is evidently not in 'trade' to chat with his customers, or maybe it just goes back to her warrant card. He is certainly more articulate than she'd given him credit for when first entering the shop though, at which she scolds herself quietly. "What was Kathleen Hodges like?"

There is a large whacking sound as Steve, with his back to her, hacks a pork joint in half, pieces of fragmented bone flying in all directions. Slowly, he half turns. "I barely spoke to her."

It's difficult to challenge that assertion she must admit, but she's not going to give up completely, not yet anyway. "How long have you worked here?"

He doesn't even bother to look in her direction this time, hammering another joint into submission instead.

"Mr Baker?"

"I've been with Joe for four years and his father for eleven years before that. I came straight from school. My first job was to look after the small abattoir out the back."

"You kill on site?"

His long eyelashes twitch at the word, though the flat timbre of his voice remains the same; no sign of any change to the vocal landscape arriving any time soon. "Much of it comes from the wholesaler these days but we do have a few local farmers who get a better price directly from us. Harry used to look after them well."

"And now you and Joe take it in turns to run the front of house?" She chooses her words carefully, assuming the middle-class vernacular of the Arts will be as alien to him as tofu.

He simply drops the meat cleaver onto his bench and

turns, fully. “Why are you here, asking these questions? I didn’t invite you.” He is just about audible now: this must be the closest he comes to raising his voice.

“We’re following up on the deaths in the village. This is purely for background. You’re not in any kind of trouble.”

“Brenda died in her sleep, as I understand it.”

“She did, but Kathleen didn’t.” She must be careful here as there is still a hold on any further details reaching the public, though that will have to change soon if they don’t make more progress quickly. She plays him at his own game of short sentences, all the time watching for any reaction.

He is either completely disinterested in other people’s business or he already knows far more than he is allowing to permeate the gristle and the bone. His face remains impassive, but she can almost feel the tension in his beefy arms as he turns his back on her once again and lifts what could once have been a large lamb.

“It must have been very difficult for Joe: losing his mother suddenly.”

She has found the key at last. He drops the carcass with a crash, causing knives and a hacksaw to jump into the air. It’s like some kind of update of the Sorcerer’s Apprentice and she hopes fervently that the sharp instruments will quickly calm themselves down again. She can see the blade of a huge knife glinting in the sunlight, longing for action.

“Joe has been under a great deal of pressure. As I said, the meat trade is going through hard times; many of our loyal customers who’ve shopped here for years are dying. The last thing he needed was for his mother to leave him too."

His eyes are bulging in his head now, either in anger or the same kind of terror experienced by one of their offerings on realising that the unexpected but nice morning drive down a country lane would be their last.

"Presumably the family rallied around?"

"Fred and Pat, you mean?" His demeanour changes completely as a sardonic smile replaces the tight lips he has treated her to so far. "They'd be no more likely to come over and see Joe than they would their own mother."

"They didn't get on?"

"You'll have to ask Joe about that." The shutters have come down again, just as a burly, elderly gentleman enters the shop.

"Morning Steve. How are you doing this fine morning?"

Steve merely tilts his head back slightly. The man – no doubt a regular code breaker and purveyor of rhetorical questions – orders a small chop.

Farren leaves the men to it.

CHAPTER FIVE

He says he enjoys it – being outside – but I'm not so sure. I don't just mean like when it's raining, although it hasn't rained for days now; more like when someone tells you something because that's what they want you to hear.

He was covered in soil and other smelly stuff when he came in tonight. It transpires that people need to spread all kinds of shit to cover things and make them grow up (pardon me for swearing. I'm sure they'd teach us how to handle words like that if I was properly trained).

It's just that he seems so tired lately. I suggested he go and see a doctor but that didn't go down too well. I think he might be frightened they'll find something wrong, and he'd rather not know. I would though. Know, I mean. I also wonder if he doesn't want to go to that surgery because of all the times we had to go there with Mum. Sometimes I glance over at him without him realising and he looks anxious. Perhaps knowing is better than not knowing after all.

I made him his favourite supper of toad in the hole. It's the least I can do while I'm waiting to hear. He said he enjoyed it, and I believed him. You can't really hide that can you? Not when you have a nice meal put in front of you. The oven chips weren't great. Just when you think they need another couple of minutes they go black around the edges. You just can't trust them.

He watched the football while I streamed the latest album from *Broccolive.* It was OK but I didn't think it was a patch on their electronica phase: 'The Green, Green Grass of Chrome.' Dad said the football was boring, but he'll still be watching it at the weekend. I don't mind because he seems to be happiest when he doesn't have to think about anything else. I suppose that's the same with all of us.

He hasn't mentioned money lately – not since I got upset last time. I did go and speak to Mum about it as he suggested. I'd bought her flowers and that expensive chocolate from the Post Office that she likes (I didn't tell Dad about that bit, obviously) but I don't think she even noticed. She wasn't in the mood to listen, not to me anyway. That's the problem, isn't it? Most people love to talk but not many of them want to listen.

I dusted the cottages in the village today. Gran would have been pleased; well, she didn't know about the accident, although she probably does by now! I'm going to try and look around the little house tomorrow like she suggested. Not sure how I'm going to get in though. Perhaps Dad will take me after work. I know he's still got a key.

***

Taylor has yet to finish her ice cream which is beginning to drip over her fingers in the heat of the day. She hopes they won't find the solicitor's building just yet as it isn't a good look.

Naturally, Harcourt, who is walking just ahead of her, devoured his almost immediately, like a child enjoying an unexpected day at the seaside. "This street we're walking along - Mealcheapen Street – was once a passageway between two of the city's churches." Seeing that Taylor is preoccupied and unable to speak he continues happily. "St Swithun's at the top there is Georgian – don't be fooled by the Tudor tower. That's from a previous church on that site.

Taylor isn't fooled (hasn't ever considered it) but is at least able to wipe her sticky fingers on an old tissue - unexpectedly found in her skirt pocket - which smells suspiciously of crisps.

Her impromptu tour guide is still going. "Old St Martin's down on the Cornmarket is also Georgian, built on the site of a previous fourteenth-century church."

She feels the need to ask a question, not as a police officer for once, but just to humour him. "Why is it called 'Old' St Martin's? I thought all churches were old."

She'd expected a withering stare in response to her crassness, but he is too far gone in his history lesson for that. "They built another church dedicated to St Martin's – up on London Road – so it's to distinguish between the two."

He seems to find the past so much easier than the present; at least a past that isn't his.

They still haven't found the solicitors' offices, so he continues, excitedly. "There is a legend, somewhat shrouded in mystery, that suggests William Shakespeare married Ann Hathaway in the fourteenth-century incarnation of Old St Martin's."

He waits for her to respond, which she does with a much more straightforward question right out of the Hendon police manual: "Is there any truth in it?"

"We do know that they came into Worcester to get a wedding licence and St Martin's was certainly on the route out of the city and back towards Stratford that they would have been most likely to follow."

"Circumstantial, I'm afraid, sir." She smiles to let him know that she isn't trying to steal his thunder and turn it into silence.

"I know." He smiles back. "Unfortunately, this is where the real mystery comes in. The relevant page in the church's marriage register on that date in 1582 was torn out. That would have given us the hard evidence we'd have been looking for. Still, there is no body of evidence to say that it didn't happen either. I think most people would prefer to believe that it did."

'As You Like It' thinks Taylor mischievously, and very much to herself.

Fittingly, a black timber framed Tudor building proves to be the building they are looking for. None of the tiny windows appear to be on the same horizontal plane as any other and the bulging once-white infill panels appear to bend over them, throwing them into shadow for the first time that day.

A suitable olde italicised name panel featuring white letters is attached to a much more ancient oak beam just above the only door in (or out). It informs them that they have reached the offices of 'Garfield, Rawlings, Edgar, Edwards and Donaldson.' Taylor wonders how ancient the occupants are going to be, and how they feel about having to share an entrance.

A surprisingly young (well, middle-aged) receptionist in a neat white blouse and dark skirt welcomes them in a formal but not unfriendly fashion.

"Old Mr Rawlings will be down shortly." She waves them towards two comfortable-looking brown upholstered armchairs in the 'entrance hall' (though no larger than a cubby hole).

"Bet he's called Martin!" Taylor whispers into her superior's left ear as they sit, enjoying the cool relief from the burning heat of the afternoon beyond the ancient wall.

"Probably very worthy" Harcourt replies, still smiling.

Moments later a grey-haired man of indeterminate age (but no less than sixty) appears at the gap left by an arched door which has opened outwards from the off-white wall. He is wearing a charcoal black three-piece suit yet shows no sign of sweating. Not that solicitors often do, thinks Harcourt.

He spots the two of them and strides over to Harcourt, pumping his hand. After a short but discernible pause, he similarly greets Taylor.

"Welcome. Welcome. Please do follow me." Stocky but surprisingly nimble he takes the stairs of a winding staircase two at a time. The detectives don't.

They follow him into a cool, gloomy room thanks to just the one leaded window behind a large mahogany desk. The room is pocket-sized with the right-hand gable of the building defiantly restricting much of the useable space on that side, where Harcourt is standing. He feels compelled to bend his head to his left for fear of catching his head on the low roof, even though it technically isn't necessary.

The desk is clear of papers, although several piles of well-thumbed books glare back at him – and them –

daring someone to open them; to be swallowed up by centuries of accumulated knowledge.

Old Mr Rawlings has clambered up onto his black, upright chair behind it. Two relatives from the same tree await them and they are beckoned to sit on the hard surfaces, each instantly regretting having to leave their leather cousins, twice removed, downstairs.

"Tea, coffee?" Rawlings isn't out of breath at all – possibly due to the number of times he makes the journey from top to bottom and back again – but he has noticed that his guests are.

Harcourt glances at Taylor who declines by simply staring back at him. "No. Thank you, sir. We're fine." They are both keen to keep the meeting short.

"Very well. How may I help you on this beautiful day?"

"We're here in connection with the late Brenda Wilkins, sir, and also her next-door neighbour, Kathleen Hodges."

"In what capacity?"

"In our capacity as police officers investigating two deaths, one of them definitely murder."

Harcourt can see that he has had the last word on the as-yet-unspoken matter of confidentiality. While murder closes things down it also opens things up.

The older man's eyes widen momentarily before they are hidden behind a pair of rimless silver glasses which he has extracted from his inside jacket pocket.

Taylor watches him pulling an ordinary-looking manilla folder towards him; not that much else in this room could reliably be described as ordinary, including its long-term tenant.

"I'm sure I don't need to remind you both that our meeting here today is on a strictly confidential basis. In such circumstances, I would certainly be able to furnish you with essential details of my late client, but I do remain the family solicitor of the three surviving children. Harold Wilkins first became a client of mine in 1970 when his own father – Herbert – passed away. They are a decent, hard-working family and this firm is honoured to represent such.

The two detectives nod sagely, like attentive children in a classroom.

Their teacher is continuing. "There are protocols for me to follow and I shall be representing them going forward – should the need arise. However, I am happy to provide you with as much detail as I am able insofar as it would be necessary for your murder investigation."

Taylor recalls what Flowers had said about the man they had met outside Kathleen Hodges's house, more particularly his way of speaking. Designed to communicate or confound, she is never entirely sure.

Harcourt thinks Mr Rawlings is a prat. "Thank you, sir, and, yes, I can confirm that we will treat any information you're able to give us with the utmost confidence."

"There's no doubt about my client's death I hope."

"Indeed not, sir. I can assure you that she is indeed dead."

If the learned man before them had detected a note of facetiousness in the detective's reply, he is old enough and experienced enough to outwardly brush it off. "A death through natural causes?" His question is, again, measured.

"Yes, sir. The circumstances of your client's death are not in question, although a question has been raised about the exclusivity of the will."

"Exclusivity." Rawlings lifts his head, an amused look on his face. "Is that the actual word in question?"

Harcourt can sense himself tensing, noticed by Taylor and no doubt Rawlings too. "It is. It has been suggested that there might have been more than one will: that Brenda Wilkins made a second, later will."

The smile does not leave the solicitor's lips. "By whom, may I ask? A disappointed claimant perhaps?"

"I'm not at liberty to disclose that, I'm afraid, but suffice it to say it is an angle we are pursuing."

"Well, I hope you have more success with that than the Saxons did!"

Taylor knows what's coming next, she can feel it in the same bones in which their ancient ancestors somehow absorbed similar truths.

"Oh, I think it was the Danes that were the problem if I might say so, sir. The kingdom of Mercia was indeed settled by the Angles by the eighth century and did come under attack and eventual subjugation but under the Danelaw. However, it was the Saxons who held firm and eventually defeated the invaders, uniting with the Saxons in a country and a people that thus became known as 'the English.' I'd favour a meritocracy over an elite any day."

Harcourt had not been lucky enough to attend a private school or, more precisely, his parents had not been rich enough. He had picked up a few nuggets along the way though and deeply resented it when members of a supposed superior class tried to infer that their superior educational opportunities validated such elevation.

There is a stunned silence in the room. Taylor is frightened that the delve into history might become more permanent and so attempts to move things on. “Could you please confirm that in the will – in the will that you executed – each of the three children receives equal shares in Brenda’s estate?”

Rawlings is still looking long and hard at Harcourt, barely turning his head towards her but he does reply, icily. “It isn’t quite so simple as that I’m afraid.” He allows the word ‘simple’ to metaphorically stick to the young detective’s head, like an unwanted and unmerited Post-it note before continuing slowly. “Brenda left all of her remaining worldly goods to 'my children' i.e. a 'class of beneficiaries' rather than any named person or persons. If an individual had been named but subsequently died, that person's estate would still have benefitted. If not, as in this case, the money would go back into Brenda’s estate and would be subsequently divided by the remaining beneficiaries.”

Harcourt is trying to process the niceties of the will, only to find something that has gone bad, probably many years ago. “What conclusions do you draw from that?”

“I don’t draw.”

“But I do. I spend my life trying to join up the dots to form a picture I can recognise or at least understand.”

“I’m not convinced that what you’re describing is drawing though, is it?”

Taylor can see that Harcourt is showing remarkable restraint. She hasn't seen him lose his temper often – his unthreatening demeanour usually elicits better results – but he is close to the edge, if not already on it. "Let me try to make this 'simpler' for you then. Look at this another way: why would anyone not name their children individually in their last will or testament? Presumably, they were loved equally, or they wouldn't have been lumped together in this 'class?'

"Pure conjecture, I'm afraid." Rawlings leans back in his chair, ignoring the sudden cracks of protest from his seat of learning which makes both detectives visibly jump. "I can only report on what I see."

"And Mrs Wilkins – Brenda Wilkins – didn't give you any indication either way?"

"She did not. Mrs Wilkins came to see me some while before she died and asked me to draw up this will which was signed, witnessed, and which we are now executing. I can tell you that probate is far from being granted."

"How long do you suppose that will take, sir?" Harcourt wonders if he has overstepped the mark a little, but he is feeling hot and angry. Still, he gives himself top marks for rattling this pompous individual.

"I suppose that will depend on all of the due processes that need to take place."

Harcourt's head is about to burst.

Rawlings continues, smoothly and quite unruffled. "Probate involves a significant amount of legal and administrative work which can be very time-consuming although we do pride ourselves in our experience of getting these things done in as speedy fashion as possible for our clients."

"So how quickly are things... proceeding?"

"As quickly as possible." Neither Harcourt nor Taylor expects this bland response to be elaborated upon but Rawlings has got into his stride now that he is on the safe and familiar ground of operating procedures. Harcourt understands that feeling well. "Harold Wilkins had taken out a life insurance policy when he turned thirty."

"Pretty young for someone to be thinking about life insurance, isn't it?" Harcourt is spurred on by the look of distaste on Rawling's face at being interrupted in full flow. "Most people don't even consider a pension until it's much too late to make the necessary contributions."

"Quite. Harold's father - Cyril - died quite young, which is when Harold took over the butchery business."

"How did he die?" Harcourt has a sudden flashback to Kathleen Hodges's prone, lifeless body after a piece of butchery business.

"He died as a direct result of feeding a sheep."

The silence in the room is broken only by the regular ticking sound of a round Victorian clock mounted just below the ceiling on the wall behind both detectives. Neither of them had spotted it when entering the room. Rawlings watches its long pendulum moving from left to right and back again as he has done so often when trying to fill voids in his time such as this.

Taylor isn't at all sure that she has heard him correctly. "I'm sorry, sir; could you repeat that please?"

"I can do better than that, Sergeant: Cyril Wilkins's

family owned a farm just this side of Hereford. It's long since gone now, of course – barn conversions and all that. Cyril used to help his father and uncle to feed the animals, some of which will have been destined for the family's retail arm, so feeding them up was particularly important, even though these were generally years of austerity.

Harcourt recalls the farms of his youth. In contrast, they were mainly arable farms separated only by the wide open spaces of the Cambridgeshire Fens. "The 1950s?"

"Correct. Cyril had noticed that one or two of the sheep he'd been feeding were salivating rather more than usual. It transpired that they had somehow contracted the rabies virus. By the time the doctors had diagnosed this, Cyril was dead. Five days was all it took... and less than an hour to destroy the rest of the flock as a precaution."

"What a dreadful story." Taylor is genuinely shocked each time she becomes aware of yet another story of rural hardship and heartbreak."

"Isn't it? And I'm afraid the 'happy ending' became even more distant after foot-and-mouth hit them two years later. A new flock, same result, though one can easily forget why they were being farmed in the first place of course."

"Even so, the human tragedy of it all!" Harcourt remains reflective.

"Not so superior, after all!" They both stare at Taylor expectantly. She is no vegan, not even a vegetarian but animal cruelty has always upset her, ever since a visit to a city farm when she was much younger. She's never forgotten the barbed wire and tiny sheds. At the same time, she would struggle in life without bacon rolls. She knows she would.

"I only heard Harold talk about this once." Rawlings, though he deals with death, knows that salvation can only come from life going on. "He said he never fully got over the sound of the ewes screaming for their lambs until there were no screams at all. Undoubtedly because of this event, he took out life assurance when he did. Unfortunately for the beneficiaries, the policy was bought up by a company based in Austria and communications are..."

"Difficult?" Harcourt offers.

"Slow. There was a provision in the policy that monies would be paid out to the benefit of his estate which then passed to Brenda. However, it was somewhat irregularly structured in that the amounts would be paid annually over the five years following Harold's death. There is therefore still a year of retrievables outstanding and they seem, shall we say, reluctant to correspond.

There is also the issue of the Probate Registry, which may slow things down considerably anyway. We've been using the Bull Street office in Birmingham for years but it's about to close. Something about the need to redeploy 'resources.'" He waves his hand in the air as though this is some kind of trick akin to black magic. "Things are therefore in a bit of a turmoil up there and this sorry state shows no sign of abating until a new, online service is up and running."

For some unknown reason, Taylor finds it so offensive that someone of his age should use terms like 'online' so freely. For her, the digital age is meant to free the masses from the tyranny of bureaucracy. Sadly, given the number of times she has failed to successfully complete the online application for a new passport, she does wonder if it's simply become another form of red tape: control by curser perhaps?

"Assuming the executors can successfully discharge the will, and probate is subsequently granted, I see no other issues that would stand in its way."

"There was no dispute over the will then. Everything was fairly agreeable?"

"I rarely find death and bereavement agreeable, Inspector."

"Chief Inspector actually, sir. So, each of the children got what they were expecting?"

"I'm not entirely sure what they were expecting, Inspector, but that is what they stand to inherit."

Harcourt ignores the sleight. Life is too short, and it feels even more so when discussing matters such as these. "No surprises then?"

Rawlings does not reply at first but he is plainly struggling with disclosure versus denial. Eventually, he leans forward and somewhat conspiratorially offers. "I don't think either of the children experienced any consternation. However, the only grandchild – Hazel Band – may have been a little disappointed by proxy."

"What does that even mean?" Taylor feels that she may encounter bad dreams about dictionaries later.

"It means that Hazel's father, Charles Band, was a little curious as to why there had been no 'per stirpes' distribution whereby his daughter – Brenda Wilkins's granddaughter - would have been named individually as a contingent beneficiary."

Thankfully, and much to Rawlings's disappointment, one of the nuggets Harcourt has picked up along the way is how to translate legal jargon. "What you're saying is that Hazel – or her father at least – thought that Hazel would be named in the will in her own right. Why would he have thought that – expected that?"

"He attended the reading with Joe, Fred and his wife, Pat Band - the only surviving daughter of Mrs Wilkins. It transpired that Hazel was, how should we phrase it: 'the apple of her grandmother's eye.' As such, he was surprised that there was no named provision for her."

"Surely Hazel would come to benefit – in time – when her own mother died?" Taylor is beginning to piece things together. "Assuming she was to leave everything to Charles, and he subsequently made provision for Hazel?"

"Indeed, and that may not be long."

"Why do you say that?" Harcourt is immediately on high alert.

"Have you met Pat Band?"

"Not yet."

"Well then, I'll leave you to make your minds up about her independently. Whatever that opinion should turn out to be, there is a survivorship clause in the will which means that each of the beneficiaries must survive a minimum of 28 days in order to inherit. Therefore, by my reckoning, there are still twelve days to go before this can even be considered for probate. The executor will make sure of that."

"I assume that, as the eldest son, Joe Wilkins is the

executor?"

"Wrong again, I'm afraid, Inspector. Fred Wilkins is the sole executor of his mother's will."

***

Farren and Flowers return to Bishop's Lacy the following morning after their colleagues on a 'regular traffic patrol' phone through to confirm that it is, indeed, Joe Wilkins who has opened the butcher's shop that morning.

They park just behind the church and Flowers makes to open his car door.

"Give it a few minutes," Farren suggests from the passenger seat. She is wearing a short, grey cotton skirt and a light-blue blouse. "Let's make sure that his chatty colleague doesn't come in to relieve him?"

Flowers giggles at her sarcasm whereas once he might have taken it much more seriously – and personally. He tries not to look at her long, bronzed legs, though he has stolen several glances in that direction on the journey over here. He had casually imagined her on the tiny patio behind the equally tiny flat they'd all been invited to when she'd first moved to Worcester, more than a year ago now. No doubt she sat out there in the evenings, trying to grab whatever remained of the sun's rays. He and his mum had had their tea in the garden last night and he has a red forehead to prove it this morning.

"Not many people about yet?" He offers lamely.

"Full English is probably still a regular breakfast item here, rather than a treat!"

"I had tea and toast."

"Me too, without the toast."

He grins, looking at the church building behind them. "No doubt the DCI would be able to give us chapter and verse on the church here."

She turns in her seat as if surveying the huge grey blocks of stone. "No doubt. Did you see Gabby's message about their meeting in town yesterday?"

"With the solicitor? I did."

"What did you make of it?"

"Her bit about Shakespeare or..."

"Or the real-life acts being performed?"

He reddens. "I wasn't sure about the per stirpes clause, to be honest."

"Nor me. I had to look it up!" The atmosphere, not helped by the growing heat in the car despite each of them having wound down their windows, immediately feels lighter (to them both). "It seems that if someone writing a will wanted to make absolutely sure that a member of the family – or anyone else – beyond their immediate beneficiaries gained a specific amount or percentage for themselves they would name them specifically."

"Not that unusual then?"

"Not at all. It's just the term for it which the solicitors like to write down on parchment with their quill pens."

"I thought they left all that sort of thing to their clerks?" Flowers laughs.

"They do. The clerks just have different titles these days – like 'Legal Executive.'"

"So, it's of interest to us because Brenda Wilkins did not

name her granddaughter specifically when everyone was led to believe that she was the favourite?"

"Maybe not everyone! It is a bit strange but, again, not that uncommon. Changing your will is still a pretty big deal, and at a late stage can seem like a lot of hassle, especially as you grow older. It's probably easier to assume that your children will do the right thing and pass the inheritance down the line in due course, despite someone like a grandchild being more 'present', shall we say?"

"Unless one of the other beneficiaries got wind of the fact that Brenda was considering making a change and thought their share might be at risk? Tried to persuade her out of it if that's what she'd been intending to do."

"Could be, but we haven't found anything to support that yet, have we? A second will might be a completely different matter, but that hasn't turned up either."

"Do you think it will?"

"It depends if anyone else knows about it or takes it seriously if they do. If you're one of the three children standing to gain what you expected to gain, why would you worry about it, unless, of course, you considered yourself to be like one of the pigs in Animal Farm?"

Flowers is on safe ground with literary references. "Some are more equal than others?"

Farren nods. "The survivorship clause is more intriguing though."

"Because?"

"Because you'd only really use that if one of the beneficiaries was, themselves, seriously ill or maybe about to take part in a dangerous activity that was going to put their life at risk. If you thought that to be the case, you'd be more likely to leave the bulk of your wealth to one or other or all of your other children, thinking they'd be more likely to get the benefit of it for longer."

"Except that Brenda left everything equally to the three children, but still put a survivorship clause into her will."

"She did. I wonder if somebody else put that idea into her head?"

***

A few minutes later Flowers walks around the church wall, noting the green clumps of daffodil leaves all along its base. Long gone now but never forgotten. He arrives at the High Street and turns to his left, walking slowly towards the butcher's shop down on his right. Glancing over to check that it is indeed Joe who is serving a customer – a bent-over, elderly lady wearing a dark coat and what looks like a misshapen mince pie on her head – he turns and heads back up the street.

As the street bends and narrows to become Rectory Lane the steady hum of lawnmowers hangs on the breeze above lovingly tendered lawns behind the pretty row of cottages to his left. He spots Joe's residence ahead of him. Fixing his gaze on his destination in case it should somehow try to move out of his vision, he spots a very large man leaving Joe's house. Before walking carefully down the uneven stone steps and stepping out into the lane, he looks slowly and deliberately to his right and his left, then to his right again – like a child crossing the road in the way they'd been taught: alert to the dangers of both cars and people.

He is dressed in a scruffy dark shirt and dark tracksuit bottoms, which might have been a good disguise at night-time but stand out quite alarmingly against the creamy stone of the wall he is now walking alongside. He is carrying a sort of brown satchel, pulled over his head, its strap supported by one bulging shoulder. To Flowers's trained eye it looks quite full and possibly quite heavy.

He approaches Flowers with his head down, neither recognising the other, though Flowers has a theory about the man who has just passed him, based on Farren's previous description of him.

Deep in thought, he climbs the steps of the cottage and knocks firmly on the door, wondering if anyone will answer it. Knowing it won't be Joe. The door is opened almost immediately, with an inner force as though the occupant had expected 'trick or treaters' to be loitering on her doorstep, doing a dry run for Halloween perhaps?

It is the woman from the garden who Flowers and Farren had spotted previously. Presumably, she wishes she was still out there. "Yes?" This isn't going to be friendly. She is wearing a very tight white t-shirt which accentuates her substantial breasts. Equally tight blue jeans complete the outfit, along with a pair of impossibly white plimsolls.

Flowers shows her his warrant card, all the while making a conscious effort to look straight into her eyes which are cold and hostile. "Mrs Wilkins?" (A garish, silver-plated necklace around her neck spells out the name 'Camilla'), "We're investigating the recent deaths in the village, and I wonder if I could have a few minutes of your time?"

Wordlessly, she stands to one side to let him pass, sideways. Maybe it's a test all male visitors must go through. He shimmies past her quickly and then waits for her to lead him into the now-familiar kitchen space. Everything is as neat as before: a barely lived-in look. "I haven't got long." Mercifully, she folds her tanned arms over her chest but remains standing.

"We were wondering if you could tell us a little more about Kathleen Hodges."

"I thought you'd already asked my husband about her!" She is and remains unmoved.

Flowers detects a London accent, Essex possibly. "We did, yes, but we are speaking to as many people as possible."

"Law of averages, is it? Eventually, you're bound to find someone who knows something?"

Flowers takes in the heavy make-up and the perfectly sculptured hair which has almost certainly never been blonde. She must be in her late forties at least. Although she has left her roots behind, the aspiration to be a chav has never left her. He tries to change things up a bit. "How long have you lived here?"

"In this village or this house?"

"Both if you like."

"It's up to you, isn't it? You're asking the questions. In this shithole in the back of beyond, twenty-six years. In this house, just over three. We moved in the springtime."

"You know people here pretty well then?"

"Why would you say that?" The woman runs her hand through her hair, less a come-on than a sod-off.

"Just that it's a small place and everyone seems to know everybody else in a place like this."

"If you'd lived in hillbilly country, you'd know what it was really like." She sneers in the direction of the front door. "Once an outsider, always an outsider. Not that you'd want to become one of them, mind. Nosy old bags, most of them."

Flowers glances outside. The lawn is cut neatly and the sun lounger is still in position. Everything is in its place. A large glass vase contains a vibrant combination of dahlias and lilies.

"These are lovely. Lilies are my mum's favourites."

"Oh, they're Joe's. I don't particularly like lilies; they remind me of death. That's another thing Joe suggested: that I join things, like the 'flower arranging club.' Try to fit in a bit."

"Not much of a choice in a small place like this though!"

"Exactly! Why would I join the library when I've got my magazines? I hate tennis, and if I'd wanted to join the Wild Indians, I'd have sent smoke signals up."

"You must have felt like a fish out of water? How is it that you met Joe in the first place?"

"Online. I'd had a recent breakup and just wanted to meet a different kind of man than those who'd always let me down. Joe was certainly that."

"You were quite a long way away from Bishop's Lacy though."

She shakes her head. "I was staying with my sister at the

time. She lives near Cheltenham, so it wasn't too far to travel."

"And Joe?"

"I think he'd always struggled with relationships. A big bloke who works in a butcher's shop is probably only going to attract a certain kind of woman, isn't he? That wasn't enough for Joe. He wanted something more, someone different."

"So, you met and everything clicked?"

She produces a smile like a long-forgotten tin of fruit from the top cupboard that nobody can be bothered to reach up for any longer. "It was alright for Joe; he'd lived here all his life, as his dad and granddad did before him. He's never been anywhere, known anywhere different. And he won't. Not now."

"You tempted him?"

"What do you mean by that?" The arms are held out in front of her now as she leans provocatively over the breakfast bar, gravity versus granite.

Flowers can feel the same flush rise that she is watching carefully. "To move, I meant. Away from here – if only for a while. You've never thought of moving back to ..."

"Chelmsford? You must be joking. We couldn't even afford a three-bed there now." She lets the statement hang in the air between them, answering for itself. "Besides, who would have looked after the business if we had?" She straightens up again, her eyes still not leaving his alone. "It's in his blood: the family's blood. I can't see Fred taking it on, can you?"

"He seems happy to have made the move that he has."

"Physically and in every other way."

"You don't see much of him?"

There is a pause while she considers her answer. "I can't remember the last time he came over here. As for his wife, I haven't seen her for years."

"That would be Suzanne?"

"Stuck up cow. Everything she knows about comes out of books, know what I mean? Tells everyone who'll still listen that she suffers from anxiety – 'can't possibly leave the house, darling'. We never really got on."

"It must be lonely for you, then. Stuck here when Joe's in the shop all day?" Flowers is thinking about the man he'd seen leaving the house earlier.

"I get by."

"You have no other family nearby, apart from your sister of course?"

"No. And, before you start getting personal, no kids either. It just didn't happen, alright? Probably for the best."

"Was Brenda close to her children? Joe must have kept a close eye on her."

"Brenda was completely ruled by her husband – Harry. That man was a brute. For years and years, she was under his thumb, doing exactly what he said, when he said it. If she didn't, he hit her. Simple as. Once he died there wasn't much left of her. All scooped out inside she was. I'm not surprised she just wanted to spend time in her garden. Didn't have much time for anything or anybody else. At least Joe's not like him – nothing like him. Thank God."

Flowers isn't sure that there is a saviour, never has been. Perhaps that's the point. He presses on.

"Joe left her to it then, knowing that Kathleen was on hand if she needed help."

"Pretty much. We have our own lives to live, don't we? Not that Joe wouldn't have been round there in a flash if something had gone wrong."

"You got on well with your mother-in-law?"

"I barely saw her, to be honest. Apart from those times when I had to be there – like Christmas – I avoided that house. I couldn't bear to see the way he treated her, or the way everyone else just let him do it. Nobody ever tried to stop him: not my definition of 'Happy Families.' When he died, she had Kathleen for company, which suited everyone."

"Did you get on OK with Kathleen – on those rare occasions when you were there?" Flowers is trying to use neutral language though it does feel increasingly like a noisy battleground in that light, quiet space.

"She was alright I suppose. Although..."

Flowers prompts her gently. "Anything at all might be useful for our enquiries. We are finding it quite difficult to put much flesh on the bone if you'll forgive the metaphor."

She doesn't get the butcher's reference, but it has certainly unlocked something inside her: doubt, concern, contempt, or maybe a combination of all three. "I just didn't like the way she seemed to know every inch of Brenda's business. I mean I know most people here are just the same if you let them. Besides, I couldn't stop Brenda from telling her everything she wanted to know even if I'd wanted to, could I?"

"You think she got Brenda to tell her things she'd rather have kept quiet?"

"Possibly. It's more that she seemed determined to get herself in, you know."

"She ingratiated herself."

"That's just the word I was looking for, yes." She nods enthusiastically. A hair is coming loose on the side of her head in the same way that she is loosening up. "It's like she wanted Brenda to rely on her for everything – couldn't manage without her, even when she obviously could still do things for herself. She just took over and was always there, in the house or the garden."

"How did Joe feel about this? Was he worried at all?"

"Not worried, no, but he did come home one evening after visiting Brenda and said he hadn't been able to get a word in edgeways because Kathleen was 'holding forth on every subject under the sun!' I think he was so frustrated by it that he didn't visit much after that. I think he might regret that a little bit now."

Flowers nods sagely (or at least he hopes that's how it comes across, having observed Harcourt for so long). "But not enough to want to hurt Kathleen though?"

"Joe? Of course not."

"Anyone else you can think of who might bear a grudge, for whatever reason?"

"The only thing I can remember about her is that she used to play tennis. I remember seeing a racket and tennis shoes just inside the back door when Brenda was in there for some reason. Maybe she made too much fuss about her ball being called out?"

As Flowers leaves to meet up with Farren again, he considers asking his charming hostess about the man whom he had witnessed leaving the cottage earlier. He decides against it, considering it to be more useful for him to know, and her not to know all that he knows. Not yet.

CHAPTER SIX

Taylor changes into first gear as her car struggles to ascend the hill. It isn't especially steep but a sharp bend to the left just over halfway up has spoiled the best-laid plans the car's engine had had for a clear run.

A wooden welcome board confirms at last that she has reached Marston on the Hill. The minor road taking her away from the A44 had become akin to a track and, in turn, made the latter seem like a North American superhighway, not that she'd ever driven on one.

The village is more of a hamlet of Bishop's Lacy which is just a mile away down the other side of the hill. Pretty brick bungalows – some with extensions and dormer windows – line the street and she can see a village pond and possibly a building that was once a pub up ahead.

An ancient road sign with a red triangle on top tells her that there may be children ahead. Spotting the tell-tale Victorian red bricks soon after, she indicates left and pulls into a surprisingly large, smart-looking car park with a new tarmac surface covering what was probably a playing field once upon a time.

Pausing momentarily to appreciate the elevated view of sheep scattered across impossibly green fields, crisscrossed with stone walls below dark, majestic mountains which rise far higher than the humble little hill she is standing on, she makes her way to the school secretary's office.

A wraparound black, metal fence encloses the school itself and the entrance gate is usually opened via a code in a keypad. Taylor has often wondered what the priority of such protection is: keeping the children in or unwelcome visitors out. After atrocities in such as Dunblane, she assumes the latter. This is not a prison, after all. With no children present today, the gate is slightly open. She pushes it and walks through. No secret codebreaking is required.

She rings a brass bell on a little wooden desk just inside the main front door and is promptly greeted by a friendly, middle-aged woman in a neat, rose-coloured two-piece suit, with round face housing twinkling brown eyes that nevertheless remain on red alert throughout. Taylor presents her warrant card and explains why she is there.

The woman nods vigorously. "Kathleen! Yes, I remember her well. A nice lady. Well-mannered. A bit quiet if I remember correctly but the children loved her."

"Can you tell me more about her please, especially why she chose to leave so suddenly?"

The woman whose name badge tells Taylor her name is Sheila, even if she does not, shakes her head slowly.

"Or is there somebody else who is still here; a fellow teacher who worked with her for example?"

"Oh, no. We've had quite the turnover since Kathleen left, which must have been, what, five years ago now?"

"That's what we thought too."

"Terrible business that was."

Taylor is intrigued now, rather than merely interested in following up on a background enquiry. "I'm sorry. If this is a bad time, I could come back..."

"Oh, no. It's just us here today."

"How long do the school holidays last these days?"

"Not long enough! Perhaps I could take an early break. I'll ask Mrs Harris." With that, she disappears through a door behind her.

Mrs Harris, who presumably does not have a name badge that is on first name terms with either staff or pupils, does not show herself but Sheila does soon re-appear and ushers Taylor into a small side-room on the other side of the corridor.

"We have to use this room for storage as well as meetings I'm afraid." She indicates the stacks of tiny chairs at the far end of the room and what looks like a goal net on the adjoining wall. "Space is at a minimum, but we do try to pack as much into our curriculum as we can!"

They each sit on wooden chairs – mercifully made for adults, not children - on either side of a small, low wooden table.

"Please don't worry. This is bigger than some of our interview rooms!" Taylor attempts to put the woman at ease, noticing that she is far less relaxed than when the police officer first arrived. Perhaps the formidable Mrs Harris imposes time penalties if things are allowed to overrun? She continues quickly. "We're simply looking for some background information on Kathleen at this stage. She was here for quite a long time and yet she left relatively suddenly?"

"As did quite a few others." Sheila lets out a deep breath but still seems ill at ease with the story she is about to tell. "I've only been here for seventeen years myself; you understand. Kathleen worked as a classroom assistant."

"Did she work with one particular teacher?" Taylor has no children of her own and it's a long time since she was at school (seems even longer). Things no doubt work differently in education these days.

If she thinks it is a silly question, Sheila has the good grace not to show it. "In the same classroom, pretty much, yes. Not with the same teacher, though. They tend to move around the school to give them experience of different year groups, you see. It wasn't always like that; Mr Johnson had looked after Year Six for three years in a row for example."

"And Kathleen was liked, respected?"

"Not much room for 'respect' in schools these days," Sheila is much less cheery now, sad even, "But, yes, Kathleen was certainly well-liked by everyone."

"Can you tell me a little more about her: what kind of person she was, maybe even what she liked doing outside of work?"

"I can and I can't. In school, she was quiet, kept her head down, and did everything she was asked to do by the teacher, much like the little ones. I don't remember her ever being ill, or late even. She was one of those people who you see every day and yet you don't know them any better after a week."

"And outside of work?"

"I really can't help you there, I'm afraid. She used to walk here and then back again, no matter how bad the weather. I'm pretty sure that she lived alone. As to what friends she had or where she went with them, what she did, I wasn't one to pry. At the same time, Kathleen kept her private life very much to herself."

"From what you're saying – or what you haven't quite said yet – I get the impression that something changed and that this had something to do with Kathleen leaving?" Taylor asks kindly, suspecting that a gift is about to be passed her way.

Sheila glances over her shoulder towards the closed door, then, satisfied that she can't be overheard, leans in towards the younger woman. "Ofsted is what happened." She is whispering now; the conversation has become even more confidential than had Taylor issued a caution first. "One day's warning they gave us. One single day!"

"Was the school struggling in some way?"

Sheila snorts in disdain, but not at Taylor. "They don't need a reason, those people. Marched in here on a Thursday morning they did, bold as brass and louder than woodwind. Tore the school apart with their criticisms and suggestions bound up as threats. People were very upset. We all were."

"Including Kathleen?"

"Especially Kathleen. We knew something was up when the inspection went over into a second day. That usually means you're being considered 'outstanding' or inadequate.' The children were happy and passed their SATs with mostly good grades each year. The parents were happy – those that took an interest at least – and we were a happy team, not that they came to see if we were happy or not. We were all aware of that."

"So they considered the school to be inadequate?"

Sheila nods, remembering, remorseful. "So officious those people were. Tim Easterly. He was the man in charge. You knew that straight away because he was the most patronising. 'Process-driven' was his answer to everything.

Kathleen was supporting her teacher in a Maths lesson (they call them 'deep dives' these days). One little girl – Bluebell – was asked if she knew what a triangle was. To be fair, she was a confident little thing for seven and came straight back by saying it was a musical instrument made of metal."

Taylor senses that Sheila is on a roll now, so lets her run with it.

Which she does. "The Headteacher called a meeting of all the staff when the report was made public. Among many other 'points to note' it said that there was considerable confusion between certain subject areas – particularly Maths – where 'lateral teaching methods' were unhelpful. Kathleen used a drum in one of those classes to sound out the beats in counting exercises. She was merely an Assistant so, of course, she wasn't named, but she took the whole thing personally. She felt that she'd let her teacher, the school and – most importantly in her eyes – the children down."

They implied that some of the staff had been here too long and most teachers had to attend re-training courses. Some did and then left. Others didn't even bother. He was like a child with the devil in them, only he wasn't a child."

"I've never understood why educationalists – or those who use that word as cover – try to drum parallel thinking out of young children when it is their creativity that is coming out. Perhaps it's because I've never had children of my own?" Taylor is as passionate about this as she is about the sexist assumption of power. The latter has never been an issue with Harcourt but Hunter-Wright is another matter altogether.

"No, you're right." Sheila leans forward in a gesture of support. "Young children are like sponges, absorbing everything they possibly can, but that doesn't mean they all express themselves in the same way, does it? A structure is fine, of course, essential according to Mrs Harris, but it has to provide enough space for children (and adults) to be individuals. I've never had children either, but you don't need to work in a school to see that."

"He doesn't sound like much of a grown-up people person either." Taylor reflects on how such a person could ever have wanted to have a 'career' in education. Perhaps he hadn't.

Sheila shakes her head, furiously, red in the face now. "I don't think he could ever get his head around why people like Kathleen could be content just to do the job they did, do it well and just leave again at the end of each day. Mrs Hughes, who Kathleen was working with that year, overheard him talking to one of his male colleagues during lunchtime (well, you have to open the windows to let fresh air in, don't you?). He said he couldn't understand why someone like Kathleen didn't go and work in a supermarket instead!"

"Not a very educated approach." Taylor has heard about these kinds of impromptu visits which are made in the name of standards but is genuinely shocked to hear of such unmeasured callousness. "Kathleen never got over it?"

"Like I said, her and most everybody else. Once Mr Sutcliffe was forced to leave at the end of the Christmas term (he drinks!) Mrs Harris became the only person remaining from that time. They made her up to Head so that she'd stay. She wasn't the best teacher, but she knows her way around a budget."

"Kathleen must have been very upset about it all?"

"She was inconsolable. Handed her notice in as soon as she could get another job."

"She became a carer."

"That's what she did here! Cared for the children and did everything she could to help them: prepare them for their lives ahead. She didn't need to leave here just because one arrogant man and his acolytes did not care about her!"

Shortly afterwards, as Taylor is heading back towards the front door, Sheila places a soft hand on her left-hand shoulder. Again, keeping her voice down for fear of unknown reprisals she announces. "I've remembered one thing though."

Taylor half-turns to look back towards the office. Perhaps she has caught Sheila's habit, or maybe it is muscle memory from her own school days. "What is it?"

"Kathleen loved films. Always films, never 'movies.' She used to tell us about the latest film she'd watched and which one she'd got lined up next. I can't think of anything else that grabbed her imagination in the way that they did."

"Did she mention any of the local cinemas she used to

go to or anyone she might have gone with?"

Sheila is anxious to return to her post, Taylor can see that. "No. The nearest one must be a fair step away from here, I'd say. There's the Conquest in Bromyard, but I don't know if that one got all the latest releases. Worcester's probably the nearest. We're a small community here in Marston; miles from anywhere some might say. We do have quite a lot of community events here in the school hall, serving all the villages around, much like the school itself does, but I don't remember seeing Kathleen at any of those. Perhaps she preferred to be by herself in the darkness – especially after what happened. Some people do, don't they?

"The darkness?"

"Watching other people's lives play out on the silver screen."

***

"This is lovely!" Daniel is sitting on one of the straw-coloured wicker chairs as Kate Shelbourne reappears with two mugs of coffee which she places on a small, glass table between them. She is wearing a yellow T-shirt with 'I'm just happy being me. OK' emblazoned in red letters over her slightly chunky frame. In relaxed mode, then; if that ever applies to journalists any more than 'off the record' means it ever truly is.

"Thank you." Kate is genuinely pleased as she also sits and looks towards the fence beyond them. I don't get many visitors; kind of forget what it must look like to them. I was determined to have a south-facing garden. I didn't need much outside space, obviously, so I took up the option of a little conservatory instead."

"You bought it off-plan?"

"I did. They only built two of them on this street – in-fill – and it suits me just fine. The lounge and kitchen are quite small, and I would have preferred another room downstairs as opposed to the three bedrooms. Would have been more useful to me, but I use one of them as a little office anyway. Well, I've got a small desk and sometimes work from my laptop up there. It's not as posh as it sounds!"

"Good location on the main road out of Evesham though."

She laughs. "Quick escape route you mean?"

Daniel pulls a face of mock horror. "You know me better than that."

Smiling still, she leans over and pats his arm, glad to see that he doesn't attempt to move it. "We can't all live in the Lenches you know! You are right about the road though. I can be out and about quickly, without having to face the traffic lights in town each time."

"They're still only letting three cars through at a time then!"

"Less if you're talking about estate cars; they don't seem to use those words to describe them anymore, do they?"

"I've no idea. My old 'saloon' got me here; whether it will be able to get back up Hipton Hill is another matter altogether..."

"How's the writing going?"

"None of my own. I call it 'writer's block' which is about as general an excuse I can come up with!"

"Except that you've probably got other people's books

coming out of your ears, and you're dealing with a lot more than most, at the moment anyway."

He nods, gratefully. "It isn't helped by the latest project they've sent me. It's supposed to be 'historical fiction' but it's more of an old story in new, very inexperienced hands which are doing their best to crush the charm out of the original. Punctuation's terrible, especially the hyphenation. The author persists in using the term 'pre-Anglo-Saxon period' without the first hyphen. Anglo-Saxons are hyphenated, to begin with, but they then forget that we also use a hyphen when the prefix precedes a capitalized word. It's driving me slightly mad."

"Sounds as if you're longing for a comma so that you can have a short break!"

He laughs out loud, although some internal safety catch warns him against providing any further examples of grammatical inexpertise.

"So, have you contacted the police about the Bishop's Lacy deaths?"

Daniel understands that he is taking up the journalist's valuable time which, with no significant information of his own, is akin to asking an escapologist, sealed in a vat of water, whether they'd recommend deep breathing exercises to relieve stress (and without possessing a key to let them out either way). "I've got an appointment with Harcourt this afternoon."

"Good. I haven't got any further with it I'm afraid. I know that a different Worcester journo is planning to put a piece out linking the two deaths though."

"Is it anyone I know? The journalist now handling the

story?"

"Lindsay Pittevils (her father was from Belgium)."

Daniel shakes his head slowly. "No. After my time I think."

"I'm not surprised. She sounds about eleven on the phone and looks even younger. One of their trainees who they couldn't risk keeping on making rubbish tea."

"Is she any good though? Seriously."

"Seriously, she wrote an article about footfall on Worcester High Street last Christmas and described *Lush* as specialising in animal cruelty products..."

"Ouch!"

"Especially if you're an animal."

Daniel shakes his head again, more quickly this time. "OK. I think I'm getting the picture. Is there any substance in connecting the two Bishop Lacy deaths do you think?"

"None at all as far as I can tell. The police have been unforthcoming though. They haven't offered them anything, so they're going for a more provocative approach."

"To see if that elicits a response?"

She nods, moving slightly nearer to her guest, to shield her eyes from the sun which is temporarily hanging out behind the upright of one of the plastic window frames. "If they deny it, which I presume they will, they might share some kind of insight as to why they know that not to be the case and, at the same time, provide us with information on what they think did happen. A blanket denial with nothing to back it up - however small –

would just sound hollow and make people think they don't know anything more."

"Perhaps they don't?"

"Or haven't been able to gather enough evidence to go public yet. Or they don't feel they need the help of either the public or the media at this stage. It doesn't stop people wondering what happened though, does it? Worrying for the most part. Especially women living on their own."

Daniel considers Kate herself. She's lived alone ever since he's known her. There haven't even been any temporary house sharers as far as he knows. He tries not to dwell on it. "Kathleen Hodges was certainly pretty upset."

"She had just been to the funeral of the person she'd spent time caring for." Kate tries not to make the obvious sound too damming.

"I know. I know." Daniel isn't offended in the slightest. He picks up the mug and begins to sip at the contents. "She was upset as in angry rather than sad though."

"People do grieve in very different ways though, don't they?"

"They do but you know DCI Harcourt. He'll get to the bottom of it, I'm sure."

"DCI? He's finally got his promotion then?"

"Only just. I understand that this will be his last case with this unit; they're opening a new Cold Case Unit which he'll oversee."

"Are they indeed?"

"Probably classified for now!"

"Did Harcourt tell you this himself?"

"No. I had a call from Hunter-Wright two nights ago."

"How is that poor man?"

"Difficult to say. He never gives much away either, does he? An old colleague from the Met had called to say they'd had another possible sighting of his son."

"Michael, wasn't it?"

"It is, yes. I could tell that he was trying not to get too excited, but it must be so hard mustn't it."

Kate nods. "I don't know him that well. Our paths have crossed a few times over the years but nothing significant since he first came down here. Is he going up to London to check it out?"

"He didn't say. I would be mortified if all of this is just a wild goose chase. I have told him lots of times – in every meeting we've had – that whatever I can do to help him is far from being an actual contact report. Not by any means."

"He must have known that from the outset, though, surely?"

"Yes. He did, but hope outweighs hard evidence sometimes, doesn't it? I'm sure it happens with long-running police cases quite often: when there's no evidence forthcoming you must just get so tired and frustrated that you're hoping and even praying that you'll get a lucky break."

"Or they call you in!"

Daniel returns her smile. "Except that the very lack of exactitude makes my insights vulnerable – 'unsafe' a court of law would most likely describe them as."

"I think you're being very hard on yourself. You know full well that your gift has made a real difference in lots of cases." She places her mug down on the table, firmly and with unarguable certainty.

"I know it has." He is encouraged by her support, yet still feels unworthy of it. "It can be like trying to nail down thin air though. I can't just switch it on or not, and I have absolutely no idea, even after all these years, whether I'm going to see something or nothing."

"And what you do see can be right but also wrong, can't it? I remember you telling me that after the Weston-super-Mare chase."

Daniel closes his eyes momentarily, remembering vividly the two young people who could quite easily have fallen into the sea and lost their lives. But they didn't. He opens them again to find her staring at him intently. "I can sometimes see the right people in the wrong place or the right place at the wrong time."

"All the same. You did materially see Kathleen Hodges after the funeral, and I'm pleased you're going to tell the police about it."

"I do too. At least there isn't the usual caveat of 'this may not be accurate' with that observation."

"Did Charlotte go to the funeral with you?"

"She did and, yes, she was with me when the two of them were arguing outside. I can't get her involved though. If my thoughts are barely coherent (even to me), she could never be described as a reliable witness. More's the pity."

"Has she… declined?" Again, Kate reaches her hand out to her friend.

Daniel takes it and holds it gently, enjoying the extra warmth that even the sunshine cannot match. "We're in a different stage of the disease now. At least that's what her specialist at The Royal thinks. Some dementias attack the back of the brain and your vision and spatial awareness. Eventually, your brain can't make sense of what is right in front of you and so you become functionally blind. We don't know if this will happen with Charlotte's form of the disease or not.

There's lots of research going on though, as with all forms of dementia, which tells me that medical science is struggling with it still, just as she is (believe me, I've read a lot of the literature since her diagnosis). I sometimes wonder if there's that much difference between science and psychometry, but I know that's just me being silly."

"It may seem silly, but you and Claire are struggling too. That's real. It's an awful situation for all of you to be in," She is watching him intently, clearly moved but unmoving.

"I just wish I could have predicted some of this, for Claire's benefit if not my own." He gently takes his hand away from Kate's, stands and walks slowly towards the window. "I used to be able to do that sometimes. It wasn't exactly a gift in the same way – not my 'specialism' if you like, and as unpredictable as anything else. But that's the great irony, isn't it? I am able to access forms of second sight and yet I didn't see what was happening to my own wife right in front of me! When you love someone with dementia you lose them more and more every day. 'Ambiguous Loss' the doctors call it, caused by a rapidly shrinking brain."

Kate stands and walks towards him, putting her hand around his shoulder. "Would it have made that much difference if you had been able to predict it?" Her voice is gentle; caring.

Daniel turns and lets her fall into his arms. They hold each other tightly. At length, he moves backwards slightly, and their eyes meet. "I don't know what's going to happen, I never did. Neither does anyone, it seems. That must be terrifying for Charlotte most of all: not knowing the future. Perhaps not knowing the past is even worse."

"As long as she has the two of you, she at least has something to hang on to. Don't forget that you're probably the only threads still connecting her to reality."

"Which makes everything so flimsy when she used to be so strong. One day soon she's going to wake up and not recognise us either. What does she do then?" They both note the anguish in his voice as the sun moves back out from behind the cloud it's been hiding behind. "And there's another thing."

She waits, unsure of what is coming next, as she so often is with this man.

"What if I can't see her again once she's passed? You'd have thought wouldn't you that of all the people who worry about never seeing their loved ones again, I might have been an exception to the rule?"

Kate moves forward and very gently kisses him on the lips. "I think you are exceptional. I don't think your gift has deserted you at all. I think the stress of Charlotte's illness itself has blocked it somehow; maybe you're not completely over the redundancy either. I know that was a huge shock too. The more you've worried, the less accessible your insights might have become."

"I never thought I'd sing the virtues of proofreading but at least the rules are clear with that (Hart's or otherwise). Dementia does not follow rules or timings. Verbs do follow subjects but actions do not follow outward symptoms, it seems." He hugs her once again then pulls away, suddenly. "Thank you, Kate."

She watches him pass through the conservatory door and whispers back: "No. Thank you for being in this world, at least for some of the time."

***

Farren is sitting in one of the window seats just inside the village's only pub: 'The British Grenadier.' She'd remarked to Flowers on their way over here that it was a strangely provocative name for a hostelry, given the region's close history from Offa's Dyke through to Welsh devolution. Perhaps it was meant as a reminder of the strength of the Union, although that strategy had nearly gone so badly wrong in Scotland just five years earlier.

An empty glass once filled to the two-thirds mark with orange juice sits on a grimy beer mat on the sticky table beside her. She glances at her watch again. It's late morning now and her colleague should be concluding his interview with Joe's wife soon. She isn't in the best of moods. The short, tubby barman had earlier told her dismissively that 'Britvic' was merely a brand name when pouring out his preferred choice.

"All alone?" A burly, red-faced man is looming over her. She hasn't heard his stealth-like approach (what kind of police officer is she?).

She looks beyond him to find three other men sitting at the bar, dressed in the regulation uniform of checked shirt and jeans as befits the status of 'rural regulars' (or 'bearded bar flies' if she was being unkind). Her gentleman caller is dressed slightly differently, in a brown short-sleeved shirt and thin, woollen tie in an even darker shade of brown, all over a tell-tale paunch squeezed into dark, non-descript trousers.

"I'm just waiting for my colleague." She manages to hide her surprise at his sudden presence, or at least she thinks she might have got away with it.

"Ah. That's what they all say, isn't it?" His broad accent is that of a man who has rarely if ever left his childhood home of Herefordshire farming country.

"Is it?" Farren is back in police mode, knowing that he won't have perceived any amendment from a 'single woman sitting by herself' in this bastion of male supremacy.

"May I?" Without waiting to receive her assent, he sits on the small wooden stool opposite. "What's such a beautiful woman doing inside on an equally beautiful day like this?" His brown teeth are studded with black fillings, and she can smell his beery breath even before he leans over to invade her space further.

"She's on surveillance." Farren whips out her warrant card and watches as her uninvited guest lean back again into the darkness from which he'd emerged.

"I see." He looks around furtively to see if the others have heard her, or maybe they're part of the same undercover team! "What – or whom – may I ask is the subject of your watchful eyes?"

She watches in disgust as his eyes appear to be trained on hers before lowering to her blouse, then quickly back again, certain that she wouldn't have noticed their little trip into forbidden territory. "I'll ask the questions if that's alright with you?" She notes with satisfaction that his pupils have stopped dilating; his eyes open wide in alarm. He isn't used to having to respond to other people's enquiries.

"My name is Portugil. Fire away."

"You own the garage at the top of the hill, yes?"

He nods, disinterested in where this strand of the conversation is leading.

"How's business?"

"Slow. We mostly do MOTs (that's an annual government test of a car's roadworthiness)."

She ignores the sarcasm and the less-than-surreptitious scratching of his crotch. "I believe my colleagues have already been in touch with you and your wife about the time leading up to Kathleen Hodges's death?"

Recognition breaks out over his ruddy cheeks. "Ah. So that's why you're here?"

"Neither of you saw or heard anything, I understand."

"I'm afraid not, my dear." He relaxes again, on safer ground, his eyes narrowing once more. "We still have active lives and sleep soundly as a result." He winks at the inference; feeling back in control.

Farren's breakfast, which she last saw about three hours earlier, is threatening to make an unwelcome reappearance. "Did you know them well? Brenda and Kathleen?"

"Not that well, though they'd been our neighbours for years. I knew Brenda's husband – Harry – better."

"From the butcher's shop?"

"That and the pub, yes. More of the latter I'm afraid." Another wink.

"But you can't tell me anything further about Kathleen?"

"Allow me to buy you a drink and we'll see how it goes!" The lascivious grin is back.

"I might remind you, sir, that we are conducting a murder enquiry. A brutal murder in fact, with the killer still at large." She has raised her voice slightly and the three beards have turned their way as one; even the barman has stopped his meaningless, repetitive polishing of a beer glass while trying to listen in.

"Of course." He is far more interested in his peers' perceptions than hers. Probably one of those tiresome lesbians that seem to get everywhere these days, he considers, although didn't they usually have short hair?

"So? Kathleen Hodges?"

"Kept herself to herself." His response is terse now. He wants to be away from her or for her to leave. He sits quite still but the tables have turned.

"No visitors you can tell me about – not just on the night in question but more generally?"

"I'm not in the habit of spying, Sergeant."

"Yet she was a lonely woman; would probably have been glad of some company?" Farren delights in watching him rub his hand behind his hot, sweaty neck: a classic sign of discomfort.

"The only person I ever saw going around there was that irritating little man from the other end of the village. Ex-solicitor: you can always tell, can't you?"

"Simon Short?"

"That's him. Was there at all hours. I did happen to see her walking away from her house quite late at night on several occasions. Presumably off to spend time with him. A very strange couple they made – like Laurel and Hardy."

"Except that this isn't funny."

He remains silent, as is his right at this stage.

Farren can make out the figure of Flowers walking past the grubby window. Time to bring this to a close, but on her terms. "What did you make of Mr Short?"

"Nothing much – there isn't much to consider is there? To be honest, I'd always thought he was a queer?"

A barely stifled snigger from one of the beards only encourages her further. "Is that your considered opinion? You're familiar with the gay community around here, are you? I mean leering at single women is one thing but using it as cover is something else entirely."

Shocked silence accompanies the horror on his face. Ultimately he decides – needs – to respond. "I can see that I'm going to have to talk to your superiors about you." He is trying to sound firm, but Farren will report later that she heard a distinct wobble in the older man's voice.

"Good plan." Flowers is approaching them now, a slightly puzzled look on his face. "Perverting the course of justice is a serious matter, especially when the emphasis is not on 'the course of justice."

She swings her bag over her shoulder and steers Flowers back towards the entrance, where they exit, fully aware of the murmuring discourse on current affairs that has already begun, with one particular item having just become the main news story.

***

"A trust fund?"

"Assuming she survives for the full 28 days, yes."

"Are you out of your mind?"

"No, but Pat is. For much of the time. I know that; you know that. We all know it. That's why Fred persuaded Mum to put that clause in the first place, wasn't it? You remember how she was after that last time! Nobody expected her to come back from that."

"She couldn't have known. It doesn't prove that she's incapable of making her own decisions."

"What? To use or not use?"

"You know exactly what I mean. It was the cutting agent, wasn't it? Fentanyl? More dangerous than the heroin itself. How would she have known?"

"Camilla says the dullness would have given it away."

"Oh, so Essex woman is now the be-all and end-all of drug prescriptions, is she? You wanna watch it: she'll be going for a job at Boots next. How will you ever keep tabs on her then?"

He is undeterred; not prepared to be blown off course by someone who has already abandoned their family. "At the very least it should have sent an alarm signal to her brain if she'd been thinking straight. But she wasn't;

doesn't think straight does she? Hasn't done for years."

"So, you think that just because of one bad batch, she's incapable of any kind of choice."

"Not any kind of choice. Her addiction doesn't present her with a choice, does it?"

"And you seriously believe that putting Brenda's money into a trust while she attempts to get better is going to solve this? She's never going to get better. I should know. I stood by her while she went through every counsellor, every therapy, every self-help programme there was."

"But you're not now, are you?" The tone of his voice is darker, menacing. "Standing by her."

"Kathleen Hodges isn't standing at all."

"Meaning?"

"Just that someone relieved us of that complication."

"There is no 'us.'"

"Oh, but I think there is. Us versus them; in this case Kathleen."

"What are you gabbing on about?"

"What if there was another will that was leaving everything to her? It wouldn't be that much of a surprise, would it? Brenda may even have told her that's what she was doing. Why ever would someone murder her otherwise, if not for greed? I don't see revenge or envy as factors do you?"

"Whoever it was that murdered Kathleen tried to frame me for it. There is no us."

"Perhaps it was your conniving little brother. Never did get over your being Daddy's favourite, did he?"

"That's not true."

"It's what Pat told me."

"She'd tell you the evening clouds were coated in marmalade if you gave her what she wanted, needed."

"It's Fred you should be speaking to, not me."

"None of this is anything to do with him."

"Oh. I think it is. I think everything that's happened is to do with him. None of you bothered with Brenda, certainly never cared for her. Of the two people who did, one of them is dead and the finger's pointing fairly and squarely at you."

Without missing a beat, Joe responds. "If we're being strictly accurate, you mean fingers. Who is the other person?"

"Who do you think?"

"Don't play games with me."

"What would you plan on doing about it if I did? It's your brother who's the joker in the pack. You'd better have a word with him – or ask your wife to, if that's easier. I bet he won't agree to this little plan of yours either."

It is as though he hasn't heard or has chosen not to dwell on the threat. Again, he doesn't even break stride. "I would be one of the trustees and we'd need at least one other – someone who isn't a named beneficiary."

"And presumably not me because I then have something to gain if Pat does die."

"Hardly. Hazel, possibly, but not you; never you. At least this way my sister can't just blow her inheritance via her nose."

"I'll advise Pat to fight this, you know that?"

"Why would she listen to you? She won't even let you into her house."

"Hazel then. She can get a doctor to testify that she is of sound mind."

"Except that she isn't. We're going round in circles here."

"You're right as usual. Just like your father. I can see that this is, as you suggest, another circle that needs squaring."

***

Harcourt watches Farren distribute four polystyrene cups of equally unnatural coffee on each of their desks before presenting him with his. While thanking her he grimaces at the smell of it: a promise of something even worse inside.

"No Detective Superintendent today, sir?" They never make coffee for Hunter-Wright, for whom hot beverages should only ever be presented in china vessels. Perhaps he knows much more about the staff drinks machine than he needs to admit to.

"He's in London today, Linda." Harcourt places his cup on the table beside him, just in front of his office door.

"Business or pleasure?"

"Neither I should think."

Farren knows not to venture further. In any case, her colleagues appear at the door and take their seats, nodding gratefully for their drinks, while inwardly groaning at the lack of still-living plants to share them with later.

"You've caught the sun again, Ian!" Harcourt has always been amused by the two-tone nature of the younger man's skin: either pale white or red raw, not to mention the regular blush which forms a kind of halfway house: rosé perhaps?

"I have, sir," he replies cheerily, "I should wear a hat, but it's just so hot."

Everyone smiles. It's good to have the old team back together, which also means that Ian Flowers is hopefully well on the road to a full recovery (unless death is the only eventuality that can truly put an end to bereavement).

Farren begins by telling them about her latest visits to Bishop's Lacy.

"So 'Big Steve' wasn't falling for your charms then?" Harcourt is careful how he phrases this, given the feistiness Farren has sometimes displayed when her femininity has been mentioned. Half a lifetime of being ogled at, he supposes. Whenever will his younger colleagues learn to keep it in their trousers?

Farren flashes him a smile. "I'm losing my touch, obviously."

Flowers shifts slightly in his chair, but it is Taylor who speaks next, politely but firmly which isn't like her. "What did you make of him? Is he going to be of interest to us?"

"Until he's ruled out, I guess." Harcourt is delighted by the response, as would a promotion board be. He knows full well that she never guesses either – only educated ones at least. Farren is continuing. "What I would say is that it felt like he was hiding something."

Quite perceptively each of them leans towards her, even Harcourt who has remained standing at the front.

"Maybe not hiding, exactly, but containing something inside. I felt like he might explode at any moment, although he kept it under control for the most part and remained soft-spoken throughout. I struggled to hear him at times."

"But capable of violence, do you think?" Taylor again.

"We all are, aren't we? He certainly knew how to handle his tools, but what motive he might have for Kathleen's death I wouldn't have any idea about at this stage. Seemed quite protective of Joe."

"He would be though, wouldn't he? I mean Joe is his food and drink, isn't he? He's not going to bite that hand." Flowers worries that they might think he is trying to be clever with words again, even though he isn't. He needs to rein it in a bit.

"Indeed. You saw him leaving Joe's house though, while Joe was safely out of the way?" Harcourt notes the blush, as regular as sunrise and sunset.

"Yes, sir. I haven't met him – not to speak to – so he wouldn't have recognised me. He did seem keen to keep his head down though, like he would have preferred not to have been noticed by anyone."

"Difficult with all the gossips in that village." Taylor again. She is much more vocal than usual, Harcourt notes. Linda Farren has spotted it too. "It was also in broad daylight, so he couldn't have been that bothered about it."

"And the lovely Camilla! You wouldn't put the two of them together?" Harcourt and Flowers have had their own albeit brief conversation about Joe Wilkins's wife.

"From what DS Farren says, I wouldn't, sir, but opposites do attract don't they? How many times have we been caught out by two or more of the most unlikely of people working together – being together?"

It's all in there, Harcourt considers, happily, as his young DS continues.

"She didn't like Kathleen Hodges, or maybe that's just because Joe didn't? I got the impression that they were kind of stuck with her while Brenda was alive. Not only was she the carer, but she was also the next-door neighbour."

"Thick as thieves?" Taylor again, more relaxed now.

"I wouldn't describe either of them as 'thick.' Farren is a little less friendly. "As to thieves, well, it's possible – if there was a motive. If we're to take seriously the way Kathleen's body was left, either actually or staged, it implies some kind of warning doesn't it? There would have to be a pretty strong motive for that wouldn't there, beyond naked greed I mean. Revenge, desperation...hatred?"

"I agree with Linda," Flowers stares at Harcourt, like a new child in the class finding his feet and trying to impress the teacher (and yet Flowers isn't new and doesn't need to work that hard if only he'd come to realise it), "For such a degree of violence to have occurred in their village, nobody seems to be that interested in what did happen to Kathleen. They certainly don't know for a fact what we saw at the murder scene because neither we nor the media have released anything, have we?"

"You mean they're not interested, or one or all of them already knows the truth? You may be on to something there, Ian."

"Thanks, sir. I mean Fred Wilkins wasn't curious about finding out details – any details - neither was Camilla, Joe or Steve. The only person who was even remotely curious was Simon Short."

"When are we bringing him in, sir?" Taylor nodded her approval of Flower's contribution, almost unnoticeably. Harcourt noticed.

"We tracked him down by phone. He is in Sidmouth; taking a few days' break."

"Convenient timing." Farren isn't surprised. There was something about that man that she had found deeply unpleasant.

"Maybe. He isn't a suspect though – not at this stage anyway – so we can't force things. We've asked him to return to be interviewed here in Worcester as soon as possible."

"Thinking back to the murder of Kathleen, sir, how serious should we be taking it? The severed hand and fingers I mean." Taylor isn't buying it; hasn't done since her colleagues had described the scene. The knife held by the garden gnome had done it for her.

"All murders are serious and very rarely without motive. I know there are events such as road rage that get out of hand or killings fuelled by drink or drugs. The simple truth here is that someone in a crazed state of mind is unlikely to have staged things in the way they did afterwards. They'd have had their misguided moment and fled. I do believe someone was trying to send somebody a message here. The knife: I'm not so sure about it. On the face of it, it was meant to implicate Joe or Steve, but I think that's a bit amateur. Strikes me as an afterthought."

"And the fishing line?" Taylor persists. "Doctor Graham was examining the material used to stitch Kathleen's lips together?" She shivers slightly at the thought.

"SOCOs have been all over it. No fingerprints on anything. The murderer was almost certainly wearing gloves. Nothing else on the body or clothing either. Again, it rather adds weight to my view that this was planned as a cold-blooded killing as opposed to the result of some hot-blooded passion. Organised Crime might not be behind it, but it was certainly well organised."

"And the will situation, sir?" Taylor won't be forgetting Old Mr Rawlings for some time. "I don't see that it gives any of the siblings the grounds to kill off Brenda's neighbour?"

"I agree," Harcourt replies, thoughtfully. "They're going to inherit anyway, although I did wonder at the survivorship clause. DS Farren and I are off to visit the daughter, Pat Band, tomorrow morning to see if she can throw any light on this. Brenda Wilkins must have had a legitimate reason at the time to have her solicitor place that clause in there."

"Or someone persuaded her to do it; strongly persuaded her to?" Flowers again.

"Could be, but why? It's the same with the so-called 'other will' that Simon Short spoke about. As I say, we'll see what details we can glean about it when he returns."

"What if the 'new' will Simon Short spoke about is actually the will that Rawlings drew up for her just before she died.?" Taylor has been troubled about the will ever since their 'conversation' in the solicitor's office, and not just because of his barely disguised sexist and almost certainly racist attitude. "He implied that it was a new will, didn't he."

"He did and he didn't," Harcourt responds gently. His younger colleague had been very upset after the meeting though she'd done her best to cover it up as she usually did. "It might indeed have been a new will, but that doesn't mean it was a replacement will from Brenda. She might never have made a will up until that point."

"True." Taylor is deflated but he can see that the cogs are whirring which is always a positive.

He continues quickly. "If there's anything at all in the staging of Kathleen's body, it's 'see nothing, say nothing, hear nothing.' Don't listen to rumours. Keep quiet. I'm not aware of any great effort being made to see if an alternative will does exist; maybe there is, and we just don't know about it. As I say, you'd think the impetus for that would come from the siblings and they're beneficiaries anyway, so why try to change things?"

"Unless the alternative will left everything to someone else?" Farren's words hang in the air for a moment.

"In which case you'd be all over Brenda's house wouldn't you? Trying to find it?"

"Or you just discredit it as rumour by doing absolutely nothing?" Taylor again.

"Maybe so. I'd like you and Ian to visit Charles Band

tomorrow please, while we are at Pat's. There's her daughter too, who lives with him not her. Let's have a chat with her too?"

"The only other immediate family member we haven't met is Suzanne Wilkins – Fred's wife." Farren has been scribbling away in her notebook as usual.

"Ah yes. The elusive butterfly who suffers from anxiety."

"Camilla Wilkins most definitely had no time for her, sir." Flowers hasn't written anything down.

"Jealousy among sisters-in-law perhaps?" Farren interjects.

"Because Fred is an upwardly mobile estate agent and Joe got landed with the family butcher's business you mean?" Harcourt would love to send Farren in to fight it out with the two women.

"Possibly, sir. I still can't get my head around why she is so disinterested in what happened to Kathleen; same as all the others."

"I think she thought Kathleen was possibly on the make somehow – with Brenda I mean." Flowers confirms. "It might just be Camilla being bitchy about her though. There's no evidence to support that view and very difficult now they're both dead."

"Unless Brenda did leave everything to Kathleen in this other will?" Farren has stopped scribbling.

"Or the killer thought that was the case, even if she didn't."

"In which case we're back to one of the beneficiaries aren't we sir?"

"It is unless there's a whole hidden world behind

Kathleen Hodges that we don't know about."

"The school had little new information, sir." Taylor takes his lead. "As I said to you before, the only thing Sheila could remember from Kathleen's school days was that she liked to watch films."

"This whole scene could be right out of a fantasy!" Flowers quips. "I just don't see a real Godfather pulling strings."

Harcourt nods. "And the carers agency couldn't tell us much either, Gabby?"

"I'm still waiting for them to send me the actual employment records, sir, but I don't imagine they're going to be of much use to us – neither the records nor the crack team that prepared them. If we were in court relying on those two, I can imagine the jury seeking medical help for brain injuries!"

"OK. Disappointing, but let's see what tomorrow brings."

"Talking of schools, sir, I did find something in Charles Band's records – Pat's husband." Farren is concerned that they might think she's been wasting time in idle, tenuous searching, but she perseveres. At least they haven't caught her browsing on Amazon. "Not sure if it's at all relevant or not. He attended the local Catholic primary school in Pershore. It seems that he was bullied. It comes up a few times."

"At least somebody noticed it, "Flowers offers, "Too often it goes under the radar, doesn't it? Still."

"You're not wrong. "Farren agrees. "One of the reasons that this probably didn't is because there was an incident in the playground when he was just eight. It seems that a whole gang of them were found hitting and kicking him."

"Dear God!" Harcourt exclaims in righteous indignation. "Was he badly hurt?"

"He wasn't, but another child was somehow wounded in the melee. Not seriously, but he had to be taken to hospital. Made a full recovery."

"And Charles?"

"No other reports of physical violence against him."

"Doesn't mean they didn't happen though, does it?" Harcourt shakes his head. "By the way, Daniel Reed has asked to see me this evening, here at the station."

Nobody responds though they all want to ask if it concerns Hunter-Wright. Possibly his visit to London.

Noting their silence, he concludes, enigmatically. "I'll let you know if anything comes out of it that is pertinent to this case."

They all rise, as he does, watching him return to his office. He in turn watches Taylor head off towards the toilet before turning in the doorway.

"You both might like to know that I had a phone call from Nigel Jennings at the British Grenadier in Bishop's Lacy earlier this afternoon.

Farren and Flowers turn to face him, their attention duly captured, as was the plan.

"Be careful how you talk to people in public. I appreciate the shortcomings of many of the people we encounter in our daily work, but I will not tolerate rudeness. Understood? People may not appear to be interested in our case, but I can assure you that they'll still be hanging off every word you say – looking for clues or meal tickets from the local press. We must always remain professional and impartial."

"Yes, sir" They acknowledge in unison.

"Remember also, it's not just the public you have to show that face to, or me. Nobody promotes their cause by getting angry: not killers nor those of us trying to track them down."

CHAPTER SEVEN

"Come on in." It's almost the end of a long, tiring day, but the sun is in no mood to go to bed just yet. The windows of the police station facing west towards the river are flooded with evening light which, as Daniel Reed has remarked on reaching their floor, 'still has some heat in it.'

"Drink?" Harcourt is genuinely pleased to see the man who has both helped the police and helped him personally when he needed it. They didn't talk about the latter at the time, and won't now, of course, but those moments of kindness can't be unlived.

Daniel is unsure whether this is one of those 'I'm on duty but the whisky is duty-free' you see in police dramas. He has also tasted the offerings from the machine in the far corner so takes the safest option and, holding his hands up as though he isn't at all thirsty, declines.

"Probably wise!" Although it's getting late, Debbie is out at Pilates until after nine, so he's in no rush. Harcourt beckons his friend to sit and wheels his chair out from behind his desk so as not to appear divisive or, worse, confrontational. "Now, how can I help you?"

Daniel sits and crosses his legs, more comfortable now that he's here, but less so than he hopes to appear. "I think it's more a question of how I might be able to help you!"

"Sounds familiar," Harcourt responds happily, though he senses the man's unease. It isn't unusual for those visiting a police station of course but Daniel has been here so many times and, apart from a DS from the vice team at the far end of the room, there is nobody else here to see him, hear him; judge him.

His visitor describes the scene outside the church in Bishop's Lacy but notices that Harcourt only begins to listen actively when he mentions the funeral itself. "I'm sorry for not coming to see you earlier, but I wasn't sure if I would be telling you anything you didn't already know. It was Kate Shelbourne who encouraged me to speak to you, just in case."

"Kate?" Harcourt has a soft spot for the journalist, which isn't the same bog in the west of Ireland he reserves for so many of her colleagues. "How is she?"

"She seems OK. A lot more circumspect these days, or maybe that's just because other, younger journalists are more gung-ho!"

"I always found her to be pretty reliable; shared most information, most of the time, which is probably the best you can realistically aim for!"

"I was at her flat this morning. It's all very nice, but very singular if you know what I mean?"

"I do." Harcourt is slightly piqued that he's never been invited to the journalist's flat; their meetings have only ever taken place on 'neutral ground.' Maybe it was that same police presence that made people feel so uneasy. "Kate always struck me as quite lonely; attached to the job because there was nobody to be attached to outside of it."

"Not like you then?"

"Thankfully not." Debbie had mentioned something about a lasagne in the fridge and possibly cooking times. He'd have to work that one out later. "Before we go on, how is Charlotte? I remember you being worried about her being out by herself..."

Daniel uncrosses his legs. "In some ways, I'd be pleased to be worried about that – for her to be up and about I mean." He reflects on his earlier meeting with Kate; has found it difficult to concentrate on much else. That afternoon he'd written a paragraph haranguing an editor to allow so many split infinitives in a draft brochure, except that when he'd gone back to re-read it, he'd spelt infinitive incorrectly. Perhaps infinity was more than a feeling after all.

"Has something significant happened?" Harcourt can see the genuine concern on the other man's face.

"Yes and no. It is significant in that the illness has entered a new phase, but nothing has drastically changed. I don't know, living with it I worry that I don't notice the small changes enough. It's a bit like when you haven't seen someone for ages and when you do, you notice how much thinner, fatter, or older they now look. They and their immediate family probably don't see it in that way: they're far too close."

"Is there anything that can be done to slow the disease down, even if it can't, you know...?"

"Be stopped in its tracks? There may well be. I've read so many studies on dementia in the past few months that it's difficult to find a way through them, especially as research is ongoing. Even the conclusions drawn by the bigger studies are inconclusive, but I suppose the medical experts have to cover themselves, don't they? Each does suggest that mental and physical exercise, as well as a good diet, are likely to be positive factors."

"Which presumably you've explored?"

"Diet has always been fine. Claire's borderline vegetarian and neither of us has been what you might call big red meat eaters. We've cut a few other things out as well but, you know, how do I know – how would I ever know – if they're making a difference? Charlotte will just become an insignificant number in a much wider universe of statistics eventually, won't she?"

Harcourt so wishes he could help this man who tries so hard to hide his suffering in the way he does himself.

"Not insignificant to you and the rest of the family. What about exercise?"

"Mentally, that was never a problem. Charlotte was – is – a lawyer which isn't so very different to proofreading if you think about it. She and I also did the daily crossword in The Guardian each day; now, it's just me. Charlotte just started filling in the blanks as best she could."

"But physical exercise must have been good. I remember you telling me about the lovely walks you used to take, especially along The Wychaven Way."

Daniel pauses, reflecting. "We did. Unfortunately, I can't let Charlotte go out on her own anymore because she got lost several times and found it hard to describe where she was so that one of us could go and find her. We tried Google Maps – dropping pins and so on – but she kept forgetting to take her phone. I do miss those times. They were among some of the happiest moments we ever spent together. Out there in the hills and the fresh air the world just feels so full of possibilities, doesn't it?"

Harcourt nods sympathetically. "How about at home: exercise, I mean?"

"The research suggests that proper physical exercise – you know, when your heart level is properly raised and sustained - needs to begin as early in life as possible. Both of us were too busy for any of that. It all sounds a bit hollow now. Blinkered. I suppose you only concentrate on medical things when you have something wrong with you. Goodness knows the paper often ran stories about mental and physical illnesses and what people in the area were doing to try to overcome them. We did try yoga – all three of us. Claire found a series of YouTube videos which we tried to follow in the lounge, but it didn't turn out that well."

"Carpet burns?"

"Those and the fact that Charlotte became freaked by the male instructor staring at her. She claimed he was just standing there, waiting for her to go wrong, which of course she then did."

"And Claire?" A bit of a cowardly move, Harcourt nevertheless feels the need to change the subject as there is very little else he can say, although listening to Daniel is probably equally if not more useful to him right now.

"Fretting about exam results. She's fine. I'm so glad of the company, to be honest. I do notice that and appreciate it. I sound terrible, don't I?"

"You'll miss her when she's gone."

Daniel is momentarily thrown. "Claire or Charlotte?"

Harcourt is appalled at his clumsiness, just as he was trying to be so empathetic. "I'm so sorry Daniel... I meant Claire, but of course..."

Daniel recovers his composure more quickly than Harcourt does. "It's fine. Honestly. I - we - have had to face up to the fact that Charlotte is not going to be with us for very much longer. Goodness knows we've had long enough to prepare for it. It's the thought of – the watching – her just drift away quietly which is the hardest part now. Previously I thought they were just episodes and that she'd come back again. I don't think that's going to happen now. I just wish we were standing there at the altar again, reading our vows: a prologue to our life together."

"Time may be a great healer but only after it's cleared up its mess!"

"Indeed. I worry most about Claire. She's the sequel to our story isn't she - as the lives of their children should be for every parent? If she gets the grades (which I'm sure she will) she should be going off to York. Her second choice was Worcester."

"Not so bad?"

"Not bad at all, except that I know she only had it down as an alternative in case she needed to look after me, after..."

"I see." Harcourt really does see. "Difficult to appear to be independent when all she's offering is kindness."

"Exactly. We're off to look at student houses in Worcester later in the week. I may put a deposit down on a room in case she does choose to stay – before the hordes come back - but, in the nicest possible way, I hope she doesn't. York would be better for her, I think. It would do her good to get away; right away. She's secured a place in Halls if she does go there, but I guess we're trying to cover all bases."

"The results must be out soon?"

"Two weeks."

"Not long to wait then; for either of you."

"True." Daniel collects himself, remembering where he is. "So, were you aware of the possibility of another will?"

Harcourt suspects Daniel has somewhere to go. Maybe he wants to be at home with his daughter and wife which is understandable. "We are aware of the suggestion, yes. In fact, it came from the same source: Simon Short."

"What has he got to say about it - if you're allowed to tell me of course. No problem if not. I just feel better for sharing what I know, to be honest."

"You're fine! We haven't spoken to Mr Short since my officers encountered him outside of Kathleen Hodges's house. He's been away but we're expecting to speak with him tomorrow."

"That should be fun for you. He talks like a man from a distant age."

"I feel like that myself some days!"

They laugh out loud as a young, uniformed officer knocks and drops an ominous pile of files on Harcourt's desk. "Thanks, Cindy!" The irony is not lost on her as she smiles before, as wordlessly as she arrived, sensibly leaves them to it.

“Tell me about the other people at the funeral. I assume you knew some of them if you were there?”

“Quite a few, yes. I grew up over there.”

“I’m so sorry. I completely forgot.” Harcourt interrupts. “Charlotte’s brother still lives over there doesn’t he?”

Not for the first time, Daniel marvels at Harcourt’s memory which, for many people it seems, only arrives on sticks these days.

“He does. He’s the vicar at St David’s – Welsh proximity and all that. We don’t get over there that often, what with Charlotte getting stressed about travelling, well, any kind of change to her immediate environment. As I said, the anxiety is hard for her to shake off, despite all our best efforts. I think it helps when we do see him, though I think he probably benefits more from it than she does.”

“But you knew Brenda?”

“I did, though I rarely saw her. We used to see Harry in the shop most weeks of course. I’d occasionally bump into Brenda who was friendly enough, but I never went round to their house. I remember Fred telling me it wasn’t very big and that he had to share a room with Joe when they were children.”

“You were at school with them?”

“I was. Fred was in my class; Joe was three years above and Pat two years behind us.”

“We haven’t met Pat yet. We have an appointment with her tomorrow as it happens.”

Daniel frowns. “She had so much going for her, did Pat. She was the brightest of the three of them. Harry paid for her to go to King’s in Worcester when she turned 11. He was very ambitious for her. I think he was hoping for Oxbridge. She’d have been the first in that family to make it that far.”

“Except that she didn’t… get that far?”

“She wanted to get away from her parents alright, from Bishop’s Lacy. She had talked about going abroad, travelling and ‘broadening her mind.’ So she went to Wales – Aberystwyth!”

“That’s where you went isn’t it?”

“English Literature, yes. Same course except that I only ran into her in my final year, after she’d arrived.”

“Did you know she had chosen to go there?”

“Not at all. It was a complete surprise. Fred and I had barely spoken since we left Sixth Form, although I did run into him once when I was up in Birmingham for a concert. He seemed fine – just the same really – but, you know, we just drifted apart after that.”

“And how was Pat?”

“Changed.”

Harcourt rolls his eyes. “Drugs?”

“Not right at the beginning but pretty quickly after that, yes. It broke Harry’s heart. I remember, after one ‘difficult’ phone call, that he’d told her she could have stayed in Worcestershire if she intended to widen her horizons in that way. All that money for schooling! I’m not surprised he was disappointed.”

“And yet his wishes, carried through by Brenda, were

that his money should be divided by all of them. He didn't cut her out."

"That's love for your family though, isn't it? He always stood by them; never gave up hope that they'd eventually go on to better things I suppose."

"We were under the impression that Fred was the bright spark." Harcourt feels as though he has struck a seam of gold with this unlikely source of information.

"He was, is. Fred didn't apply himself as Pat did though. Was the class joker. He did OK. Went to Birmingham to study Economics I think but fell into estate agency work when his big plans to be a merchant banker failed."

"He didn't have the brains for it?"

"More like he didn't have the right background. Harry may have died hoping for better things for them, but he wasn't prepared to throw any more money away, not after what happened with Pat. Fred had to try and convince the moneymen in the city to give him a job with only a middling degree from Birmingham in his credentials. I think being 'just' the son of a family butcher probably did more damage."

"He did seem resentful, or maybe we mistook that for being driven. The butcher's shop passing down to his elder brother didn't seem to be a concern."

"I don't think that would have fitted in with Fred's plans at all. If anything, the butcher's business had held him back, socially. I think he always knew that Joe would get the shop, and he and Pat would get their inheritance when Brenda died."

"Except they got equal shares: both of them got less

than Joe in real terms because he'd inherited the shop already."

"You're right," Daniel replies thoughtfully, as though the thought had never struck him until that moment. I do know that Fred was always jealous of Joe, but that had nothing at all to do with the shop."

"What do you think it was?"

"Fred was always attention-seeking as a child; needed to be at the centre of things. I remember that he was just that, pretty much, during school time. When he went home, it was all about Joe 'the eldest son' or Pat 'the clever daughter.' He did often tell me that he was 'going to show them' and I do think that drove him on, or out."

"Interesting. I wonder if he is as resentful now that he has carved out his own life; it seems like he has a pretty good lifestyle, or at least tries very hard to project that image."

Daniel smiles, though he knows Harcourt is being provocative rather than naïve. "He is an estate agent after all!"

Harcourt returns the grin. "What about his wife?"

Daniel shakes his head. "No idea, I'm afraid. I didn't even know he was married. I suppose that must have been her at the funeral, but we never got to talk. I was hoping for a word with Fred afterwards, but they had to go off to the internment. I was keen to get Charlotte away in case she became uncomfortable with so many new faces around, including those she would have recognised in different times."

"What do you, or did you make of Joe?"

"I never really knew him; he never spent much time

with us. You know what it's like when you're young – a three-year age difference seems like two decades. Our paths hardly crossed. I never saw Joe with a lot of friends though. He was certainly a bit of a loner. He didn't run around the playground playing kiss chase, for example. You'd have been more likely to find him sitting on his own somewhere. I don't think he was unpopular and certainly not bullied or anything like that. Joe was big, even then, maybe too big for the other children to feel comfortable around?"

"And going back to Pat. Her problems got worse, not better?"

Harcourt glances deftly at his watch, thinking Daniel hasn't seen it. He doesn't admit that he has. "She didn't complete her degree. I think she left in the autumn after I graduated. I honestly don't know what happened to her after that. She looked terrible though: the kind of 'sunken cheek chic' they presented as 'cool' in Nineties Britannia."

He stands, silently acknowledging that Harcourt needs to leave.

"Good to see you again and thanks for coming in; this has been extremely useful." Harcourt gets to his feet a little too quickly (Daniel can feel the invisible blood rush). "We're not making very speedy progress I'm afraid, so any extra detail we can glean is very useful at this stage. We don't buy the whole mobster-style staging of the body, but someone must have felt it necessary."

"Even if their reasons weren't exactly logical."

"Meaning?"

"Just that antisocial personality disorders can manifest themselves in psychopathic or sociopathic behaviour."

"You think that's what we're dealing with here? The pathologist – Jenny Graham – did wonder about that too."

"Well, for sure it's antisocial behaviour, isn't it? If it exhibits a degree of control or manipulation, you're more likely to be looking at a psychopath. I sincerely hope that you're not because they can be far more difficult to spot."

"Would you consider helping us again, if we were to ask you?"

"It would depend very much on where I am with Charlotte. Time is precious and it's running out. My priority is equally with Claire. It's a rubbish time for her anyway, but to have all of this on top of that just makes the stress worse."

"So, it's a 'yes' then?"

"It is. No promises though. I told Rupert that, right at the beginning."

"I'm sure he understood."

"Me too, except you don't always want to believe what you understand do you? He's on the South Bank again today, chasing shadows."

"No shadows without sunshine though." Harcourt doesn't believe that either as he accompanies Daniel down the metal stairs to the front reception area.

"Please do stay in touch, and we might well be."

***

"Thanks. I'll have a latte... skinny."

"Since when did you start considering your weight?"

"You wouldn't have noticed if I had."

"You don't even like latte!" Suzanne Wilkins is sitting opposite her husband, her long legs folded under the wicker table. That must surely be a metaphor for their relationship these days; these weeks, and these years.

"Come here often?" Once upon a time, Fred used to make her laugh. If only she could have seen then the lack of a happy ending on the distant horizon. They are at Jody's farm, a shop selling fresh produce and an outdoor café, with tables mercifully accompanied by sunshades. She's no idea who Jody is or whether it was ever a farm. The view is nice: over the Cotswold Hills towards nearby Chipping Campden.

"Why are we here?"

"What's wrong with it?" He has that smug expression on his face, as though all questions can be batted away with as few actual words as necessary.

"That's not what I asked."

He shrugs. "It's so hot in the house at the moment, I thought some fresh air might do us good; do both of us some good."

"The house is only hot because the 'ultra' air conditioning system you installed at great expense doesn't work properly, either remotely at the tap of a screen or when we're in the house, flicking an old-fashioned switch. Isn't that how the marketing blurb went; how it seduced you?"

"I thought it would be good for both of us." The grin has gone, which is a start she supposes, unsure over whether he's talking about the failing air con or the need to get out, here, anywhere.

"In a different life, we could be meeting here as illicit lovers, parking our cars in different parts of the car park. Is that how it works Fred?"

"Keep your voice down."

"Or what. What will you do? Allow that famously even temper to erupt again?"

The young waitress in jeans and a dark T-shirt with *Jody's* in white lettering in its top right-hand corner presents a tray of coffees in tall glasses, a silver jar of wrapped sugar and sweetener sachets, two wrapped biscuits and spoons (not silver).

"Thanks very much!" Fred flashes his teeth at her, his eyes not looking at the logo.

"What is it that you want?" She tears the wrapper off one of the biscuits in a single, expert pass.

"I don't want anything; I just want to talk."

"I've read enough books and watched enough run-of-the-mill dramas to know how this goes."

"No. Not in this case. For once, you have no idea what I'm about to say." His voice is firm. The deal needs to be closed and he is the only person who can do it. It's easy for her to recognise the play and easier for her to just let him get on with it.

He takes a mouthful of coffee, wipes his mouth with a serviette and rubs his hands on his trousers. Maybe not so assured then?

"I think Joe killed Kathleen Hodges."

"Joe? A murderer? What shot have they put in your coffee?"

"This is no joking matter."

"I wasn't joking." He's right: she hadn't seen this coming. She would never have considered it. "All the police have told us – and the press people haven't been any sharper - is that Kathleen was stabbed. You are aware that other people use knives too – that not only a butcher could have committed such an atrocity?"

"Of course not. But what if it's a double play."

"If that's part of your seemingly never-ending armoury of jargon I'm afraid you'll have to enlighten me."

"You can be as sarcastic as you want, and yet I didn't see – hear – you complaining when we moved from one beautiful house to another!"

The elderly couple near them are looking in his direction. A cup rattles in its saucer; nerves or a warning not to fracture English table etiquette, no matter what.

He lowers his voice, accordingly, pulling his chair under the table to get closer to her even as she bends backwards dramatically to get further away from him. "I believe," he whispers (if she can't hear him, then tough. He's making an effort), "The obvious use of a knife might have been designed to put everyone off the scent."

"You're not in the middle of a crime scene; this isn't some cheap novel. Ah, sorry, books are beyond you, or below you, I always forget which."

"Suzanne, please!" She sees the pleasing furrow in his brow; hears the beseeching request of a little boy trying to make himself heard. How weak he is - always was.

Her coffee is still slightly too hot despite the refreshing

breeze that appears to have got up at last. “What you’re saying is that Joe stabbed Kathleen in a deliberate and calculated attempt to achieve the opposite effect. Everyone – even the police - would consider it much too obvious that it was the work of a butcher and therefore wasn’t him. Hiding in plain sight as it were?”

“Exactly.”

“Except there is one fairly serious flaw in your expert theory.”

“Which is?” He hides his deflation behind the tilted glass as he finishes his coffee, like the man full of hot air he truly is.

“Why would he act in this way? Why would he wish to kill the woman who had looked after his mother in the latter days of her unremarkable life?”

“Careful! That’s my mother you’re talking about.”

“Incredibly, I am fully aware of that. Also that neither you nor Joe bothered that much about her and certainly not since your father died. Not enough to kill someone, for any reason I can think of. This isn’t a passion play you’re describing, more an unlikely episode of an unbelievable soap opera.”

“Could you just stop being so downright clever for once!” The volume of his voice is rising again, as do their neighbours who glare in his direction as they walk back towards the café to pay (or escape). The woman shakes her head, but only from the safety of her husband’s shadow.

“I thought it was my brain that you were first attracted to. Subsequent events have rather thrown doubt on that haven’t they?”

"Are you going to listen to me or not?" With nobody else nearby, he is giving full vent to his inner angst now (though he probably wouldn't describe it like that, not in so many words anyway).

"Carry on and calm down. With all that excess weight you're carrying you'll do yourself a mischief."

"I think," he hesitates to see if she will interrupt him again, but only his pausing does so, "Joe killed Kathleen because he got wind of another will being written by Mum which left everything to her instead of us."

"'Got wind of.' From whom?"

"Let's just say he 'phoned me last night to say he was worried someone was trying to frame him, and that the only motive for killing Kathleen must be because one of us was worried about our inheritance."

"Well, if this is part of some unlikely subterfuge along the lines you so painfully suggest, it must be you or Pat if it's not him, and I can't imagine, in my wildest nightmares, her doing it – though she probably wouldn't remember anything about if she had."

He is shaking his head, but not because he is necessarily agreeing with her. "Neither can I, but he now wants her money to go into a trust: to protect her."

"To 'protect' her. Who is he kidding? That will just hold everything up. Didn't your solicitor tell you there were already delays with probate?"

"He did. They haven't even got that far yet: the survivorship clause, remember."

How could she forget? The breeze is stronger now. Goosebumps have broken out on her bare arms. "I do. I also know why it's in there. This could mess everything up and we can't have that can we?"

***

'I've just got home. I managed to get the last bus into Hereford and then the train from there to Pershore. Good job I did get that one as the one after that terminates in Great Malvern for some reason. Dad was busy so couldn't take me (not that I asked him to in the end) and he's still out so I didn't have to tell him where I've been either. I wouldn't mind him knowing; he knows I'm looking for whatever it is that Nan mentioned, and after all, she gave me the house key, not him, even though it lives on the hook in the hall next to his car keys.

I told Auntie Sue about it as well. I don't see her very often, but she emails me all the time with ideas for books I might like to read. I think she's trying to 'stretch me.' She didn't like the idea of my going over to Nan's on my own though. Not sure why. Maybe she's worried about strangers? Auntie Sue has always seemed to be frightened of pretty much everyone.

Mum left a message to say that the police are going to visit her tomorrow, and what should she do. 'What should she do?' How would I know? I don't even know what they want to talk to her about, but I can guess. I wish she'd stop bothering me.

I could pop up there; it's not too late. I've had my shower now though and am in my bedroom. I can't believe how hot it is in here, even with both windows wide open. I certainly won't be needing the quilt again tonight. Dad doesn't approve of me having the windows open at night, you know, with us being so close to the pub. It does get very noisy late on, but more so at weekends. It doesn't always wake me up.

I didn't find anything before you ask. I took everything out and then put it back again. Sweat was running down my back and I worried all the way home on the train that I might smell. You can't smell your own sweat, can you? I didn't really know what I was looking for: a letter perhaps? All I found were a couple of watering cans, a load of string and flowerpots. I counted them out and then tried to stack them up in the same-sized columns as I found them. Hopefully, nobody will notice. Who's going to be looking though? The blue and white tape still had Miss Hodges's house next door surrounded.

It felt funny to be in Nan's house again. It smelled so familiar. Everything seemed to be in exactly the same place apart from her. Dad told me it would take a long time yet for things to get sorted out. I'm pleased about that because it means I can go over there again, sit in the chair opposite hers and pretend she's still there – to talk to I mean. Don't tell anyone but I did that today, just for a few minutes. Silly really; she couldn't answer any of my questions, but I asked them all the same. I miss her. Dad does his best, but Nan was the only one who properly listened to me; understood me.

Nan's garden looked a bit sad too. I don't suppose there's anyone to water it is there? Uncle Joe lives just up the lane but there was no sign that he or anybody else was taking care of the flowers. They looked so thirsty, so I did give them a sneaky drink, using water from the old black water butt. It was nearly empty though, so I don't know what I'll do next time (whenever that is). Nan used to have a long, green hosepipe, but I couldn't see it anywhere. Not that I know where the outside tap is either.

It was a bit scary when I left. I locked the door and pressed the door handle down a few times, just to be sure – like she's always shown me. When I shut the garden gate behind me, I saw a big man at the end of the road. He was just standing there under that big old apple tree, in the shade (not that there was much sunshine left by then anyway) so I didn't get a good look at his face. I thought it was Uncle Joe at first, but he didn't wave so it couldn't have been, could it? I walked away quickly but just before I turned the corner I looked around; he was still there, not following me, just watching.'

***

"What do you mean: you don't know anything about it?"

Harcourt smiles at Debbie as she enters the room and makes a 'T' shape with her fingers. He'd heard her key in the lock just before his mobile rang. He makes a thumbs-up gesture with his free hand, by way of reply.

"Exactly that, sir. I had no heads-up or any other conversation with them."

"Why not?" I thought you and that Shelbourne woman were as thick as thieves?"

Harcourt moves away and into the small dining room where they might eat once a year. Hunter-Wright is clearly beside himself, and he doesn't want his wife to have to put up with a late-night argument, not of his making. Not that these occur as often as they used to – certainly not for more than a year now. That's good but he has an equally bad feeling about Bishop's Lacy. Maybe he doesn't want Debbie to overhear anything about Kate and jump to the wrong conclusion (even though it would be a leap in completely the wrong direction).

"You mentioned that it was a Worcester News piece, sir. Kate Shelbourne is attached to the Evesham Journal." He knows that this probably won't go down well, but he can't help himself.

"Attached? Connected! All I ever hear these days is about making connections – being linked. They're part of the same group and, even if they weren't, no doubt there are 'private networks' where they all chat about opportunities and share pictures of what they had for breakfast."

"Indeed, sir."

"Deeds, not words, Harcourt. They're saying the two murders are linked and that the police are 'keeping an open mind.'"

"Because they don't know what's on our minds, sir. We've kept this deliberately low-key, especially given the nature of the crime scene. We haven't wanted to frighten people unnecessarily."

"Except that it is now: necessary to feed them something. We can't have a vacuum. These people would have a field day. Imagine how I felt when I read the headline on my tablet: 'The Bishop's Lacy Murders.' I'd barely got to Moreton-in-Marsh! Still had half an hour until I got home. I was thinking of ringing you from the train, but the damned signal was in and out."

'Small mercies!' thinks Harcourt.

"We don't have anything to connect the two people or

causes of death, do we?"

"No, sir..."

"Then we must say so without delay. We don't have to officially deny anything or cow tail to these wretched people."

"Of course, not..." Interrupting him in full flow is usually pointless, like trying to hold the waves back.

"You're not buying the whole gang thing now, anyway, are you?"

"It was just an obvious angle for us to consider, sir." Harcourt bristles at the inference that he would be so one-dimensional. "However, given the theatricality and staging of the crime scene, and the risks the killer would have had to take to make it look that way, I do think that this is personal in some way."

"A clear message being sent to someone rather than everyone?"

"Yes, sir. We just don't know who the recipient or recipients were meant to be... yet."

"Well let's tell the general unwashed that there is no obvious connection between the two deaths. Don't give any details of the crime scene. None. Understand? If this is one-to-one, we don't want the many to pile in unnecessarily."

"Yes, sir."

"Let's see if anyone will come forward though – genuine individuals of interest rather than just voyeurs - and at least tell us more about Kathleen Hodges. Your team appear to have gleaned little information beyond the colour of the dress she was found in."

"Yes, sir." Harcourt's heart is pounding with indignation. Debbie brings him a mug of tea and places it on the table in front of him. He mouths 'thanks' before addressing his superior's badmouthing of his team. "With respect, sir, there seems to be very little to tell. Kathleen Hodges was, how shall we say, 'bland.'"

"Which gives her the perfect cover to suspect that nothing untoward is going on under the surface. Everyone has secrets."

A click in his right ear indicates that the storm has abated – for now.

Debbie pops her head around the door. "Bad news?"

He nods before pulling out a second dining chair and beckoning her to join him, which she willingly does. "Good for selling newspapers, bad for trying to solve murders when you're already getting precisely nowhere."

"I'm guessing he's had another bad day?"

"No end in sight." Harcourt stares through the window at the darkening sky while his tea eventually goes cold.

CHAPTER EIGHT

Harcourt admires some of the Georgian architecture that Pershore has to offer as Farren drives them through to the far side of town.

"They used to have an annual Plum Festival here." He muses out loud. "My wife and I attended it a few years ago – towards the end of the summer. I might try it again next year."

"Parts of the town do look very old, especially these huge archways." This isn't what Farren wanted to talk to her boss about (and she certainly doesn't share the passion for ancient buildings that she knows he does), but, as with so many interviews with suspects, finding some common ground to build upon is usually beneficial.

"Very grand, aren't they? In years gone by they'd have had to be tall enough to allow private horses and carriageways to pass through into courtyards behind this main street. There's also a fifteenth-century bridge over the Avon here!" He is warming to his theme, while Farren is feeling merely warm. "It was built by the monks after their Abbot (Upton I think his name was) drowned after falling off the stepping stones they'd previously used to cross the river."

"How do you know all this stuff, sir?"

"Oh, it's amazing what you pick up here and there,

Linda; things you store away. Some are useful, others not so much. Although I suspect that depends on very much who you're talking to!"

"I wish I knew more."

"To know history is good; to make history is great."

Undeterred and him having called her by her first name, she ventures forth. "I am so sorry if my – our – behaviour towards Mr Portugil in Bishop's Lacy was deemed to be rude, sir. It would never have been my attention to let the service down in such a way."

Harcourt raises his hand in the air, indicating for her to stop right there. "It was the landlord who contacted us, as I said."

"I think it was probably Portugil who put him up to it though."

"That's as maybe, but you should know that uniform has had their eyes on Jennings for a while."

"Late nights?"

"Those, yes, but mainly dealing on the premises. I've no doubt Jennings would take great delight in trying to throw us off the scent, or at least seizing an opportunity to make us keep our distance by filing a complaint."

"Was it actually that, sir: an official complaint?"

"Relax. He wouldn't do that because then we'd be all over him rather than further away. He must have told himself the timing was good for a warning shot. I can pretty much guarantee that he won't be taking it any further. It's all part of the game."

"All the same, I did allow myself to get pretty riled by Mr Portugil." She isn't sure if she feels relieved or not.

"And yet technically it was DS Flowers who warned him off?"

"He just came in at the end of it; could see I was upset."

"Well, then, let's just put it down to good teamwork. I haven't recorded anything officially so there's nothing on either of your files. This isn't at all like Z-Cars. Plenty of letters come before that."

"Thank you so much, sir." Now, she relaxes.

"Just be careful though. Some people will do anything to protect themselves or whatever it is they convince themselves to be theirs. It doesn't matter if they're right or wrong: if they believe it to be true, they will act accordingly. That's the real point."

Farren reflects on those very words as they turn into Elmley Road, a seemingly unremarkable street of grey, Victorian terraces, periodically broken by archways that were only ever intended for people dutifully walking in single file to tiny backyards.

It seems to take an age for anyone to answer the battered-looking blue front door, although both detectives are grateful for the brief respite from the sun. The weather update on the radio over there had promised yet more hot, sunny weather – at least until the end of the following week.

Some promises aren't meant to be kept, Harcourt laments inwardly as he fiddles with the damp collar of his shirt. He is wearing a beige tie, despite the heat. He'd much rather not do so, but a collar and tie is a part of the uniform and he hopes that at least some of the people he comes into contact with would still expect that; even respect it.

There is no glass pane in the door, so Farren jumps slightly back as it is suddenly opened, unaware of approaching footsteps from behind it. She watches as an elderly, grey-haired lady, dressed in a grubby, blue nylon dressing gown fills the gap – or just a part of it as she herself is so thin.

They hold up their warrant cards simultaneously, but it is Farren who speaks first. “Good morning. We’re looking for a Mrs Pat Band.”

“Just Pat, not ‘Mrs;’ not for years now!” She snaps back, allowing a blast of fetid breath to make good its escape.

“Is she in, Mrs er…” Harcourt is anxious to get past the gatekeeper.

“She is!” There is a triumphant tone to her reply this time. “You’re looking straight at her!”

They have both been trained to disguise their feelings as best they can at times like this (Farren had even been to a seminar in Wolverhampton on the subject, wittily entitled ‘express relief’) and yet the surprise must have shown on their faces, as Pat Band’s dry and cracked lips have formed themselves into a satisfied smirk.

“What do you want, anyway?” She crosses her arms over her tiny chest, in the process revealing a glimpse of pale flesh, pot-marked with darker tell-tale bruising.

“May we come in?” Harcourt is aware of the curtains twitching in the front room of the house next door.

Pat glances to her left. “Oh, don’t worry about them,” she is practically screaming, making her point. “Nosy parkers round here, the lot of them. Never give me any peace.”

Farren flashes Harcourt a meaningful glance implying

that the boot may well be on the other foot. "All the same, it might be better if we don't do this on the front doorstep."

"Suit yourselves." With that, she turns and heads back into a long corridor leading to a dark, cluttered back kitchen. She opens the curtains and sunlight floods in, revealing dirty dishes piled up in the sink and at least three mugs of cold tea in various stages of being drunk. Farren notices the skin on the surface of the one nearest her before its regal badge and faded legend proclaiming its owner to be 'The Queen.'

"Don't ask me for tea or coffee because I haven't got any of either." Their host simply stands by the oven which is free of pots or pans and looks remarkably clean in comparison with every other surface.

Probably never used, thinks Harcourt as he stares at the woman's skin, remembering the description of that and the hollowed-out cheeks given to him by Daniel Reed the evening before.

"We're investigating the murder of Kathleen Hodges, your late mother's carer, and were wondering if you could help us at all."

"Never heard of her."

Harcourt is momentarily tempted to ask whether she is referring to Kathleen or her mother, but doesn't, of course. "We believe that she helped your mother on most days – spent a lot of her time with her."

"People can believe what they want. It's a free country, last time I heard."

They both hear the wheeziness in the woman's chest. Farren takes up the 'conversation.' "When was the last time you'd visited your mother, Pat?"

"At her funeral. She didn't say much though." She looks at the two of them for any signs of amusement but finds none: there is a time and a place for black humour, and this fails on both counts.

"Before that?" Farren is as unassuming as ever.

"Can't be sure. I'd have to consult with my diary secretary." Again, she glances around, finding only the same stony faces. "Well, you two aren't much fun, are you?" She turns her back on them abruptly, hunting for something among the debris.

"We don't find brutal murders to be that funny Mrs Band," Harcourt adopts a similar, soft voice, though both women cannot mistake its sarcastic edge.

Pat swings around to face him. "Like I told you before: my name is Pat, plain and simple. Don't you be looking down your perfumed little nose at me either! Looks fade, you know."

Farren continues to stare back at her, considering the adage that 'you're only three bad decisions from disaster.' She's thought of this often even if she can't now remember when she first heard it or from whom.

Pat has barely drawn breath. "I had a private education and a retail career of my own. My husband didn't like that; didn't like it at all. That's why he left."

"Did he find someone else?" Harcourt helps his colleague out.

"He wasn't looking; still isn't as far as I know. Our daughter went with him, but she'll be off to college in September I expect."

"They still live in Pershore at present."

She nods her reply, still staring angrily at Farren.

"Where do you work now?" Farren knows the answer but wants to hear the woman say it.

"Asda. In Worcester: Silver Street. I work shifts. Satisfied?"

"That's quite a trip each day. Couldn't you find anything closer?"

"Yes." She flings the observation back at the police officer, like a stone. "I could find plenty; did find plenty, only nobody wanted to take me on. They know me around here, see. 'Better the devil you know' doesn't usually work in my favour."

"Whereas Asda..."

"Much the same, except that I had an old friend there. She and I used to work together, and she vouched for me. I work on the tills. Nobody notices me so it suits everybody just fine. You'll have to go soon. I start at two o'clock today and don't want to be late for my bus."

"You didn't see much of your mother in later years then; didn't go over to Bishop's Lacy often?" Harcourt senses the animosity between the two women.

"I don't have a car. Charles took it. Couldn't just swan off over there whenever I wanted to, could I?"

"And your brothers. Were they close to Brenda?" Farren continues.

"Joe lived just down the road, but I don't think he had much to do with her. His flighty wife would have seen to that. Always wanted to be out, that one."

"And Fred?"

"Fred wouldn't have bothered either. I'll bet he was the one who put that thing in the will."

"The survivorship clause. Why would he have done that?"

"Not much of a detective, are you?" While she is waiting for his response, she suddenly slams her bony hand hard on the table in front of them causing the liquid to jump out of one of the mugs and a collection of bacon rinds to fall off the edge of an egg-stained green plate. She lifts her hand to reveal a dead fly which she promptly picks up and hurls towards the closed window.

"You were saying... about Fred?" Harcourt persists, the acrid taste of bile already in his throat.

"I've not been well. Fred knew that. I can only think that Hazel must have told him or that snobby cow who thinks she's such a cut above."

"Hazel is your daughter?" Farren asks another closed question which is completely ignored anyway.

"Why would your mother have agreed to it, though," Harcourt has a theory now, "I mean you were – are – her only daughter. Surely Brenda would have wanted you to have your fair share, especially as Hazel would have benefitted eventually?"

"Fred can be very persuasive. My mother hung off his every word. Dad used to take Joe off alone – all that 'eldest son' crap – meaning that Fred had her ear more often than not."

"And you?"

"I let them down, didn't I? Dad never forgave me, so she didn't either. It isn't just inheritances that pass down the family line."

"Fred persuaded her that you were so ill, you might not live long enough to benefit from the inheritance?"

"And no doubt also gave her some kind of promise that he'd look after my daughter if the worst happened."

"Would he? Look after her I mean?" Farren has no desire to offend the woman, however offensive she is.

"I expect he has his hands full looking after that fancy woman?"

"Suzanne? His wife?"

Before she can respond there is a loud knock on the back door. A figure looms beyond the upper half-panel of grubby opaque glass.

Pat strides over towards the door, pulling the gown tight around what remains of her body, like a shroud. She opens the door wide, just as she had the front door earlier.

A plump woman is standing there, her dirty blue housecoat on top of a dark tracksuit which has certainly never seen a track. "You going in later?"

Harcourt grimaces as the mouth reveals more gaps than teeth. What is it with dentistry around here: a lack of fluoride in the water perhaps?

"Afternoon shift." Pat acknowledges. "What do you need?"

"Eggs and cheese if you don't mind." The woman hands over a ten-pound note. "But not the free-range ones; I'm not made of money."

Farren blushes slightly, feeling much the same about inflated supermarket prices that are pushed up by perceived customers' desires – needs – to be seen to be friendly towards animals (although humans are often exceptions to this 'rule').

"And I'll have the change."

Pat slams the door on either her neighbour's ingratitude or maybe a bad-tempered acknowledgement that she has short-changed her on a previous occasion.

"We were talking about Fred – thinking you were ill."

"I have my ups and downs." She raises her head defiantly. "Who doesn't?"

"You seem well enough at the moment." Harcourt knows he is stepping into dangerous territory.

"Clean you mean?"

"Are you?" He has just noticed the woman's toenails, long and curling up towards their conversation, as though trying to listen in, like miniature satellite dishes.

"Suppose so," she replies sulkily. "Don't have much choice, do I?"

Like all addicts, thinks Farren uncharitably. Where there's a will, though, there's always a way. "You should inherit your share of Brenda's money then when it's finished going through probate."

"Unless my darling brother gets his knives into me first!"

***

"We're assuming this was just a figure of speech aren't we, sir?" Farren needs to change her stride pattern to keep up with her colleague who is positively marching towards the short-stay car park.

"Was that figure of speech in there not enough for you then?" He smiles back at her.

She giggles. "Not pleasant! You think she was just messing though?"

"About the knives? Probably. I don't think she's bright enough to have deliberately put the idea into our heads to cast doubt on Joe, although someone did do that in Brenda Hodges's garden."

"And she did benefit from a private education!"

Now Harcourt laughs out loud as they reach the car and climb in. "Each time we see a tragedy like that, I wonder to myself at the circumstances that triggered it and then kept the poison flowing." He reflects on a previous scene, miles from here. The night sweats have thankfully almost stopped now, but the pores remain open, exposed.

"At least you're curious about it, sir. We're all on individual journeys, aren't we? Some people never get to appreciate the beauty all around them, while others see only decay."

"I think you might have been spending too long with DS Flowers!"

Farren smiles in her response. "It's important to ask the questions I think: the 'how' and the 'why' rather than just the 'what is it?' or 'what does it look like?' I think that's one of the main reasons I joined the force – to understand people better and try and help them if I can – difficult though it can be, like in there just now. If it hadn't been the police, I think I'd have liked to have trained as a paramedic."

"I'm sure you'd have been successful in almost anything

you put your mind to, Linda."

He watches her as she turns away from him for a few seconds; stares out of the driver's window. What would people looking back at her see? Embarrassment? Insecurity? The 'how' and 'why' applies to every one of them, even (especially) after they've died.

"You are on to something though, aren't you, sir? I can always tell." She is back on track.

Harcourt leans back in the passenger seat, loosening his tie. "I think Fred is one greedy individual. His house was all about the show and tell, not slow and dwell."

"Sir?"

"It wasn't like a home at all: somewhere where you can slow down and chill out. There were no family photos, just artwork that you'd find in any mid-range hotel. If they ever have friends over – because I'm pretty sure it would be friends rather than family – I imagine Fred doing a show round and being very keen to know what they think of it. That's not at all the same as inviting people into your home to relax is it?"

"What did you make of the 'fancy woman' bit? Pat didn't confirm whether she was talking about the wife or not, did she?"

Harcourt closes his eyes, thinking and breathing deeply.

Farren recognises the signs. She continues in the background. "Do you think Fred did resent Joe having the shop and also a third of the inheritance?"

"I think he probably did. Pat would probably have agreed if she hadn't been off her face so much. I do think Fred saw an opportunity to effectively cut Pat out of the money so that he'd get at least half; equal things up a bit, not that it does."

"If she actually did die?"

"Maybe he was relying on that happening; perhaps he still is? It does look as though he influenced Brenda (possibly pressurised her) in her decision to put the survivorship clause in the will. I thought it odd at the time that he was named as the sole executor of the will, rather than jointly with Joe – or even with Pat. I think he had a strategy right from the very beginning, which could even have included murder if necessary. I'm not sure why Brenda listened to him, though; did what he told her to do."

"And Joe."

"A clumsy attempt to discredit him perhaps. I certainly think he has a motive for killing Kathleen Hodges. None of them would want to risk the money going to her instead, would they?"

"It will be interesting to hear what the others make of Charles Band."

"Indeed, it will. Now, let's see what the seemingly fragile little flower Suzanne Wilkins has to say about it. I don't necessarily believe in 'fragility.'"

"Sir?"

"Have you ever seen crocuses gently poking their heads through a gravel drive in the springtime? It isn't to question what you see, more of a why did they do it?"

"To gain nourishment through sunshine and rain and, I suppose, bees, pollination, growth?"

"All of those things. But how on earth does a tiny little stem like that push its way through that weight on top of it, with all that pressure holding it down?"

"Determination?"

"Needs must."

***

Just over a mile away Flowers and Taylor draw up outside a compact semi-detached house on one of the sprawling estates just off Station Road. A row of small family cars separates them from the tightly packed buildings but Flowers spots a parking space a little further down.

A group of barely dressed teenagers are sitting on the wall opposite in front of another house, divided into two, which could be a carbon copy of the one they're about to enter. They watch them getting out of the car but it's only Flowers who they notice. Taylor senses their eyes on him, and his embarrassment.

A slight but tall, ginger-haired man opens the door to them. "Do come in; we've been expecting you." He leads them into a compact front room with an armchair and two-seater sofa arranged around a small TV set in the corner. "No large screen TVs for us, I'm afraid, not that we'd have the room."

"That's fine. We haven't come round to watch television!" Taylor flashes him a beaming smile, pleasantly surprised to see the tell-tale lines of a recently vacuumed carpet. Everything is clean and tidy, not that there is much on the shelving unit that runs behind the chairs, apart from a few DVDs, an ancient (and large!) black telephone answering machine and several ornamental china houses.

Charles Band follows her gaze. "We only keep the

answering machine on in case Hazel's mother needs to get in touch with us. She doesn't have a mobile phone and I don't want her to feel vulnerable, you know, living on her own. At least if she needs help she can leave a message so that one of us can get back to her as soon as we're back in. The cottages are Hazel's. She calls them her 'village.' Her grandmother used to give her them as Christmas presents and sometimes birthdays if she was feeling flush."

"The grandmother being Brenda Wilkins?" Flowers is seated on the sofa next to Taylor: comfortable enough despite sitting close to the edge.

"Yes. Poor Brenda. We're all still getting used to her not being here. I'm dreading Hazel's next birthday if I'm honest."

"She was close to her gran?" Taylor again.

"I think they shared a lot of secrets! When we first moved here, I was keen that Hazel had someone she could share things with that maybe she couldn't talk to me about. Women's things mostly."

"She missed her mother?" Flowers has picked up on a sense of sadness in the eyes of this gentle soul."

"I think she missed her mother while we were all still living in the same house together. I'm sorry. Where are my manners? Would you like a drink?"

The officers wave away the request, thanking him all the same.

"When did you move here, sir?"

"Charles, please. It would be just over two years ago now."

"You're quite settled?"

"As much as anyone can be I suppose. We only rent it; It's basic but it suits us. Mind you, if the rent continues to rise as it is, we may have to consider moving again."

"Things are tight for a lot of people at the moment."

"Sure, and there are many who are much worse off than us. I see people sleeping on benches all the time – they don't have anywhere they can call home: probably haven't done for a very long time looking at some of them. It's not right, is it? Here's me worrying about not being able to afford a big deposit on a house for us.

Pat – Hazel's mother – sends her a small allowance each month, but it's a bit hit and miss, you know. At least that allows her to have some treats. I'm afraid all my spare money goes on food."

"You and your wife still get on alright, even though you no longer live together?"

"It's all very amicable, yes, apart from when she 'forgets' to send Hazel any money. She lives in Pershore too, but we don't see her, although I made it clear to Hazel at the beginning that she's welcome to go over there whenever she wants to."

"Where were you before this? I hope you don't mind me asking." Flowers is going to ask the question anyway.

"Of course not. We used to have a little house up in Bishampton if you know it?"

"I do indeed." Flowers nods, encouragingly. "We live over in Upton Snodsbury."

"Ah. I used to ride my bike around there: down to Peopleton and back through Flyford Flavell."

"I think the hills would have done for me."

"Me too. That's why I stopped." Band laughs out loud. "Besides, I get plenty of exercise at work."

"You work for the Council I believe." Taylor brings things back on track before the two of them can head off on an imaginary road trip together.

"I do, yes. I work for the Parks Team, or 'Parks and Green Spaces' to give it its' official title."

"Based here in Pershore?"

"Out of Queen Elizabeth Drive, yes, but we don't spend much time there. There are quite a lot of wetlands and nature reserves to look after as well as the parks here in the town. I was at Broadway Gravel Pit yesterday, for example - you know, the one they flooded? Quite a beautiful, peaceful spot now if you're interested in that sort of thing. The lilies are stunning, although the mud on the bottom can be a bit sticky when we're trying to clean some of the aquatic weeds out!"

"It must be nice to work outside, especially in this weather?" Flowers is sitting back now, relaxing into the conversation.

"It is, although we do have our moments with the bees when everything's in full bloom! Worth it, though. They sell jars of organic honey there sometimes."

"I do love honey!" Flowers grins.

"Me too. I'm up there again the day after tomorrow; I'll get you one if you like?"

Flowers nods his approval.

"I've always loved nature and wildlife," Band is continuing. "I grew up on army bases so the countryside was my sanctuary, you might say."

Before he can elaborate further, they hear footsteps on the stairs and, shortly after, are joined by a teenage girl, also with ginger hair, and dressed in a smart white T-shirt and jeans.

"Hello," she greets them confidently, "I'm Hazel."

After the exchange of pleasantries, Flowers leaps up gallantly. "Do sit down."

"It's fine, I'll get a chair from the kitchen."

"We don't get too many visitors I'm afraid," Charles confirms, smiling at them as Hazel returns with a wooden chair and sits on it. "Thank goodness!"

"Thanks for joining us." Taylor is quite taken with the girl's appearance and demeanour. "I hope we're not interrupting anything?"

"Oh no. Not at all. Dad and I are off for a walk later, aren't we? I'm just trying to fill my days as best I can, to be honest."

"Hazel's waiting for the exam results," Charles explains. "Not that she's anything to worry about, I'm sure."

"Are you hoping to go off to Uni?" Flowers asks.

Father and daughter look at each other knowingly.

"Maybe." Hazel's reply is enigmatic.

"She wants to do Media Studies at Worcester, well, she wants to be a writer, but she's worried about me being on my own."

"Nice though." Taylor acknowledges. "In my experience, most children can't wait to get away from the family home."

"Did you? Hazel has turned towards the older woman. "Want to leave home I mean."

Taylor shakes her head. "Actually, no I didn't. I still spend a lot of time travelling back and forth to make sure my parents are OK, so I get it."

Hazel looks relieved. "Family's everything to me."

"I'm so sorry about your grandmother. Your Dad and I were talking about it before you came down."

"It's alright. I'm a bit better now. I have had time to think and get things back in perspective. I do miss her though."

"Did you know her neighbour – Kathleen – well?" Flowers has his notebook out now. "That's really why we're here."

"She died soon after Nan, didn't she?"

Flowers nods. "Quite soon after, yes. We don't believe the two deaths are connected though, despite what you might have read in the papers – or online."

Hazel nods. "I did read something about it, but it wasn't a very good piece – didn't say very much and there were a few typos."

Charles beams. "That's why they need someone like you to lick them into shape!"

Taylor also considers that this confident, astute young lady has all the makings of a great journalist, provided she doesn't get dragged down by the need to make money above that of necessarily always telling the truth at whichever media outlet she joins. "Back to Kathleen in real life. You must have seen her around?"

"Oh yes. She was always there. Nan used to like her

company I think, and Kathleen didn't seem to have many other friends – apart from Mr Short - so I guess it worked well for both of them. Kathleen helped Nan with all her pills from the box and made sure she always took the right ones on time. I do remember that."

"What was she like: Kathleen?"

"She never really said much to me, but she was always very polite when I visited Nan, asked me how Sixth Form was going, that sort of thing. She used to leave Nan and me alone together when I was over there, which I guess was her respecting our privacy."

"Did Kathleen ever mention any family at all?"

"Not to me, no. Nan did once tell me that Kathleen had nobody else. I think she felt a bit sorry for her, to be honest. Kathleen and I did once have a chat about Jane Eyre!"

"The Brontë character I hope – not the name of one of the villagers." Taylor notices that Flowers's interest has been piqued as she knew it would be.

Hazel laughs. "Yes, that's the one. Thankfully Kathleen's house didn't look big enough to have an attic though!"

"How did you get round to Jane Eyre?" Flowers asks, leaning forward now.

"Kathleen had seen the film – the one with Michael Fassbender as Rochester – when it first came out. I suppose there have been so many versions of it haven't there? We were studying the book in English, and she wanted to know if I thought it was a good representation. I think she might have fancied Michael really but..."

"Do you know who she went to the cinema with?"

"I assume it would have been Mr Short. They went to each other's houses to watch films – DVDs and so on. I suppose they could have gone on cinema trips too, but I wouldn't know that for certain."

"Did you ever meet Mr Short yourself?"

"Only in passing."

"You didn't like him." It is more of a statement than a question. Taylor senses a reluctance to speak about the man.

"It wasn't that so much. I just found him a little bit up himself. He used to ask me questions but never listened to the answers."

"Not like us then!" Taylor is keen to lighten the mood again. "Did you meet Mr Short, sir?"

Charles shakes his head. "No, but I remember Hazel mentioning him once or twice. From what I can gather he was just a bit of a know-all. You get people like that in all walks of life, don't you?"

Both detectives nod, before Flowers asks: "Did you ever visit Brenda with Hazel, sir."

"No. She used to get the train and I tried to meet her at this end if I wasn't at work. I did pay the fares though!"

Hazel squeezes her father's hand.

"But you got on well with your mother-in-law?" Flowers persists.

"Everybody did, Sergeant. I don't think anyone would have had a bad word to say about her. Harry was a different kettle of fish though; get on the wrong side of him and you'd have a mountain to climb to get back in his good books again."

"And Joe and Fred. No problems with either of them?"

"None that I can remember, no. Joe has always been the quiet one, never says much to anyone, though I don't suppose he gets much chance with Camilla."

"And Fred?"

"I haven't seen him for some time. The family weren't big on get-togethers once Harry died and, even then, only under sufferance. I'm afraid Fred and I don't move in the same circles." He smiles at them all. "I don't think even he could describe this as a 'des res.'"

Hazel throws her arms around his neck. "It's home and that's all that matters."

***

"Nice chap." Flowers remarks as they each clip their seatbelts into place. "They had a lovely relationship didn't they: caring for each other."

"They did. She's old before her time, that one. Amazing that she talks with such conviction about family love when hers seems to have been torn apart!"

"It can work better that way though, can't it? Parents get on better when they're no longer under the same roof; usually nicer for the children in the long run, although I suppose it depends on how old they are when everything blows up. Anyway, I hope she passes her exams." Flowers nods his head as they pull out of the estate.

Taylor curses herself inwardly, remembering that Flowers hasn't seen his father since he left them before her colleague had even started school. She glances across at him, knowing that he will already have read her thoughts.

"It's fine. I barely knew my dad. At least I have a photo of him. He'll be smiling at me forever in that won't he?"

"He could still come back into your life you know – probably when you're least expecting it." She speaks softly, even as a short, stocky man sways off the pavement almost walking right in front of her. She lets her car horn do the talking.

"Maybe. But he'll never get to know Rob, will he? Not like Mum and I did?"

Then it would be his loss, she considers, sadly. She pushes on. "It won't be easy for Hazel either way – leaving her father or not being able to. I was a bit surprised that he wasn't bigger, muscly, given his occupation."

"Sorry, were you expecting one of your fireman fantasies to finally come true?" He dodges a sweet paper she has hurled in his direction. "You know that physical appearances can be deceptive, right."

"Ha Ha." She grins back at him, feeling better. "I wish we'd had time to talk more about his ex-wife and what happened there before Hazel came down. It didn't seem right to talk about her mum in front of her."

"The others will probably be able to fill us in. I'm intrigued to see what you make of Simon Short."

"Is it this afternoon he's coming in?"

"It is. We'd better get learning how to genuflect."

***

"Come on. Just one more to look at." Daniel Reed has turned into Ellsford Avenue and is walking briskly towards a nondescript 1950s house, long divided up into flats for students at the nearby university.

His daughter Claire is a couple of paces behind, the distance between them reflecting their different levels of enthusiasm for the project. "York was nicer!"

"Or the York campus that you visited was nicer?"

"We did head into the centre after the tour of the department!" Her reply is defiant, but she isn't - not really. She saw plenty of streets like this from her train window. 'You can't just hide from your history, any more than it can hide from you.' She can't remember who it was who told her that. Someone from her past. She takes a slightly different tack: "I thought you said this place was described as a 'village in the city?' Doesn't look very villagey to me."

"You remember Chief Inspector Harcourt? I met up with him the other night and he told me this whole area used to be an independent township – up until the early nineteenth century at least."

"Still doesn't look much like a village. The one down in Woodstock Road was prettier; nearer to town as well."

"Except that you won't even notice how pretty it is or be worrying about trips into the heaving metropolis of Worcester because you'll be studying so hard!" He grins at her and receives a lopsided version in return.

Petra Halliday is waiting for them just outside the front door. She couldn't have looked more like a down-market estate agent if she'd tried: cheap, dark suit with flat heels and thick make-up designed to cover up any visible flaws.

She leads them inside past a pleasingly large and tidy front room (except that it serves up to five 'tenants' and no doubt their friends at any one time) and a poky kitchen smelling of burnt fat, with regulation wall cupboards marked with the peeling labels of their previous custodians. "As you can see, there's plenty of space and this westerly aspect brings in lots of lovely light in the afternoons." They follow her adoring gaze towards a small window – the only window – with a dirty net curtain pulled across it. They are forced to use their imaginations as she does, effortlessly, being the consummate professional that she is.

Heading up a steep staircase with occasional dark carpet covering the wood below they arrive at the bedroom which is 'currently available.' Daniel takes in the faded bed cover and dried wallpaper trying to make its escape from the wall in the far corner (a sure sign of damp, but best not to mention it). He is taken back to his student accommodation in Aberystwyth. Time has performed its favourite tricks such that he doesn't remember it being as awful as this but it probably was; maybe even worse.

"Plenty of desk space and shelves for shoes!" Petra winks at Claire conspiratorially. Claire's eyes are set: unmoved, as is the rest of her. She takes one more look around as though she is taking it all in, fixing the image for the photo library in her mind, before following Petra out of the door and along to the fresh horrors of a bathroom still sporting old hairs as 'night out' trophies.

Daniel is about to follow them before spotting something on the far side of the two grubby pillows, glinting in the half-light. Not wishing to accidentally touch the bed cover by leaning over it, he has to walk sideways right around to the other side to reach it (all the time being careful not to knock his head on the sloping roof).

He gently picks up the earring by its gold stud, long since parted from its butterfly partner. He has a sudden flashback to a pair of earrings he bought for Charlotte on her fiftieth birthday. He feels slightly ashamed that this is more than eleven years ago: the relentless progression of time again. His guilt is made worse by recognising that he is now the only one likely to remember it at all.

This stone looks as though it might be a cheap diamond – certainly more expensive than most students might wear, apart from maybe special occasions. Do people still celebrate 'special occasions?' They do in the books he reads, but out here, in real life...

The questions quickly fade away, as does the room. Answers don't matter. He is aware of a charge between his fingers, like an electrical current, growing warmer, stronger. He is aware of Claire in the doorway, saying something to him that he can't quite hear. The woman on the bed isn't like her. Not at all like her. He knows that much even though he's equally certain he's never seen her before. According to the naked man lying beside her, moaning and whispering her name, this earring belonged to somebody called 'Camilla.'

***

The police were very nice; not at all how people talk about them around here. Then again, we've done nothing wrong, have we? Dad got a phone call from Mum just after they left. The police had visited her too. I don't think she was as impressed by them as we were.

She was pretty angry at Dad for some reason. I could

hear her shouting from the kitchen, not that it's very far away but you know what I mean? Dad didn't say much, just listened. What can he say to her that will make her stop?

I did hear him mentioning money again, thankfully not like the other day when he lost his temper. He was quieter this time, but his voice was just as firm. I heard my name mentioned a few times which upsets me. I don't want to have to rely on either of them. I do want to stay at home and look after Dad but be able to help properly by having money for food and bills.

The sooner I can get a student loan the better. I know that Dad doesn't see it that way though. It's all about what's right for the family with him. He's always been like that. I know that's why he stayed with Mum as long as he did, even after the awful things she said to him and about him. Calls like today's don't help, but she's probably not aware of what she's saying. I must keep believing that. We don't have very much money now either, but we're managing. That's all you can do, isn't it?

***

Dressed in a voluminous white dress, Suzanne Wilkins seems to float across the impossibly green lawn towards them, like a Victorian ghost. Miss Haversham perhaps? No, she wasn't actually dead, was she? Harcourt corrects himself as he hears Farren introducing them both.

"We're in the garden." She flashes a set of perfect, white teeth to go with her outfit while he tries to remember what the daughter was called: the one Pip fell in love with, just as he was supposed to.

Farren raises her eyes at Harcourt, silently questioning the 'we' but, seeing him deep in thought, simply follows their hostess around the side of the house to a series of comfortable-looking garden chairs with large, comfy cushions.

Suzanne appears to be quite alone. Perhaps Fred is about to join them after all, even though they'd noted that his car was missing. "Do take a seat. I thought fresh orange juice might be preferable to tea or coffee, but I can pop the kettle on if not..."

Harcourt raises his hand in happy acceptance of the cool drink. He has been feeling slightly sticky all over since leaving Pat Band's house and isn't convinced that the external heat is entirely to blame.

He smiles at the woman nicely, taking in the lush golden locks and perfectly manicured fingers and toenails which aren't so vulgar as to be carrying any shade of varnish. Without shoes – even sandals - the woman appears to want to convey an image of simple purity. Except that things are rarely that simple.

Farren thinks of the figure before them as an actress, performing on her stage, with them as her captive if not captivated audience. She can't explain why but all she can think about at that moment is one of the glossy chocolate adverts on TV suggestively playing on everyone's temptation. Living just down the road from Bournville there'd been a lot of chocolate. She can see already that Harcourt isn't buying it though.

A book lies face down on the seat beside her. A hardback book. Farren tries to edge around to see the title on the spine but can't quite make it out. It looks heavy. Not a problem she experiences with her Kindle, though she hasn't told anybody – especially not her colleagues on the force – about her penchant for crime fiction.

"Thank you for agreeing to see us," Harcourt starts proceedings, "You're quite a hard woman to get hold of?"

"Am I?" The answer is meant to be quizzical, enigmatic even. She runs a hand through her hair before letting it hang down over her neck, partly covering one side of her face.

"We've phoned several times." Farren feels slightly queasy. Maybe it's the lack of chocolate after all.

"I'm sorry. I like to walk."

"Alone?" Although Harcourt is staring right at her, he isn't taken in by her startlingly blue eyes.

"Usually, yes. I prefer that. I don't mix well with people you see. I don't venture out far from home. Sometimes I don't even venture out of my bed."

"Are you recovering from some kind of illness?" Harcourt asks the question kindly but any classical scene featuring a wronged female convalescing after having her heart broken would be as unfamiliar to him as if it was depicted in a painting in a gallery he would never think to visit.

"Anxiety is a silent disease, Inspector. I've suffered from it on and off for most of my life."

Now Farren feels positively sick. "Is there anything or anyone you've been especially worried about lately?"

Suzanne bends forward for Harcourt's sake, allowing the front of her gown to fall sufficiently far for it to be apparent she'd decided not to wear a bra today when 'venturing forth' from her bed chamber. "It doesn't really work like that."

"How does it work then, if you don't mind me asking?" Farren persists and they can both see that this is not how the woman prefers to play the game; not being in control.

"It's a general feeling of unease. It can latch on to specifics and yet, when certain hurdles have been crossed, it persists in the background. I find sanctuary in books usually."

"You worked in publishing I believe." Harcourt is sweating quite badly now and mops his brow with a handkerchief that had been clean when Debbie presented it to him this morning. For him, that represents true love, not fantasy.

"You have done your homework." Suzanne smiles approvingly. "What else do you know about me; or want to know?"

"You gave up your career at Schickstirs – in Russell Square, wasn't it?"

"I do miss Town. I had to give it up when I married Fred and moved down here."

"He swept you off your feet?" Farren tries to make the notion sound as utilitarian as she possibly can.

"In a way. We met at a party in Belgravia. Not really his scene you understand. He'd been working with a developer who wanted to convert an existing Cotswold hotel in Little Slaughter into a high-end party destination. Sad little people."

"The existing hotel staff or owners."

"Oh, both. The owners had no vision of their own which is why the place was overpriced and those foolish enough to pay their prices were served by supercilious staff who looked as though they'd raided the dressing-up box. Nothing fitted properly."

"You make it sound as if you're speaking from first-hand knowledge." Harcourt remains polite despite feeling increasingly hot and even after liberating his drink from its cut-glass receptacle.

"Fred took me down there after the party. A group of us went including Hugo (the property guru). It was ghastly. They rushed out to greet us in the car park with warm champagne. Probably from Sainsbury's. The beds were much too soft – squeaky springs and you know what that means?"

Neither detective is quite sure how to respond, so they don't.

"Nothing came of it. They boasted that they regularly hosted what they laughingly called 'society weddings' but that the villagers complained about the slightest noise in the evenings. More harp than hip hop. It was never going to happen, not that the owners weren't holding out their greasy palms in hope though."

"And you and Fred became an item after all this?" Farren feels like she might need a lie down after all this talk about beds.

"How prosaic! He told me he was going to build me a fabulous home in the country, and I told him that was fine so long as I was also allowed to sit in it and read all day. I was already feeling the pressure of work and I think he saw it as a way of making me better."

"But it didn't."

"Nothing can."

"Still, it's no doubt good for his business too – having a show home like this. Does he still get involved in developing property!" Harcourt sticks a small needle into her lovely arm.

"I'm not sure he was ever going to. Once a salesman and all that. My husband is not as self-confident as he may appear. Once he has money, he's very keen to not lose it again. He watched his father struggle in the latter years."

Oh, the perils of being in 'trade' thinks Farren unkindly. "So, he wasn't too upset about not inheriting the shop then; not unhappy that it was passed down to Joe?"

"God, no. All that dead flesh! Who would want to spend their lives up to their armpits in blood?"

"Do they get on? Fred and Joe?"

"What a curious question." She brushes her hands over her dress, smoothing out the folds. "As well as any siblings I suppose. We rarely see each other."

"And Camilla? What is your relationship with her like?"

He watches her stiffen slightly but she doesn't miss a beat. "We're quite different people, Chief Inspector, which you'll probably know if you've already met her. We walk in very different circles."

Yet they all come back to the same place, he thinks, amused by her use of the same vernacular as Charles Band who would presumably barely make it as a walk-on artist in a personal film adaptation of one of her precious books. Perish the thought of him becoming a gamekeeper! "And Pat – your sister-in-law?"

"She probably thinks I'm Boudicca, even when she's not stoned."

"Whereas I suspect you see yourself rather more as a Roman goddess – Venus perhaps?"

"Well, you never know until you've tried it, Inspector." Her cold stare says far more to him than the words do.

"What can you tell us about Kathleen Hodges?" Farren throws a curve ball into the pantheon.

"Ah, yes. The lady who was murdered. I was wondering when you were going to get around to the real reason for your visit."

"Well?" Harcourt glances at his watch, unconcerned as to whether she has seen it or not.

"I never met her, I'm afraid."

"Not even when you were attending family gatherings in Bishop's Lacy; maybe when Harry was still alive? She was their next-door neighbour long before she started caring for Brenda?"

"Unlike her, I never cared for Brenda. I didn't attend what you so quaintly describe as 'family gatherings.' I've never played games like Happy Families."

"This being a murder enquiry, we'll still need both your fingerprints and a DNA sample I'm afraid." Harcourt isn't. "It's purely for elimination purposes. We've asked all the other members of the family and they've each complied."

"Can somebody come out here; I'm not too good in towns and cities these days."

"As you wish. We'll arrange that for you."

"It must have made it difficult for Fred - your refusal to accompany him?" Farren has been studiously making copious notes as usual.

"Not at all. He has always known about my nervousness around other people. I have absolutely nothing in common with Joe and even less with Pat Band."

"You wouldn't miss either of them?" Farren's question is blunt. Even the butterflies have stopped fluttering around them for the time being.

"I wouldn't miss someone I barely have any contact with, would I? It's like an old contact falling off the Christmas card list, not that anyone seems to send cards now, more's the pity. You just strike a line through it. You don't miss the person behind it, do you: not if you haven't seen them, for years? You may even consider how they made it onto the list in the first place. The coldness makes contact with the much warmer air. A storm may be on the way. "Pat had everything going for her: a doting, indulgent father and then a doting, indulgent husband. She chose to sidestep both."

"Did she really, though?" Farren won't let it go.

"Oh, please. Don't go down the path of helpless addiction. Save it for second-rate novels that are permanently discounted on Amazon, solely because people continue to advertise them and their inadequacies. If someone did persuade Brenda to put that clause in her will, it may not have been the selfish, self-serving person you appear to have decided that they were. Or maybe there was nobody else involved at all?"

"Go on."

"Have you never once considered, in your two-dimensional little world, that Brenda may have been minded to insert it herself: to try and encourage Pat to think about the life she was living – to seek help? Shock tactics if you like. Harry never really got over her change of direction – her change of personality – once she'd gone away to college, away from his 'protection.' The only way he could reconcile it was by telling everyone who would listen that she'd 'got in with the wrong crowd.' Perhaps the clause was Brenda's final act of loyalty to Harry (and also to Pat, actually) to try and get her to do something about her life. The clause may not have been that important in itself. The important thing was that there was a clause: a condition."

Harcourt is curious now and has to admit that up until then they had assumed that Brenda had been influenced by either a member of the family or Kathleen or someone who hadn't yet crossed their radar screens. "What do you think?"

"Me, Inspector!" She places a palm against her dress in faux modesty. "I think that Pat Band had been very ill, and so somebody was watching that situation very carefully."

It is a flatter bat than the one used by Chris Tavaré at Edgbaston many years ago when Harcourt had been lucky enough to get tickets for the Test against Australia, and unlucky enough to witness a morning session when the defensive cricketer had barely moved from the crease, scoring a handful of runs in what seemed to be many more hours than had passed.

"Has Fred mentioned Kathleen to you at all?" Harcourt thinks that he must have, although his mind is spinning now. They need to move things on.

"In passing. He likes to read me news headlines from his iPad now and again – makes sure I'm still conscious I suppose. Her name did come up, but he didn't dwell on it: no money in it you see."

"Are you quite sure about that?" Harcourt's voice is much sharper now. His words scratch the surface of the thin air between them.

"Quite sure!"

***

"No love lost there, sir."

"I'm not sure she had any to start with." He starts the car but brakes suddenly, pulling to a halt at the entrance, even though no cars are approaching from either direction. "I've just remembered her name!"

"Whose name?" Farren is perplexed, as she so often is by his impromptu exclamations.

"The orphan girl in Great Expectations. It was Estella!"

"What larks, Pip…" Farren is as surprised as he is, but far from displeased.

CHAPTER NINE

"Have you ever visited Sidmouth, Inspector?" Simon Short's bronzed forehead resembles a Brazil nut.

"I haven't had that pleasure, sir." Harcourt watches as his interviewee takes a sip of water and places the plastic cup back on the table between them. This whole process can tell them so much about states of mind: nerves, confidence, defiance. On this occasion no obvious nouns present themselves.

"Oh, but you must. It's a wonderful place. They call it 'God's waiting room' but that's fine by me; I read a whole Rebus in a single afternoon." He smiles benignly, his white and brown checked shirt unbuttoned slightly to reveal or suggest further tanned skin below. No tie. He must still be in holiday mode.

"Were you staying there alone, sir?" Taylor has watched him studiously avoiding her gaze.

"I always holiday in solitude... Sergeant?"

She ignores his intended put-down, remembering instead a rock group by that name a few years back – from Scandinavia possibly? Or has she just made that up? Not really her scene but then music has never really captivated her. Too busy trying to keep up to allow her mind to chill out.

"Thank you again for popping in and going through the identification checks." Harcourt smiles warmly. "It's purely for elimination purposes at this stage, especially as we believe you may have been one of the last people to see Kathleen Hodges alive."

"Poor Kathleen. I needed to get away. It was a devastating shock."

Harcourt isn't convinced that it was 'devastating' or necessarily a 'shock.' Yet. "You were concerned about her on the night that she died?" Not so concerned that it couldn't wait until the following day though, he muses.

"I'd arranged to meet her on that fateful evening, yes. She'd asked me over to watch 'Tinker Tailor.' She'd just got it on Blu-ray. I hadn't seen Gary Oldman's take on it yet so was quite looking forward to it; not that anyone could have usurped Alec Guinness of course, larger screen or not!"

He sits back, pleased with his little joke and seemingly oblivious to Harcourt's lack of response. He probably wouldn't have noticed if Taylor had, in the meantime, decided to blow her cover, jump up and point a Makarov pistol at his chest.

"Would you mind telling us again what time this was, please?" Taylor notices the ever-so-nice, unassuming tone of Harcourt's voice.

"Of course." he nods, excitedly. "We'd arranged to meet at eight o'clock that evening."

"You weren't worried about walking home afterwards – in the dark I mean?" Taylor knows full well that he didn't walk; she will make him look at her. She will.

"As I believe I explained previously," he continues to stare at Harcourt, ignoring everything he considers to be peripheral in his vision, "I drove over and parked around the back of the cottages. I usually do that unless we're... unless we were planning to imbibe something stronger than hot chocolate. Kathleen did make the most stupendous hot chocolate. Belgian I suppose."

"You never stayed over?" Harcourt is less friendly now.

His gaze is unflinching. No stray muscles giving the game away. "Our friendship was based entirely on books and films. I am far less active than my wife was, you understand."

"Please go on."

"As I told the officers already, I knocked on the front door but there was no answer. I called out her name, but all of the windows were shut so she may not have heard me had she been awake."

"You think now that she was already dead?"

"I try not to think about it all, Chief Inspector. What I meant was that she may have fallen asleep."

"Was she in the habit of falling asleep in the evenings?"

"Not usually, but I wasn't there every evening so it would be hard for me to provide you with any data from which you could compute a significant probability."

Taylor stores that phrase away to share with her colleagues later. Flowers would love it.

"Please continue." Harcourt isn't loving it.

"I walked around to the wall at the back and shouted out her name but, again, no reply."

"You didn't think to ask the neighbours – Mr and Mrs Portugil - if they had seen Kathleen that evening?"

"I didn't consider it, no. There would have been little point. He would have been in the Grenadier (like the hero he never was) and she's as deaf as a post. I doubt she'd even have heard me knocking."

"You returned home and, presumably, phoned her?" Taylor senses that something is off; something indescribable, no matter what vocabulary Short prefers to use.

"I did and I did. There was no answer. As I inferred earlier, I assumed that she had fallen asleep early. It had been a hot day so there would have been little surprise there. We're all getting on a bit..."

"And yet the windows were shut?"

"Storms had been forecast. Kathleen had a fear of lightning."

"So, you phoned her again the following morning?"

"I did but, again, there was no reply. That did surprise me as Kathleen was an early riser. She'd had to be to keep up with Brenda."

"Then you phoned us?"

"You've pieced the chain of events together beautifully."

Harcourt doesn't return his grin. "You went up there, spoke with our colleagues and then went straight to the coast?"

"Fleeing the scene of the crime? Is that what it looks like to you?"

"Not exactly, although I would have thought you'd want to stick around – to see what had happened to your friend."

"And help you with your enquiries?"

"That too."

"Do I need a solicitor, Chief Inspector, or shall I attempt to defend myself?"

"I'm not sure that you need to have any defence, sir; you haven't been charged with any crime."

Short blows out an exaggerated breath of mock relief.

Taylor pounces. "Did you, in fact, call it in?"

Short glances in her direction as if his pupils have temporarily lost their forward-facing equilibrium. "What an interesting phrase. It reminds me of a boating lake in my youth. Tenby perhaps? 'Come in number seven.' Lost on you I presume!"

Taylor isn't lost. She has found a way through the human shield. She knows she has. "Using a Northern Irish accent for cover?"

Harcourt watches the man begin to sweat, even though the air-conditioning has, mercifully, kicked in. That only usually happens just before Christmas. "You didn't want us to know that it was yourself who reported it?"

"I was conflicted, Inspector."

"Chief Inspector." Yes, there was the tell-tale flush, from the neck upwards. A good job he wasn't wearing a tie.

"My mistake and my apologies." He bows slightly before continuing. "I was concerned enough to report it, but also sufficiently wary of getting involved, with it occurring so quickly after poor Brenda's murder. I considered that an accent was the best arrow to use from my dwindling quiver. I'd never make a spy, of course, but my accent isn't too bad for one day trip to Londonderry many years ago. Wouldn't you agree?"

"Do you remember the scene in the film where we

all cheer inwardly as the character we've been led to detest is charged with perverting the course of justice?" Harcourt has quite regularly been accused of swallowing a dictionary. The infuriating man in front of him has added a thesaurus as well.

Short swallows noticeably. The swagger and fanciful orchestration of events are gone for now at least.

Harcourt doesn't miss a beat. "You mentioned a second will to the officers at the scene?"

"Is that a question or a statement of fact?" When neither of them indulges him, he continues. "Not second, no. There could have been more than one alternative will and that word implies only two were in existence, doesn't it?"

"But you were aware of at least one alternative to the will that was read out upon Brenda's death?" Harcourt has never had much time for semantics, even less at this moment in time that the clocks appear to have forgotten.

"Correct."

"Because you said that you'd signed and witnessed it?"

"Quite so."

"Do you have any idea as to its contents or why Brenda may have felt compelled to write a second – alternative – will?"

"The last will or testament is recognisable as a confidential matter. I didn't share that kind of confidence with Mrs Wilkins I'm afraid. Even if I had, I wouldn't deem it fitting to share it with you now. Kathleen asked me if I would be a witness to it as she felt that she might be compromised in some way, being the carer. She also didn't want it to look suspicious to the three children."

"Suspicious?"

"That was the word she used."

"I assume you have no idea where this document could have been hidden, or you would have informed the solicitors acting for her, even if you hadn't deemed it fitting to share it with us?" Sarcasm has made its way to Harcourt's lips as patience has finally given up on its gatekeeper role.

"I have absolutely no idea if it still exists!"

Taylor thinks laterally, in the hope it might move them out of this literal cul-de-sac they seem to have become stuck in. "Do you know if Kathleen left a will, Mr Short?"

"Unlike Brenda, I'm not sure that she would have been contemplating death quite yet." Short reddens again at the mention of the word, or perhaps the finality it describes. "She certainly never mentioned it to me but, as I said, we just met up from time to time to escape from the world together."

"Did she have many other friends that you're aware of? We haven't been able to track down any family members."

"You make it sound like Davy Cockett looking for footprints or smoke signals!"

"If you could just answer the question, please, sir?"

"No." His tone is impatient now; the idea of life after death and a possible reunion with Kathleen is far less appealing than the usual sequels he experiences. "She was a broken woman in many ways. She'd wanted nothing more than to work with children and that odious, pompous little man broke her heart."

The irony is not lost on them. Even though there are no mirrors in the interview room.

"Mr Easterly, the Ofsted inspector and his not-so-merry men?"

"Ruined her life. No doubt he took it upon himself to destroy the reputations of many other good people too. Kathleen told me that some of her erstwhile colleagues never taught again. I'd like to teach him a lesson or two, I can tell you."

"But no other friends she may have talked to; confided in?"

"As I have repeated on numerous occasions," he stands, "She may well have had other friends, but I was not introduced to any of them. She certainly never mentioned anyone else to me. As to family, they were probably as distant to Kathleen as Brenda's so-called family were to her."

***

"Nothing of interest on Short, sir." Farren stands to kick off the meeting. The station's air conditioning system is working normally today, which means it's cold. She pulls her blue cardigan tighter while Harcourt puts the jacket back on which he had just hung on the back of his chair.

"Local?" He asks.

"Hereford, sir. He was effectively a conveyancing clerk for Cauldrons for many years. Only two colleagues remain from his time there. You'll remember that scandal about expenses being loaded?"

Harcourt looks blank but Taylor steps into the fray. "Joanne Briskett 'worked from home' except that she worked for a rival company at the same time. Played the two off against each other and duplicated expenses."

Harcourt is nodding his head now as the detail begins to form in his mind like mist clearing to reveal a signpost, even though he can't read the words on it quite yet.

"DS Taylor is right, sir. It caused a storm at the time and there was a lot of fallout among other clients."

"I bet there was!" Flowers can't remember it at all.

"Also, other staff were implicated so there's been a real shake-out. Most of the people I spoke to have no recollection of Mr Short either."

"Short wasn't involved though?" Harcourt so hopes that he was.

"No, sir. The gentlemen who remembered him both spoke of a diligent solicitor who never strayed from the process, literally to the letter of the law. One of them is now a Partner – a Mr Foster – told me that's probably why Short never really progressed. He was so obsessed with the detail himself that he couldn't delegate the drudge work to others."

"He enjoyed the drudge?"

"Seems like it, yes. Both said that although he was mainly dull, he was reliable. Whereas Joanne Briskett had the glamour to entice new clients into the firm, she overlooked important details (apart from those that led straight to her personal bank account, obviously.)

"So, as a character reference, Short comes over as an

honest pedant!"

"Indeed, sir."

"Thanks, Linda. Gabby, what news on the fingerprints? I guess you won't have all of the DNA analysis to hand yet?"

Taylor remains sitting as she has no desire to try to make Farren or Flowers feel inferior. There may be a promotion in the offing but, for now, she is just another member of the team.

"I do have quite a bit, actually, sir." She is comforted by his warm smile. "We only have fingerprint matches for Kathleen herself and Mr Short on Kathleen's property. Mr Short's fingerprints are on both the front and back doors of her house, but we know that he was a regular visitor there, so it isn't so surprising."

"Kathleen's back door was open though." Flowers reminds them.

"It was, but the front door was shut and locked. If Short is our man he was already in the house, instead of knocking on the door or shouting Kathleen's name from the outside as he would have us believe. He must have enticed her into the back garden and then killed her because he wouldn't have been able to carry Kathleen's body out there on his own. He's quite a lot smaller than her."

"And then left through the front door?" Taylor isn't convinced and the doubt in her voice spreads out until it fills the small room. "I go with our original thought that whoever killed Kathleen did so by coming through into the garden from Brenda's house. I think Kathleen's back door was open because they'd somehow attracted her attention from the back garden. I'm still not sure why her windows were closed on such a hot, sticky night but maybe it was because of her fear of lightning from storms that had been forecast, although I'm still slightly queasy about that, given it was Short putting the idea into our heads?"

"The results of the tyre prints from that place at the back of the houses have come in." Harcourt consults a sheet of paper he's printed off from the PC he's happy to leave behind. "The older set is almost certainly from Short's Fiesta. We know he would have parked there when he was visiting Kathleen in the evenings. He probably just strolled up during the day.

It's a 2010 plate and MOT records show he hasn't had them changed for a few years. One was borderline illegal when he had his last test a couple of months ago; certainly, an advisory. He could have had them changed since then, but I'd say he doesn't generally do a lot of mileage. Probably just pootles about the village on his snooping missions! The other set was much newer, again from a smallish car. Obviously, we can't check ownership of those without much more information to go on."

"I don't buy it anyway, sir." Farren stands again. "I agree with DS Taylor - about Short I mean. I think he probably was telling the truth about the thunderstorms too. We have established that his character is essentially honest. He's never had any involvement with the police until now. Besides, what would his motive be? He was Kathleen's friend and, to flip things, she may have been a loner but so is he. Kathleen's may have been the only significant company he got to enjoy."

"Unless they had a sudden falling out over something?" Taylor agrees with Farren but is feeling mischievous.

"That suggests spontaneity doesn't it, or passion?" Harcourt also agrees with Farren. "I can't imagine Short being passionate about anything. He leaves that for the characters in books and films. Heroes by proxy if you like. It certainly doesn't fit with the staging of the scene or the sending of messages which is suggestive of much more planned (and cold-blooded) behaviour – unless Short had let his imagination run riot for once. I can't imagine it though."

"Do we know yet if Kathleen left a will?"

"We do!" Flowers is triumphant. "I found out just before the meeting. Cauldrons again, which may or may not be significant. Anyway, Kathleen left everything she owned – which was basically the value of the house and £3,900 in savings accounts – to Marston Church of England Primary."

"The school where she was probably happiest." Taylor is delighted by the news, as she knows Sheila will be.

"The will is very specific. The money must go towards books and school equipment for the children. It also has a clause stipulating that no amount from the legacy may be used by the church or for church purposes."

"I guess they never gave her much support in her life." Harcourt is reflective.

"Or the school," Taylor confirms.

"Which means that Short didn't stand to benefit from Kathleen's death." Farren moves things on.

"If he even knew about it. He told us he wasn't aware of a will and there's nothing to suggest that he thought he would have gained from it anyway. He didn't seem that bothered about Kathleen's death, more excited to be at the heart of a real-life murder investigation. Kathleen was his wife's friend first. I think they just filled gaps in each other's lives."

"I agree. I don't think he's our man at all. Was there anything else from forensics, Gabby?"

"Fingerprints of Joe and Fred Wilkins on the back door of Brenda's house, and also Hazel Band."

"Pat's daughter?"

Taylor bobs her head. "Yes, sir. None from Pat though, so it does seem to be the case that she hadn't visited Brenda recently. We didn't find anything from her husband, Charles, or the wives of the other two – Camilla or Suzanne."

"Suzanne I can understand, although there's more going on there than the dust jacket suggests. Camilla surprises me a bit. I'd have thought there'd have been some trace."

"Hazel's DNA was also found in the garden shed, sir, on three of the pots to be precise."

"We do know that she spent more time with her grandmother, don't we? Maybe she helped Brenda in the garden when she visited."

"I wonder if Brenda disliked her three children equally?" Flowers blushes as the question pings into each of his colleague's brains.

"Go on." Harcourt has been quick to judge Ian Flowers in the past. Not anymore. He's been proved wrong on too many occasions since then.

"Well, sir. We assume that a will implies an equal liking of each recipient, but what if she felt equally bad about all three children? They never seemed to visit her from one week to the next. Her daughter-in-law – Camilla – lived just up the road but preferred to stay there. She clearly wasn't interested in Brenda's welfare at all."

"But Brenda left nothing to the one person who did visit her every day, and who seems to have genuinely cared for her." Farren remains sitting this time, her point made.

"Who is now dead." Agrees Taylor.

"There was another person who cared for her though, wasn't there? Not every day, admittedly, but that's probably more to the distance involved." Flowers isn't going to give up on this easily.

"Hazel." Harcourt sits forward. "And yet, the will not only doesn't name Hazel specifically, but with the survivorship clause it puts her mother's inheritance – and, by definition, Hazel's – at risk if that's the right phrase? If anything, it moves Hazel not only down but potentially out of the pecking order altogether."

"Which is why she may have made a second will, potentially leaving everything to either Kathleen or Hazel directly. We do know that Kathleen and Short were talking about it. It's just that if it does exist, we haven't found it yet." Flowers is as earnest as ever.

"Then Joe or Fred – or one of their wives – gets wind of that possibility." Harcourt sits back in his chair, which is usually a sign that he is feeling on safer, more solid ground, despite the wheels. "They need to quash it straightaway by killing Kathleen and leaving a sign for the other two children that there is no truth in it and to be aware of who or what they listen to. I wonder if Smug Mr Short feels under threat for the same reason? What did they say during the war: 'Talking costs lives.' Maybe we're looking at a family at war here in trying to protect itself or its individual interests within it. I've seen the same and worse where inheritances are involved."

"My money's on Fred Wilkins being the killer, sir." Taylor makes her move. "What if Suzanne knows this and that's what she's hiding behind that floaty façade? He probably put Brenda up to putting in the survivorship clause too. Maybe he was angry that Joe got the shop as well as an equal share in the will – which, as you said, wasn't entirely equitable. I sensed a ruthless streak when we visited him. The whole theatrical framing of his brother, Joe, was probably meant to frighten him off at the same time as throwing suspicion on him, feeble though it was."

"I'd go with that. I think Fred has a greater motive." Farren has a determined expression on her face. "Joe Wilkins was closer, though. It would have been much easier for him to do it and, by the rather bizarre, amateurish staging of the scene and seemingly throwing suspicion on himself, perhaps he was trying to throw us off the scent."

"Unless his partner Steve was involved in some way?" Taylor still feels the need to compete with her colleague.

"I just don't know what motive Steve would have though. Why would he kill Kathleen and then throw suspicion on Joe? You don't generally bite the hand that feeds you, do you?" Harcourt senses another impasse failing to pass him by.

All are in silent agreement.

Harcourt's phone rings and he heads into his office to answer it. "Is he? OK, could you bring him up, please? Thanks."

He returns to the others. "That was the front desk. Daniel Reed has something to tell us. He says it's urgent."

Farren is still to be convinced of the benefits of psychometry if that's what this relates to. "He came to see you the other evening, didn't he, sir?"

Harcourt hadn't broadcast the fact. He likes Daniel but is equally aware that it is difficult for some of his less-impressionistic colleagues. What he is impressed by is the fact that Farren knows about the visit. Once a detective... "He did, yes. That's how we got to know about the discussion between Simon Short and Kathleen Hodges after Brenda's funeral. He was also able to give us some background on the Wilkins family. He used to live out that way so knew them reasonably well when he was growing up. Everything aligns pretty much with the profiles we held for each of the siblings."

"Did he have any thoughts on who might have killed Kathleen Hodges, sir? I don't mean second sight, just based on what we can all see." Flowers is secretly delighted to be meeting Daniel again. He's seen him a couple of times when Hunter-Wright has asked him over to the station, but not to talk to – or listen to.

"No, he couldn't come up with any motive for it, other than this whole idea of a second will. Without it, we don't have any substantial motive, do we? Kathleen's back story doesn't provide us with any plot or memorable characters, apart from that vicious, officious man who effectively ended her career at the school."

"And she did try to address that in her will," Taylor adds, approvingly.

"Not only that," Harcourt acknowledges the point but continues at pace, "We have no evidence to put any of the Wilkins family – or anybody else for that matter - at the scene of Kathleen's death; only our usual bedfellows, theory and supposition, which are driving us around in circles and driving me mad."

"And we can't have that!" Daniel Reed walks across the room towards them, wearing a cream T-shirt and faded, blue jeans, as Harcourt raises his head in thanks to the young PC who smiles briefly as she closes the door behind him.

"Daniel!" Harcourt holds out his hand and shakes the others warmly. "You know everyone I believe."

"I do, yes. I've heard that the dream team may soon be broken up though." He pauses for a reaction but then proceeds quickly, seeing the confusion on young DS Flowers's face. "The new Cold Case Unit. Exciting times."

"You'll know what the deep freeze feels like soon enough." Farren has meant it as a joke but sees that the punch line has hit her in the face instead. "Wearing just a T-shirt in here – the cold air appears to be unconditional!"

Harcourt laughs a little too loudly while Taylor and Flowers exchange glances. She thinks she's recovered the situation despite the way Daniel continues to stare at her – through her.

"Thanks for seeing me." Daniel does now rub his

bare arms, whether consciously or not. "I thought you might find this useful." He hands over the earring he had found in the room in St John's and describes his experience, while walking towards the incident board, covered in images and arrows and various notes written over those that haven't quite been rubbed out.

"You think that Camilla Wilkins is having an affair with another man?" Harcourt summarises for himself and his team.

"I know that she is, Inspector. What's more, I also know who the other man is."

"Please do share." Farren's voice remains cold, like the rest of her at that precise moment in time.

Daniel points at the last of the three faces towards the top of the board. "Camilla is having an affair with her brother-in-law, Fred Wilkins."

***

It's no good, Charlotte cannot find keys to either the front or back doors. She's tried all of the places she can remember: in the drawer of the wooden thing in the hallway; on top of the time machine that hangs on the wall just above it, and on the platform that runs underneath the windows in the cooking area. They are not there, so where are they? Perhaps there never were any keys, in which case why aren't the doors opening when she pulls down the levers and pushes them?

She's feeling hot again, although she can see that the highest windows in the cooking area are open. She can just feel the air on her face as it moves into the house without bothering to knock first. Things can come in, but they can't get out. She's trapped. Perhaps that young girl forgot that she was in the house when she closed the door this morning.

She'd heard the door slam shut, or was that in the dream she was having: the one about lying in a different wooden box while someone who looked a lot like Daniel read over the top of it? He was always reading but it couldn't have been Daniel because, of course, he'd left years ago. Dear Daniel: the most patient man yet living with me must have made him feel like a patient a lot of the time. At least he'll get the chance to recover now.

That woman from next door is here again, sitting on one of the chairs next to the entrance to the tunnel. She's seen it swallow people up, their desperate attempts to escape borne out by arms and legs frantically swirling around in the abyss, drowning inwardly. Perhaps this woman is a double agent. Is that why there are never enough chairs? She's taking them away, one by one. A fleeting memory of white party dresses comes into her mind. Why? Is that all part of the disguise? Why won't her eyes focus on the details? Why can't they focus on anything or anyone for more than the shortest of time?

The girl is back. She hadn't heard her come in so there must be another entrance somewhere. Maybe she bent down and came in through the flap in the back door? Maybe she can make herself very small like Alice? Then big again. She's complaining that her pin doesn't work so she can't open her notebook. How can that be? Since when did you need a sharp object to open a book? Is the pin blunt?

She's leading her to one of the remaining chairs, but Charlotte doesn't want to sit down. She wants to run and shout to the air outside: 'It's alright for you but they're keeping me a prisoner in here for some reason. What do they suspect me of; what have I done wrong?

***

'Dad brought a cup of fruity tea up to my little room when he got in earlier – the lemon and ginger one he knows I like. There was no extra honey in it because we'd run out. We'll have to get more from Tesco at the weekend. He looked really tired, and his face was as red as a cherry. He told me they'd been mowing lawns for most of the day, and he did have that fresh grass smell you get on summer days when it's just been cut.

He sat on the end of the bed as usual and asked me about my day. I suppose all fathers do that if mothers aren't around to look after their daughters anymore. I didn't want to keep him up for too long. I could see that he just wanted to get a shower and go to bed. He could sense that I was upset though like he always seems to.

I'd been looking through an old photo album of Nan and me when I was little. Mum was on some of them but not many. Dad looked so big and strong – not that he isn't now. Well, maybe not quite so big or perhaps it's just that I've grown so much. Nan is smiling in all of them. There was even one of Grandad Harry: a family shot. Everyone was in it apart from Auntie Sue.

He told me it was alright to be sad and that everyone would have expected me to be – maybe even more so. I haven't wanted to worry him so he wouldn't have known that I've been trying to always keep a smile on my face for him, whereas my stomach's been churning away inside. I do think the exam results have been part of that too. I certainly haven't cried as I did straight after the funeral, but I think now that it might have been better if I had.

Dad started talking about when he was younger and lost his own father. I never knew Grandad Band, but I do know that he fought in the Falklands War and then in Iraq. He never came home from the desert. Dad always said that 'luck' had deserted him.

When I was very small and beginning to learn about the world outside of Worcestershire Dad once showed me his 'stamp album.' He told me that he'd stand by the front door every day, waiting for the postman. If he got a letter, then he knew that his father was still safe. Many of the stamps looked identical to me, but each one of them was a moment in time that he could treasure.

There were lots with 'Falklands Islands' and the Queen's head, sideways like in Britain, but the ones I remember had pictures of Princess Diana on her 21st birthday (although she was married by then) and one of 'The Beagle' which was the ship Charles Darwin sailed on when he went exploring.

The Iraq stamps had Arabic writing all over them; I can still remember colourful pictures of a Bazar on some. Dad said mail from there was sometimes sent differently through the British Forces Post Office using a new service called e-blueys which used the internet. He thought that had now been replaced by something called 'Intouch.' I think that's a more suitable word (if it is a word) as it describes better what it does. I suppose they wouldn't have been allowed to send texts back then, either, even if they'd had mobile phones. There weren't many stamps from Iraq. Then there weren't any at all.

Dad never mentions Granny Band who also died before I was born. I've never even seen a picture of her. At least I've got my photos which captured my memories with Nan. Dad said that I should always try to remember her and all the nice things she did for me. I do know one thing: when I do eventually leave home, it won't be far away from him.'

***

Pat Band is unimpressed at having to wait, especially as every passing child in King's School uniform – ties askew and blazers stuffed into sports bags – seem to be looking across at her and then whispering loudly to their little friends.

One of the 'Free the Spirit' people had crossed the road earlier to offer her a Bible. A pale, frail man had asked her if she wanted to 'talk about God.' Surely it would have been more helpful if she had found a way to talk to God directly, not via some worthy middleman?

There they were, standing to attention outside the black railings of the Guildhall, behind their table of books and pamphlets, on the lookout for victims of circumstance (like her?) The words of God had never occupied key places in the paragraphs describing her life; not even when she had been surrounded by words.

She sips at her coffee. Why they call it Americano she has never quite understood. Makes it sound vaguely South American she supposes. Just as with Ceylon tea – reinforces where the raw materials have come from. Not sure how Earl Grey fits in? She would have preferred tea, but they don't do it in pots, just dangle teabags in cups and charge you double for the dangling. Then you've got to take the bag out and put it somewhere

– anywhere - before you can add the sugar and stir. Impossible to do it without it dripping hot tea all over your fingers and everything else. Her mother would have had a fit if she'd sat at a table without a tablecloth, but it would have been far worse if she'd spotted stains.

"You took your time!" It was her brother who had arranged this 'meeting' not her.

"My fault." He is as meek and mild as ever. "I got it into my head that I'd said the Costa in St Martins rather than the High Street."

"Would have been much easier for me."

"I know. I'm sorry. Have you finished your shift or are you on your way over there?"

She points to her shopping bags that are loaded with groceries. "Doesn't mean my time isn't precious." She barks, satisfied at seeing him cringe.

"Dinner party, is it?"

They both know that he isn't suited to sarcasm. The temporary silence confirms it.

"Do you want another coffee?" He offers at last.

"I haven't finished this one. You go ahead."

"It's alright. I had one earlier."

"So why arrange to meet at a coffee shop?" She can't help getting irritated. It always happens when they meet. Which is why they rarely do.

He pretends he hasn't heard the question, either because he can't answer it or because it just confirms how useless he is at this kind of thing.

"I needed to see you to discuss Mum's will."

"What about it? I thought I just needed to hang on for a few more days."

"I had nothing to do with that clause."

"Someone put the idea into her head, and you were the closest." She spits out the last word as though it were poison.

"I promise you, Pat, I had nothing to do with it."

"Our thieving brother then? They say that money goes to money, don't they?" She flicks a strand of her greasy, matted hair away from her eye, watching as a young girl who has just sat down does the same. Her blonde tresses (that have been washed to within an inch of their natural life) sufficiently swept back, their eyes meet fleetingly before the younger version of who she might have become turns away quickly.

"I do know that Fred went to see Mum just before she had the dizzy spell."

"How convenient!" She finishes her coffee in one gulp and slams the cup down on the metal table, making an old man jump as he gazes at her disapprovingly.

"Mum didn't like it when I warned her about Kathleen. She became not so much a 'carer' as a guard. She was always there. When I did go round – which, I admit, wasn't nearly as often as it should have been – I could never really chat to Mum. She was never allowed to be on her own; that woman saw to it that nobody else could get close to her. Mum and I were barely on speaking terms by the end."

"You can't blame me for that."

"I know. I wasn't."

"You brought it all on yourself."

He bows his head slightly, the weight of recent history heavy despite the lack of years in its creation. "I thought Mum would understand."

"Whatever made you think that?" Mum was from a totally different world. On top of that, Dad made sure that she knew where her place was: in the home, whenever he went out and whenever he came back in."

"Probably why she enjoyed being in the garden so much – later on I mean."

Pat doesn't generally do light entertainment and today is no exception. "People didn't have 'relationships.' They met, got married and then the husband threw away the key. That's how it was."

"It wasn't like that for you – not for a long time." Joe splays his huge hands on the table, palms up.

"It was."

He decides not to challenge her on it. Not in this mood. "She wouldn't listen to me; wasn't even prepared to hear my side of things."

"Because she didn't like the tale you were telling. Like so many things in life, she just closed her ears to it. Hoped it would go away."

"You think she wanted me to go away?"

Pat suddenly yells at a young, male student riding past. "Oi. Bikes aren't allowed on the High Street until after six!"

He gives her the silent finger as he continues, quite unperturbed.

She raises her voice even further. "What makes you so

special anyway? You won't be so smug when all those woofters get their willies up your backside in jail!"

There is a stunned silence as other customers around them greedily drink in the unexpected drama that has unfolded before returning to their drinks amid excited, barely hushed voices.

"I'm sorry. Pisses me off how people like that have no respect for others."

Joe has been rendered speechless as usual, so she continues as though nothing at all has happened. "Mum had lots of practice in getting by with as minimum amount of disruption as possible. You must remember her telling us not to 'make a fuss' whenever Dad said or did something we didn't agree with."

"All the time." He has found the lost words.

"All I'm saying is that not all stories have happy endings. Hers didn't, did it?"

"Perhaps she would have been more tolerant if that poisonous woman hadn't turned her against me – against both of us. I certainly wasn't going to keep paying for Mum to enjoy the privilege of her dubious company."

"Is **she** with you?"

"Camilla? Yes, she's on the other side of town."

"Shopping?"

He looks up, suddenly. "Of course. What else would she be doing?"

He takes in the fleeting smile which she doesn't try too hard to hide. "So, what is it about the will that you're suddenly so concerned about?"

"I think... we think it might be sensible to put your share of the money into a trust for a while. Somewhere safe. At least until you're properly better."

"What do you mean by 'better'" She snaps, raising her voice such that the good people opposite bury their faces in the literature they themselves hadn't read until that point.

"You haven't been well for a long time, and it's getting worse." He speaks gently but his voice isn't soothing.

"How would you know? How would any of you know?"

It's clear to him that the situation – one of his own making – now needs to be contained. He looks around and behind him, seeing others quickly look away as he does so. "The funeral. It was a shock."

"They generally are."

He's twisting his fingers, just as he did when they were small. Not that he was ever small. "I didn't mean that. Seeing you. It was a shock."

"Wouldn't have been if you'd made more of an effort to visit."

"Like you did, you mean?"

"I had a lot on my plate. Charles leaving when he did..."

"Did that cause a relapse?" He seems earnest now. Keen to know the truth.

This in turn calms her, at least for a few, precious moments. "There was no relapse. I've been clean for over a year now. I'm not saying it's easy. Sometimes it's very, very difficult and that won't ever go away. No amount of 'therapy' is going to sort it out. Charles worked that out, eventually."

"How did you – he – get to that point?"

"I think he just came to realise that he couldn't save me. The funny thing is that I thought I was saving him. He was quite broken before I even went to college."

"When you first met him – at TK Maxx?"

"The same. I probably never thanked you for all those Saturday evenings when you came in to pick me up after working in the shop all day."

"You probably never did."

"I do need the money now though. Please help me."

"I don't want to take it away from you. Quite the opposite. What's the rush, anyway?"

Now it's her turn not to answer the question; not directly. "Charles keeps badgering me about money for Hazel."

"She is your daughter!"

"Don't I know it?"

"Didn't you agree on an allowance for her when it all blew up?"

"We did. It's just that I'm finding it difficult to pay for everything else as well: food, energy bills. They keep on going up. I don't need to hear about how expensive it was to get his car through its MOT."

"Perhaps you should ask for a pay rise?" He means well. She knows this to be true.

"I'm not in the same position as you, am I? I'm lucky to have the job. Plenty turned me down first. I can't push it now or they might use it as a way of 'letting me go.'"

"Now you're just being paranoid."

"Yes. I am! Well done. That's something else in my life that will likely never go away. Mood swings and behaviour patterns which are, how do they describe them: 'out of character.'

"Time might change things, especially if you can stay on top of the addiction."

"Let me tell you something else: that poison was in my blood, in my veins, long before anything else was."

"Dad?"

"All that expectation, all that pressure. It was alright for you: you were always going to get the shop. He was there with you for years before that, showing you how things needed to be done. How he did them."

"You make him sound like a teacher."

"If you like, yes, he was. He might have been one of those old-style fascists who used the cane first and reluctantly answered questions afterwards, but you at least had someone you could ask. Who could I talk to about life skills generally or university in particular? Nobody in our family had ever been, had they? Leaving the village was like leaving NASA in an upwards direction: unearthly, unknown?"

"You could have tried Fred?"

"Haha. You know as well as I do that he'd just have talked himself out of anything he didn't want to do and into whatever it was that he did. If it didn't affect him, it didn't concern him."

He smiles. A genuine smile rather than a facial construct to fit the occasion. "But you were still the clever one."

"Just like Hazel is now. I see a lot of me in her you know, despite Charles's best efforts to dilute any genetic input I may have had. She'll be fine. She has her head screwed on like mine was until 'Lefty Loosy' seemed much more attractive."

"She still needs you though. Every child needs its mother."

The poignancy of the words is not lost on her. "I have tried to talk to her, but she doesn't return my calls. I can't go around there. I promised Charles that I wouldn't. I know I can't fill any of the gap left by Mum – certainly not now – but I do know how to paper over things until they become a bit less painful. I've had to do it often enough."

He nods, satisfied that his sister is being sincere. "I know how you feel: about expectation I mean."

She puts her hand over his, her withered fingers barely covering half of it. "So, understand me now."

"What are you saying?"

"I'm saying that I need to get away from here – from all of this: the school, the places I've worked at, the doorways I've thrown up in; the mess I've made of my life and nearly did of Hazel's and Charles's."

"You can't blame yourself for everything."

"I don't, but I need to leave it behind. I could give Hazel a little lump sum for college or to make up for all the times I spent her pocket money on smack. Mum's money would help me to do that. I know I'll still look like rubbish and people will draw their own conclusions, but at least I'd have a chance. It would be a fresh start for me. If I stay here, I'll cross the finish line much sooner. You all know that and so do I."

"Where would you go?" Several seagulls suddenly fly up and away from the pavement beside them, screaming in the late afternoon shadows.

"That's the wonderful thing about it. I don't know. For the first time in my life, I'd be able to move forward without someone else trying to point me in the 'right' direction, which is just another word for where they think I should end up; what I ought to be doing with my life. Even when I've tried to do that, I've always made a mess of everything."

"My life hasn't been a great success!"

"But you've found happiness now. You could do the same. In a place like this people who know something about you assume that they know everything about you. They make their minds up and then just as quickly close them. Neither you nor I can ever change that, not while we stay around here."

"Maybe it's our destiny?" He leans back in his chair.

"No. It isn't! It's just one of many destinations. You can choose to go a different way; you've done it before."

CHAPTER TEN

"You'll have to be quick. I have some very important appointments this afternoon!" Fred Wilkins is unimpressed about being led to a police interview room.

"If you have an appointment here with us, it's usually serious, sir." Harcourt is as composed as ever. Few storms are allowed to adversely affect the surface calm.

"It better not take long, that's all."

"Or?" Farren has adopted the same tranquil interview style, even though she is rarely able to abide by it.

"Or I'll be calling my solicitor. Perhaps I should?"

Dressed in a crisp, white open-necked shirt and red chinos finished with white 'tennis' shoes he looks very much like the property manager about town (or, curiously, Harcourt considers: the human embodiment of the historic flag of Belarus).

"You're not in any kind of trouble, as far as we know, and certainly not under arrest, but if you'd like your solicitor to be informed about this little chat then, obviously, that's your prerogative, sir." Harcourt sits back, quite relaxed, and watches the words flow quickly from the man's ears up to his brain and slowly back down to his eyes.

He continues to glare at the detectives opposite, but

clearly, there is now a self-preservation filter in place in his head. “Fine. What do you want?”

“We thought it would be more dignified to invite you into the station.” Farren is loving the sense of intrigue that has replaced the outrage. “Particularly in the circumstances.”

“What circumstances? Just get to the point.”

“Tell me about your brother’s wife – Camilla Wilkins.”

There is a swift dilation of the man’s pupils. In Harcourt’s head, the traffic lights have gone straight through amber to green.

“What about her?” His defiance isn’t fooling them, and he probably knows this although he is an estate agent so might be assuming that he can buy some time while thinking about his next move across the chess board (although there are no knights in shining armour that can help him here).

“When did you last see her?”

He shrugs. Still planning his strategy then. “Maybe last year?” One tried and trusted way would certainly be to brazen it out, believing that the lies he hears coming out of his mouth are somehow him telling the truth.

“Or maybe not.” Harcourt didn’t like Fred Wilkins before and is beginning to loathe him now.

“What’s this all about? Camilla is married to Joe – in theory at least.” He smirks. “Perhaps you’ve accidentally asked the wrong brother in for tea and biscuits?”

“Accidents do happen.” Farren can see that her superior officer is on the verge of displaying his superiority. “Throw the prospect of a lot of money and a dose of age-old sibling rivalry into the mix and family values suddenly don't seem so valuable, do they...sir?"

"You seem very uptight, Sergeant. You should learn to relax more. I could help you with that..."

Now it is Harcourt's turn to wipe the leering smile off their interviewee's face. No more 'sir.' He leans forward suddenly, catching both of them off guard. "The point is that we know you're having an affair with your sister-in-law, Camilla Wilkins."

Farren watches the man's face closely – the blood rising to form an uncontrollable blush, followed by beads of sweat breaking out all over the closely shaven cheeks, matching those on his forehead. It's cool in the interview room, so Harcourt's words are causing the effect, not meteorology for once.

"How could you possibly know that." Fred's voice is softer, almost resigned. If he'd meant to ask 'How could you possibly accuse me of that' it would have been subtly different, but significantly so. The two of them had discussed the gamble beforehand and agreed to go with it if only to observe Fred's reaction.

Harcourt is more believing in Daniel than Farren has been in the past. Despite her reluctance, she had to admit that they had very little else to work with. Having considered all of this, a single earring found in a bedroom of a house of multiple occupation could hardly be classed as evidence of anything other than detachment from its owner. Deductions or projections beyond that represented a huge leap of faith or, as a defence lawyer would interpret it: a stab in the dark without a knife.

"When did it begin?" Harcourt can smell blood.

Fred holds his hands up. "Whoa! This is a private matter. It has nothing to do with Kathleen Hodges's death."

Farren senses a kill too, especially as he has passed up on a second opportunity to wholeheartedly deny their adultery or react as a wronged man would do by surely protesting loudly and railing against the allegation. "Why would we believe that?"

"Because I'm telling you so." Fred has recovered some of his swagger, but not all.

"If that is the case," Harcourt adopts the most annoying, patronising voice that he can muster, despite his excitement, "You must know who did kill her."

"How so?" The detectives are delighted to see that vulnerability is still in the room - very much alive and kicking. Kicking it is then.

"Because you are effectively discounting any person known to you and Camilla Wilkins who might have been affected by such an affair. Nobody could be so certain of such a thing unless, as I mentioned, you know who did kill her."

"Including yourself." Farren can't help herself.

"Now wait just a minute! You have no evidence that I was involved, or you'd have arrested me before now."

Funny how he never asked how we could prove the affair though, Harcourt muses with satisfaction. "It was just a thought; a philosophical meandering if you like. I haven't cautioned you but perhaps you should proceed with caution."

"What do you mean by that?"

"Well, I don't imagine that Joe will be too thrilled when he finds out about you and his wife. He's a big man, Joe. I imagine he could do some serious damage if he lost his temper."

"'Lost his temper.' That just shows how little you know, Inspector. Joe couldn't and wouldn't hurt a fly, even if it was crawling over his porky loins."

"Everybody has a boiling point, I can assure you, particularly when shocked."

"Except that it wouldn't come as a shock to my big brother, would it? He's known about it for a long time."

"Did your mother know?"

"Not at first."

"How then?"

"That witch next door saw me go into Joe's house one afternoon when Joe was at the shop. Went and told Mum."

"How did she react?"

"How do you think? Joe had always been the favourite. She wasn't thrilled to learn that he wasn't Camilla's first choice."

"Except he was though, wasn't he?" Farren joins in again. "She married Joe before you got your hands on her; all over her."

"It wasn't like that."

"Oh. The other way around, then? She got bored with big, silent Joe and was attracted to smooth-talking Fred who promised her what: excitement?"

"Perhaps she became a vegan?" Harcourt offers, not quite innocently.

"You've no right to talk to me like that. I could just walk out of here if I chose to."

"Does Suzanne know about it – the sordid affair you're having with her sister-in-law I mean?"

"Of course, she does. That's why she wants to leave me."

Not the only reason, surely, Farren deduces. "So why hasn't she packed up all her things in a book bag and headed off?"

"Because she needs my money, even if she doesn't need me."

"And you wanted to spend your money on your mistress instead?"

A bulb explodes in Harcourt's head. "So, your mother dying was a gift."

"I didn't see it like that. No son would." His attempt at affrontery doesn't come off.

"Loving son as well as a loving brother? Let's stop playing games, shall we? You saw your inheritance as a means of paying Suzanne off so that you'd be free to..."

"I wasn't 'paying her off.'"

"What then?"

"We'd reached an agreement."

"Agreements by estate agents aren't the most watertight I've ever known..."

"Just let me finish! We'd agreed to separate. I'd already agreed an amount; it was just a matter of time."

"But you got greedy. Decided you'd have your sister's share too. That's why you forced your mother to put the survivorship clause into the will?"

"I didn't force her to do anything. I didn't need to. She was as worried about Pat's health as I was."

"Heartfelt." Farren addresses Harcourt, not Fred.

"You people with your cheap suits and peppermints! Alright, I found myself pushing at an open door."

"Where does Kathleen Hodges fit into all of this?" Farren's question hangs in the air.

"I don't know. I don't know whether she does - did." Fred rises and heads towards the door. "My wife lives in a fantasy world of her own making. She chooses to go to places in her mind – in those endless novels - where she cannot be hurt by anybody or anything any longer. It's her choice to do so; a protective shield if that's your thing."

"It isn't, but nice work if you can get it?" Harcourt raises his eyebrows in mock amusement.

"Not everybody can choose to spend their life daydreaming, Inspector, hoping to make all the bad in their real lives go away."

"Especially when those dreams turn into nightmares: an unforeseen death, an unfortunate ending…"

"Quite."

"By the way, it's Chief Inspector to you. Did Suzanne ever need you, do you think?" That annoying voice from Harcourt again.

"The only thing Suzanne has ever needed in this world is money."

"And you?"

He turns to face them before replying, quietly: "I thought I needed her. It turns out that I was wrong."

***

Daniel can picture Hunter-Wright in the big house just this side of Droitwich. He's only been invited there once but remembers it clearly. A three-storey Edwardian 'villa,' it was situated off a narrow, private road and stood quietly waiting behind a tall hedge which seemed to surround the house, whether by design or by stealth.

The house was smaller inside than he had expected, and tidier. He'd somehow expected more mess, given his previous experience of police officers' proclivities to live and work 'on the job.' All polished wood floors and square bay windows, the house was flooded with light regardless of nature's assault from beyond.

Hunter-Wright is probably sitting in the same small sitting room at the front of the house, increasingly consumed by the early evening gloom, and quite alone apart from the company of a group of musicians he can just make out in the background. A plaintive, country rock sound. The Eagles possibly?

He glances over at Charlotte who is sitting in the chair by the patio windows, half looking in and half looking out. A paperback is sitting, open, on her knee, forgotten now as is much of the story of her own life. But not by him. Never by him.

"Are you alright, darling?" He whispers, although if he'd shouted, she still wouldn't have heard him, acknowledged that he was there. But he is. He always will be.

The voice on the telephone brings him back to his current location. "Martin has been filling me in on your latest vision." Is there an edge to his voice?

"Thanks. I hope it will help them in time."

"Indeed. They've certainly been taking their time; much too much of it." Yes, there is. He's unhappy.

"DCI Harcourt has asked if I'd be prepared to help with the enquiry."

"'Be prepared' is that still the motto of the Boy Scouts? So, are you happy to be on standby?"

"I am." Daniel glances across the room and then, in a softer voice owing to respect if not reason, continues," As long as they know that my family life – my wife in particular – must take priority. Especially now."

"I'm sure they do. We all do." Again, there is a separation: a staccato movement only. There is no flow to the conversation.

Unable to grasp the meaning behind it, he clutches at the details instead. "I believe that Fred Wilkins didn't deny the affair."

"Correct."

"Progress then?"

"Of sorts. It isn't technically a crime (although perhaps it is, morally) and there is nothing to connect it directly to our murder enquiry. No hard evidence, that is. Harcourt was excited though, so that's something at least."

No more 'Martin,' then. Back to normal. The music plays on: 'No more walks in the wood. The trees have all been cut down…' The words are haunting.

"It does also raise Fred Wilkins' suspicions." It's as though the detective is doing a voiceover.

"Suspicions?"

"Over how we've discovered it. He will be suspicious of us but also of all those people around him. He'll be wanting to find out which of them has spoken to us about his 'arrangement' with Camilla Wilkins, and why? I'm not sure that a lion running wild is healthy when we've yet to put a net in place – in case we need to catch him."

"Hardly a lion!"

"Definitely wild though. We're keeping a close watch on his movements in case he leads us to something more interesting."

Daniel can hear the resignation in his voice, in each of their voices. "I'm sorry we haven't made more progress in our own 'enquiry.' An ominous silence fills in for the lack of reply. "I could have been wrong about the whole 'Waterloo' thing. It's just the word that kept coming into my head."

"So many words in our mind's eyes, aren't there?" Thankfully, he resumes contact. "Some of them enter and leave again; many of them stay."

Not for the first time, Daniel wishes that he had an antidote for life's disappointments. Charlotte shifts in her seat, her eyes firmly closed now. He is not alone.

"Please don't lose hope!"

"Ah. 'Hope.' Miriam speaks of it often. She used to hang on to it until it became a dirty word. Like an autumn leaf clinging to the branch of a tree, just beyond her reach, before inevitably being blown away and brought down to earth. Crushed in the cold, unforgiving mud beneath her feet. Out of sight."

***

"Taking bribes, Sergeant?" Harcourt picks up the jar of honey from the younger man's desk, noting the clearness of the contents, even if the 'Cotswold Buzz' label replete with multiple images of bees does seem a bit busy.

"Of course not, sir!" Flowers reddens and stands to attention as if to prove that he has taken the allegation entirely seriously and can explain.

"Relax Ian. I was only joking. Nice honey though, by the looks of it."

"It does look good doesn't it." Flowers beams as he takes his seat once more. "Charles Band dropped it in earlier. He said he would when he was next passing. He's got a check-up at Specsavers today, down on Pump Street. It's been two years so..."

"Too much information!" Harcourt holds his hands up in mock surrender. "Did he mention the case at all?"

"No, sir. Should I have perhaps asked?"

"Not at all. I was just wondering whether he'd thought of anything that might help us, that's all."

"I'm afraid not, but I'm sure he will if anything comes to mind. He used to live quite close to me."

"But he's in Pershore now – since he split with his wife?"

"Yes, sir. He and his daughter, Hazel."

"She must be the same age as Daniel Reed's daughter. Waiting for the dreaded A-level results?"

"Yes, sir. I haven't met Claire Reed, but I doubt that Hazel Band need have any concerns. She seemed to have her head very tightly screwed on."

"Still nerve-wracking though – your whole future

depending on a series of papers written in unnatural conditions, usually on the hottest days of the year."

"Sounds like you're speaking from experience, sir!"

"I wake up at night in cold sweats; even now. You?"

"It's a 'no' on both counts. It wasn't quite so critical for me though. I never wanted to go to university."

"Didn't want to spend the rest of your life in debt?"

"Something like that. I can see the value of education but it was a much easier decision to make for those who already had money. We never really did – not that I'm complaining. My childhood was full of love, although some have described it since as simple, country living."

"Not a lot wrong with that."

"I have very few regrets. It was good enough for Rob and me. I still love being surrounded by nature – a bit like Mr Band I suppose. I think a lot of my friends from that time consider that they've moved on. I never felt the need to, personally."

"You joined the force straight after Sixth Form, didn't you?"

"Yes, sir. Again, I didn't feel the need to travel first to 'find myself.'"

The two men laugh.

"Just keep the needle of that compass pointing in the direction it is and I'm sure you'll be fine." Harcourt pats him on the back before hurrying back into his office to answer the phone which always seems to sense when it is time for him to get back on track.

***

The big man is unnaturally still. Farren can see that he's

breathing, but there is no movement beyond the rise and fall of his chest. He's bent over like a runner when his race is run. Not out of breath though, just preserved for essential bodily functions. No sense of relief here. Just regret.

"Mr Baker!" The response officers have already told Harcourt that this is how they found him when they arrived at the scene just forty minutes earlier. He must have called the incident in and then returned to the scene of the crime; the very heart of it.

He isn't even blinking. Just staring into a space that hadn't previously existed; not as a vacuum anyway.

"Steve." Harcourt holds out a hand and hooks it under the man's arm, gently pulling him into an upright position. Whether it is the ongoing shock or the head rush caused by the rising temperature, he sways slightly. Luckily, Farren is on hand to help her colleague lead him to a wooden chair at the back of the shop. They help him to sit while Harcourt signals through the window to the older of the PCs to call for an ambulance. A second ambulance.

The detectives are dressed in white gloves and matching white protective suits with incongruous blue plastic slippers to complete their outfits. Two SOCOs are already at work in the front, along with the pathologist who had arrived just before they did. Harcourt is disappointed that it isn't Jenny Graham but, if he's completely honest, relieved too that their game of banter has been postponed - for now. This version is older and plumper. The grey moustache completes the makeover.

"Please take your time, Steve." Farren is sitting next to

him, perched on what looks like an old wooden crate of some sort. Steve looks as though time is the least of his problems, but they both understand that it may all too soon become the worst.

“You found him lying there?” Harcourt is as sympathetic as he tries very hard to be on occasions such as this. When one or more human beings have done something like this to another. He’s had plenty of practice at it but, still, the need to move on, to detect and then to avenge through justice, is coursing through his veins. He’s after blood.

The man simply nods. He is either broken or deliberately disassembled.

“What time was this?”

He looks up, seeming to be aware of Farren for the first time, but addresses Harcourt instead.

“I wasn’t supposed to be here at all. Joe had given me a day off.” Farren recalls the softly spoken voice: unusual in such a big man. Unheard of in any other butcher’s shop, she’s ever visited. “We usually split them. It’s unusual for me not to be here for at least a part of the day.”

“What then? You’d popped in to see how things were going?”

“Joe phoned me first thing to tell me not to come in today. I was down to do the morning shift you see.”

“Go on.” Harcourt is pleased that Farren isn’t being as defensive as she can sometimes be - hasn’t jumped in for once. If he holds the communication cord connecting Steve with the outside world right now, then that’s fine by him. He just wants to help the man.

They both do.

"I was a little bit worried about him. He seemed distant and Joe isn't ever like that." His voice is strained. The man is replaying every moment of the scene in his mind, frame by frame. "Not like he hadn't been sleeping. His voice wasn't slurred or anything like that. It was crystal clear. That was it. It had clarity. He was thinking clearly."

"Are you saying that he was normally vague, muddled perhaps?"

"Not muddled, just conflicted sometimes. Joe tried to please everybody all the time. That's not possible though, is it? Something has to give, sometimes."

"Or somebody?"

Steve doesn't reply. They both make mental notes of this: to be discussed later.

"Was his wife – Camilla – with him when he made the call, do you know." Farren is unable to remain quiet for long.

Now he does turn his face towards her and sees her dangling her legs over the crate like an expectant child eager for him to tell her a story. His face is less crumpled by loss, more filled with something approaching anger; hate even.

"I wouldn't know. I couldn't hear her if that's what you mean?"

"How would you describe their relationship?"

"With difficulty. There was no relationship to speak of."

Recalling the sighting of Steve leaving the family home, she dangles a different scenario in front of him. "And how did you get on with Camilla Wilkins?"

Yes. Hate now. No holds barred. "I didn't."

"Meaning?" Harcourt joins in.

"I didn't get on with her. Joe was very protective of her."

Much good it did him, Harcourt considers. He is keen to share what they know about Camilla and Fred Wilkins but reflects that it may be more valuable to keep his powder dry for now. At least they've got the man talking after taking him on a slight diversion before bringing him back to the matter at hand. "

"You arrived at the shop, then. I assume it was closed?"

"Thankfully, yes." He shudders.

"That would have been unusual I take it?"

"In the middle of the day, yes. Mr Wilkins – Harry, that is – used to prefer lunchtime closing, but you can't do that these days. If you inconvenience customers now, they'll just take their money to a supermarket that's open 24/7. They won't come back even if the meat's not up to scratch (like it always would be here)."

"You have your own key?" Farren is watching him curiously. She is certain that he knows far more than he is currently sharing. He'd never make a social media 'influencer.'

He nods.

"Out of interest, who else has keys to the shop?"

"Just the two of us, and his wife." He practically spits out the last word.

"OK. You let yourself in. Were the cuts of meat still laid out on the counter as they normally would be?" Harcourt remains focused.

"Yes. Everything was as if he had been standing there, ready to serve, just moments before I walked in."

"Could he have just taken a quick toilet break?"

"He may have done. That did sometimes happen, but we'd normally have just nipped out the back and busked it. Wouldn't have bothered to put the Closed sign on the door for such a short length of time."

"Very trusting?" Harcourt observes.

"We're not exactly inundated. That's why we did the split shifts - so that we could be open pretty much all the time."

"And not too long to wait if you did need to go!" Harcourt's attempt at lightening the mood even slightly is poor. He acknowledges the frowns from both Steve and Farren alike. He tries a different approach: "That sign on the door: it had been turned round to Closed then?'"

"It had. Yes. But if Joe had changed it, he must have intended for it to be just temporary because there was no indication of him starting to clean things up."

"Unless he had only just changed it?" A theory is forming in Farren's mind.

"I'm sorry?"

"Well, maybe he had just that minute decided to close for the day and hadn't had a chance to start putting things back into the fridges?"

"Before his attacker arrived." Harcourt continues for her.

"Who must have been known to him or he'd have pointed to the sign and told whoever it was that the shop was closed." Farren agrees as Steve simply looks on.

"Or the attacker arrived first and then changed the sign? They could have used a key – maybe Joe's key – to lock the door behind them and then again when they left."

"Perhaps they were already in the shop? Is there a back door?"

Steve shakes his head.

"One thing's for certain: they wouldn't have risked being seen while the shop was still open," Harcourt concludes, acutely aware that Steve may be gleaning more from their exchange than either one of them is.

"The blinds weren't down." Steve barely raises his voice, despite his bulging eyes registering a key breakthrough, in his thinking at least.

"In which case anyone walking past the shop would have seen the attack?" Harcourt runs with it.

"So, the attack happened elsewhere, and his body was arranged behind the counter?" Farren is still watching Steve closely. She doesn't have to wait too long.

"Arranged! You arrange flowers, not bodies." He stands now, his bulk almost completely blocking Farren from Harcourt's view. Each of them had forgotten how big the man is, especially at such close quarters. Spittle escapes from his bulbous lips as he rages. "Someone's hit him over the head with something hard. They've then dragged him out there and dumped him like a piece of meat."

Irony draws a pattern in the air – like a speech bubble in a children's cartoon – which just as quickly disappears. Steve remains animated throughout. Harcourt tries to calm him whilst recognising anger as one the most common first signs of grief that they encounter. "The experts will work out what has happened here and then we'll bring whoever did this to justice."

"You don't class yourselves as experts too then?"

Before Harcourt can detect sarcasm or something else equally hurtful, they are interrupted by the pathologist who turns out to be Mr Armstrong, looking like an astronaut and strolling in like his namesake who strolled on the moon fifty years earlier.

"May I have a word please?"

By way of reply and, more importantly, privacy, Harcourt asks Farren to take Steve out to their car where he promises to join them shortly. As Steve shuts the door behind him, possibly for the last time, Harcourt turns to Armstrong. "Shoot."

"Scuff marks on the tops of his shoes and knees do indicate dragging. He was a big man so that would have taken some doing."

"More than one perpetrator then?"

"That's certainly the most likely scenario or at least someone who was physically very fit. It doesn't look as though he was killed out here."

"Because?"

"Because there's no patently human blood splatter on any of the surfaces. He was hit with something hard. The surrounding air would have been full of it – momentarily."

"Presumably it's complicated by this taking place in a butcher's shop. I mean they're hacking and slicing meat all the time?"

"They are but we're doing a comprehensive sweep to try to eliminate that activity."

"Sounds like a plan."

"It does." The man seems put out by Harcourt's abruptness, yet he must surely face this every time he leaves his lab. "Though it will be a lengthy process."

"So, we need to be patient. That's what you're saying."

"I am. At least we have established that, unambiguously."

"In terms of establishing the cause of death, I know it's early days but do you think the blow to the head is what killed him?"

The 'tut' is almost imperceptible but Harcourt's trained ears pick it up like a speck on a radar screen. "It would certainly have disabled him had he not already been disabled by something else. As to the causa mortis, it is, as you rightly say, early days."

Harcourt loves History but he has never loved Latin.

"I can illuminate things a little further..."

Harcourt waits for the metaphorical light bulb to start flashing above his thinning grey hair. "Any light you can throw on this dark day would no doubt be useful."

"There are some tiny fibres in the gash on the victim's head – even to the naked eye. I'd say they are going to have come from some other animal."

"And you're not including humans in that species of animal?"

"I am not. You could have a similar episode to 'Tales of the Unexpected' on your hands."

"I never really liked Roald Dahl – too fanciful for me."

"Me too. My favourite TV programme was Emergency Ward 10, but I don't share that thought with many people. Ages me far too much."

Harcourt surveys the greyness of the man before summarising. "What you're saying is that he might have been hit over the head with a leg of lamb or something similar?"

"Indeed. I've suggested the SOCOs look for matches with any of the heavier pieces of meat – out here or in the fridge or freezers in the back."

"Which means that if there are no matches, we are looking for the wrong murder weapon or the murderer took it away with them?"

"Probably wrapped it up and placed it in one of those blue, plastic bags down there. It would have been quite usual and wouldn't have attracted any attention."

"You think this was calculated rather than a sporadic act of violence then?"

"Very definitely. It could have been a sudden attack from behind - in the heat of the moment – but either way, it looks as if we have a single blow here. Certainly, no struggle."

"Joe Wilkins was a big man. It would have taken someone at least as tall as him to be able to hit down on his head with the requisite force, particularly if they had a heavy object raised above their head."

"Hair raising! Yes." The learned man pauses to consider his joke – not the reaction normally expected by stand-up comedians. "Let's see what we can find when we get the body back to the lab. I should be able to tell you more then."

***

Taylor greets him warmly as they return to the office, also nodding sympathetically in Farren's direction. It's never easy to be in the presence of dead bodies (or their spirits, as Flowers had somewhat enigmatically informed her earlier). "Fred Wilkins has been on the phone, sir."

"Wanting to know what we know?" Harcourt sighs as he sinks into his office chair, which also does its best not to sink any further into the carpet than it already has. He's had his fill of the heat now; just fed up with it.

"He seemed pretty upset. Said his sister was too."

"Understandable if you've just lost a brother… or killed him."

Farren and Flowers both look up from their monitors. Taylor exchanges a glance with Flowers who is looking genuinely shocked. "The Carers people also phoned me back earlier, sir."

"The agency Kathleen Hodges signed up to?"

"In Bromyard. Yes, sir. 'We care so that you won't be scared!' Glenda finally retrieved the 'back office' files, probably from her garden shed!"

Harcourt licks his lips, smiling and forming his own vision of the woman his sergeant had so eloquently described. "Go on."

"It seems that Kathleen only ever worked for two people while she was on their books. Initially, she was sent out to a Mr Coffee, as well as Brenda."

"Tell me about Mr Coffee." He can already hear Farren

sniggering in the background.

"She didn't work with him for long." Taylor consults her notebook. "Just under eighteen months. He lived alone, just on the Bromyard side of Hereford as you head in. Kathleen visited and did a bit of cleaning and occasionally some grocery shopping for him. I think it was the company he was paying for."

"Before he sadly passed away, I assume?"

"No, sir. He didn't. In fact, he is very much alive. Mr Coffee is a retired clown."

Mini explosions of laughter can be heard behind her. Both Farren and Flowers raise their hands in silent apology.

Taylor lets them settle down before continuing. "He applied for a job as a joke writer on the Late Lennie show. It's a late-night cabaret thing on BBC Midlands. I've never watched it."

"Funny that!" Harcourt can't resist it. "Just shows that there's more to life than a hot drink and a good book when you get older. Kathleen didn't visit him after that?"

"Glenda says he was too busy; saw out the notice period and the contract was terminated."

"At least he wasn't lonely anymore, not with a whole new production team to interact with?"

"I suppose not, though I'm not sure how much of it was virtual – him sending material in and getting feedback. Glenda did say he was much better at IT than she is, but that isn't saying much."

"Kathleen just worked for Brenda after that?"

"According to their records, yes, sir. The interesting bit is that it was Joe Wilkins who was footing the bill for Brenda's care, but then it all stopped suddenly about a year ago."

"Really. Do you know why?"

"Not yet, sir, but I'm working on it. Glenda said that he contacted them and like Mr Coffee, went through the termination process and that was that. Kathleen took herself off their books at the same time and continued on a voluntary basis. They were next-door neighbours after all; it's not as if she had to travel or anything."

"And this Glenda had nothing more to tell us?"

"No, sir. She kept banging on about how proud she was of training Kathleen, as though she was trying to cover her tracks if something had gone wrong."

"No longer their problem, was it?" Harcourt has a good mental picture of the agency 'professionals' Taylor encountered. "Probably just a kneejerk reaction. Nothing did go wrong on their watch, did it? Apart from Kathleen dying of course."

"I'm not sure if it's relevant or not, but neither Glenda nor Sybil showed the slightest interest in why we were asking about Kathleen. If they were feeling insecure about something, wouldn't you have thought they'd have been more curious?"

"Or they already knew what had happened to her?" Harcourt has the beginnings of a headache: too much fluidity and not enough fluids.

"I wonder if this was just down to money on Joe's part," Farren has recovered, "Or whether there was a different reason for him being no longer prepared to cover the expense of his mother's care?"

"Perhaps he thought it was too expensive to go through the agency any longer?" Flowers joins in.

"Or didn't think Brenda was getting value for his money?" Harcourt agrees.

"Or that Kathleen would go on caring for his mother for nothing anyway – even if it was on a sort of ad hoc basis?" Taylor throws her hat into the ring.

"Or even that she would stop caring for Brenda if she was no longer getting paid for it as per the bank statements showing us that there was no more money coming in? Perhaps he thought Kathleen would withdraw and be less present in his mother's life?" Harcourt is deep in thought now, especially given so many alternative explanations. They often called it the 'crime d'or.' Flowers had come up with the play on words when there were too many 'ors' to be funny anymore.

Taylor is speaking again. "Camilla did tell us that Kathleen was getting on their nerves – driving a wedge between Joe and Brenda. Perhaps Joe miscalculated and Kathleen really was getting her feet too firmly under the table. If Brenda knew that she was now caring for her for free, that could have driven the very wedge between mother and son that he was anxious to avoid?"

"And yet she still left him the same share of the money as the other two." Harcourt is concerned. Something doesn't add up here; that is his personal takeaway from it, and now that Joe has inconveniently got himself killed, they can't ask him to explain himself.

***

"What did they say?" Suzanne Wilkins drops her car keys on the granite worktop with a pleasing crash that she knows will upset her husband.

"Harcourt wasn't there. They said he was at the scene of the crime." Fred elucidates the last few words individually as though they are more important than the sentence itself, overemphasising them.

"What happened?"

"I don't know. I wasn't there."

There it is again. She must be wary, aware of how hurtful he can be; the damage he can still cause her. "So, all we know is that they found his body in the shop, lying behind the counter?"

"That's what the uniformed officers who came round said, yes. He'd been hit over the head with something heavy. That's all they could tell us. Oh, they asked if we knew of any reason why anyone would want to cause Joe harm."

The ensuing silence replicates what would have been his reply to them, she knows this without needing to seek confirmation.

Fred placed his empty coffee cup on one of the onyx coasters he'd picked up in Bulgaria on one of his weekend breaks with Camilla that spring. "They also asked if we wanted a trained officer to come and stay with us for a while. I told them it wouldn't be necessary."

Again, she feels a sudden coldness on her neck: a frisson of fear or something else? "I assume they've been in touch with Pat too?"

"Who?"

"The police of course."

"She phoned me here about half an hour ago. Very upset, as you might well believe – especially with that famous imagination of yours." His voice has now taken on a menacing tone which both of them can clearly hear.

She takes a slight step backwards. "Are you going to see her?"

"Why on earth would I do that?"

"Because she's your sister!"

"Ah. So she is. Part of the same happy family you graced with your presence for so many long years."

Why did she leave her car keys on the table? She can't possibly get to them now and the spares are God knows where.

"Where have you been these last couple of days?"

"I told you on the phone. I went down to see Jennifer in Stroud and decided to stay for a couple of days."

"Of course, you did." He smiles but not with his eyes. Usually, that wouldn't have concerned her; hasn't done for a long time. He can keep his dirty secrets, but it seems that hers are somehow different. "Except that I phoned 'Jennifer' in Stroud. It wasn't so very difficult with a surname like Eccles. Like the cake or apparently a pop song years ago. Take your pick. Anyway, Jennifer was unsure of herself I thought. Caught off guard you might say. She told me she hadn't seen or heard from you since Christmas."

Why would he do that? Why would he go to all that trouble? What should she say? What can she say? She says nothing.

"Don't think I don't know what you're up to." He snarls.

She grimaces, her confidence – her self-esteem – blown away. He's raged at her before but never like this. Suddenly, the penny drops. She stops. He's frightened. Fear is driving him and all that assurance of where he is going with his life, and who with, has gone. This is him, stripped down and naked and abhorrent.

"What happens..." She pauses, aware of the annoying quaver in her voice. Still, his icy eyes are fixed on hers, but she is no longer stuck in reverse. She is standing her ground and makes a second attempt: "What will happen with Joe's share of the will?"

"Always money with you, isn't it?"

"That's rich."

"Isn't it?" His face is ugly, contorting itself into a kind of rage. "But do let me stop you right there if you're already planning on getting more than we agreed. Pat received an anonymous call which the police are following up on, although it seemed to her that they didn't hold out much hope of success. The caller – who she didn't recognise because they put on some kind of foreign accent - said that she'd be next unless she 'did the right thing.' So, you see, dear wife, if we're being targeted by some madman or woman, I might be next. Then you'd most likely end up with absolutely nothing."

CHAPTER ELEVEN

"At least we now know that the murder itself did take place in the back room of the butcher's shop." Harcourt is standing in front of the whiteboard with the others gathered around in a semi-circle. It reminds him of his time at school when boards were black, and they hadn't listened nearly so politely to the lessons being taught by their teachers. Perhaps they should have.

"Was Armstrong able to give us anything further on the blood splatter he found there, sir? Farren is the first to engage, as usual.

Harcourt shakes his head. "I'm afraid not. It is human blood though and he has absolutely no doubt that Joe Wilkins was murdered there. It's his blood for sure but no other DNA traces, apart from big Steve Baker's of course. You'd expect that because he was in that room at least every other day."

"No fingerprints from the door, I'm guessing?"

"None that we could usefully or inexpensively separate and use. That part of the site is effectively contaminated by each of the customers who would have come into the shop, pushing the door handle or even the door itself. Apart from Steve and Joe none of the other family members' DNA is prominent on that door but, as I say, it's compromised by all the other regular activity. It would never stand up as evidence in court, shall we say."

“Joe must either have let the killer in, or he was already in there when the incident took place.” Taylor takes the lead from Farren’s assertiveness.

“Or they let themselves in without Joe realising, as we said before.” Flowers isn’t particularly interested in promotion, not yet anyway.

“We assume the killer was known to Joe, either because he let them in, or they were there already; or they had a key.” Harcourt summarises for the benefit of all of them but especially himself. The question then becomes one of motive. Why would they want to kill Joe?”

“I know this is a bit left-field, sir,” Flowers has no idea how much his boss looks forward to such insights, “But we don’t think there is any organised crime involvement here, do we? I mean, what if the shop was a front for some kind of money laundering activity – if Joe had got in too deep with something he couldn’t get out of.”

“The shop wasn’t exactly busy when you visited was it?” Taylor is happy to back up her colleague’s theory. “Perhaps Joe was more in need of the money than he let on.”

“Or he was planning a future life without his wife, rather like his brother?” Harcourt joins in. “It would also account for why Kathleen might have been killed with such a theatrical flourish. Perhaps it was a warning after all.”

“Do you think the murders are connected then? Farren prompts.

“I do and I don’t. Joe’s murder appears to be as cold and clinical as Kathleen’s but what if it was opportunist?

Someone lost their temper and just hit him over the head with whatever they could find to hand."

"No news on the murder weapon I suppose, sir?" Taylor again.

"None. Nothing obvious on any of the meat cuts under the counter or in storage. The big carcasses hanging up would have been far too heavy. Armstrong has confirmed that the hairs found on Joe's head were sheep hairs though."

"Maybe they did take it away with them then. As we said before, if the killer is that self-assured, it wouldn't look at all out of place walking down a village High Street with a leg of lamb in a carrier bag." Taylor is getting despondent. They seem to be walking in circles with plenty of motives but no actual evidence connecting anyone to either scene.

"Money has to be the key, somewhere – somehow – down the line!" Farren doesn't even blink. "What other motivation could there be here? Revenge – especially after infidelity – is a powerful driver, but it doesn't fit here."

"Certainly not with Kathleen Hodges." Taylor agrees.

"Or with the family members." Flowers chips in. "Camilla Wilkins would gain no benefit from killing Joe."

"Except that she'd then be free to ponce about with Fred." Farren can feel herself getting angry again at the very thought of Fred Wilkins."

Flower persists. "In fact, she'd have put her share of the inheritance and the butchery business on the line, especially if she was unsure whether Joe had made a will. It could just as easily have passed to Steve Baker, couldn't it?"

"And, from the other end of things, Suzanne Wilkins gains nothing by killing Joe in terms of Fred sleeping with Camilla. There's no element of revenge in it at all." Taylor concludes. "The only thing to be gained by her, via Fred's settlement, would be extra money from Joe's share of Brenda's inheritance."

"This has to be about the will, surely." Harcourt welcomes the focus. "Either Pat or Fred stand to gain if Joe dies and effectively forfeits his share."

"Would they still inherit if one of them turns out to be the killer, sir?"

Harcourt smiles grimly. "That is a very good question, Gabby. Yes, they would. Beneficiaries would only forfeit their rights to their inheritance if they had killed the actual testator which, in this case, is (was) Brenda."

"Which means that you could commit murder and still receive your inheritance from prison?" Flowers is slightly open-mouthed.

"Probably not via any kind of open money transfer but, yes, you could. This makes Pat and Fred prime suspects; they have the most to gain from Joe's death, although the probate process is still a long way off. I contacted Rawlings yesterday to get the latest state of play."

"I've checked on Pat Band, sir." Taylor is quietly pleased to see Farren's face drop, if only slightly. "She's understandably very upset about Joe's death, but I'd say she was nervous more than anything. If Joe's murder did occur at some point on Monday morning between about ten and twelve as Mr Armstrong is suggesting, then she has a cast iron alibi. She had a shift at ASDA from eight that morning and didn't leave until after three. I checked with her line manager who confirmed it and I'm sure plenty of others could too."

"And I checked on Fred Wilkins, sir." Flowers leaps in before Farren can. "As you suggested I visited them on my way home last night."

"How did they seem?" In 'normal' circumstances Harcourt recognises that this would be a fairly superficial if not insensitive question. But although he likes to think he is neither of those things, this is very far away from being a normal family.

"I'd say she was more upset than he was, sir. He didn't say much at all, but she almost said too much, if you know what I mean?"

"Like people do when they're in shock, you mean? Words fall out of their mouths which don't always make sense when you try to put them together again?"

"A little. I'd say it was nerves. She seemed genuinely anxious."

"We know all about her anxiety." Farren sniffs.

"What about alibis?" Harcourt has noted it too.

"They were together in the house apparently; alibied each other. He had a meeting that afternoon but didn't leave the house until half-past three. She was there all day. She said she spent most of the time in the house and rarely left it."

"Good work both of you. At this stage, I'm not sure whether they need protecting from each other or some third party we haven't yet considered. What I will say – and this concerns the whole of the Wilkins family –

where is the love? Family time is so precious, why do so many choose not to value it?"

"You don't think Steve Baker is more involved in this than he appears to be do you sir?" Once again, Flowers is thinking laterally.

"I had considered it, Ian. I did think his grief was genuine though and, besides, how would he stand to gain? Even if Joe had made a will, which I very much doubt at his age, it's highly unlikely that he would have left the business to Steve, isn't it? Why would he? In lieu of a will, everything would ordinarily go to his wife, Camilla."

"Which leads us straight back to Brother Fred." Farren's words hang in the air.

"We did find those strands of Hazel's hair." Taylor has been thinking about the lovely granddaughter. The idea of her being involved in all of this in a sinister way is too horrible to contemplate, but she is a police officer and they've been fooled on so many occasions she could write a book on smoke and mirrors. Not that she is clever enough to write a book.

"I don't think they amount to anything significant." Harcourt sees the relief on his sergeant's face. "However, why don't you and Ian pop down there and just ask her the question directly?"

***

As they pass The Royal Oak in Broadwas, Harcourt recalls an evening he had spent there many years ago; soon after he'd joined West Mercia. DCI Cummings, who lived in the village, had decided to have his retirement party in that particular hostelry so that he wouldn't have to pay for a taxi home.

Retiring he might have been but retiring he wasn't. Harcourt had taken a distinct dislike to the loud, bumptious man and, although he and Hunter-Wright had an uneasy relationship, he did at least respect him. He can't remember much about that evening other than Cummings wearing a ridiculous party hat as he regaled them with his 'war stories' which became more outlandish with each pint.

Farren follows his eyes towards the building, seeking clues as to his latest reverie. "I didn't know that was a carvery. Have you ever been there, sir?"

"Only once, and not for the food." In truth, he had made a note of the place as a possible Sunday lunchtime drive out for Debbie and himself. They'd never followed up on it though. Subconsciously he knew that this was in part because of the risk of running into the man again when he'd have much preferred to run him over. He realises that his reply was unnecessarily blunt. "You should get your exam results any time now?"

"I'm not running down the garden path pleading with the postman to stop; not that I have a garden path – or a garden for that matter!" She smiles, reflecting his relief.

"I'm sure you have nothing to worry about. Daniel Reed was telling me about his daughter, Claire. She's waiting for her A-level results which come out tomorrow I believe."

"You forget, don't you, how important those grades are? I mean, forget GCSEs..."

"Or O-levels!"

"Or O-levels, yes, sorry sir." His chuckle encourages

her to continue. "A-level results stand at the gateway of whatever you want to do with your life don't they: university, fast-track job, whatever. If you mess them up, then you're facing at least an extra year for re-takes."

"Or facing the rest of your life with regret."

Not for the first time she wonders about Harcourt's background. He is so open and friendly most of the time, but there are certain areas that none of them venture into. Private things that he chooses not to share. She looks directly ahead as Bishop's Lacy comes into view once more.

Surprisingly and somewhat incongruously it is Steve Baker who opens Camilla Wilkins's front door to them. Looming ominously in the doorway he eventually lets them past, his body language alone letting them know that they aren't at all welcome there. Words are in short supply as ever.

Camilla is sitting on one of the stools behind the breakfast bar. She is wearing a fittingly dark t-shirt which still fits tightly over her upper body, hiding little.

"We are very sorry for your loss," Harcourt approaches her slowly. "I realise that this is a bad time but there's no time to waste if we're to catch whoever's doing these terrible things."

Farren watches as Steve sits beside her, gently placing his enormous rough hand over hers, completely covering it – even the immaculate nails painted today in shiny gold.

Harcourt has noticed it too of course. "May I ask either of you if you can think of anyone – anyone at all – who might have wanted to harm Joe."

They observe the tears filling Steve's eyes, but, curiously, not hers. Maybe she left her husband behind years ago mentally as well as physically."

"Course not!" She snaps. "Who would want to hurt him? Joe was loved by everyone – in this village anyway. He was one of them, wasn't he? One of their own. Born and brought up here. I've had no end of callers offering their condolences. Pity they couldn't have called into the shop more often – bought a bit more meat."

"He didn't mention any problems to you, did he?" Farren's voice is not that sympathetic as she takes in the false eyelashes and ribbon of pink lip gloss. She knows that she shouldn't judge women on sight – not like most men do.

"What sort of problems? The business was struggling but it was a long way from going under."

"Personal problems." That firm voice again, echoing off the gleaming cooker hood.

"No. Not to me. What kind of personal problems?"

Harcourt has been watching Steve throughout. He still hasn't uttered a word. What is going through that man's mind?

"We're not sure." Farren beats a retreat, both uneasy and suspicious of what Steve might know, even if Joe's wife appears not to. "We're following up on all kinds of theories as to why Joe may have been attacked and murdered."

"What theories? Conspiracy theories do you mean?"

Harcourt can see her floundering and has no desire to watch her drown. "We have no evidence to suspect anything untoward Mrs Wilkins; just covering our bases. It would be completely remiss of us not to do that. It may even be that the person responsible set out to attack Joe, even if not fully intending to kill him."

Camilla exchanges a look with Steve. Neither of them speaks.

"I'm afraid I must ask this Mrs Wilkins. Where were you on Monday morning last between the hours of ten o'clock and two o'clock?"

"Are you going to caution me for some reason? I've done nothing wrong. Nothing at all."

"You're not a suspect Mrs Wilkins. This is just routine. We're working on a process of elimination."

"Worked well for Joe that, didn't it? He was eliminated. Supposing I'm next in line? That reporter woman seems to think we're all potential targets."

"Who would that be – the reporter you mentioned?" Harcourt already has a pretty good idea of the name she will answer him with.

"Kate somebody... came to the door yesterday. Said she was following up on the murders in the village. That's what they're going to call them now isn't it: The Bishop's Lacy Murders!"

"Please try not to be alarmed." Farren tries again in a much softer voice. "There's no reason to suggest that anyone is being targeted."

"No reason. No reason! You're the one who's lost her reason. Alright, Brenda might have died of natural causes, but Kathleen didn't, did she? And Joe most certainly didn't." Camilla is shrieking uncontrollably now but it is Steve whose voice they can just make out above the storm.

"I spoke with Pat on the phone last night," Farren remembers that gentle, faltering whisper - seemingly so incompatible with a working world of knives and meat cleavers. "She agrees with Camilla. Someone is out to punish us, all of us." With that he dissolves into tears, heavy sobs of angst or grief or both.

'Well, I think this is going well' Harcourt hears Debbie's voice and phrase that she uses whenever he's done something especially stupid, like absentmindedly pouring boiling water onto his cereal instead of milk. What is that compared to murder and death though? The attack on Farren was unwarranted but understandable. They do not have a clue who is responsible for this; any of it.

Camilla offers Steve a tissue before passing him the whole box. Eventually, he calms down.

"You've had a bit of time to think since we last met." Harcourt proceeds gently, still not entirely convinced by the histrionics or their real cause. "Can you think of anything at all that might help us – even the tiniest detail?

"I did see the granddaughter – Hazel – in Brenda's garden quite late one night, last week. I don't know if she saw me or not. I hid in the shadow of the hawthorn bush at the top of the road. I didn't see what she was doing there, just saw her leave by the front gate and race down the road. It's probably nothing but you did say 'anything.'"

"Thank you. Is there anything else?"

Again, an almost imperceptible look between the two of them. He seems to make his mind up at last. "Yes, Inspector, there is."

Farren feels a frisson of excitement, as though they're on the verge of a breakthrough at last. This is why she loves the job. She has often tried to recapture such moments – to experience the build-up of suspense and then the revelation. Unlike Kathleen Hodges, she isn't a big cinemagoer but give her a boxset and that TV has her full attention for however long it takes.

"Steve, you don't need to say anything. It doesn't - can't - affect Joe any longer." Camilla is holding his hand now, wiping his cheeks with one of the tissues.

Harcourt's synapses are pulsing all over the place. Did they get this so badly wrong? Is it Steve who Camilla is having the affair with, not Fred? Did Daniel get it wrong? He's always made it very clear to them that his 'gift' is hit and miss. If so, why would Fred have confessed so readily following Daniel's vision after finding Camilla's stray earring? Is she having affairs with both of them? Flowers had seen Steve leaving the house previously, knowing that Joe was already serving in the shop.

Steve slides off the stool, takes a glass from the wall cupboard next to them and half-fills it from the tap. Steadying himself he sits back down and looks directly at Harcourt.

"I loved Joe, Inspector. I loved him with every part of my being. I loved him in the shop, and I loved him here. I often stayed over when Camilla was away. It wasn't easy. Not here in this sad, insular little place. I kept an eye on Brenda's house for him. It was difficult for him to see the house empty. I walked up there each evening to check there were no obvious problems from the outside: door and windows. I never went in there, not even when

Brenda was alive. It wasn't that Joe was ashamed of me, us. He did tell his mother about it in the end, but he was never quite sure what she thought about him after that.

That's the real reason I hid from Hazel. You get used to darting into the shadows, not wanting to be seen unless people talk even more than they already do. Oh, I know they do in the pub – probably in each other's houses too."

"I'm so sorry." Harcourt genuinely cannot think of anything else to say at that precise moment in time.

He needn't have worried too much as Steve is evidently keen to get it off his chest – all of it. He continues to whisper but all around him is silent now; everything and everyone listening to him for once. "They talk about 'coming out' don't they? Come clean. Stand up for yourself. Well, that's all very well if you're newcomers or planning to leave home. In places like this, you're known for who they want you to be: the person they've pigeonholed to do and say the things they expect you to do or say. There isn't any room in there for change. They won't allow you to move on, evolve. Even if you finally accept who you are, they can't. They won't."

Farren is feeling ashamed. Too often she has had to remind herself (or be reminded) that not all men are intrinsically programmed to fit the stereotype that she and so many others are guilty of perpetuating, even though she might have very good reasons for that personal default.

Steve is continuing and she fervently hopes that she hasn't missed anything else. "I could have tried to be brave for myself, for Joe: for both of us. Joe couldn't though, could he? He wouldn't have stood a chance. All I know is that neither of us would have harmed a hair on his big, beautiful head."

Camilla pulls the huge man into her slender arms, hugging him as he rocks backwards and forwards. He may not have thought himself to be brave, but she recognises his courage at a time when he has, literally, just lost the love of his own clandestine life. "I never left Joe; you see." She looks from one detective to the other. "Joe left me so that he could be himself, finally; and long before Steve came to the village and began working in the shop. I know you've had me down as being some kind of 'scarlet woman' but, I promise you, I never stopped loving Joe either. Joe and I were family right up until the end."

***

Neither of them speaks as they head back down the lane and past Joe's shop, closed now with the awning pulled in and grey blinds pulled down to the sills. Harcourt can see specks of blood towards the foot. Some might call this an ongoing murder scene.

"Oh no!" Farren mutters.

Harcourt sees him then, just ahead of them on the other side of the High Street but walking in the same direction as them. He gets the distinct impression that the other man's journey had only begun once they had reached Joe's shop, like a relay runner waiting in the zone for the baton to be passed over by their teammate. As though Simon Short had been waiting for them to appear - warming up for some gossip.

"Good morning, Mr Short." Harcourt's loud voice stops him in his tracks. He had pretended not to have noticed them, but years of surveillance confirm that the furtive little backward glances are not borne out of any kind of surprise. "Had you been waiting long?" He knows that it is provocative but big Steve's heart-rending sobs are still resident in his ears.

Whether it is the inference or simply being shouted at by a policeman in broad daylight, he scuttles across the road to join them. His head is burned red from the sun overhead and he is dressed incongruously in a bright pink flannelled shirt over beige slacks, looking rather like a matchstick that could spontaneously combust at any moment. "I hadn't been waiting for you or anybody else, Inspector. I assume citizens are still free to walk the streets of towns and villages up and down the country, providing that they are mobile of course."

Farren takes in the reedy voice and sickly smile; also, the way his lascivious eyes linger much too long on her breasts. "This is the second time we've bumped into each other like this."

"Hardly bumped!" His pupils dilate with lust.

"Were you wanting to talk to us about anything, sir?" Harcourt wants to scream out loud for them both.

"Not unless you have any updates on the village murders. I saw you heading up to poor Mrs Wilkins's house earlier. This must be such a difficult time for her."

There it is! The lack of genuine empathy and ignorance of others' feelings makes Harcourt's mind up for him before he even realises it himself. "It is and I would suggest you keep well away from her. I should remind you that idle tittle-tattle is rarely helpful."

"Oh, I don't know about that!" Again, he stares at Farren's chest, making little effort to disguise the object, not the subject, of his attention. "I find that comments made in less guarded moments to often be the most telling. Your colleague from the newspaper seemed much more receptive to my witness statement."

"'Witness statement?' What statement would that be, exactly?"

"Exactly? Well, she asked me if I'd seen anything unusual lately or, more particularly, anyone out of the ordinary – different – hanging around. The kinds of questions I assumed you might be asking of all residents: perhaps you haven't got around to that part of your investigation yet?"

Harcourt bridles at the man's sarcasm while Farren picks up the reins. "If you have something useful to tell us which might be pertinent to our enquiries, please do so."

"Pert eh!" He licks his dry lips leaving a line of spittle just below his nose. "Let's just say that the other lady was – and I mean no disrespect – very attractive as well as very interested."

"While obstructing us could easily be construed as perverting the course of justice. I thought I'd made that perfectly clear." Harcourt's bellow makes them both jump.

"There's no need to take that tone with me, Inspector. I might have to take it up with your superiors. I do still have plenty of old contacts in the force."

"You'll soon be making some new ones who'll be happy to throw away the keys unless you stop wasting our time. And it's Chief Inspector."

The smaller man's face becomes serious, hard even. "Did

you ever see *The Green Mile*? No, I don't suppose you did. I'd commend it to you though. You'd recognise the brutality if not the guilt… I did see somebody untoward close to Joe Wilkins's shop on the day of the latest murder. Pretty tall, dressed in a black hoodie thing and some kind of dark trousers. Work trousers I presumed."

Farren notes the way he practically spits out the word 'work.' More spittle. "At what time was this, roughly?"

"It was at eleven fifty two precisely." He smiles with satisfaction. His eyes locked onto hers now, which makes her feel almost as uncomfortable.

"You were 'just passing' I assume." Harcourt isn't having it.

"Only because the butcher's shop was closed you see. I had to make do with fish cakes."

"Was it a male or female?" Harcourt again.

"Oh, I didn't hang around long enough to ascertain which sex they identified with, Inspector. The hood was up so I didn't catch sight of the person's face."

"But your gut reaction?"

"Empty." He holds his hands up in mock surrender. "It was lunchtime, and I was getting hungry."

***

"Tell uniform I want them to add his address to their regular patrols around the village." Harcourt has been bitten by an even smaller but no less annoying creature on the way back to their car. He scratches at the pink welt on his forearm.

"Do you think he knows more than he's telling us?"

Farren feels mentally and physically exhausted as she pulls the seatbelt on.

"No. I don't. I think he'd like us to think so, just as all village gossips do."

"You don't think there's anything in the fact that he always seems to be on the edge of a crime scene?"

"I think that was probably always the case. He probably had an office next door to colleagues who were called out all the time to represent their clients in criminal cases while he had to concentrate on retrospective planning permission for rogue conservatories."

"See-through, you mean?"

Harcourt smiles fleetingly. "That and listening in to actual conversations while letting his overactive imagination fill in the blanks."

"I'll circulate the description."

"Thanks. We'll keep an eye on him although I don't see him as a person of interest. I'd go as far as to say that he isn't nearly as interesting as he perhaps wishes he was."

"Lonely?"

He nods. "Especially now that his only film buddy has left the scene."

***

Taylor kills the second call from Harcourt in the last five minutes and relays news of their latest encounter with Simon Short.

"We can ask Hazel about him too. "Flowers pulls up at the traffic lights just beyond Pershore's Civic Centre. "Maybe she saw him loitering outside Brenda's house as well as Kathleen's. She seems to be the only family member who ever visited regularly."

"Linda said he made her skin crawl - again." Taylor pulls her jacket around her protectively.

"'Caveman just drew what they could see:

The world beyond a fantasy…'"

"Is that from a song?"

"Just poetry."

"You couldn't make it up."

"No. I just did. Really!"

She laughs out loud, feeling better if not necessarily enriched. "You didn't go for your Inspector's then?"

He engages gear as the lights switch to green. "I do want to progress – like everybody else." His eyes are firmly on the road ahead. "It's just that, with Rob and everything, I didn't think the timing was right. I only passed my Sergeant's exam a year ago and that felt too soon at the time as well."

"Is it ever the right time though?" Taylor is gentle, aware of everything her colleague (and probably her best mate) has been through. Sometimes though he needs a push – just a little one but a push, nevertheless.

"Probably not." He indicates left and heads back into the housing estate they left just a few days earlier. "Mum is OK, but I don't need the extra pressure right now. Late nights and all that. One day I'll come home to find that she's gone away. I hope that's not for a long time yet, but you never know, do you?"

Taylor pats his arm and then holds on to it before looking across at him. "I don't know what she'd have done without you over these last few months."

"And I don't know what I would have done without you." He watches her blush as she gently removes her hand. "All of you." He adds.

Hazel opens the door to them. Taylor has forgotten just how vivid her copper-coloured hair is, especially above the plain white T-shirt and light blue jeans she is wearing.

"Dad's at work, I'm afraid." She smiles brightly at each in turn. "You're welcome to come in though."

"If that's alright?" Taylor grins back.

"Course." They head back into the living room just to the left of the front door.

"Would you like a drink?"

Both shake their heads. Flowers confirms with an even bigger grin. "Thanks, but we got a sneaky McDonalds on the way over!"

"I see." Hazel sits down on the chair opposite the two of them, folding her legs beneath her. Not great for the salt intake though!"

She must be all of five feet five tall thinks Flowers who has taken the other sofa alongside Taylor. "I didn't realise..." he begins.

"It's fine." Hazel is laughing. "I love their nuggets. So does Dad although he always pretends that he doesn't. We do eat pretty healthily, to be fair. Lots of veggies and fruit."

Taylor notices that the fruit bowl is piled high with bananas, large, red apples, and a couple of pears. She's pretty sure there were bananas last time too – so these green ones must be replacements.

"Thanks for agreeing to see us today, Hazel. Is it tomorrow?"

She nods, still smiling. "It is. The weeks seem to have each taken months this summer like they put the clocks forward but that just slowed everything down."

"Do you think you'll have done alright?" Flowers is hugely impressed with how articulate she is. Then again, why wouldn't she be – even at that age?

"I think so. You can never be sure until you've got that piece of paper in your hand though, can you? Even an email attachment can be Photoshopped."

Flowers considers how product names have so quickly and easily become verbs for, if not his, then certainly the generation below him. He'd have to mention it to Daniel Reed when he sees him next; he's bound to have a view on it.

"We just wanted to have a few words about your grandmother's house in Bishop's Lacy. I think you spent a good deal of time there?" Taylor watches Hazel as she crosses her legs now, completely relaxed and at ease with them.

"Not as much as I would have liked."

"The coursework?"

"Yes, but I often took my stuff over there and had my books out all over Nan's dining table. She never actually ate in there, so it didn't matter. It was more to do with the fact that Dad couldn't always take me, and the buses are a bit of a faff. I know that's as bad an excuse as the dog eating them, but I literally couldn't get back sometimes. It was fine if I was going to stay overnight."

"Did you do that often?"

"I did at weekends. Usually, the Friday and sometimes the Saturday as well. When things got a bit tough at home Nan gave me a house key. She said I could go over there and stay at any time. I didn't need to phone her or anything first, I could just turn up and she'd take care of me. Said I could stay for as long as I liked."

"That must have been nice – just knowing that she was there?"

"It was. She understood me and I loved her so much. I'd rather have known that Mum was there for me to be honest though. All she ever seemed to do was get angry with Dad."

"I guess you were out in the garden quite a bit – especially on a day like this?" Taylor is gradually getting to it and doesn't want to stray off course.

She nods, her young eyes recalling (reliving) afternoons of rough and tumble with Grandad and helping Nan water the many pots and troughs all around the edges of a lawn that always seemed to be cut short – just for her to play on. "Nan loved her garden. She was always out there. Grandad built me the little house to play in when I was a child so that I could be with her, even when it rained. Whatever I wanted it to be that day – a hotel or restaurant – Nan would always be my most important customer. She once asked me for a room with a bidet. That did throw me a bit - I was only about eight!"

They all laugh, Taylor and Flowers politely, Hazel reflectively as she looks beyond the house opposite in both time and space.

"Your Nan used it latterly to store pots and other garden equipment." Taylor wants to be tender, but they do need to know what Hazel had been doing in there. "I guess you would have helped her with the gardening too?"

Hazel shrugs. "Not really. Miss Hodges from next door did. As I told you before, she used to do lots of things for Nan by then, lifting heavy stuff and so on. Nan and I never stopped calling it the 'little house' though. We shared all our secrets in there."

Flowers interest is piqued by that. "It was a special place."

"It was, still is even though Nan can't come to the door now. When she was in the hospital, just before she died, she told me to go and look for something in the little house. I suppose it's just a shed now, isn't it?"

"It will always be special; nothing and nobody can take that away from you." Taylor leans forward. "What was it Hazel - the thing she'd hidden in there - did she say?"

"No, but she kept going on about it. She said the others would never find it in there, only me."

"You went over there, to look for it?" Taylor is slotting the pieces together.

"Yes, one evening, but I didn't find anything. I did see a big man just beyond the gate when I left. He turned away from me though, as if he didn't want me to see him, almost like he was trying to hide."

Taylor remembers the conversation she has just had with Harcourt. "Can you remember what he was wearing?"

"I couldn't be certain of the colour, but it was a sort of summer jacket – either white or cream."

"Not a hoodie then?"

Hazel laughs at the apparent absurdity of the question.

"No, not at all. It would have looked very strange on a man of his size. Extra, extra-large at least."

"But you can't think of anything that your grandmother might have been hiding for you?" Flowers recognises the cul-de-sac they had wandered into.

"No. Nothing. I didn't find anything so I can only assume that Nan wasn't thinking right by then. They had given her a lot of drugs and she was sweating ever so much. The doctor told me they were having a lot of trouble keeping her temperature down."

Delirious or determined, Taylor wonders but not out loud.

***

"That's brilliant news!" Daniel half skips, half runs across the room to throw his arms around his daughter who has quite understandably been crying tears of joy.

"I got the email and the school link but waited for the post to arrive. I knew it was silly – unnecessary – but I just wanted to have the piece of paper in my hand. It was Nigel and he was late as usual. You know how he loves to chat. Apparently, old Mrs Bryan was concerned about her chickens. Couldn't find any of them anywhere. She thought the fox had got in again then remembered that she'd sold the last one to Peter at the farm at the weekend."

"Poor woman. But she and he got there in the end!"

"I practically tore the sheet in half opening the envelope."

Daniel releases her from the bear hug and holds her at arm's length. He gazes at her happily; pride and joy personified.

"Have you told Mum?"

"Of course. As soon as I read the form and checked the grades, well, after reading it several times I went straight up to tell her."

"How was she?"

"I think she smiled but it's like with a baby isn't it: it could just have been a bit of wind."

"It will have been a smile." Daniel is far from convinced either. "She will have been as thrilled as I am. Did she say anything to you later?"

Claire shakes her head sadly. "No, but she's been asleep for most of the morning."

"I'm sorry I wasn't here when you got the news. The police called me first thing and asked me to head over there to see if I could help with the Joe Wilkins's murder (the butcher in Bishop's Lacy). I was only in there for a little before we were interrupted by some senior officers arriving from Birmingham. I've got to go back in the morning."

"Were you able to help?"

"Not yet and not sure if I'll be able to. You know how it works – or doesn't. I got the impression that they're really up against it now. Anyway, enough doom and gloom, this is your day. Have you contacted York yet; confirmed your acceptance?"

"Not yet." She sits down opposite her father. "I wanted to talk to you first."

"Go on." An alarm bell rings at the back of his head, barely audible at first but becoming louder as the seconds tick by without him being able to switch it off.

His lovely, clever daughter has started to cry, and he realises now that joy was far from the only source of the tears earlier.

"I'm just a bit mixed up!"

"About York or Worcester? Honestly, Claire, York runs the better course, doesn't it? You told me that when you made it your first choice."

"I know I did, and it is. It's just that Mum was different then. Not different exactly, more the same: like she used to be. Quieter, but still Mum."

"She's still Mum, darling. She would want you to do the best thing for you. She'd probably have had you on the phone as soon as you got the email!"

Claire laughs and wipes her face with yet another tissue. "I know she would. I know that. I wish I knew..."

"How long she's going to be with us?" Daniel is less bullish now, the void in their lives – including Charlotte's – suddenly impossible to get past, jump over or try to pretend out of existence.

"I don't know how long I have left with her and the thought of deliberately walking out of this house, knowing that she's lying there so quietly upstairs..."

"You're overthinking it." He leans towards her and takes her hand, just as he did on that first day of primary school. She grips his fingers now as she did then. "I do understand that fear of the unknown but what have we always said?"

"We're never alone!"

"That's it. Besides, you've got six or seven weeks or so before you physically go. Enjoy being with Mum until then. That's all you can do, and that counts for both of us. The staff at the hospice said that there's no rush unless she starts getting distressed again." He feels slightly guilty at the thought that Charlotte would be unlikely to understand the situation now, either way. He wants to hold on to the idea that she'd back his judgement in encouraging Claire to go away as planned. Except she hadn't had the same choice. None of it was planned and yet she's still going away.

"What will you do though?" Claire has seen the dark cloud slowly crossing his face. Does she technically need to go to university to understand body language better? "I hate the thought of leaving you alone with Mum or... all on your own."

"But I wouldn't be. As we just agreed."

"If I went to Worcester, it would solve the problem."

"There is no problem, only an opportunity for you to learn from the best and show the rest of the world the best that you can be. I'm so proud of you. We both are."

"Not nearly as proud as I am of you, Dad."

***

'The results were even better than I'd hoped for. I did worry about History with that trick question about appeasement in the 1930s – a good job Mrs Hesketh warned us about that one. If Mr Chamberlain had her as a teacher, world history might have taken a very different course!

English was the main one. If I hadn't got an 'A' in that I'd have been disappointed, especially as I thought my Jane Austen essay was one of the best I'd ever written. Not sure that means anything though – not in the overall context of the thousands of essays that must have been written about her work. I'm just a poor schoolgirl living in a town that's seen better days, aren't I? Still, if Bridget Jones was right, there's a Mr Darcy out there for all of us!

It's all just fiction, isn't it; you make-believe as soon as you're able to suspend the reality of your own situation, however good or bad it really is?"

Dad's still not back so I haven't been able to tell him yet. I know he'll be pleased that I've chosen to stay here, although my grades would certainly be good enough to get me in. I don't know how he'd cope on his own with little or no family around him.'

***

"You mustn't get so worked up." Debbie is holding on to her husband having coaxed him back into bed, away from the window and an escape which isn't what it seemed. "You've been dreaming again. That's the third time you've woken up in the middle of the night this week."

"I'm so sorry. I truly am. "Harcourt pulls the quilt away from his legs. He is sweating even more than usual and this has been going on for seemingly days now. The bedroom smells of damp sweat despite both windows being wide open. It's getting lighter but even the birds haven't realised this quite yet. "I didn't mean to wake you. Go back to sleep; I'm sure I'll be able to get off again soon."

"Your heart is thumping in your chest. "Debbie places a wonderfully cool palm against his skin. "Remember what the doctor told you before. You've got to be careful. Was it that dream again?"

"The river? No, not this time. I can't remember what was going on, other than that the window was a trapdoor, and I couldn't work out whether it was a trap or not."

"I wish I could help you to let it go – at least here at home."

"I know." He pats her shoulder in acknowledgement that she is concerned about him, trying her best to look after him while the evils of the world outside keep trying to break in. "It's just that we have three deaths – two of them unequivocally murders – and not a shred of evidence to connect anyone to them, or even the two deaths to each other. We have possible motives for several characters, but they've then been cancelled out by perfectly believable alibis in every circumstance we've examined."

"There must be something (or someone) you've overlooked."

"Honestly, these cases seem – feel - more like those dreams when every road you take is blocked."

"No, that'll be Worcestershire County Council having far too much budget left for 'essential' road repairs as usual."

"And far too many bollards!" He knows that she is smiling in the darkness, even if he can't quite manage it.

"You'll have even less chance of working things out if you're tired before you even start!"

"I know that too. So do the new guys they've drafted in. Each of them determined to make their mark while I'm pensioned off to cold cases."

"If it's any help at all, you're certainly not cold at the

moment! Probably much warmer than you think."

CHAPTER TWELVE

Daniel sees before he can hear that Harcourt is on the phone in his office. DS Flowers is sitting at his desk, but the floor is otherwise empty.

"Good morning, Mr Reed, how are you?" Flowers wheels round to face him.

Daniel takes one of the nearby chairs and sits down, similarly rotating. They are like cogs in a watch's mechanism he thinks, heading in different directions at different speeds perhaps, but coming together often. He refuses to consider which of them may be moving the fastest; equally whether moving in circles is pleasantly reassuring or frustratingly set in time.

"I'm well, thank you. You?"

Harcourt waves in acknowledgement of his arrival but seems to be in the middle of a deep conversation which Daniel is keen not to interrupt. He can wait.

Flowers also looks in his superior's direction, then lowers his voice. He moves his chair closer to Daniel's, slowly but deliberately. "It looks like the boss is going to want me to join him in the new Cold Case Unit."

"That's good news, isn't it?" Daniel isn't sure or not whether this represents a quiet cul-de-sac which would suit Harcourt more than younger officers who might have preferred to stay in the fast lane of policing.

"It is in the sense that we work well together. It's nice to be wanted, isn't it?"

"It certainly is." Daniel isn't convinced that he's been told the whole story yet, so he says nothing more for now.

Sure enough, Flowers continues, unabated. "I'm just not sure it's what I should be doing."

"Should or want. They're very different things."

"I'm not sure that I should be heading in this direction at this stage in my career, but part of me enjoys the backtracking and uncovering of mysteries that others have given up on. Like the Julie Beech case for example."

"OK. So would that be enough to make you want to move over or do you feel you still need something more challenging?"

"I probably would have felt that only the DCI has told me I have to actively work towards my Inspector's exam even if I do join him."

"So, you'd still have that challenge and would feel as though you were still moving forward."

"I would, yes. I think that would be enough. I'm not cut out to be a highflyer. It's probably a weakness but I'm too much of a family man for that."

"It isn't a weakness, and you can never be too much of a family man." Daniel sees Harcourt hang up and rise from his desk.

"DS Farren has passed hers." Flowers half-whispers. "She'll be staying with Major Crimes but with a new team."

Daniel hasn't mentioned Farren's insecurities to anyone

else. Farren obviously hasn't spoken to him about them either. Nevertheless, he senses that uncertainty each time he meets up with her, even if her colleagues and suspects do not. Perhaps one day he would see where they came from, and why they continue to drive her in the peculiarly aggressive way that they do. "Will Taylor stay with her?" Daniel considers that to be an unlikely if not ultimately unworkable prospect.

"Not sure! She's still deciding but I'm working on it." The younger man grins as he rolls back and around to face Harcourt who is fast approaching them.

"I'm so sorry, Daniel."

"Not a problem. You're a bit light in here this morning – apart from DS Flowers of course. Quality if not quantity!"

The other two men beam at him. "They're in Bishop's Lacy with our new colleagues."

"New colleagues?" Daniel looks to Flowers for a clue, but none are forthcoming.

"Just temporary," Harcourt responds a little too quickly. They've been sent down to help or 'facilitate a faster solution' as the official line goes.

"Aha. No pressure then!" Daniel stands and follows Harcourt who is heading back towards his office. As he passes Flowers's desk, he spots what looks, inconceivably, like a jar of honey.

"Sweetener, Ian?"

"Sorry? Oh, no, a recent interviewee brought it in for me. I was going to declare it as a 'gift' but the boss said he would cover it.

"I bet. Especially if a nice rustic loaf was also involved. May I?"

Farren passes it to him. Daniel has barely turned the jar around to examine the label when he spots a tall man right in front of him. Except that there is nobody else there apart from the three of them.

"What is it, Daniel?" Harcourt has himself turned around to see why his friend has stopped following him. He notices the faraway look in his eyes – a look he has seen a few times before.

"There's a tall figure directly in front of me," Daniel whispers, taking note of the look of concern on Flower's face who has double-checked that nobody else is present. "They're wearing a dark black diving suit and have what looks like a long butcher's knife in their right hand."

***

Suzanne Wilkins parks her Vauxhall Corsa on the empty drive outside her house. Fred has already left, thankfully. She vaguely remembers him muttering something about a morning meeting. She stopped bothering to concentrate a long time ago – when work and pleasure became so entangled in his sad little life.

She enters the house, heading for the kitchen, only the hum of the dishwasher acknowledging her presence. She flicks the switch on the kettle and places her latest collection of book purchases on the counter next to it. She has always dreamed of travelling to some of the far-flung places in the novels she reads. Perhaps now she can start to plan rather than just daydream; look forward rather than sideways - and maybe not alone either?

That busybody neighbour of Brenda's has been dealt with. Far too influential she'd become. Once she'd started mouthing off about an alternative will, that was it. Something needed to be done and something was done.

Her brother-in-law had been a different matter. Quietly keeping his secrets while allowing his wife to treat him in such a shoddy way. Suzanne is genuinely surprised that he let it go on for as long as he did. As for an outward show of still caring for Pat, where on earth did that come from? Never mind. All's well that ends well.

If men took control of their lives as she has done: sat down and properly planned what they needed to do to earn their freedom – real and lasting freedom - they would be sitting as pretty as she is now. Men aren't always the heroes. Readers might be led to believe in the beginning that this is going to be the case, but the evidence can subsequently prove otherwise.

Tea or coffee? Earl Grey or ordinary? Whatever choices she makes now, her 'cup runneth over.'

***

"Charles Band didn't turn up for work today," Harcourt shouts into his mobile as he and Flowers race down the stairs of the police station. "They say it's never happened before. I've got cars heading for Pat Band's house and out to the Fred Wilkins's property. If the remaining family members are being picked off one by one, then Charles could be a potential victim too.

Response officers are on alert for any sighting, initially in a radius of ten miles from Pershore. We're heading down there now to offer our support. The diving suit explains why we've never found any of the murderer's

DNA at the crime scenes. We have potential motives but absolutely no evidence that would stand up in court, so we'll need a confession. Sorry? Yes, I do believe in what Daniel saw. Hunter-Wright still believes in him as well. He signed off on the budget so if this does turn out to be a wild goose chase, I'll most likely be in cold storage myself rather than merely investigating cold cases."

He ends the call as Flowers draws up in the car. "There's a problem at Sneachill, sir, so I suggest we take the 4084 past Norton – where the new railway station's going to be."

"That's fine, Ian, but you'll need to put your foot down. That back road is quite bendy. Use the lights if necessary."

Flowers heads for Worcester's one-way system, glad to be on the move at last. They both are.

"DS Farren is doing her nut!" Harcourt holds the side of the car as Flowers cuts inside a van indicating right. "She always wants to be at the heart of the action."

"I think we all do, sir." Flowers isn't sure if it was meant as a personal slight or not. "If we wanted to be office-based we'd have gone into administration."

"Metaphorically or literally?" Harcourt laughs out loud, momentarily relieving the tension he can feel in his pounding chest.

Similarly relieved and pleased to see the traffic thinning as they pass the cathedral on their right, Flowers continues. "Where does Camilla Wilkins stand in all of this, sir – now that her husband is dead, I mean."

"Concerning the will?" Harcourt is glad, for now, to be able to focus on something slightly tangential to their immediate situation. “Brenda only listed her children as beneficiaries. No other names were included, which is why Hazel misses out. She would only inherit via Pat if she in turn left everything to her only daughter.”

“I can’t see that there’s anyone else she’d want to inherit. She and Charles are barely on speaking terms.”

“Indeed, and Pat herself still has to survive for two more days. If she is a target and dies before then, any inheritance she would have had from Brenda’s estate is null and void.”

Flowers beeps at a slow-moving jeep at the Larkhill lights. The driver promptly looks up into their rear-view mirror and waves.

“OK. Hit the siren!” Harcourt hasn’t got time for this.

As the siren sounds and the lights begin to flash, the jeep pulls over sharply onto the pavement on the left and Flowers shoots past it. Harcourt turns in his seat as they pass the driver – a small man with bottle glasses who even now is trying to hide under the steering wheel – and waves back, nicely. He then clutches the side pocket as Flowers blasts up Red Hill. Perhaps this is not the time to mention that it got its name through being a place of execution.

“Sorry to keep going on about it, sir, but does that mean that Camilla gets nothing from Brenda’s will, Joe having died before probate goes through?”

It does.” Harcourt is hanging on to the front fascia as they fly over the M5 flyover. “Even if Joe had made a will leaving everything to her, which seems unlikely.”

“So even if Joe and Steve Baker had been formally married, Steve would have missed out too?”

"He would. Joe's share now goes back into the pot, leaving Fred with a much bigger pot. Bigger still if Pat were to die."

"Although Pat would inherit all of it if she did survive and anything now happened to Fred! Suzanne would be like Camilla is now – empty-handed – as far as the family inheritance is concerned."

"She would, although if things play out as we expect them to, Fred and Camilla will become a public item so Camilla won't miss out apart from losing her husband which I'm sure Fred will help her to get over. She would probably get the butcher's shop too as next of kin unless Joe had made some other arrangement we don't know about."

"And Suzanne will get a generous payoff from her husband - even more than she had planned. That's if Fred was telling us the truth about his intentions of course."

"All other things being equal, which they rarely are. Just ask Steve Baker."

***

Hazel's eyes had been drawn immediately to the flashing red light in the corner of the room when she'd come down earlier. She'd had the best sleep for ages, probably because she'd been worried about the exam results for the last few days, at least subconsciously when the natural guards of denial were down.

She heads into the kitchen first. The cereal bowl is sitting patiently in its usual place. She never starts a day without her Weetabix. A spoon sits beside it, watching her; waiting.

Hazel lifts the electric kettle from its cordless cradle and notices that its body is cold. Puzzled, she glances over at the washing-up rack next to the sink. There is neither a recently washed bowl nor a plate there. Even if her father hadn't had time for cereal, he would always have had a slice of toast before leaving the house.

Concerned now at this break in their morning routine, she rushes out of the kitchen and up the stairs. The door to his room is open and his bed is made. She creeps over towards it (she couldn't explain to herself later why she'd crept in, almost furtively, despite there clearly being nobody else present). Slipping her hand below the duvet, the bed is also stone cold. Surely a warm patch would have lasted longer?

Despite the sunshine pouring through the window, Hazel shivers. She heads back down the stairs, much more slowly this time. Perhaps she is already resigned to the words which will seal her fate, although she doesn't know yet what they will say or what her immediate future now looks like. She just senses a shift in the air – in all of the elements that have made her what she is, up until this moment.

***

The streaks of sunlight on the hills below him have gone now. The purples and oranges in the early morning clouds, informing a world no longer sleeping that it is, indeed, a brand-new day, have faded in the bright light that has replaced them. That light, which is sent to warm them and help them to see more clearly. How ironic that it simultaneously washes away the small details of life itself.

'The bigger picture' everyone calls it nowadays. What

has happened to the vignettes that evoke the smaller of life's episodes, no less significant and no less real? He remembers his father hugging his mother in the hallway before leaving them; before his mother did too. Nobody else will be able to describe that scene, even know that it took place. No 'family history' project will capture those tiny moments like the camera in his head does.

Sheep are bleating down in the valley, close to the ribbon of water that is the River Avon. He grins helplessly at the fate of the leg of one of their forebears – in a different field somewhere between here and Bishop's Lacy. These are the survivors who will gladly greet the cold air that is surely coming, before longing for the warmth of a mother's love.

He suddenly picks up the smell of manure – organic waste – but, honestly, it has been a long time coming. He raises himself from the Cotswold Edge, running as far into the distance as he can see. Along with the skylarks chirping high in the sky above (almost impossible to see individually but undeniably there), he surveys the steep drop beyond the ancient stone wall.

Voices assault him from the east. He recognises the police officer who visited them. A local man. Somebody who understood what it was to be present in nature without the need for human intervention.

He watches too as an older man scrambles up the hill behind him, red in the face and puffing heavily. It's now or never. Whatever happens, it's over.

***

The scream shatters the silence, before a torrent of tears floods downwards, like a dam that has been burst by some unexpected force.

Hazel picks up a pen and pad they keep (kept) on the work surface for recording the weekly Tesco list, as though she is going to take notes where each of the letters might form different words, a first impression magically corrected. She presses the Rewind button and then Play again. A familiar voice fills the room as it has done each day until now.

'Hello Hazel

I was hoping to talk to you but perhaps this is the coward's way out for the person you had always thought of as such a hero. I know those new tapes only last about a minute and a half so I'd best get on.

I realise that this is all going to come as a great shock to you but please believe me if I could have saved you from it, I would have. I have always tried to do my best to look after you – to provide for you - but this time my best has not been good enough. Not been 'good' at all.

After my father died, all those miles away and all those years ago, I didn't know what to do, what to say. I think you may be feeling much the same now. Let me just say that you will get over it, just as I did.

I am so proud of your school achievements. I did want you to know that first. I always said that you were much cleverer than me (I failed my A-levels at what was then just Pershore Comprehensive). I'm sure Mum will be proud of you too.

At least you had a nicer school life than I did. The powers that be might have decided that Hail the Redeemer is outstanding now, but it wasn't when I was little. They all turned a blind eye to the violence that took place; prayed that it wasn't happening.

One day I'd had enough. The gang came out from behind the bicycle sheds as usual, but I was prepared for them. I had my compass divider in my blazer pocket and stabbed one of them in the arm. That was enough for him, for all of them. It was in the wintertime, and I was wearing gloves, so handling the instrument made things a bit awkward. I was going for his eye but missed it. That sounds about right! It did give me the idea years later though.

My mother married another man. He could never have filled the gap left by Dad, but he didn't even try. As soon as I left school, they left me. Set up house elsewhere. Didn't ask if I wanted to go with them. Didn't even leave a forwarding address, just had the post redirected by the Post Office.

My dole money kept me going for a little while. I didn't know who was paying the house bills, but it wasn't me. Then, one day, a man stuck a 'For Sale' sign outside. I told him he must have got the wrong house, but he was adamant. He also informed me that they'd be bringing people round to look at it and I'd best make myself scarce.

I only really went back there to sleep after that, before a friend at work offered me a room in his house. It was really small but they needed someone to help with the rent and I was effectively a beggar by then, wasn't I?

As you know, I'd worked with Mum in Worcester for a while then met up with her again later, at Foregate Station when she was on her way back to Wales. The best chance meeting I ever had. I've never stopped loving your mum; I just couldn't live with her anymore. That night, when she took the money I'd saved up for our tea (to feed her disgusting habit) was the last straw for me. But that didn't stop me from caring about her. Like that nice copper said when he came round to the house: 'The first rule of policing is to never blame the victim.'

It's just that money got so tight, and I wanted you to be able to go to university, like your friends; just in case you changed your mind about going. I had no way of providing that for you so, as I said earlier, I completely failed you.

All I ever wanted was a quiet, family life. Mine was ripped apart by first a missile and then a mother who didn't want to care for me. Couldn't have cared less about me. I couldn't believe how your uncles behaved when Nan died. Whatever happened to family unity? It was just a fiction I'm afraid. I needed to send them a message from real life.

First, that Kathleen woman started talking about a different will. At least you might have inherited something from your mum one day. Far too late for university I know, but surely better than nothing. I couldn't have some busybody – somebody from outside - taking that possibility away from you, from our little family. Dragging her backwards with the garden twine from the shed was easy enough. I stabbed her three times in the heart – just to be sure I'd stopped her. One for each of the children she was trying to disinherit by being heartless.

I had my wire cutters with me of course, so cut and re-used a piece of line from the gnome's rod and put the knife in its place. I was trying to throw suspicion onto your Uncle Joe, even though I knew at the time it was much too clumsy. What's the phrase – 'not fit for purpose?' What I did want to do was close down any conversations about there being an alternative will. To be fair, I never did hear anything else about it. Maybe Nan was just trying to be nice to you while having Uncle Fred's greedy voice in her head?

Once Uncle Joe started talking about Mum's money going into a trust fund, I knew that I had to do something about it. I hoped that Uncle Fred might sort him out but, of course, he didn't. All mouth and no action that one. If Nan was serious about you having some of her money, I wasn't going to have you waiting any longer for it than necessary. I thought if your mum inherited it, she might have given you a share. I'd like to think, even now, that she would do exactly that.

I went over there with a big screwdriver in my bag. You know, the one we used to re-direct those IKEA screws on the wardrobe that time? I didn't need it in the end. Joe had been cutting up a lamb, so I picked up a leg and hit him over the head with it in the back room. I don't know where he was when I arrived, but I was able to hide in the back behind the main freezer, waiting for my chance.

He wouldn't have realised it was me as he didn't even have time to turn around. I wore the diving suit I sometimes use for work. I thought that I would get away with it if there was no DNA left behind – just like when I wore those gloves in the playground. I probably would have done but I would never have got away from myself, would I? All those quiet moments with your father: a murderer.

I don't know where they'll send me, but I don't want you to think that you have to visit me. Not there, not like that. I never saw my mother or father again. Your Granny Band didn't die though, not like I told you. Your mum has always known the truth, but I couldn't bring myself to tell you, even after Nan died. I don't know if she's still alive or not. I've never heard from her but that doesn't mean anything. Perhaps you could try and find her through records and so on. What I do know is the grandmother that you did know loved you more than all her children put together. You never left her, not like they did.

I must go now before the machine cuts out. Remember how much I love you, just as my father never stopped loving me.

Bye-bye'

***

"But he left you everything else!" Fred Wilkins is pacing up and down across the Karndean floor of his sunlit lounge. "Even if we can't argue that Joe's own will leaving his share of his mother's inheritance should pass down to you, it will just go back into the pot and that part of it will come to me – us - assuming Pat survives until tomorrow and the probate process eventually comes to an end!"

He'd intended the last sentence to lighten the mood a little, but Camilla Wilkins isn't so easily appeased. "It's not that I wanted the shop, but it had been passed down through the family. I can't understand why you're not more upset about that."

"Dad left it to Joe. He was always going to leave it to his eldest son. That's when any attachment I had to it ended." He turns his back on her as he has tried so hard to turn his back on each of the others, on a past he takes no pleasure from.

He can hear her blowing her nose. "I'm not even sure that Steve will want it either. Every time he steps foot in there he'll be thinking of Joe."

"That's up to him, isn't it? Maybe they talked about it."

"He didn't talk to me! I didn't even know he'd made a will. He never told me."

"Not the sort of thing you talk about really, though, is it?"

"Have you made one?"

He turns back towards her. "Of course not." He lies easily, pretending to be affronted by her even asking the question. "Why would I? I've got years ahead of me yet unless I get worn out earlier of course…"

She picks up on the inference but hasn't time for any of that now. It's always been far more important to him than her. "There's more to life than sex, you know!"

"If it wasn't for sex there'd be no life…"

She hears the glib comment as if it had come from an audiobook, just before this character – the loser, leering at her now – met with an unfortunate death. On that note, she continues, sullenly. "Perhaps we could make a joint will, once Suzanne is out of the way?"

"She's already gone."

"What do you mean?"

"Cleared out. Clothes, perfume, the lot."

"Did she say anything to you before she left?"

"She said her solicitor would be in touch about the money."

"Anything else?"

"That she'd be back for her books."

***

"What will happen to Charles Band now, sir." Flowers is driving them back to Worcester, far more slowly than when heading in the opposite direction earlier.

"He'll confess to at least one, probably both murders. We have absolutely nobody else in the frame for either and still no hard evidence so let's hope that happens."

"And if he was responsible for just one or the other?"

"Then we're back to square one – two, at most. I don't think that will be the case though. Brenda Wilkins's will ties all of this together. I think it probably always did."

"What if he doesn't confess – to either I mean."

"He will. He didn't argue with us taking him in, did he? If somebody didn't want to be found they'd make it as difficult as possible for us. In some circumstances, they'd have made it impossible. He parked his car in a public car park in Chipping Bumstead. Not exactly undercover, is it? You'll find that the tyres are an exact match for those we found in that lean-to behind Kathleen's house in Bishop's Lacy."

"Do you think he planned to kill himself?"

"I think he may have thought about it. I think he may often have thought about it. The only reason I can think of for him not attempting to do so would have been the thought of never seeing his daughter again. At least he can carry that hope forward, however slim it might be. When his father died, and then his mother left home he didn't even have that."

"He seemed such a nice man. Brought me that honey!"

"He probably is – most of the time. Psychopathic behaviour is incredibly hard to spot and yet it is in there. There are no standard signs to look out for, but charm is a characteristic we often find and also anti-social behaviour."

"I wouldn't have described him as anti-social, sir; quite the opposite."

"Not in that sense, no. We think of it being characterised by aggression, don't we, rather than the much more passive Charles Band you spent some time with? But think of the incident at school and also the fact that he appears to have no friends – or none that have ever been mentioned to us – only his family. His childhood experiences may have brought it to the surface once before but then it has lain hidden for many years until recent events provoked it."

"When we were in the hospital with Rob, I remember the nurses talking about another man who had been rushed into A&E with symptoms of meningitis. I didn't realise until then that it's a bacterium that lives in our throats. I certainly didn't know that most of us have it during our lives or that it can 'migrate' for some reasons the doctors aren't entirely sure about yet. It's similar though, isn't it? Lying dormant until aroused."

"It is. As for the honey, he would have wanted you to have it. He wouldn't have had a problem with the police per se; he wasn't playing games with us. We hadn't done anything to upset him so why would he?"

"It was all down to the dysfunctional family he'd married into?"

"Charles couldn't cope with people not doing the right thing; his mental state must have been severely put to the test when his marriage with Pat failed. All of this on top of it pushed him over the edge, especially when greed was involved. I don't think greed or duplicity were drivers he could ever really understand. What he did came from his interpretation of – his disappointment with – that family's actions. All of it through a narrow focus of wanting Hazel to have a fair crack of the whip. None of them was being fair to her."

Flowers brakes suddenly as a family of ducks decides to head in single file to the promised land of water and plenty on the other side of the carriageway. "Even Kathleen by suggesting that there was another will."

"Especially that. That was the trigger. I think he thought that she had wheedled her way into Brenda's affections and stood to take everything away from her family. Had they not acted in the way they did, both she and Joe would probably still have been alive today."

"I cannot even start to think how Hazel is going to react to her father being arrested?"

"Family Liaison are on the way over there. DS Taylor is on her way back too. I'm going to ask Daniel Reed if he'll meet and go with her in case she asks questions about how we came to suspect Charles in the first place."

***

Just over an hour later, and much to their surprise, the door is opened by Pat Band.

She nods at the two of them before standing to one side

and muttering at them to come in.

Hazel is sitting in the front room, much as before, in the single chair. She greets them warmly, although Taylor can see the shock etched in her young, pale face. She sits down on the floor beside her, holding the younger woman's hand.

Daniel immediately appreciates the connection they have. Taylor has told Daniel Reed on their way over to Pershore that she will be joining Flowers and Harcourt in the new Cold Case Unit, although she'd had to think long and hard about it.

One of the doubts in her mind was that she'd be less likely to be working with younger people like Hazel, helping them with past traumas such as this, and whether Family Liaison would have been better for her. Daniel had listened before replying that all families needed closure, however many years it takes. The age of innocence could last a lifetime if truth and honesty could not be found.

He looks through the window at the passers-by, on their way into town or returning home, laden with goods and promises.

"Thank you so much for coming." Her voice sounds older than he had expected, before turning back around, he sees Pat Band in the doorway. "I'll be off now. I'll call in again later, Hazel."

She doesn't move to get up, but he can see the appreciation on her face. When times are tough you just need your mum. Daniel accompanies the ravaged woman to the front door.

"She's strong. She'll be OK." Pat is trying to convince

herself as much as the man she has just met, as she struggles into a tatty coat which smells suspiciously of white spirit. "Stay with her a while, won't you?"

Daniel opens the door for her. "We will. Take care." He watches her amble off down the street, as do several young heads that have turned in her direction, smiling and nudging each other. Daniel cannot see what will happen to them. He doesn't have the energy, but he can guess that it won't amount to much.

He goes back into the house and sits next to Taylor, opposite Hazel.

"Hazel was telling me about her A-level results." Taylor is pleased to bring him into their conversation.

"I heard. Very well done!"

"Thank you. I believe your daughter – Claire is it – also got the grades she wanted."

"She did. Thanks." He wants to tell her how Claire is busily planning her future, although simultaneously conflicted with leaving her mother and him at home. He is much too sensitive to do so, something many of the writers of novels he proofreads simply do not get.

He looks over Hazel's head to the row of miniature houses on the shelf behind her. "Those look beautiful. May I?"

She nods, pleased at his interest, and stands to retrieve the nearest item from her collection. Taking it from her he marvels at the detail. It is heavier than he expected but also colder. He can't explain it easily. Something about the collection is missing but, after a quick survey of the cluster of houses, can't see what it might be: a pub perhaps, or a church?

"Is this the complete set?" He asks gently enough but a force is coursing through his veins.

"Are you alright, Daniel?" Taylor is concerned, as is his hostess.

"I'm fine. Just came over a little woozy, that's all. I just felt that there should be more heat, somehow: that the house would have been hotter."

Taylor seriously wonders if he has become delusional. Perhaps the stress over his wife's illness and his daughter's exam results has finally caused him to lose his mind – hopefully only momentarily.

Hazel does not think this. She knows exactly why he has asked the question. "There is another piece. I don't have it on show because…" Unable to say more she moves across to a small cupboard, almost out of view below the shelf – the sort of place where you hide junk that isn't quite good enough to have on display or that you're fed up with dusting.

Reaching in with her hand, she lifts out another piece in the same style as the others, yet much bigger. "I broke this one. It was Nan's favourite. She told me so just before she had her attack. It was the last time she visited. Simon Short brought her and Miss Hodges over for a ride."

"Go on, Hazel; in your own time." Taylor is encouraging while Daniel Reed's face is even more manic than it was a couple of minutes ago.

"After she'd gone, I was putting it back on the shelf when I dropped it." She bursts into tears again.

"It's alright, Hazel. It's going to be fine." Taylor's voice is consoling but neither of the other two appear to be comforted by it.

“The chimney broke off, see!” She turns the model around to show them where the chimney stack would have been, revealing a hole. They both gasp as they realise that the building she is holding is a replica of Joe’s butcher’s shop albeit with a little house attached.

As Taylor quickly moves across to cover Hazel with tissues and kindness, Daniel notices a sliver of white paper inside the main shop part of the model. He pulls it out gently to reveal two neatly folded single sheets, not stapled or joined by paperclips. Each is covered in typescript. He unfolds them carefully. The first begins:

‘I, Brenda Hazel Wilkins, being of sound mind and judgement...’

***

Meanwhile in Waterlow Park, just to the southeast of Highgate Village in north London, a slight, gentle soul contemplates what he will do for his birthday if anything. He’s in his thirties now and, although he has long ago resolved the need just to keep moving, some kind of destination would be nice. He smoothes the creases of his embroidered waistcoat as he watches the dark clouds rolling in overhead. It had been sunny earlier when he’d looked out of the first floor landing window of the local hotel where he works.

He is standing by the statue of Sir Sydney Waterlow who bequeathed the park to the public one hundred and thirty years ago as "a garden for the gardenless." He tells a lot of people about this gentleman but never mentions his father. He’s not even sure if he’s still alive. If he is, does he remember his only son? Has he ever come looking for him? Probably not. Policemen always find the truth of things in the end if they truly want to, don't they?

It's better this way. He bundles up his sandwich bag and pops this along with the empty orange bottle into the recycling bin. Better that they've each had to make new starts in life. Maybe one day it will be somebody else carrying his baggage... This is the journey he's on now. He's got to be heading somewhere. Right?

***

'I've had two weeks to think about it all. Not sure even that is long enough, to be honest. Perhaps you shouldn't mention that kind of time in a straight line; it's much more up and down and side to side.

The solicitor was on the phone this morning to confirm what he said in the meeting. It's going to take a little while for everything to go through – but it will. Nan did leave it all to me and so it's now up to me to sort things out.

I'm going to give a chunk of it to Mum so that she can finally become somebody else - get a new face - although I've made her promise that she won't ever forget that she's still my mum. I never really understood what made her the way she is, even though she's been a lot more open recently. I think she was very unhappy when she went away to college and needed someone or something to help her through it. She didn't find anybody.

That's why I don't want to go, not while I'm feeling so sad. Daniel Reed said that I could go at any time so maybe next year. He's been ever so nice to me. So has Gabby (only special people are allowed to call her that!). Daniel invited me to his house in Wood Lench so that

I could meet and chat with his daughter, Claire. I think we're going to be good friends and can't wait to go up to York one weekend soon. I might even have found someone to share my secrets with – finally! There's been nobody since Nan died, just this diary.

He also introduced me to Miss Shelbourne (Kate). What a lovely lady! I've taken her up on her offer and am going to be a trainee journalist. I can learn from her each day and the job will be flexible so that I am free to study the basics when I need to. So, I'm on my way and lots more words to come from me – hopefully!

Kate is going to help me find a flat in Evesham so that we can be closer to work. I think she's a bit lonely too, so that should work out well. She says I'll be able to afford to buy, but I think I'll carry on renting for now. Dad and I were very happy here and I'd rather buy something closer to him when we know where he's likely to be. That's the beauty of renting, isn't it? I know it might be money down the drain, but I don't have to pay for the drains if they get blocked.

Mr Harcourt keeps in touch and says there's a lot to do still. He let me go and see Dad. I would never have believed him capable of doing those things, especially after putting up with Mum's tantrums for all those years. He never fought back. I think that incident in the playground all those years ago frightened him – made him scared of what he was capable of. We all have our limits, don't we?

I know that he did it all for me which seems so tragic now we know that none of it was necessary. None of it ever was. Anyway, I shall write to him every week, just like his own Dad did. I've bought a new pen already. It's a bit more personal than just a text or an email I think.'

***

Christmas won't be long now, not if all those predictions in the shops and on the television come true. Daniel is sitting by the log burner, watching the flames as he's taken to doing in the dark evenings.

He has his laptop on his knee of course. He prefers to be downstairs these days rather than up in his study. It feels closer to her and there's nobody to interrupt him now. No noise. Nothing to listen out for. He might even bring his desk down and make the dining room his new workspace. He's not going to need it for meals – they rarely did – and the family card games they used to play on the dining table have been placed carefully back into their packs and stored in the kitchen cupboard where they've always lived.

Claire has just phoned to say she's safely back in York. He always asks her to – not to be the kind of controlling father he's always deplored – just to know that she got her connection in Birmingham OK and is safe. He knows that one day she'll forget to do so. Even when that day comes, he hopes it's for the best of reasons.

Everything went as well as these things can. Even Lucy was pleasant to him. He was very touched to see all four of the police colleagues in attendance. DI Farren, in particular, seemed very keen to make the effort to speak to him. What do you say though? What can you say? Even Kate Shelbourne seemed to find it difficult to form sentences.

Maybe there is some redemption in being able to help others to find their way again; one day he might even forgive himself for not reading the clues about

Charlotte's illness which were there, right in front of him, all along. It didn't need some special gift, just the willingness to read between the lines.

He has been gazing at a faded dark stain on the carpet in front of him before turning back towards the kitchen counter. The two mugs are still there, empty and unused. Some habits are going to take longer to change. He looks across at her chair and hopes more than anything else that one day he might see her sitting there once again.

The End

ABOUT THE AUTHOR

Mark Rasdall

Mark Rasdall was born in Peterborough in 1960 and brought up on the edge of the Cambridgeshire Fens. A writer of fiction and history, with a professional background in content creation, curation, and online search in London's advertising sector, he is based in the UK, in a small village on top of a hill in the beautiful Worcestershire countryside. For a few years he ran a sweet shop on Worcester High Street with his wife Michelle.

Now retired, this is the third in his series of Inspector Harcourt crime novels set in a changing rural Worcestershire.

You can visit his website at www.markrasdallwriting.com and follow Mark on Facebook, X and Instagram.

MAILING LIST

If you enjoyed this book please look out for the next title in the series:

Bread of Heaven

Previous titles:

The Proofreader
Water, slaughter everywhere

Please also join our mailing list for the latest news, including about forthcoming books in the series: https://23e39b8f.sibforms.com/serve/MUIFANz0yGHzWd78toV2l8aQF4W9OEv6OK0gKWoa-Gj_LjT9GSzpHGYX1GZwsXLSNxUGcQezK_H6jsvjgnPYBvhl8ctfHQAvxgVvCJuQNos4F2bRHEYFYH-kgQwGBlyUisLxTZPgufZAQLICtjX5mM83Cf-osZw3dmXqTi-1JvRa9dIBPgcaePmVrm8DnlEhBrWJHSqRbJ9LKKuC

Printed in Great Britain
by Amazon